Praise for the *New York Times* bestselling author Jill Gregory

THUNDER CREEK

"A transfixing blend of fiery romance and spine-tingling suspense." —*Booklist*

"For tales of romance and adventure that keep you reading into the night, look no further than Jill Gregory." —Nora Roberts

"A compelling tale that works on two levels, as a well-structured mystery and a first-rate romance. Gregory . . . writes the stuff that romance readers yearn for. If you haven't yet read her, you're missing out on a great treat." —*Oakland Press*

"Fans . . . will be pleased by her treatment of the protagonists' relationship and drawn in by the book's cozy, small-town setting. . . . Once the action revs up, readers will gladly sit back and enjoy the journey." —*Publishers Weekly*

"Greg . . . will drive a herd o . . . eartfelt family drama . . . -paced action, romance . . . s the fiery attraction between . . . s fever pitch." —*Publishers Weekly*

"Gregory's heroine is a breath of fresh air with her whip-smart commentary and charismatic confidence, and her leading man is the perfect sparring partner, making for a duo as captivating as Hepburn and Tracy." —*Booklist*

"Few authors have command of the West like Jill Gregory. . . . Adding a true feeling of the era and the setting is a gift. Jill Gregory has that gift and we are lucky to have her share it with us." —*Romantic Times*

ROUGH WRANGLER,
TENDER KISSES

"This is the first Jill Gregory book I've read, but if the rest of her tales are as well told as this one, I've got many hours of great reading ahead of me." —*Oakland Press*

"Jill Gregory crafts stories against the backdrop of the Wild West and creates characters that are so real they are easy to understand and empathize with. She bases her romances on how her characters learn to trust in the power of love to heal and ease away the pain of the past. Her faith in love renews our own. Thank you for this invaluable lesson, Ms. Gregory." —*Romantic Times*

COLD NIGHT,
WARM STRANGER

"You will be enticed from the first chapter. . . . You will cry and cheer for these wonderfully beloved characters, who will do nothing less than capture your heart. . . . Jill Gregory has done it again. Her talent shines through in this sensually captivating novel—she shows us once again that love can conquer all." —*Rendezvous*

"Jill Gregory's western romances always pack a wallop. *Cold Night, Warm Stranger* is true to form. Strong characters that engage readers' emotions and an action-packed story with a powerful plot makes this a not-to-be-missed western." —*Romantic Times*

NEVER LOVE A COWBOY

"A western version of *Romeo and Juliet* . . . This is a who-done-it with strong elements of suspense . . . but the emphasis is definitely on the romance. This book has wonderful, tender scenes. . . . Jill Gregory creates not only a very human hero and a likeable heroine but also very evil villains with interesting motivations."
—*Romance Reader*

"Sensual . . . Enjoy *Never Love a Cowboy*. . . . A western, a suspenseful mystery, and a good book. Combining grit, sensuality, and a cleverly plotted mystery takes talent."
—*Romantic Times*

JUST THIS ONCE

"Refreshing characters, witty dialogue, and adventure . . . *Just This Once* enthralls, delights, and captivates, winning readers' hearts along the way." —*Romantic Times*

"Here is another unforgettable story that will keep you captivated. She has combined the Old West and the elegance of England into this brilliantly glorious tale. The characters are undeniably wonderful. Their pains and joys will reach through the pages and touch your heart."
—*Rendezvous*

ALWAYS YOU

"*Always You* has it all. . . . Jill Gregory's inventive imagination and sprightly prose combine for another bell ringer." —*Rendezvous*

"Compelling . . . definitely a winner!" —*Affaire de Coeur*

"A sure-fire winner . . . remarkable . . . A delightful romance with both tenderness and tough western grit."
—*Romantic Times*

MORE PRAISE FOR JILL GREGORY

"A wonderfully exciting romance from the Old West. The plot twists in this novel are handled expertly. . . . It's great from start to finish."
—*Rendezvous* on *When the Heart Beckons*

"A fast-paced Western romance novel that will keep readers' attention throughout. Both the hero and heroine are charming characters."
—*Affaire de Coeur* on *Daisies in the Wind*

"A charming tale of dreams come true. It combines a heartwarming love story with an intriguing mystery."
—*Gothic Journal* on *Forever After*

Doubleday Book Club and
Rhapsody Book Club Featured Alternate

Books by Jill Gregory

Thunder Creek
Once an Outlaw
Rough Wrangler, Tender Kisses
Never Love a Cowboy
Just This Once
Always You
Daisies in the Wind
Forever After
Cherished
When the Heart Beckons

JILL GREGORY

NIGHT

THUNDER

Toledo Public Library
173 N.W. 7th St.
Toledo, OR 97391

A DELL BOOK

NIGHT THUNDER
A Dell Book / July 2004

Published by Bantam Dell
A Division of Random House, Inc.
New York, New York

All rights reserved
Copyright © 2004 by Jill Gregory
Cover photo © Jeff Vanuga/Corbis
Cover design by Marietta Anastassatos

No part of this book may be reproduced or transmitted in any form or by
any means, electronic or mechanical, including photocopying, recording,
or by any information storage and retrieval system, without the written
permission of the publisher, except where permitted by law. For
information address: Dell Books, New York, New York.

If you purchased this book without a cover, you should be aware that this
book is stolen property. It was reported as "unsold and destroyed" to the
publisher, and neither the author nor the publisher has received any pay-
ment for this "stripped book."

Dell is a registered trademark of Random House, Inc., and
the colophon is a trademark of Random House, Inc.

ISBN 0-440-23735-1

Manufactured in the United States of America
Published simultaneously in Canada

OPM 10 9 8 7 6 5 4 3 2 1

To my wonderful friend Karen Katz.
And as always, to Larry and Rachel.

"Oh what lies lurk in kisses!"
—*Heinrich Heine*

NIGHT THUNDER

Chapter 1

WHEN JOSY WARNER ANSWERED THE PHONE that warm April day she thought it was going to be her lying ex-boyfriend begging her for a second chance. Instead it was Ricky Sabatini—her childhood ally and protector, and the closest thing to a big brother she'd ever had.

"Jo-Jo, it's me. Listen, I'm in a jam and I don't have much time. Sorry to ask this, but I need a favor. A big one."

"Ricky!" Josy sat up with a jerk, sloshing coffee over the rim of her cup and onto the sketches scattered across her desk. She grabbed a handful of Kleenex and blotted frantically at the drawings, her pale blonde hair falling into her eyes as she tried to rescue them. But as the summer sun glittered through her one-bedroom apartment on the Upper East Side that Saturday afternoon, high above the roar of Manhattan traffic, she saw it was too late. The sketches were smeared, soggy—ruined. She tried to keep the dismay from her voice and to focus on Ricky instead.

"What do you need, Ricky? I'll help any way I can," she told him, clutching the soggy wadded Kleenex and trying not to moan at what was left of her carefully drawn images of lean pants and tailored blazers.

"It's a big favor, kid. Think about it for a second. Shouldn't be too much of a problem, but no guarantees."

The warning note in his voice struck her then. Her stomach knotted. She hadn't heard from him in several months, but she knew Ricky's life was a mess—possibly even more so than her own. She'd left messages for him when she'd read the accusations against him in the newspaper, when she'd learned of his suspension from the NYPD and the subsequent internal investigation. But he hadn't called her back, and she'd become distracted by her own problems. Her own carefully built, hard-won life had been falling apart, piece by precious piece, and lately it was all she could do to keep going, trying to salvage what she could.

First there'd been her breakup with Doug, now her job was on the line . . . it had been one thing after another, and Josy felt like she was frantically trying to stay afloat and sinking a little more each day. But if Ricky needed her, no matter what, she couldn't say no. Not to him . . . not ever.

"You still there, Jo-Jo? I don't have a lot of time here."

"Sorry, Ricky. I'm really sorry—about the investigation, everything. I tried to call you . . ."

"Forget about it, kid. It'll work out." His voice sounded the same as it always had—rough, hard, hurried.

"Do you want to meet for a drink . . . to talk?"

"Hey, you worried about me? That's nice. But I don't need a drink. What I need is this favor."

She took a deep breath. "Name it, Ricky," she said quietly. "As long as it's not illegal, it's yours."

"You don't believe that bunk they wrote about me in the papers, do you? That I was on the take? That I colluded with Caventini?"

There was a sudden edge to his voice and she immediately felt guilty about adding that "illegal" part to her condition. Ricky had been far more than her foster brother when they'd both lived in the Hammond home for two years. He'd been her rock, her shield against the Callahan boys who'd ruled their Jersey neighborhood, and against Karl Hammond and his unpredictable temper. If not for Ricky . . .

She shuddered, unwilling to imagine what might have been if not for him.

"Of course I don't believe it," she said quickly. Then she added in a low tone, "Not if you tell me it isn't true."

"That's exactly what I'm telling you. I'm a clean cop, Josy, always have been, since day one on the force. I never took a dime from the mob, or from anyone else. Not a dime. I went undercover like I was told, and I nailed some big-time asses, and then I got set up—set up by someone in my own department. It's all going to come out in the trial—"

"I'm on your side, Ricky. What . . . what do you need me to do?"

Maybe he's going to ask me to show up at the trial, be a character witness or something—give him moral support, she thought. *Maybe he needs a friendly face in the courtroom.*

No, that can't be it, Josy realized immediately. Ricky had never needed anyone in his life. He'd always been able to rely on himself, and he'd given her some valuable lessons in how to do that very thing.

For a moment her eyes closed and she could picture herself back in her old Jersey neighborhood, back in the run-down, weed-choked yard of the foster home owned by May and Karl Hammond, the home she'd lived in longer than any other of the five separate ones she'd grown up in after her parents died.

She could smell the fried onions and sauerkraut and beer wafting from the kitchen window, see the Camel butts littering the porch stoop and the driveway, hear the bawling of the television announcer in the broiling July heat as Karl watched the Yankees game from his tattered plaid easy chair in the living room. And she saw the three Callahan brothers from the next block, riding their bicycles on the broken sidewalk, sticking out their tongues at her, calling her names. Laughing . . .

"I had a package delivered to you," Ricky was saying, and she jerked herself back from her reverie of Jefferson Street to the present, to her own airy little apartment with its sleek cream leather sofa and hardwood floors, its carefully chosen prints, snazzy chandelier lamps, and striped red and cream throw pillows.

"Your doorman's holding it for you. Go get it. Put it away and keep it safe for me, just for a week—no more, until I need it back. Okay?"

"Well, yes, but . . . what's in the package, Ricky?" A prickle of uneasiness ran through her. She sat up straighter, speaking evenly into the phone. "You're going to tell me, right?"

"No can do, sweetheart. Just trust me. You know you can trust me, don't you?"

"Yes, but—"

"Whatever you do, don't let the cops get hold of it. They're trying to fry me, but I'm not going down. I'll call you and set up a meet when I'm ready to take it back."

"But—"

"Thanks a million, kid. You're my girl."

And he was gone, leaving her holding a dead phone and sensing that somehow she was going to regret this.

But Ricky would never do anything to hurt me, she told herself as she rode down the elevator to the lobby. And he wouldn't have taken any money from the mob. He was tough—he'd always been tough—and he liked to cut corners, but he'd always known what was right.

Even when he was fourteen and you were twelve and he caught the Callahan brothers dragging you through that garbage dump . . .

The elevator door opened and she pushed the images from her mind. She didn't like to think of those days, when she'd been a scared, skinny foster kid, bumped from one crowded, noisy home to the next. Until she met Ricky, she didn't know how to stand up for herself. But now she did. She'd come a long way from the pale, knob-kneed little ghost who hadn't spoken a word for three months after her parents died, who'd worn nothing but hand-me-down patched shirts and jeans, who had to borrow Carol Walinsky's older cousin's dress for the prom . . .

Yep, she thought, glancing down at her baby-blue capris and her skinny white tank top, at the Prada sandals that bared her seashell-pink-painted toes. She'd come a long way. And she was never going back.

"Afternoon, Ms. Warner. I was just about to call you. Got a package here for you." Len O'Brien, the spry sixty-two-year-old doorman, handed her a brown-paper-wrapped parcel about the size of a paperback book.

"Thanks, Len." As the doorman turned to consult with the super about an electrical problem in 17B, Josy stared down at the package in her hands. There was no writing on it, nothing but that plain brown paper and some wedges of Scotch tape. It looked innocuous enough. It felt solid, not squishy. Like some kind of box. What in the world could Ricky have sent to her? And why?

I'm not going to worry about it, she decided, heading back to the elevator. *I'm just going to forget all about it until Ricky calls and wants it back.*

She stuffed it in the bottom drawer of her dresser, beneath her winter sweaters and socks, and pushed it out of her mind.

It wasn't all that difficult to do. Josy had a lot going on in her life, all of it more pressing than a small brown package tucked in her dresser drawer.

For starters, there was her once skyrocketing career, which was on the verge of plummeting into the toilet. And there was her boss, Francesca, who desperately wanted Josy's completed sketches for the new ready-to-wear line and had been calling every day from Italy for a week, demanding to know when she could expect them.

"As soon as I finish them," Josy had been repeating, over and over. "It won't be long now, Francesca."

"Damn it, I'm trying to get a merger going here." Francesca's clipped voice had hammered like a Jimmy Choo stiletto in her ear. Despite her Italian name, she'd been born and bred in Beverly Hills, the only daughter of famed film director Marco Dellagio. Which was appropriate, Josy had reflected on more than one occasion, since Francesca had the imperious Hollywood diva bit down cold.

"After last season, that damned disaster of a season, I need an infusion of money. And before the Andiamo team agrees to *anything,* they need to see the new line. And *I* need to see it first. What about this don't you understand?"

"I get it, Francesca. I'm . . . trying." Josy had forced

herself to keep her voice even, as Jane Boyd, the junior creative assistant, and Reese Ashley, the design firm's business manager, both gathered in her office doorway, rolling their eyes.

"Things just aren't . . . clicking right now. I'll have a breakthrough any day—just be a little patient. You told me you didn't need the sketches for another month—"

"At the latest!" Francesca snapped. "Two weeks would be much much better."

Two weeks. Two weeks to come up with a complete fall line. Josy's temples throbbed. Somehow or other, her creative muse had gone AWOL seven months ago, roughly the same time she'd found out that Doug Fifer, the clean-cut, funny, effortlessly charming investment banker she'd been dating for the previous six months, was a married man. A married man with two kids. The thought of it still made her sick to her stomach. For the first week after she'd found out, she felt like someone had taken a two-by-four to her head. She'd been stunned and furious, and she was still furious—and badly shaken by her own abysmal judgment in character.

And ever since, she hadn't been able to come up with a single inspired vision for the beautiful clothes she loved to design.

"I'll do my best," she'd told Francesca, her stomach roiling.

"There are dozens of girls, hundreds of girls, who'd give their eyeteeth to work for me, Josy. You can be replaced in less time than it takes me to put on my lipstick."

Fortunately Francesca had slammed down the phone before Josy said something she'd have regretted. Standing up for herself was one thing, but getting herself fired was another—especially in the current job market. She needed this job, at least until she had a few more notches of success on her belt and a comfortable financial cushion to fall back on in case she was out of work for any length of time.

But if she didn't have the sketches done in two weeks—a month at the latest—that point would be moot. She *would* be out of a job—and up a creek.

If only she could just get past this mental block, relax, and come up with an *idea* . . .

She went back to her desk and picked up the sketches. Coffee stains or no, they weren't that good, she realized, her heart sinking. Adequate maybe, some possibilities to work with . . . but . . .

The individual pieces lacked cohesion and . . . something else.

Flair. Freshness. *Inspiration.*

Frustrated, she sank into the chair and dumped the sketches in the wastebasket. She dragged her hands through her hair, trying to picture the runway at the spring show, the models all dressed in the new line from Francesca Dellagio. *And what were they wearing?* she wondered, closing her eyes, trying to see the suits and jackets and skirts and dresses draping the models' bodies. They were wearing . . . they were wearing . . .

Nothing. She saw nothing.

And that's what your future will hold if you don't shake off this block, she told herself furiously, opening her eyes and pushing back her chair. She began to pace through her apartment. She thought better when she paced.

But all she could think about was how much she was going to miss working with Jane and Reese after she was fired.

They'd both hurried into her office after that last nasty phone conversation with Francesca.

"That bitch ought to be kissing your feet!" Jane had exclaimed. "The only reason Francesca Dellagio Designs made it in the first place was because of *your* ideas! You've been letting her take the credit for three years, when you're the one who came up with every single element of the collections!"

"And look what happened this season, when she vetoed your stuff and went ahead with her own," Reese pointed out, as they both dropped into the chocolate suede chairs opposite Josy's desk. "The fashion writers crucified her. She knows the new line has to be a stunning success. You're her only chance."

"Start your own company and I'll come with you." Jane leaned forward, her blue eyes dancing beneath her crown of short, spiky red hair. "Wouldn't you, Reese?"

"Yes, if everything was in place. If Josy had the resources and was ready," Reese had said slowly. She'd studied Josy with frank appraisal. "I don't think you are right now, are you?" she'd asked thoughtfully. "You're still figuring out what direction you want to go in." At thirty-four, she was tall and lean as a model, with dark hair, flawless olive skin, and a master's degree in business from Yale. And she'd been married and divorced three times before she was thirty.

"Ever since Doug Fifer burned you, you've been . . . different. Distracted. You can't let a man get to you like that, Josy. Don't take men—any man—so seriously. They'll only bring you down."

"I'm not down. I'm just . . . blank. Every time I get an idea, I discard it. Nothing's ringing my bells." She'd pushed a bunch of papers around her desk, hesitated, and finally told them the truth. "It's not just Doug. It's not just because I feel like an idiot for not *knowing* he was married, for letting him deceive me all that time. Even though, God knows, I do."

She'd taken a deep breath and looked from one to the other. "There's . . . something else. Something that I found out about right around the same time. And . . . I can't stop thinking about it."

"Oh, my God, you're pregnant!" Jane gasped.

"*No.* I'm not pregnant!" Appalled, Josy stared at her in shock.

"You're sick?" Reese's eyes moved over her, as if searching for some sign of disease. "What have you got? Whatever it is, if it isn't advanced, we can take care of it. My first ex-husband's brother is the chief of staff at the Mayo Clinic. I can call him and get you in for a second opinion by the end of the week—"

"I'm fine," Josy interrupted her. She shook her head. Maybe it wasn't such a good idea confiding in Jane and Reese. "It's nothing that . . . earth-shattering. Well, maybe it is. Sort of. To *me.*"

"Tell us!" Reese demanded.

"Now!" Jane's eyes were wide.

Josy looked from one to the other of them. "I have a grandmother," she said quietly.

For a moment there had been utter silence in the office. Then Jane had burst out laughing. "Doesn't everyone? . . ." she'd begun. And then she remembered.

"Oh. Sorry. I mean . . . I know you were an orphan, but . . ."

"I thought you said your grandparents were all dead or in nursing homes when your parents died," Reese interjected.

"That's what I thought. But this is someone else. Someone . . . new. I found out recently that I have another grandmother—a birth grandmother. It turns out that my mother was adopted."

"You never knew?" Reese asked.

Josy shook her head. "I had no idea. But my mom apparently found out about it when I was still a little girl. She was given up for adoption by a woman named Ada Timmons."

Ada Timmons. How many times since she received the adoption report had she stared at that name, trying to picture the woman it belonged to?

"She's my biological grandmother," she continued in a low tone. "The only person left in this world who's my flesh and blood."

"Wow." Jane stared at her open-mouthed. "Oh, please, tell me you come from some rich family and you're going to inherit a vineyard somewhere—or a plantation outside New Orleans—or an oil empire in Dallas—"

"Hardly." Josy smiled. "She's from some little town in Wyoming. It's nothing but a speck on the map. But . . ." A note of excitement crept into her voice. "I did some online research into public records and found out that she married a man named Guy Scott in 1949, so her name is now Ada Scott. And she's still *there*. In Thunder Creek." She moistened her lips and looked at each of them. "I've been thinking about going to see her . . . making contact."

"Okay, start from the beginning," Reese had ordered her, tapping a long exquisitely manicured finger on the desk. "Tell us how you found out about all this."

And so she'd told them then, told them about the papers, her mother's papers, which had been accidentally discovered in a misnamed file by social services a few months ago—more than a decade after Andrea and Gene Warner had been killed by a drunk driver, more than a decade after Josy, with no living relatives able to care for her, had been placed into the overworked maelstrom known as "the system," a labyrinthine network of social workers, bureaucrats, red tape, and foster homes.

She'd told them what those papers and a few subsequent phone calls and Internet searches had proved—that she *did* have family left in this world. She had a biological grandmother named Ada Scott who was alive and living in Wyoming—in a community of fewer than six hundred people, in a town called Thunder Creek.

Thinking of their astonishment, their arguments for and against making contact with her grandmother, she reached into the center drawer of her desk on that mild Saturday afternoon and pulled out the manila folder that Gloria Renfrew of social services had belatedly discovered and had mailed to her.

Her fingers shook a little as she lifted out the adoption report for her mother, Andrea Salenger Warner, which had been found among her parents' papers after the accident. Her gaze fell on the name of the town where her mother's birth mother lived—Thunder Creek.

And as the vibrant, overcrowded city of New York pulsed and raced far below her window, a breeze of a long-ago memory once more stirred her heart and ruffled something deep in her soul.

For Josy had been to Thunder Creek. Once. She'd gone on a trip there with her parents when she was very young, perhaps seven or eight—and ever since she'd received these papers, she'd known why.

They'd flown into some city in Wyoming, rented a car, and driven to the town of Thunder Creek for a day. One day.

Josy dimly remembered the big open land of Wyoming, the sky seeming bluer than she'd ever seen it before, as blue as the dress she'd worn that year for the first day of school. She'd seen mountains, and cows dotting all the hillsides and valleys they drove through, more cows than she'd ever imagined existed in the world. And her father had pointed out some elk on a tiny distant ledge.

The town itself had been small and pleasant and quiet, she remembered. There'd been a diner with a ceiling fan where they'd eaten lunch. Afterward they'd walked along the main street and Josy had seen men wearing cowboy hats, just like on TV.

And . . . her eyebrows drew together as she fought to summon the last vestiges of memory . . .

They'd taken a drive. She could see a house in her mind's eye . . . trees down the end of a lane . . . she could just make out a figure on the porch, a woman. She was watering pots of geraniums, looking their way . . .

It must have been her, Josy thought, her fingers tightening around the adoption report. *Mom must have gone to Thunder Creek to find her birth mother.* But . . . had she met her? Was Ada Scott the woman on the porch?

She remembered her father driving away when the woman had looked up toward their car, when she'd set the watering can down on the porch railing. Had that been it, that one brief glimpse? Had that been their only contact? Had her mother ever spoken to Ada Scott or approached her? Or had she sped away after that one fleeting look?

Neither of her parents had ever mentioned anything about the adoption to her, or anything about Ada Scott. All she'd known was that her mother's parents had both passed away, and her father's parents had divorced, her paternal grandfather moving away and losing touch, and her maternal grandmother ending up in a nursing home by the time Josy was ten.

There had been no one, no one at all, to care for her after her parents' fatal accident.

But now she knew she had a relative, a grandmother . . . after all these years . . .

Something in her yearned to meet the woman. Of course she had no idea how Ada Scott would receive her, or even if she would allow a meeting. But she'd been fantasizing about making the call, introducing herself . . . seeing what would happen.

How would it feel to have a grandmother, someone to call on the phone now and then, to send a card or picture at Christmastime, or to invite one day to her wedding . . .

If she ever had a wedding. Right now it wasn't exactly a hot prospect—or a top priority. After the debacle with Doug, she'd have to vastly improve on her instincts about men before she'd even consider going out on another date, much less starting any kind of relationship.

And first, she had to secure her job.

Perhaps once the sketches were done, once she helped Francesca and Jane get production started and fabric ordered, perhaps then she'd call Ada Scott. Maybe then she could take off a few days, and if her grandmother— her *grandmother*—she repeated the words to herself in wonder—agreed to see her, she could go to Thunder Creek, find her . . . and what? See what happened?

Don't expect miracles, she told herself, going into the kitchen and fixing herself a bowl of Easy Mac. *It's not going to be instant connection, instant family, hugs, and kisses.*

Maybe it will be a disaster, she thought, moving her bowl to the breakfast counter and hopping onto a stool.

Maybe Ada Scott will turn out to be a mean, bitter old woman, someone who doesn't want to be reminded of a teen pregnancy—or that she gave her baby away. Maybe she has other family now who will resent an outsider showing up, or a husband who doesn't know anything about the child she gave up. You could ruin her life . . .

Or you might enrich it. You might enrich both of yours, she thought, picking up a forkful of macaroni and cheese, staring at it, unseeing.

She'd been spending far too much time lately thinking about the what-ifs and why-nots instead of focusing on the here and now. She needed to focus on her sketches. Her job. Her life.

She took a bite and made up her mind, working out a compromise with herself. Right now she couldn't afford to be distracted with any more personal issues. She'd been stressed and scattered enough. She had to work, nothing else. But once she finished the sketches, once Francesca was off her back and the pressure was gone, she'd allow herself the luxury of time, time to think hard about actually placing the call.

She had to go that far, at least, and then . . .

Then she'd see about the rest of it. When the sketches were finished . . . when the fall collection was set, she'd be more ready to take the first step.

Now all she needed was an idea, a theme or mood that grabbed her, that she could focus and expand upon, something that would capture the shape and colors and textures of the clothes Francesca's elegant clientele would clamor for come September. She'd been going back and forth between a chaotic blur of choices: lush peasant looks, rocker glam, ladylike chic given edge with metal or fringe, bold contemporary colors and taut lines, or soft and flirtatious little skirts and jackets with oversize belts and zippers—cowl necks and miniskirts, or skinny jackets with wide leather pants, A-line versus pencil-shaped skirts, pastels or earth tones . . .

She gobbled the rest of her macaroni and cheese, snatched a can of Coke from the fridge, and hurried over to her desk. Her face set in concentration, she tore off a fresh sheet of sketch paper and began to draw.

Six days later she was still at it. She'd worked from home half the time, gone into the design studio the other half, and torn off sheet after sheet, starting anew, adding and subtracting pieces, changing her mind.

But none of it was clicking. None of it was coming together. It was a mishmash, not so much a collection as a jumbled kaleidoscope, lacking unity, form, and drama.

In short, she thought in despair, it was a mess. She hated it, every single page of it. She was alone in the design studio Friday night, ripping the most recent sketch into shreds and hurling them in the wastebasket, when the cordless phone on her desk rang. Bleary-eyed and discouraged, she peered at her watch. Lord, it was a quarter past nine.

She hadn't even heard everyone else leave. The phone rang again, echoing loud and lonely through the high-ceilinged studio with its vast charcoal granite floor and bright overhead lighting, its oversize paintings adorning stark white walls, setting the backdrop for the mannequins and tables draped with every color and texture of rich, glowing fabric.

"Josy Warner," she mumbled into the phone, weakly remembering that she hadn't had a bite to eat since the bagel with cream cheese and cucumber slices she'd wolfed down at lunch.

"Josy, it's me." Ricky's voice on the other end of the line was raw, tight, and urgent. "I need you to get me the package back—*now*."

"Now? You mean . . . right now?" She shook her head, trying to cast off her fatigue and to digest what he was saying. Suddenly, the hard, driving urgency of his tone registered and she clutched the phone tighter.

"Ricky, what's wrong?"

"Don't ask me questions, there's no time to explain. I'm not in town, so you'll have to bring the package to this guy, Archie. He's a friend, maybe the only one besides you I can trust. Write down this address. Fast."

Her heart was pumping. Frantically she grabbed for notepaper and scribbled down the street number he gave her.

"It's in Brooklyn—Windsor Terrace—right off Prospect Park. Tell the cabdriver to wait," Ricky ordered, "and as soon as you give Archie the package, get the hell out of there. You hear me?"

"Yes, but—"

"Go now. Right now."

He hung up.

Josy stared at the phone, her throat dry. Ricky didn't sound good. It couldn't be the trial—it hadn't started yet. There'd been a postponement. But . . . why did he need the package now?

What the hell difference does it make? she thought, dropping the cordless phone into its base and springing out of her chair, sending her colored pencils clattering to the floor. He needed the package right away. And she was more than glad to be rid of it.

She left the studio at a run, hailed a cab at the corner, and gave the driver her address as she jumped into the backseat. When she reached her building she spared only a quick nod to the doorman as she strode past and punched the elevator button. She'd never heard that note of frantic urgency in Ricky's voice before. Even when they were kids on Jefferson Street, there'd been a cool toughness about him that had made it appear he had no problem keeping every emotion in check. Tonight he'd sounded almost unraveled.

What the hell is in that box? she wondered as she fitted the key in her lock.

She half expected the package to have disappeared when she opened the bottom drawer of her dresser, but it was right where she'd left it under her sweaters.

She stuffed it into her black leather work tote and in less than a minute she was hailing another cab.

It took nearly an hour to get to Brooklyn zooming straight across the Manhattan Bridge, down Flatbush and cutting through Grand Army Plaza, and by the time the cab turned onto Vanderbilt and braked before the small brick house on the left side of the street, her nerves were shot. She felt queasy, her hands were shaking, and she didn't know if it was from having skipped dinner or from anxiety, but she heard herself ask the driver to wait in a breathless voice that sounded completely unlike her own.

Clearing her throat, she climbed out of the cab and hurried up the cement steps, feeling the package swaying inside her tote. It was nearly ten o'clock, and the windows of many houses on the street were open to the April night. She heard a radio blaring rap, smelled the aroma of pizza drifting from one of the windows. Down the block, a dog yapped, rapid and staccato. She saw kids skateboarding around a corner—a few people sat on porches in aluminum chairs, enjoying the spring air.

She rang the doorbell of the silent brick house and waited.

Chapter 2

Thirty seconds dragged by. There was no answer.

She rang the bell again and followed this up immediately with three sharp raps on the door.

Still no answer. This wasn't right. And it wasn't good, not at all.

She checked the slip of paper again, confirming the address, then turned to the cabdriver.

He was hunched over the steering wheel, watching her, looking irritated as hell. "One minute," she called as imperatively as she could with her heart beating in time to the rap music, and she pounded on the door again.

Damn it, Ricky, she thought. Maybe Archie was late. Maybe she should leave the package on the front porch for him.

Or . . . inside.

She gave the doorknob a little jostle, praying it wouldn't turn. But it did. The door gave and she pushed it open an inch just to see if she could.

Damn. She didn't want to go in there. The entire situation was freaking her out. But if she went in, she could leave the package on a table or something and when Archie got here, it'd be safe.

The cabdriver leaned out the window. "Lady, I'm not supposed to just sit. You want me to take you someplace or what?"

"Yes, yes, I do. Wait one more minute."

She shoved the door open and stepped inside. There were lights on, and a window air conditioner whirred somewhere.

"Archie?"

No answer.

The house was warm, though, and cluttered, with a tiny hall and a brown-carpeted living room filled with a mismatched jumble of older furniture that contrasted with the gleaming, twenty-first-century wide-screen TV dominating one wall. There was a wood coffee table in front of a cracked black leather sofa and she hurried toward it, planning to leave the package right there, next to three empty beer bottles and a pile of laundry. But then she heard a noise coming from a back room.

Not just any noise—one that made the skin on the back of her neck prickle. It was a moan.

For a moment, Josy froze, then she started toward the sound. She heard another moan—it seemed to be coming from the kitchen up ahead.

She saw him as soon as she reached the doorway. He was lying facedown on the linoleum floor. There was blood everywhere—beneath him, on the counter, the refrigerator, the floor. The queasiness rushed to her head and she sucked in a deep breath to steady herself.

"Oh, God." Shock ripped through her. She ran to him and knelt down. He was young, tough-looking, twentyish. His face was turned toward her and she saw that his brown eyes were open. They looked glazed, sad . . . dim. She also saw the bullet hole that had torn through his thin shoulder blades and gouged out a hole in his faded green cotton shirt.

"Archie?" she gasped. "Archie, hold on, I'll get help."

She groped in her tote for her cell phone, but before she could find it, he wheezed, "No . . . get outta here. Take the package . . . get out . . ."

She ignored him and punched in 911, still on her knees beside him.

"A man's been hurt. He's bleeding. We need an ambulance." Her voice was high-pitched, rapid. "The address?" She gave it in a rush. "Yes, he's conscious, but there's blood all over the—"

Suddenly, the wounded man's arm shot out and grabbed the phone. His finger jammed against the *end* button, and then, groaning, he threw the phone as far as he could. It slid to a rest only five feet away, against the base of an electric stove.

"No . . . cops," he told her, but his voice sounded even weaker than it had before. "Get out . . . take the package . . . go . . ."

Her cell phone rang and she scrambled across the floor to grab it, half expecting the emergency operator to have traced the call and called back for more information.

But Ricky's voice yelled in her ear. "Josy, change in plans. Don't go to the address I gave you—"

"I'm already here. Ricky, a man's been shot. I think it's Archie! You're Archie, aren't you?" she asked the man on the floor, whose eyes were now closed, scaring her half to death.

"Yeah. Lemme . . . talk to . . . Ricky . . . tell him . . . Hammer . . ."

"Ricky, what the hell's going on?" she shrieked.

"How bad is he hurt?" Ricky ignored her question. "Did you call an ambulance?"

"Yes, they're on their way——"

"Then get the hell out of there, Josy. Now!"

"Oh, no. Ricky . . . Ricky, I think . . ."

The man's eyes were closed again. He wasn't even moaning now. *Please,* she prayed silently, forgetting about Ricky, forgetting about everything except the man lying in his own blood on the floor.

"Archie," she cried. She set the phone down, reached for his wrist, felt for a pulse. She hadn't done this since they'd learned it in health class in high school. She hadn't been good at it. She couldn't feel one now. Shouldn't she be doing something else? Mouth to mouth? Putting pressure on the wound?

She couldn't feel a pulse. He looked so still, so . . .

"Ricky, I think . . . he's dead!"

She heard the scream of an ambulance in the distance.

"Josy, you still got the package? Take it with you right this damned minute and get the hell out of there!" Ricky roared into the phone.

"But I can't leave——"

"Yes, you can. For me, Josy. I can't let the cops get that package, you see? Get outta there. If he's going to make it, the paramedics will save him. All you can do is get the hell out!"

She was still frozen, still staring at Archie, who hadn't moved a muscle, when she heard something else.

The front door, squeaking open. Low voices.

Pure instinct had her surging to her feet, trembling, edging out of sight of the front part of the house. She held her breath, clutching the cell phone, fear rushing at her.

"Josy, do you hear—" She hit the *end* button to blot out Ricky's shout and turned off the phone. Whoever was out there, it sure wasn't the paramedics. Maybe whoever had shot Archie had come back to finish him off. Though from the looks of it, there was no need, she thought, her gaze shifting to him and then quickly away.

She'd never seen a dead man before, but she was pretty sure she'd seen one now.

She wanted to scream, but she clenched all her muscles tight, took a deep breath, and leaned forward ever so slightly so that she could peek around the doorway and down the hall. She just caught a glimpse of a man with dark blond hair dressed all in black—black blazer, black slacks, and a black gun in his hand. *Now, there's a fashion accessory I can do without,* she thought, jerking back out of sight.

Ricky was right. She had to get out of here.

There was a side door off the kitchen. She edged toward it, praying the floor wouldn't creak. She took one last look back at Archie, who hadn't moved or spoken a word, and opened the door.

It led outside into a small unfenced yard. Carefully, she stepped out and closed the door after her.

It took a moment for her eyes to adjust to the hot darkness, but the moon riding high overhead helped and she saw a maze of backyards on either side of her.

She ran toward the left and glanced at the street, praying the cab was still there, knowing it was her best chance.

It was gone.

Choking down panic, she veered away from the street, clutching her tote close, running faster than she'd ever thought she could in sandals with two-inch heels.

She dashed through yards, past swing sets and fig trees

and marigold gardens, running, running. She nearly ran over a couple of teenagers drinking beer on a beach towel spread across the grass and slowed down long enough to ask them where the nearest subway station was.

They pointed her toward the Fort Hamilton stop, and she stumbled on. She had no idea how long she ran before she reached it. Every so often, she twisted her head around, trying to see if she was being followed. She wasn't—yet. But even when she reached the F train and sank onto a seat in the back, she couldn't believe she'd gotten away.

"Faster," she urged the train silently, as she slumped back, clutching her sides. Her head was pounding with the vision of a dead man on a linoleum floor, and another man with a gun, searching the house, looking for . . . what?

The answer was obvious. For her. Or the package.

Possibly both.

I know I owe you, Ricky, she thought miserably, *and I'll always be grateful—but what the hell have you gotten me into?* A shudder racked her shoulders, and serious nausea clogged her throat.

She pulled the tote closer and peered inside at the dark shape of the package. She needed to know what was inside it. And more important, she thought, fear eating through the inner lining of her stomach, how the hell was she going to get rid of it?

By the time she reached the door of her apartment and had to try three times to fit her key in the lock because her hand was shaking so badly, she'd decided that things couldn't get any worse.

But then they did. She opened the door at last and gasped.

Her lovely, tidy, chic, and comfortable apartment, the one place that felt more like home to her than any place she'd lived in except for her childhood bedroom before her parents had died, looked like a hurricane had blown through and left a wake of destruction.

The sofa cushions had been slashed and dumped on the floor, lamps were knocked over, the coffee table kicked aside. Her lovely rose silk bedding was in a heap on the floor and the drawers of the antique Regency dresser she'd so painstakingly refinished had been overturned, her clothes strewn everywhere imaginable.

Even her trash can in the kitchen had been upended. Garbage lay everywhere on the previously shining white-tile floor, alongside pots and pans, cracked dishes, and boxes of Cheerios and macaroni and cheese and broken chocolate chip cookies.

Shock and anger raged through her, along with the slick rush of fear.

What the hell is so damned important about this package? she thought furiously, and reached into her tote to pull it out. She glared at it a moment, then started to rip the brown paper off, but she stopped dead when her apartment phone rang.

"Josy! Josy, are you there? Damn it, Josy, why'd you turn off your cell? Answer me!" Rough fear throbbed through Ricky's voice. Somehow, she found her own.

"They were here, Ricky. In my apartment. They've ruined . . . everything."

"They tossed your apartment? Jesus. Josy, I'm sorry." She heard him suck in his breath. "You don't know how sorry I am. Things weren't supposed to go down this way. I never thought . . . listen, you need to get out of town. *Now.*"

"Out of town? No, Ricky, that's crazy. I need to call the police!" She sank down on her stripped-down bed, still holding the parcel.

"Josy, listen to me. That's the worst thing you can do. They want what's inside the package and they'll kill you to get it."

"That's why I have to get rid of it—fast." She heard her voice rising, on the brink of hysteria. "The police can take it off my hands and—"

"Josy, I'm not sure who we can trust at the police department. I was set up . . . and until I know for sure how many were involved, I can't go to them and neither can you. Pack a bag and—"

"Are you crazy? I have a job. My boss is expecting me to turn in sketches for the fall collection in two weeks. Running away is *not* an option—"

"Neither is dying," Ricky yelled at the other end of the phone.

That stunned her into silence. Ricky continued more quietly, but with that same urgency she'd heard the first time he called about the package.

"I never should have gotten you mixed up in this. I swear I didn't mean for this to happen. I thought . . . never mind. You have to get out, Josy, tonight, right now. I'm nowhere near the city, or I'd get you out myself, but I can't come back. I can't be found, not yet . . . and you can't be found either. So pack a bag, take the package, and go somewhere no one would expect. Not to any friend, anyone they could find out about or locate. Go someplace where you can get lost for a while, until I can get to you and take the package back."

"Ricky . . ." She could barely speak. Her voice was a hoarse, sick rasp. "Do you know what you're asking?"

"Yeah. I'm asking you to save your life. And mine. You know I wouldn't unless this was really important, Josy. These guys don't fool around. They can't get that package, and they can't catch up to you. They're not the type to ask questions and leave quietly, you know what I mean?"

Her heart was pounding like the roar of the subway. She felt as if she were in a movie, the loud, violent, gritty kind of movie she didn't especially care for . . . only it wasn't a movie, it was her *life*.

"How are you going to find me? Shouldn't I tell you where I'm going?"

"Not now—not on this line. Just go . . . and I mean now. Grab the package and get out—don't use your cell phone once you disappear, buy a disposable, one with no contract, nothing to trace back to you, and don't use it until I tell you. Open a new e-mail account on Hotmail and send me an e-mail when you're settled and safe. Then I'll get you instructions. Don't use my regular screen name. Middle name, Josy. You know the one. *Middle name.* Add my age. I'll contact you when I can and take the package off your hands. Oh, hell, I gotta go—"

And then there was nothing. Ricky had vanished.

Just like she had to do.

She fought down a sob, dragged her suitcase from the closet, and grabbed an armload of clothes.

Two hours later she was at LaGuardia, boarding a plane for Salt Lake City. She had her tote, her suitcase, and her sketch pad, and she made it on the plane in one piece.

That was something, Josy thought, as the jet taxied down the runway before takeoff.

There was only one place she'd thought to go. A place far from New York, where she could lose herself, lay low, have time to think, to work, and maybe put some pieces of her life together while she was trying to save that same life.

A town where a woman named Ada Scott lived. A town as different from New York as cowhide was from crystal. A town where she could try to recharge what was left of her creative batteries and meet the one living relative she had left in this world.

A town called Thunder Creek.

Chapter 3

AT TEN MINUTES PAST SIX IN THE EVENING, TY Barclay locked up his sheriff's department office and headed out the door without a backward glance. Dead tired, he shifted his black Crown Victoria into drive and headed for home. He'd been awake since 4 A.M. when he'd started the day with a five-mile run to town and back in the predawn darkness, then he'd worked nonstop at his desk ever since. All he wanted to do now was go home, crash, and not wake up, not talk to anyone, not see anyone until tomorrow.

Then, thankfully, this day—and this night—would be over.

The Pine Hills apartments were on the outskirts of Thunder Creek, five miles south of Main Street, and he passed only one car on his way—the white Ford Ranger driven by his cousin Roy Hewett.

Roy honked at him and gave a wave. Ty managed a brief, automatic nod back, but truth be told, his brain scarcely registered Roy. It was still wrapped up in his work, in the cattle rustling investigation that had been on-going for several months now without a break in the case, in the bar fight the previous night at the Tumbleweed Bar and Grill, and in the rescue of a couple of tourists lost this morning on Cougar Mountain—not to mention the mass of paperwork that had piled up on his desk when he wasn't looking.

He had to keep thinking about work in order not to think about Meg. About what today was. And tonight.

He'd only slept five hours the night before, so sleep would come. It better come. He was counting on that. And when he woke up tomorrow morning, his wedding anniversary would be behind him once again.

He swore when his cell phone rang.

"You okay, Ty?" Roy asked.

"Yeah." He suppressed the impulse to hang up after that single word. He liked Roy just fine—they were good friends as well as cousins, in fact, but he didn't like being checked up on. And they both knew that was what was going on here.

"Want to come over to my place for some supper? Corinne's cooking—roast chicken, mashed potatoes, all the fixings. We've got plenty—"

"No, thanks. I'm beat, Roy."

"Yeah, but you gotta eat—"

"Another time."

There was a silence. "Look, Ty, I know what day this is. I know it's hard on you. Why be alone? I saw your face when I passed you and you looked grim as death yourself. I mean . . ." Roy broke off and Ty heard the frustration in his voice. He was trying to say the right things. But there were no right things. Not when it came to Meg's death. And there never would be.

"I'm all right, Roy. No sweat. I'm going to zap myself a frozen pizza and hit the sack. No big deal. Say hi to Corinne for me."

And he disconnected.

There were times—too many times, he reflected, frowning—when having a big family was a pain in the butt. Like on days like this, the anniversary of his and Meg's wedding, when everyone thought he needed coddling. Ty doubted very much that he'd get through the day without calls from his brother, Adam, his sister, Faith, and his mother. That's why he turned off his phone as he pulled into a parking spot at the Pine Hills as the sun began to set over the mountains.

He sat for a minute, his hands on the steering wheel, gazing out from beneath the brim of his Stetson, but he wasn't seeing the glorious rose and gold and lavender colors of the sky, or the majesty of the Laramies bathed in shimmering light, or even the shadows of nightfall creeping nearer.

He saw only Meg, as she'd looked at the morgue the last time he'd seen her. With all the life and the passion drained from her, with only the cold marble facsimile of beauty making a mockery of the joyously vibrant, red-headed woman who'd been the love of his life for as far back as he could remember. Meg, with her cascading red curls and Irish cream complexion, her rich ringing laugh and eyes the color of a wild sea.

He was thirty years old and he'd loved Meg Campbell since she was seven and he was eight.

And he'd grieve for her until the day he died. Nothing was going to change that. Nothing was going to make him stop, or ease the pain, or make him embrace a life without her.

That was just the way it was.

Ty encountered no one as he climbed the steps to his second-floor furnished apartment. He'd gotten rid of everything after she died—all of their furniture and the stuff they'd received as wedding gifts. What he hadn't sold or given away, his parents had stored in a basement closet. He knew his mother, the eternal optimist, thought he might want some of it again if he found someone new. Married again.

There wasn't a chance in hell he ever would.

His answering machine was flickering. Two messages.

He checked caller ID and saw it was his sister, Faith, and his brother, Adam.

Since the messages would have nothing to do with work, he didn't bother playing them. For the past two years, Faith and Adam had worried about him on Meg's birthday, the day of her death, and this, May 2, the date of their anniversary. It would have been their fifth.

What did they think, he was going to kill himself? They should know better. Maybe if he'd stayed on at homicide in Philly, in the city where he and Meg had grown up down the block from one another, where they'd gone to school together, eaten hamburgers and shakes together, and eventually worked at the same precinct and hung out with all the same cops at Shorty's Pub, he might have gone crazy enough to think about doing that. He didn't like to admit it, but it was true. Being in Philly, working on the force, without Meg, had been a living hell.

That's why, when his cousin Roy had called him and said that Thunder Creek needed a new sheriff, and suggested a change of scene might be good for him, he'd actually considered and then accepted the idea.

It hadn't been difficult getting elected, not with Roy's endorsement and his own record in law enforcement. And there was the helpful fact that no one had run against him. He had family ties to the community, and as a matter of fact, the Barclays still owned a big parcel of land in Thunder Creek, land on Blue Moon Mesa that had been in the family for generations. When they were kids, Ty and Faith and Adam had spent a lot of summers here visiting the Hewett side of the clan, riding horseback, fishing, hiking in the foothills above Thunder Creek.

Those had been good years, good times. And coming back had helped. Things had settled down for him a lot since he'd left Philadelphia and started over here. He liked the town and the people, his job was more laid back than being on homicide in Philly, yet it kept him plenty busy. He'd bought himself a couple of horses, he had time to go fishing now and then, and nobody bothered him much. Roy was here, but he had Corinne, and they'd gotten engaged three months ago, which kept him pretty occupied. Sometimes they all three hung out at the Tumbleweed Bar and Grill, where Corinne worked. And occasionally, Roy and Corinne tried to nag him into dating some of the local women.

But that hadn't happened, and Ty knew it wasn't going to happen. Fortunately, Roy and Corinne seemed to have gotten the message and had recently pretty much quit trying to push a social life on him.

It was about time.

He dropped his briefcase on a chair, flicked on a light switch as the sun angled lower in the sky, and went to the fridge in search of a beer.

The sun was a molten ball in the western sky as Josy drove slowly through the town of Thunder Creek. Beside her on the seat of the Blazer was an empty foam coffee cup, half of a chicken sandwich in a Wendy's bag, and the map that had guided her all the way from Salt Lake City to Wyoming.

Inside the pocket of her jeans was a key to her temporary new home—fresh from the palm of Candy Merck, the friendly young bleached blonde rental agent who had just accepted a month's security deposit and a month's rent up front in cash and told her how to find the Pine Hills apartments.

As she cruised down Main Street, headed south, she couldn't help the surge of excitement rushing through her. For the first time in a week she wasn't running away. She had arrived. She was in the town where Ada Scott lived, and where her mother had come long ago to learn about her past.

When she saw the brightly lit diner filled with people, emotions flickered through her, running the gamut from delight to pain. All those childhood memories gushed back of the visit to Thunder Creek and lunch with her parents in that same tiny restaurant. Her parents had been gone for so long now, yet suddenly, for just a moment, they felt as close to her as the front booth of Bessie's Diner.

But only for a moment.

Her hands tightened on the steering wheel as she drove past. This street looked vaguely familiar, but it must have changed some in the past twenty or so years, she realized, glancing from side to side in the shimmering sunset light. She drove past a glass-fronted beauty salon, Merck's Hardware, a gas station—then suddenly backed up and pulled in at the last minute. She didn't need gas—she'd filled up some miles back, but she went inside and bought a can of Coke and a bag of potato chips to go with the leftover chicken sandwich that was going to be her dinner.

For a moment longing filled her, but she shook it off.

Much as she'd have loved to stop at Bessie's Diner for a real meal, something hot and homey, tonight wasn't the time. She'd start her temporary new life in Thunder Creek tomorrow, when she was fresh and rested, when she had her wits about her, not now when she was dead on her feet.

It seemed like months since she'd fled her apartment with one suitcase, her tote, and Ricky's package in tow. Months since she'd lived through that nerve-wracking taxi ride to LaGuardia, calling Reese hastily on her cell, babbling a voice mail message about taking a leave of absence to work on the sketches and asking Reese to let Francesca know. At the airport she'd withdrawn four thousand dollars, nearly all of her savings, from an ATM, and hurried onto the next flight to Salt Lake City, where she'd stayed only a day, enough time to get her bearings and buy a map and a car. A truck, really, a dented, blue, banged-up 1995 Blazer that had seen better days, but the guy at Ray's Used Cars had sworn he'd tuned her up three days earlier and she was good to go.

Ha. The Blazer had broken down in Rock Springs, developed a flat tire on the highway outside of Rawlins, and had been making a weird clunking noise for the past twenty miles. But she was here at last and all she wanted now was to get to the Pine Hills apartments and collapse.

By some miracle, she'd gotten safely away from New York. By some miracle, she hadn't been followed—or caught. Yet.

She felt like she'd been driving forever and her eyes were bleary. Her head hurt. Her shoulders and butt ached from the long hours in the car. But she was here, and in her pocket was the key to a one-bedroom furnished apartment, hers for the next month.

If she needed to stay that long. Maybe Ricky would be in touch in a matter of days, not weeks, and this entire nightmare would be over. Maybe Archie hadn't really died, maybe he'd been resuscitated by the paramedics, and Ricky had managed to clear his name, and whoever was after this damned package was in jail.

And maybe she was Julia Roberts and this was all just a very bad dream.

She found the Pine Hills apartment building with no problem. The nondescript rectangular building was only three stories high and set back from the road, flanked on either side by a meadow full of bluegrass and wildflowers.

It couldn't have looked more different from her fifty-two-story Manhattan high-rise, and she wondered fleetingly what the provided furnishings in her "furnished" apartment would look like.

It's only for a few weeks, until you hear from Ricky, she told herself as she parked in the lot facing the balconied units. *You survived foster home musical chairs and two years with the Hammonds—this will be a piece of cake.*

She dragged her suitcase out of the Blazer, secured her tote over her arm, and slammed the Blazer's door.

Ty Barclay stood in the shadows of his small balcony on the second floor, sipping his beer, alone with his thoughts. He couldn't miss the brilliant glory of the sunset sky now, but it didn't soothe him the way it usually did when he was out riding in the mountains or even driving the winding roads through the foothills. It just didn't matter.

He was thinking about five years ago today, when he'd watched Meg walk toward him down the aisle wearing her mother's ivory wedding dress, her red hair all pinned up, with just a few curls framing her face, and everyone they both knew in the world filling the seats in the church.

And he felt the tight knot of pain he lived with every day clenching inside him, more painful than ever.

Damn it, baby, I miss you so, he thought. *It wasn't supposed to be this way. Not for us.*

A car pulled into the parking lot then, making some kind of clacking sound that penetrated the darkness of his thoughts. In the rosy gold light he saw it was a Blazer, with a dent in the passenger-side door and a low right rear tire. The woman driving it parked right next to his car below, sat for a moment, and then got out.

He watched her automatically, because it was what he did, who he was. A cop. He'd never seen the Blazer before, so she didn't live here. Either she was visiting . . . or she was a new tenant.

As she pulled out a suitcase and slipped a black tote bag on her shoulder, he stopped with the bottle lifted halfway to his mouth.

He'd never seen her before, but she didn't look like anyone from around here. His keen eyes saw the sweep of chin-length silky blonde hair, the jeans that hugged her lean figure, the dainty pink tank top encasing small, firm breasts.

He couldn't see her face too well, but nothing about her that he could see looked familiar.

She's probably from Hope or Medicine Bow or Douglas and got hired on as a waitress or guest wrangler at the dude ranch, he thought, taking another swig of his beer. The Crystal Horseshoe Dude Ranch, owned by Wood and Tammie Morgan, had more employees than just about any other business in Thunder Creek, and they were always coming and going. Most of those who didn't live in the bunkhouses on the Crystal Horseshoe property lived here at the Pine Hills, which offered half of its units with month-to-month leases.

Between the dude ranch's wealthy guests and its employees, a small but steady flow of strangers came and went from Thunder Creek these days, but fortunately, even that hadn't much changed the character of the little town, which was much the same as he remembered from his childhood.

A gust of wind blew down from the mountains, ruffling the woman's hair as she started toward the door of the building, dragging the suitcase behind her. Ty shrugged, finished his beer, and left the balcony, slamming the door closed behind him.

Restlessness churned through him, almost crowding out the emptiness he'd felt ever since the day Meg died. He eyed the laptop on the desk and knew he could always work until he couldn't see straight. Or he could run—another five-mile jog might sap some of what was eating him. Better yet, he'd do both. Run now, work later. And maybe, just maybe, he'd eventually manage to sleep.

He stuffed his keys into the pocket of the sweats he'd changed into and headed for the door.

On the stairway, he saw the woman struggling with her suitcase. She was halfway up to his floor and nearly fell backward when she spotted him sprinting suddenly toward her.

"Your tire's going flat," Ty said, cruising past her.

"Ex— . . . excuse me?"

"On your Blazer. Rear tire's going flat," he said curtly over his shoulder as he reached the ground floor. Then he noted how pale and tired she looked, and how filled to the gills her suitcase was.

"Oh, hell. Give me that." He sprinted back up and took it from her before she could protest, then ran it up to the landing as if it weighed no more than his briefcase.

"Thanks . . . I . . . think," she mumbled with a small, hesitant smile, but Ty was already forgetting her. He bounded past her and out the door, plunging into the deepening cool of the night and thinking of Meg, of how she'd chuckled when he'd gotten her veil all tangled lifting it for their first married kiss, of how warm her lips had felt, of how they'd promised themselves to each other for always.

He put his head down, clenched his fists, and ran faster.

Josy dragged her suitcase down the hallway until she reached 2D. For a moment she wondered if all the men in Thunder Creek could possibly be as handsome as the one she'd just met. *Well, not met, actually,* she thought wryly. *Encountered* was more like it.

He obviously had things on his mind, but at least he'd helped her with her suitcase. For a moment when she'd seen him running toward her with that scowl on his face, she'd feared he was one of the men she'd seen at Archie's house, arriving in Thunder Creek right on her tail. She didn't know why, but she'd had a quick impression of toughness, danger, and a kind of darkness—on his hard-planed face and in the way he moved.

Or maybe, she reflected wearily, her nerves were just shot.

Her leather tote with the package inside swung against her side as she fitted the key Candy Merck had given her into the lock and pushed the door open. She flipped on the light switch and peered in at her new home away from home.

The apartment wasn't bad. It was small, with a cheap

overhead light fixture that gave out merely adequate light, but the nubby forest-green sofa against one wall looked decent enough and there was a tall maple bookcase, and two armchairs upholstered in a passable maroon twill. She tugged her suitcase inside, closed the door, and walked through the place slowly.

The furniture was inexpensive but sturdy maple veneer, the kitchen cabinets looked new, and the floors were all plain buffed wood. The white-painted walls were uniformly bare, except for one framed print over the sofa—a moose standing by a river with a backdrop of snowcapped mountains. There was a lonely looking potted silk plant near the sliding doors that opened onto a small balcony. All in all, it was pretty generic but decent, and nothing that a few rugs and prints and maybe some throw pillows couldn't brighten up a bit. Not that she was in a position to spend much money decorating a place that was going to be a very temporary home. She'd depleted most of her combined checking and savings account when she'd made the ATM withdrawal, and after paying cash for her airline ticket and the Blazer and then laying out the security deposit on this place, she only had six hundred dollars left. She'd have to count her pennies—or find some part-time work while she was here and earn a little money on the side.

In the small bedroom that overlooked the meadow she found a double bed, nightstand, and closet, but was dismayed to discover that there weren't any linens—only a mattress pad, a pillow, and a cheap polyester-cotton quilt. She'd need to buy a set of sheets, a pillowcase, and blanket . . .

Anxiety rose up suddenly and she felt her stomach clenching. She probably should have just booked a room at the Saddle-Up Motel she'd passed on her way into town. It would have definitely been more affordable. But it had looked isolated and shabby and she'd passed it up in favor of finding a bed-and-breakfast or something. But it turned out that Thunder Creek didn't have a bed-and-breakfast—only the Saddle-Up Motel, the Pine Hills apartments, and the Crystal Horseshoe Dude Ranch, which was all the way at the other end of the spectrum, far too plush and pricey for her to even consider.

The Pine Hills had made the most sense. She'd have privacy and security—and anyone searching for her would probably check in motels and hotels, not in an apartment building. *If* anyone even *was* searching for her. They were probably after Ricky, not her.

What in the world is he mixed up in? she wondered for the hundredth time. *And what does that stupid package have to do with it?*

She closed her eyes, praying he was all right, praying he'd show up soon to take this damned package off her hands.

She had a life to get back to in New York—what was left of her life, at least—and she couldn't stay here in this speck of a town forever.

But while she was here . . . Josy rose from the bed and strode to the window, staring out at the meadow and the distant mountains shadowed in darkness now. While she was here, she'd clear her head, come up with some ideas, and get them sketched out for Francesca.

And she'd find Ada Scott. She wasn't sure if she'd approach her or tell her about the connection between them, but she'd find her, and at least know what her grandmother looked like, who she was.

It would make the time go faster until she could go

home. It would distract her from the fact that she could be in danger. It would keep her from thinking about Doug.

And surely by the time she finished with all of that, Ricky would be in touch, he'd show up, he'd take the package off her hands and explain this mess to her.

All she had to do was take it one step at a time.

Exhaustion dragged at her. She'd been driving long hours for days on end, eating at truck stops and greasy spoons. What she really needed was a massage and a facial at the Red Door. A Pilates workout with Jane at the gym. She needed a martini at the Soho Grand, take-out Mongolian beef from Shun Lee Palace, and ten hours' sleep on her own fluffy featherbed complete with cloud-soft DKNY linens.

Instead, she sat on her nubby green sofa and ate half a chicken sandwich and a bag of potato chips. After a final sip of tepid Coke, she pushed Ricky's package into the shadowy recesses of a kitchen cabinet, curled up on top of the thin maroon quilt atop her bed, and fell asleep until the sun woke her in the morning, shining like a fiery opal in the pristine blue Wyoming sky.

Chapter 4

JOSY DROVE THE TWO MILES INTO TOWN EARLY the next morning armed with a shopping list and a plan. Though she was ravenously hungry, she'd discovered that her right rear tire was indeed flat, as the dark-haired stranger on the stairway had told her, so she pulled into Slade's gas station first and arranged to have the spare put on, then walked swiftly up the street to Bessie's Diner.

The morning was mild, without any trace of the chill that had pinged the air once the sun went down last night. She was comfortable in her sandals, Diesel jeans, and a red tank top as she studied the long, pleasant main street, filled with rows of shops. Some of them—like Granny's Quilts and Mrs. Brown's Antiques—looked brand-new and were probably geared toward the tourists staying at the Crystal Horseshoe Dude Ranch. Others—like the Mane Event beauty salon, Merck's Hardware, and Krane's drugstore—looked as weathered and permanent as the mountains themselves and had probably been here the last time she walked along this street—with her parents when she was eight years old.

What struck her most was the pure freshness of the pine-laced air, the vastness of the rolling gray and green expanses stretching in every direction from the town, and the gorgeous silk-blue sky that seemed to fill the universe. Her breath caught at the sight of the mountains towering in the distance, glittering snow frosting their peaks. A waterfall glinted like liquid crystal amid cool green ponderosa pine. And something inside of her, something knotted tight, relaxed at the sight of all this space and openness, at the grand wild beauty of it arrayed before her as far as she could see.

She felt at last that she might be safely, thoroughly, totally removed from New York—and from the danger that had sent her fleeing from the city.

"Morning. Coffee?" A buxom, middle-aged waitress with a mane of wiry, silver-frosted hair pulled back in a low ponytail dashed toward her, coffeepot in hand, the moment she slid into an empty booth near the back of the restaurant.

"Here's the specials of the day, and here's our regular menu. I'll be back in a sec," the waitress told her breathlessly as she finished pouring coffee. She flashed a quick, harried smile, and her dangling crystal earrings swung as she rushed over to the cash register where several customers were lined up to pay.

Josy cradled the coffee cup in both hands as she raised it to her lips. Thank God for caffeine. The coffee was hot and strong and glided down her throat. The waitress had her hands full, bringing out plates of eggs and sausage, pancakes, toast, refilling coffee cups, trying to wipe down a newly vacated table as yet more customers entered the diner and the little bell over the door jangled an announcement of their arrival.

By the time the waitress had a moment to skid to a stop

beside her table once more, she was ready to order scrambled eggs, hash browns, and toast.

"Got it, I'll bring it out quick as I can," the waitress promised, scribbling frantically on her pad.

"Is it always this crazy in here?" Josy asked with a smile, and the woman rolled her eyes.

"It's busy every day, but usually we've got it covered. Today we're shorthanded. The owner and the lady who works the cash register are in Vegas, and the owner's granddaughter was supposed to come in but her baby has a cold, so . . ." She sighed. "It looks like I'm 'it' for now. Don't worry, though, hon, we've got a great cook and he's fast, so you shouldn't have to wait too long."

And she didn't. Her breakfast arrived in a remarkably short time considering the crowd, and she dug in, famished and feeling like she hadn't really tasted anything since she'd left New York.

She savored every bite and by the time the last crust of toast was gone and she was lingering over her third cup of coffee, Bessie's Diner had pretty much emptied out and the waitress was clearing tables left and right.

"Is that it for you, hon—?" The waitress began, but she stopped in midsentence as the door to the diner opened and a lean blonde of about thirty wearing a lemon-yellow shirt, black jeans, and a slim gold bracelet slipped inside.

"Roberta, don't kill me, but the invitation list for my shower isn't ready yet." The blonde thrust a hand through her hair as she hurried across the room. The waitress sighed and set Josy's bill on the table. She turned toward the other woman, shaking her head.

"Aw, Corinne, don't do this to me."

"Sorry, I can't help it." The blonde offered a rueful, somewhat frustrated smile.

"You know I can't even start writing out those invites until you get me that list—"

"I know, I know. I promise I'll have it by tomorrow afternoon. Things have been crazy."

"Yeah, honey, that's what happens when you get married."

"*This* stuff isn't what happens—not to everyone." Corinne leaned a hip against one of the tables and continued on in an agitated tone. "My wedding gown came in yesterday—finally—in the wrong damned color! I wanted ivory and it's white. Stark snow white. I'm going to look completely washed-out. Roy will think he's marrying a ghost when he sees me. That's not how I want to look on my wedding day."

"Aw, sorry, honey." Roberta sighed sympathetically.

Corinne hurried on, her words tumbling together. "So now I have to send it back and hope it comes in right next time, and I'm deciding about place cards and, can you believe it, I still can't find shoes. Did you ever in your life see a barefoot bride? At this rate, you will."

Corinne drew a deep, disgusted breath and tugged a cigarette from her purse. Josy couldn't help listening, amusement and sympathy rising in her as the woman with the short ash-blonde hair kept talking rapidly only three feet away, in between harried puffs on her cigarette.

"My only hope is to find shoes in Casper. So I'm going to have to get there in the next day or so and pray they have something worthy of a bride in size nine narrow. On top of that, last night I promised I'd make dinner for Roy and I meant to work on the shower list right after that, but . . . dinner turned out so great. Roberta, we just ended up having this really romantic night, you know? It was perfect." She sighed with contentment, then added drily, "So perfect that I never got to the shower list." ·

"Didn't you guys even come up for air?" Roberta snorted.

"Not even. I mean, we lost all track of time and I ended up being late for work. My last night at the Tumbleweed and I was late! Elam was fit to be tied, and I thought he was going to cancel the party tonight, but he didn't and it's still on. So be there by ten, okay?"

"You know I'll be there, hon, but you're cutting it close. The shower's a week from Saturday. I need that invitation list pronto. We can't just send out invites the day before—not if you want folks to show up. Hang on a sec."

Roberta turned back to Josy, tapping a fuchsia-colored fingernail on the bill. "Sorry, I'll take this whenever you're ready. Don't mind us, just a little prewedding crisis here."

"No problem." Josy smiled at the bride-to-be as she slid from her seat. "Congratulations. These are nice problems to have, if you're going to have problems," she murmured sympathetically. *Not like having murderers looking for you and having to run for your life halfway across the country,* she thought.

Corinne gave a slow, rueful smile and her shoulders relaxed. "No kidding," she conceded. Her brown eyes suddenly glinted. "And if you saw the groom, you'd know I have no right to complain."

"He's a cutie, that's for sure." Roberta winked at Josy. "Nearly as handsome as my own poor Luther, Lord rest his soul. Now, that man of mine was a *hunk.* I'll never find another like him if I live to be a hundred."

"Maybe not, but all the widowers in town hope you'll keep trying." Corinne grinned. She turned back to Josy. "You're new to town, aren't you?"

"I only arrived yesterday."

"Welcome to Thunder Creek." Roberta spoke over her shoulder as she led the way to the cash register. "Passing through, sticking around, or visiting?"

"Sticking around—short term, at least."

"Don't tell me. I bet you're up staying up at the Crystal Horseshoe Ranch. It's one pretty place, isn't it?" Roberta's sharp hazel gaze flicked over Josy's designer jeans and pendant necklace, even down to the distinctive crystal beading on her sandals, which Josy realized must scream *tourist*.

She shook her head, bracing herself for the lies to come. "No, actually, I've rented a place for the month. I probably won't be staying much longer than that. This is sort of a working vacation. And once I'm caught up with my work, I'll need to get back to Chicago right away."

"Well, if it's peace and quiet you're looking for, you've come to the right place." Roberta met her gaze squarely. "I've only been here for about a year, but you won't ever find a nicer town."

"How in the world did you end up coming to Thunder Creek?" Corinne asked suddenly. She'd followed them to the cash register and was studying Josy curiously. "I'm not trying to be nosy, but we're not exactly on the beaten path."

"That's easy." Roberta slammed the register's drawer, answering before Josy could speak. "I bet she knows someone who stayed at the Crystal Horseshoe. That place has been getting a lot of good write-ups in the travel magazines. We've had guests from all over the country. Am I right?" she asked Josy.

"Yes, absolutely." She grabbed at the excuse like a lifeline. "A good friend of mine stayed at the Crystal Horseshoe for a week. She loved it and raved to me about what a nice town this is. Thunder Creek sounded like the perfect place for a working vacation. Nice people," she added with a smile, "and few distractions."

Josy stuck out out her hand, hoping to avoid any more questions. She'd rehearsed her "story" in the car all the way from Utah. But she wasn't a good liar, never had been, and she felt guilty lying to these two nice women. "I'm Josy Warner—I'm happy to meet you," she added, and at least that was the truth.

"You too, Josy. I'm Roberta Hawkins, and this is Corinne Thomas—soon to be Corinne Hewett, if she ever gets her act together," Roberta added with a snort. At that moment the diner's door opened and several men in cowboy boots, T-shirts, and jeans sauntered in and headed for the big table up front.

"Gotta go." Roberta grabbed the coffeepot again. "Corinne, honey, *please.* Get me that list, will you?"

She sashayed toward the men's table as Josy and Corinne moved toward the door.

"When's the big day?" Josy asked as they emerged into the sunlight. For a moment she caught her breath at the striking vista of soaring mountains, prairie, and sky. She guessed it would take some time to get as used to that view as people in Thunder Creek no doubt were.

"Three weeks from Saturday. If I make it until then." Corinne shook her head. "Thank heavens for Roberta. My dad and brother are coming in from Texas for the big day, but they weren't too interested in helping me plan a wedding. And I lost my mom five years ago. So here in Thunder Creek, Roberta's been like family to me. She and Bessie and the lady who works the cash register at the diner have helped me out with just about everything—and kept me sane. Make that semi-sane," she amended with a laugh. "I'm normally a very calm woman. But I'm thirty-four, I've never been married, and I want my wedding day to be perfect. Pretty unrealistic, right?"

"If I were getting married, I'd feel the same way."

"Thanks. That makes me feel slightly less neurotic." Corinne chuckled and took another drag on her cigarette. "What about you? No ring, I see. Anyone special in your life right now?"

"No." Too late, Josy realized that the single word had snapped out, sounding far more emphatic than she'd intended. She bit her lip. "And for the time being I plan to keep it that way," she added as lightly as she could.

"Sounds like you've been burned."

Josy didn't reply. Corinne studied her cool, closed face with knowing sympathy. "In case you change your mind, you should know we've got a herd of handsome cowboys in this town."

"Thanks, but no thanks. This is strictly a working trip."

"What kind of work do you do?"

Josy hesitated. She'd already lied about being from Chicago and not New York. It was highly unlikely that any of Ricky's enemies, whoever they were, would trace her to Thunder Creek, and she probably could tell the truth about her job at least without risking discovery, but . . .

An inner voice advised her to play it safe. "I'm an assistant to an interior designer," she said. *At least the assistant and designer part was true.* "I'm working on some sketches for an important client. He's moving into a new penthouse in the Loop and I'm coming up with a range of ideas for the home."

"Wow." Corinne stared at her. "That sounds so exciting. It really does. Maybe you can give me a few tips—I'm redoing Roy's house now that it's going to be our home. We've been living together there for over a year," she explained, "but with us getting married and everything, I want to make it more . . . well, *ours*."

"Oh . . . yes. Of course, I'd be glad to help." Josy wanted to crawl into a hole.

"Thanks. Actually, though, the house is the least of my worries at the moment. I'm about to get married without a wedding gown." A sweep of forceful May wind danced around them. "I swear if I don't have a nervous breakdown before this wedding, it'll be a miracle. I honestly think Roberta's going to kill me if I don't get her my list for the shower."

"She does sound pretty desperate."

"I've got to get caught up—I don't mean to make it hard on her. I really appreciate her throwing the shower for me. Actually Roberta and Ada are hosting it together—it's going to be at Ada's house. Sweet of them."

Josy stopped walking. *Ada's house*. Ada Scott? She shifted, trying to relax her suddenly tense shoulders. "Who's Ada?" she asked, trying to sound no more than casual. But she held her breath as Corinne replied.

"Oh, sorry. Ada's the woman I told you about—she works the cash register at Bessie's Diner. Bessie Templeton owns the place and Ada—Ada Scott—is her best friend. Roberta works with both of them, and with Bessie's granddaughter, Katy Brent, who helps out once in a while and does the books. They've all become really good friends of mine in the past year or so."

"So . . . it's Ada and Bessie who are away in Las Vegas?" Josy asked slowly. "Roberta told me they were away, but she didn't mention their names."

"Yes, that's right. Actually, they're coming home tomorrow. And if I don't have the invitation list ready by then, Ada will be on my case too." She laughed. "I'd better get my act together. Look, I don't know if this working vacation of yours includes socializing or not, but my boss, Elam Lowell, over at the Tumbleweed Bar and Grill, is throwing a good-bye party for me there tonight. I've been waitressing there for years, but now that Roy and I are getting married, I want a day job, so he and I can spend all of our evenings together. So I'll be working weekdays at Roy's real estate office. Tonight's my last night at the Tumbleweed. Want to come?"

"Oh . . . thanks . . . but . . ."

"Think about it." Corinne smiled, and gave a small shrug. "No big deal. If you want to get out, have a few drinks, meet some people, come on by. I've got to run over and meet Roy at the office real quick, but . . . maybe I'll see you later."

"Yes, maybe. Thanks." Josy stared after her as Corinne stamped out her cigarette and hurried down the street.

So. Corinne's Ada is my Ada. Ada Scott. And she'll be home from Las Vegas tomorrow, Josy mused as she walked slowly back up Main Street. *If she hadn't been away, I might have met her today in Bessie's Diner. Right off the bat . . .*

The imminent prospect of coming face-to-face with her grandmother filled her with a strange mix of emotions—excitement, curiosity, and . . . reserve. Once she did meet Ada, she'd need to decide if she should tell the woman who she was—or if she should just keep her distance and eventually leave Thunder Creek as her mother apparently had years ago, never having reached out to make contact.

After I meet her, I'll decide, she told herself. Right

now, with Ada away, all she could do was take things one step at a time.

Today she needed to buy groceries and toiletries and linens for the apartment. And she had to find a library.

She walked along Thunder Creek's main street until she reached Lucy's Grocery and Drugs, where she stocked up on crackers, peanut butter, Rice Krispies, and other essentials. While checking out, she asked the gangly young boy working the cash register where the nearest Wal-Mart might be found. "Casper," he told her without hesitation.

"And is there a library in Thunder Creek?"

Sure, but it was only open three days a week—Monday, Wednesday, and Friday.

"How do I find it?" she asked as he handed over the second bag of her groceries.

"Uh, Miller Road, a quarter mile west of town, near the high school," he mumbled, his gaze shifting to the two teenage girls in halter tops and shorts who'd just entered the store, giggling.

"Does it have a computer?"

"Yep. A computer and a printer. Wood and Tammie Morgan donated 'em both last year."

She breathed an inward sigh of relief. She'd be able to get in touch with Ricky easily after all. Tomorrow was Wednesday—she'd go to the library and send him an e-mail. With any luck, he'd read it within a few days and let her know when he'd be coming to get the package.

Ever since she'd landed in Salt Lake City, a part of her had itched to rip open the package and see what was inside. But that impulse wasn't nearly as powerful as the part of her that didn't want to know. The part that hoped Ricky would show up and take it off her hands before she had to know—and deal with—whatever was inside—whatever had cost Archie his life.

She pushed away the unspoken worry in her mind—that something could have happened to Ricky already. That he hadn't gotten away as she had. That there'd be no answer to her e-mail. And that he wasn't coming for the package at all . . .

Those thoughts made her throat tighten and the muscles of her neck clench, but she did her best to ignore them and decided to concentrate on the positive.

Thunder Creek had a library. And a computer. And very friendly people. So far, so good.

She'd just take it one step at a time.

She was hugging both bags of groceries to her chest as she headed back to the gas station, when a red pickup cruising past suddenly braked against the curb and a lean, sandy-haired young cowboy wearing a broad smile, a green polo shirt, and worn jeans jumped out.

"Those bags look heavy. Can I give you a hand?"

He looked like he was in his early twenties, with hazel eyes, a lean jaw, and the fresh-off-the-range handsomeness of a model in a Ralph Lauren ad.

"No thanks, I'm good." She strolled past him without slowing her steps. "My car's at the gas station, right over there—"

"All the way over there? Then, c'mon, let me help you."

"I don't think so."

He was following her, his muscular arms spread wide. "I promise not to run off with your groceries. And if I do, we have a crackerjack sheriff here in Thunder Creek and he'll get them back for you. You can give him my description."

She had to laugh. He had a killer grin and a Western drawl and his words brought a reluctant smile to her lips.

Her arms *were* aching a bit. Oh hell, why not?

"All right, but I have your face memorized. If you hightail it out of town with my Rice Krispies, the law will be after you before you can say snap, crackle, pop."

A crack of laughter boomed from his chest as she passed him the bags. "You've got nothing to worry about, ma'am. I'm a Wheaties kind of guy."

Obviously, she thought, as he snaked those muscled arms around the grocery bags. Only a blind woman wouldn't have noticed biceps that impressive.

"I'm Chance Roper," he said easily as he fell into step alongside her. "I'm a ranch hand at the Crystal Horseshoe Ranch. Let me guess—you're one of our guests staying out at the private cabins, right? If you were staying in the main house, I'd definitely remember you."

"I'm afraid you're wrong on both counts. Here we are."

"This bucket of bolts is yours?" He was eyeing the Blazer as if it had just crawled out of the junk heap on one cylinder. His glance immediately flipped back to her and she almost laughed, knowing he was trying to reconcile her fancy sandals and cool jeans with the beat-up, semi-rusted car.

"She's mine all right. Good old Nellie." She reached out for the bags with an amused smile. "I'll take those now. Thanks—"

"Hold on, let me put 'em in for you."

When the groceries were stored in the backseat of the Blazer, Chance Roper stood there another minute, his hands stuffed in his pockets. "You're not a tourist, then? Just driving through?"

"I'm staying on a bit. But not at the Crystal Horse-shoe."

"A mystery woman, huh?" He grinned. "Maybe I could buy you a drink sometime? Like tonight?"

"I don't think so." He was persistent, she had to give him that much. Charming, sweet, and persistent. But she wasn't here to date cowboys, or anyone else for that matter. Of course he had no way of knowing that, she told herself. Or of knowing that for her, right now, *date* was a four-letter word.

"How long are you staying around?"

"I'm not sure." She met his gaze squarely. "Look, thanks for the help, but I have to go pay for my new tire and I have a lot of settling in to do—"

He held up a hand good-naturedly. "Sure. Don't say another word. I'm outta here." He tipped his wide-brimmed cowboy hat at her. "See you around . . . uh . . . what did you say your name was?"

She did laugh then. She couldn't help it. You had to admire—or despise—a guy who wouldn't give up. But Chance Roper seemed too genuinely nice for anyone to despise.

She caved.

"Josy. Josy Warner."

His smile was nearly as wide as his hat brim. "I'll see you around, Miz Warner."

As he swung off toward his pickup, whistling, Josy could only wonder if all the men in Thunder Creek were as charmingly skillful at hitting on newcomers. Then she remembered the man she'd encountered on the stairway of the Pine Hills apartments last night. Nothing charming about him. And obviously no interest in hitting on newcomers. At least not this newcomer.

Which was fine with her. Unlike Chance, who, apart
from his cowboy hat and boots and his cute twang, was
not so different from any number of smooth, confident
guys she could meet in any club in New York, the man on
the stairwell had struck her as a dark, cool-eyed loner.
That was hardly her type and never had been.

Of course, Doug Fifer was exactly her type and look
how that had turned out.

With a sigh, Josy went in search of the gas station at-
tendant, deciding that thinking about men—any man—
was a waste of valuable time and energy. What she needed
to do now was go back to the apartment to put her groceries away, then drive to Wal-Mart for some bed linens
and towels and cleaning supplies and then back to the
apartment for the rest of the day, to concentrate on work.

Which was a great plan in theory, but in reality, she
realized by eight o'clock that night, it just plain sucked.

Sitting on her rented sofa in her tiny Pine Hills living
room after the sun went down, she stared morosely at the
doodles occuping the bottom quarter of her sketchbook.

A cat. She'd doodled a cat. And a mountain. Like one
of those she could see from her balcony. And she'd doodled the name Ada Scott. In print, in cursive. In rounded
letters, and slanted letters. Ada Scott . . . Ada Scott . . .
Ada Scott . . .

She obviously wasn't going to get any work done
tonight. Maybe it was too soon, she reflected, pushing the
sketches away. Maybe she needed to settle into her new
environment and let the muse return at her own pace. It
never paid to rush the muse. She always rebelled.

Josy didn't want to think about how for years, her muse
had never left her side, had been a part of her soul. What
had happened to that girl, the one who'd lived and

breathed and dreamed of beautiful clothes, whose creative thoughts had flowed so easily and vibrantly onto the page, who had only to envision a hot new red dress, a flowy skirt or elegant jacket, and she could see it in luxe living color and practically feel the silk of it caressing her skin? The girl who'd once visualized an entire formal ball gown and all the accessories and sketched it all in rapid detail while listening to a lecture on textile variations at the Fashion Institute of Technology in New York?

She's still here, she told herself. *She's merely gone on a sabbatical—given the creativity a break—focused on other things. Like staying alive. Hiding out. Going crazy . . .*

She glanced around at the generic walls of the apartment, feeling stifled. It was Tuesday night. If she were home right now, she'd be meeting Jane and Reese for drinks at the Plaza. They went out every Tuesday night for drinks and then dinner, usually for sushi or Thai food.

She suddenly missed them, missed New York, with a painful lurch of her heart. *Okay,* she thought, jumping up, throwing her pencil down on the coffee table beside the worthless doodle-sketches.

You're stuck here for a while, but you don't have to sit here alone in this suffocating apartment. You had two invitations for tonight, right? So don't just sit here like a scared little kid—do what Ricky taught you to do—stand up for yourself and fight. Fight for your own life, your own wants. Fight the urge to be silent and afraid. And alone. Fight that urge to retreat into a mute, silent shell, a pathetic child like you were before. Get yourself out there and into the game.

She knew Ricky's way was right. Since she'd found out the truth about Doug and his lies she'd been less social than ever, more withdrawn than she'd been since her first foster home.

Ricky had taught her how to cope with the urge to retreat. And she needed to remember those lessons now.

She unzipped her suitcase, which she hadn't yet unpacked, and tore through it for something to wear.

She was going to a party.

Chapter 5

* * *

GARTH BROOKS WAS CROONING FROM THE JUKE-box over the din of laughter and chatter when Josy slipped through the double doors of the Tumbleweed Bar and Grill and paused for a moment to scan the packed, smoky room.

It was fairly dark, but she could see that the booths against the back wall were mostly full of people, as were the dozen or so small tables scattered around a big wooden dance floor. To the right of the entrance a group of men played pool, and in the low, smoky light of the room she spotted Candy Merck and some other women at the bar, chatting up the bartender.

Suddenly she noticed Corinne, waving at her from one of the tables off the dance floor.

"Josy! We're over here!"

"Who's that?" Roy Hewett asked his fiancée as the willowy blonde he'd never seen before smiled and started toward them. She was more than pretty, with a pale sweep of hair that didn't quite touch her shoulders, sexy green cat eyes, and a walk that would have stirred the blood of a monk. In fact, her lithe figure encased in low-slung jeans, boots, and a silky, low-necked ruby-colored blouse drew more than one stare, he noted.

And if he hadn't been happily engaged to Corinne, he'd have damn sure stared too.

"That's the girl I met today in Bessie's Diner. I told you—I invited her to come tonight, but I didn't really think she would." Corinne flashed a grin as Josy reached the table.

"Glad you could make it," she exclaimed. "This is Roy, my honey." Grinning, Corinne glanced up at the tall man who had risen to his feet beside her. He had dark hair and friendly brown puppy dog eyes. "Sweetie, this is Josy Warner."

"Glad to meet you, Josy. All the way from Chicago, right? That's a long way from home. What can I get you to drink?"

"White wine sounds good."

"That's exactly what I would have guessed." His eyes twinkled. "Be right back," he said easily and sauntered off toward the bar.

"Here, take a seat, Josy. I want you to meet Katy and Jackson Brent, good friends of ours," Corinne continued. "Katy's grandmother, Bessie, owns Bessie's Diner—Katy works there too sometimes, but she couldn't make it in today because her little girl was sick."

"Yes, Roberta told me that." Josy offered a smile to the slim, beautiful woman seated across from her. "I hope she's feeling better now."

"Mattie's fever is down, thanks." Katy Brent set down her wineglass and gave her head a shake, sending the honey-colored strands swinging around her shoulders. "The poor baby had an ear infection and it turned into a cold. Thank God it was nothing really serious."

"That's the only reason why we're putting in an appearance tonight. But we can't stay too long," Jackson Brent said meaningfully, with a sideways glance at his wife.

Katy laughed. "Jackson worries if Mattie has a hiccup," she explained, and threw her husband a look of pure love. "We left her with my parents tonight, and I had to promise him we wouldn't stay here more than half an hour."

"And it's twenty-four minutes and counting," Jackson Brent retorted. "If Corinne and Roy weren't two of our best friends, we'd be home hovering over the crib where we belong," he grinned.

Josy joined in laughing along with Katy and Corinne. As Roberta came over and joined the group, taking a seat and tipping back a bottle of Budweiser, she couldn't help thinking what a stunning couple the Brents made.

Katy Brent glowed with beauty and it was clear she was madly in love with her husband. And Jackson was not only tall, dark, and handsome, he had one of the sexiest, gentlest smiles she'd ever seen. By the time Roy returned with her wine, Jackson was shepherding his wife toward the door and Katy was calling over her shoulder, "See you in town, Josy. Come into Bessie's and have a slice of pie on me!"

She called out her thanks, but wasn't sure Katy Brent heard her, because the din in the Tumbleweed seemed to be rising by the second. All around her, men and women were dancing, drinking, playing darts, or engrossed in group conversations. Just about everyone there seemed to know everyone else.

The atmosphere was warm and loud and welcoming. She didn't care much for the smoke clogging the air, mixing with the scent of beer, sawdust, and perfume, but the country music touched a chord in her as she watched a few couples swaying together on the dance floor, their arms entwined.

"Okay, everybody—get off your butts and dance!" the bartender, a big burly guy with stringy brown hair and a beard, shouted. "This one's for Corinne, for being the best damned waitress we've had in this place in years. No offense, ladies," he added in his gravelly voice, glancing at the two working waitresses striding from table to bar and back again, carrying trays of beer bottles, bowls of nuts, and glasses. "But we're sure going to miss our very own A-1 waitress, Miz Corinne Thomas. Everybody shaking their tail out on that dance floor's going to get a drink on the house!" he yelled, and there was a roar of approval and laughing applause that shook the rafters of the bar.

"Corinne and Roy—you two lead it off."

Corinne and Roy stood up, grinning.

"That's Elam, my boss," Corinne told Josy. "He's just buttering me up, hoping I'll stay on after all."

"Not a chance in hell of that." From behind her, Roy wrapped his arms around her waist, just as a bowlegged older man in a plaid shirt and string tie hustled up, grabbed Roberta's hand, and pulled her toward the dance floor. She was doing a jitterbug as she allowed herself to be swept away.

Throughout the Tumbleweed Bar and Grill, couples were swarming toward the dance floor.

Josy noticed Corinne glancing at her, hesitating.

"Go on, you two. I'm fine here."

But Roy was shaking his head. "No way, Josy. A beautiful woman like you sitting here all alone? Corinne and me won't hear of it. Besides, you heard what Elam said— everybody on the dance floor." A slow grin spread across his face. "And damned if I don't have the perfect dancing partner for you."

He turned around before she could speak and cupped his hands around his mouth.

"Hey! Ty!" he called in the direction of the men still playing pool near the double doors. "Come on over here!"

"Roy—no!" Josy murmured, her stomach sinking. Corinne placed a hand on his arm.

"Honey, this isn't such a good idea." But Roy wasn't about to be deterred. He waved his hat over his head as the group of men playing pool all turned and glanced at him.

Josy turned sharply back to the table, caught between amusement and mortification. *That's what you get for coming tonight,* she thought. *You should have just stayed in and plugged away at the fall line.*

"I don't want to dance with anyone, Roy. Seriously." She tried her most charming smile. "I'm antisocial—always have been. It's a chronic condition. All my friends will tell you. Please, just go dance with Corinne. I have my wine, I'm perfectly happy to—"

But she broke off as she heard the unmistakeable sound of a man's boots thumping against the floor behind her, moving closer.

"Ty, this is your lucky night. This lady needs a dance partner. Meet Josy Warner—from Chicago," Roy said cheerfully.

The footsteps halted right behind her chair.

"Josy, this is my cousin, Ty Barclay." Grinning from ear to ear, as if well pleased with himself, Roy clapped a hand on the shoulder of the man behind her. Resignedly, Josy craned her neck up and sideways to see who she was about to be stuck with.

Oh, no.

It was him. Mr. Not-So-Prince-Charming from the Pine Hills apartment stairwell. The tall, powerfully built man with the hard features and the wavy blue-black hair. And those cold, gun-smoke-blue eyes. Tonight instead of sweats he was wearing an open-necked dark blue shirt and well-tailored gray slacks—but the same scowl he'd worn last night.

He looked even less pleased to see her than he had when he'd nearly knocked her down the stairs.

"You'd be doing my cousin a big favor by dancing with him," Roy informed Josy, seemingly oblivious to the tense silence that had dragged on several seconds too long.

"He's done nothing but play pool and talk business since he got here, and Ed Flanagan over there could bend his ear all night about rustled cows and damned incompetent brand inspectors. Ty, I know you'd much rather be dancing with this beautiful woman than thinking about rustlers. You'll even get a free beer," he added, grinning, and Josy wished she could sink through the floor.

"Roy!" Corinne gasped, but he just pulled her toward the dance floor with a chuckle.

For a moment the silence continued. The man standing behind her chair didn't move, didn't speak.

"It's all right. I don't want to dance," Josy said firmly, turning slightly, throwing him a quick cool glance. "Not with you, not with anyone. So thank you anyway, but—"

"Great." Ty Barclay gave a curt nod, not even letting her finish. "If you're sure."

"Oh, I'm sure. I'm positive."

That penetrating blue gaze fixed itself on her face for a full ten seconds. His eyes were as dark and unfathomable as tinted glass but she sensed anger coming off him in waves.

"Great," he said again. "Thanks for the reprieve."

He strode toward the bar without giving her a second glance and Josy found herself tightly gripping the stem of her wineglass, her face and fingers frozen.

Asshole, Josy thought, and took a deep breath. She forced her fingers to relax and to ease their grip on the glass before she cracked it. After having lived in New York for the past ten years she considered herself sophisticated and fairly worldly, but she was still stunned by Ty Barclay's rudeness—and yes, by his instant and complete rejection.

Damn it. She might not be movie star material, but she wasn't exactly a dog. She hadn't been turned down for a dance or a drink or a date or anything else by a man since she was fourteen and sprouted boobs. What the hell was the matter with him?

Congenital rudeness, she thought, and took a gulp of her wine. He might be drop-dead gorgeous but he had the manners of an iguana. The charm of a mackerel. The arrogance of a . . .

Uh-oh. He had stopped just short of the bar and turned around. He was looking at her, she realized, her heartbeat quickening. And now, he was . . . coming back.

She set the wineglass down carefully, trying to control the anger surging through her.

"Look, that was rude—even for me." He stopped beside her chair and his mouth twisted ruefully. "You're not the one I'm mad at. Roy keeps trying to—oh, hell, never mind. It has nothing to do with you." He cleared his throat and started again.

"I don't suppose one dance will kill us—either one of us. What do you say?"

"I say maybe we're better off not finding out."

A hint of a grin touched the corners of his lips. "I had that coming. But you know, sometimes it's good to live dangerously."

As her eyebrows shot up, he said in a reasonable tone, "Besides, if Roy finds out I gave you the brush-off he'll be on my case for a week. He'll probably even call my mother and tell her she raised a rude son-of-a-bitch and then she's likely to cry. So what do you say?"

He held out a hand and she stared at it. His hand was big and it looked strong, capable. Like him. But he didn't strike her as a man who'd have a mother who would cry over his being rude. Or like a man who'd care what anyone else thought of him. He looked tough and self-sufficient, like a man whose emotions were always under control, who did what he pleased and didn't much care who didn't like it.

But the funny thing was, he did sound sorry. And he was standing there with his hand out, patiently waiting for her answer. The languid thrum of the music caressed her senses. Everyone in the place was dancing. "What do you say?" Ty Barclay asked again.

"I wouldn't want to upset anybody's mother," she muttered. She rose to her feet but ignored his outstretched hand, hurrying ahead of him toward the dance floor, wondering why she was even bothering to go through with this.

A slow country song flowed from the jukebox and the floor was packed with couples dancing closely together. As his arms went around her waist, drawing her to him, Josy couldn't help but be aware of the rock-hard strength packed into his six-foot-two-inch frame, and of the whip-cord tension she felt in those broad, sloping shoulders. Maybe it was her imagination, but a hot jolt of fire seemed to quiver through her when the fingers of his right hand closed around hers.

It means nothing, she told herself as they began to sway to the music. *Except that I haven't gotten out much lately.*

She'd danced with men she didn't know in Manhattan clubs a hundred times or more, but here in the Tumbleweed Bar and Grill in the middle of Wyoming, it felt different. Maybe it was the country song playing in the darkness, or the sultry night, or the clean scent of soap and the sage-scented outdoors on the man whose arm encircled her waist, but somehow there was an intimacy here that felt completely unlike the typical scene at Suede or Nocturne.

"Did you get that flat tire fixed all right?"

His words yanked her out of her thoughts. "Oh . . . yes. I did." She forced herself to say the word. "Thanks."

There was silence then between them as the music flowed, and she might have relaxed a little except that she was intensely aware of the heat where his hand touched her waist.

"That rig of yours looks like she's been ridden hard and put away wet."

"I beg your pardon?"

He shook his head as if she were a dimwitted child. "Never mind." He was glancing over at the pool table, no doubt regretting the fact that someone seemed to have taken his place there. Josy felt a surge of annoyance.

"Look," she said. Her chin angled up so she could meet his eyes. "I appreciate your trying to make up for before, but it isn't necessary. You don't have to be nice to me or try to make small talk with me. The song's almost over. Your torture will be ended soon."

His eyes glinted like cobalt through the dim, smoky light. "You're the one who seems tortured. I'm holding up just fine."

"Are you?"

"Considering."

She gritted her teeth. "I can't imagine why your cousin is so eager to set you up in a dance with a complete stranger. With your charm, you must be able to score plenty of phone numbers on your own."

Ouch, Ty thought, amused. This one could bite. He let the sarcasm slide and glanced at her again, this slim lithe blonde with the cameo face and eyes the color of new Wyoming grass. She looked elegant and delicate, as if a strong wind would carry her off. As if she didn't belong here in this town, or in this bar, but someplace sheltered and protected, someplace soft and tame.

"I'm not into scoring phone numbers," he told her with a shrug.

"Obviously." She saw Corinne and Roy dancing only a few feet away, both of them looking dreamy-eyed. It was the only reason, she told herself, why she wouldn't kill Roy Hewett the moment the song ended. She sighed. "So what *are* you into?"

"Now who's making small talk? You don't want to know."

"Oh, c'mon, try me. What else do I have to do?"

He looked her dead in the eye. "Guns, handcuffs, and Krispy Kremes."

"*What?*"

"I'm a cop." He deftly turned her so that a huge cowboy dancing with a woman almost as tall as her partner avoided smashing into them. "More specifically, I'm the sheriff here in Thunder Creek."

The *sheriff*. Josy lost track of her feet and stepped on his toes. "Sorry," she murmured, as he glanced downward. Her three-inch boot heel must have dug into his big toe, but if it hurt at all through the leather of his own boot, he didn't show it.

"You're not . . . wearing a uniform," she stammered.

"I'm off-duty." He was looking carefully at her, she realized in dismay. Examining her face. He appeared torn between amusement and something else. Like the beginnings of suspicion. "It seems to bother you that I'm a cop. Why is that?"

Josy drew a deep breath. She wasn't about to tell him, though he'd no doubt be fascinated to learn that he was dancing with a woman on the run, a woman hiding out from other cops, cops like him. And from whoever had killed Archie—and ransacked her apartment—and framed Ricky.

"Don't be ridiculous," she heard herself say in an airy tone that sounded just a little too shrill. She tried again. "It doesn't bother me," she assured him. "It's just . . . you don't *look* like a cop."

Actually he did. Like Ricky, he had an alertness about him, a toughness. And that same flat, intense way of looking at you that seemed to be x-raying your brain.

He was doing it now.

"So, what do you do for a living?" he asked, making it sound like a casual question, but Josy wasn't fooled.

"I'm here to catch up on some work. I just needed to get away from it all." *Yes, like murderers, the people who trashed my apartment, and possibly the entire NYPD.*

"What kind of work do you do?"

"Creative stuff. I'm sure you wouldn't be interested," she said hurriedly. "The music's stopped."

"So it has."

He was still watching her with those piercing eyes, no doubt trying to recall if he'd ever spotted her face on a mug sheet. Josy tried to fight the panic thumping in her chest. Why had she been so snotty to him? Why hadn't she just kept her mouth shut, put up with the dance, and done nothing to attract his attention?

"Thanks for the dance. You've done your good deed for the night." She forced a smile, hoping she looked polite and natural, and not on the verge of a meltdown. "I'm sure your mother will be proud."

He grinned suddenly, and it was like a punch to the gut. He was *much* too attractive and even more so when he smiled. Which, she told herself, he probably did only once in a millennium.

To her dismay, he escorted her back to the table, where Corinne and Roy had already returned. Roberta was still dancing, this time to an upbeat song by Shania Twain. Her long frosted ponytail bounced as she swung on the arm of a thin sixtyish man in a bright yellow shirt. Josy remembered Corinne's comment about Roberta and all the widowers in town. *At least someone's having fun,* she thought as the middle-aged waitress and her dance partner showed off their moves.

"Hope my big cousin didn't step on your toes," Roy said as she slipped into her chair.

"Actually, I stepped on his. But I don't think I hurt him too much," she managed to say in a light tone.

"If you did, no doubt he had it coming. Don't worry, he's pretty tough. Big-city cop and all—" Roy broke off at her shocked look.

Big-city cop?

"What? He didn't tell you?"

"He . . . said he's the sheriff here." Josy threw Ty a sharp glance as he dropped into the chair next to hers.

"Well, yeah, he is, but he used to be a homicide cop in Philadelphia. He's been decorated, shot, honored by the mayor, the works. You were dancing with a hero."

"Cut it out, Roy." Ty signaled the waitress passing by for a beer.

Corinne jumped into the breach, talking fast. "Roy, did you know that Josy works for an interior designer? She's going to give me some tips for redecorating your place . . . I mean, our place. After the wedding, of course." She looked hopefully at Josy. "You'll still be here after the twenty-second of May, right?"

"I'm not sure. I . . . think so."

"Interior decorator, eh?" Ty Barclay's sharp gaze flicked again to her face. "Goes to show what kind of a detective I am. You got more out of her than I did, Corinne. She wouldn't even tell me what she did for a living."

"That's probably because you scared her, cuz," Roy put in.

"Can't imagine how." Ty gave a slow, hard smile, but his eyes were too keen for comfort. Josy heard alarm bells screaming in her head.

Damn it. She'd stirred the suspicions of a cop after only twenty-four hours in Thunder Creek. This wasn't good. It wasn't good at all.

The only thing she could do now was try to act as normal as possible. She had to try to stop Ty Barclay from wondering about her, or checking out her background.

I'm sorry, Ricky, she thought. *I'm not very good at lying. But I'll try to fix it.*

"It's just . . . my ex-boyfriend was a cop," she heard

herself saying, before she could think twice. "And it ended badly."

At least that much was true. "So . . . it shook me up a little when you said you were the sheriff here in Thunder Creek. I'm over it now," she added with a pleasant smile, determined to douse any suspicions Ty might have about her before they could spark into dangerous flames.

He nodded and leaned back, not saying anything, not even looking at her anymore. *He's lost interest,* she thought with a stab of hope. *Good.*

Corinne pushed back her chair suddenly. "I'm going to powder my nose," she announced. She grabbed Josy's arm. "Come with me."

Josy hadn't traveled to the ladies' room in a pack since high school, but she was only too glad to escape. Corinne charged through the door showing a cowgirl holding a lasso and dragged her inside the small two-stall restroom, which reeked of drugstore perfume and cigarettes.

"Sorry Roy pushed you into dancing with Ty," she said immediately. "He meant well, but . . . it was a bad idea from the start. Roy and I have tried setting Ty up with lots of girls since he moved to Thunder Creek, but he's not into dating these days, not at all. I'm sorry if he took it out on you—we're the ones he's really annoyed with."

"I did get the impression he'd rather be doing almost anything other than dancing with me."

"That's no reflection on you, honey, believe me." Corinne had whipped a deep pink lipstick from her purse, but she paused after snapping off the cap. "Ty lost his wife two years ago. She was with the police department in Philadelphia just like him, and this criminal got loose in the station house and grabbed a gun. It hit Ty really hard.

She was pregnant at the time. Ever since then he's blocked out just about everything except for his work."

"I'm sorry . . . that's awful." Josy was stunned.

"Yeah." Corinne looked grim. "It was awful. Roy says he and Ty have always been close, but now Roy can't even get through to him. Ty won't let his brother or his sister get close to him anymore either. He's basically shut down his personal life."

"That's too bad." Josy thought of the frown on Ty Barclay's face the first time she met him in the stairwell. "He must have loved his wife very much," she said slowly.

"Oh, he did. According to Roy, they had this fairy-tale thing. This magic . . ." Corinne glided the lipstick carefully over her mouth. "But even so . . . he's got to get over her sometime, right? When he moved here, we gave him a few months to settle in, and then we figured he'd want to meet some women, start getting back into the swing of things, but he only went on one or two dates and he never called either woman back again. And, honey, I assure you, there's plenty of girls in this town who'd love the chance to help him forget his wife. But he's not having any of it."

"I'm sure he will when he's ready."

"It's been two years. To tell you the truth," Corinne sighed, "Roy and I are starting to think he won't ever be ready." She dropped the lipstick back into her purse. "That's why I didn't want Roy to bulldoze you two into dancing together. I had a feeling Ty wouldn't like our pushing him toward someone again. So if he seemed standoffish or . . . rude, or anything like that, it's not *you*. It's him. He might be drop-dead gorgeous, smart, and the best shot I've ever seen, but right now, Ty Barclay is poison for any woman's ego."

"My ego's intact, Corinne. Don't worry about it."

"I heard Chance Roper threw his hat into the ring."

"I beg your pardon?"

Corinne finger-combed her hair and her eyes danced. "He came into Bessie's Diner today and pumped Roberta for information about you. Told her all about how he saw this knockout blonde on Main Street, and how he carried your groceries even though you wouldn't give him the time of day."

"Oh, God. So what they say about small towns is true. News travels fast."

"Speed of light." Corinne chuckled. "A new woman in town is always big news. Most of the ones who stay at the dude ranch don't get to meet many people beyond the ranch hands there. Tammie and Wood don't mind some flirtation between the guests and the employees—they think it adds to the business. But you must've told Chance you're not part of the tourist crowd and he wanted all the deets he could get. Bessie's Diner is sort of the unofficial town center, and he figured if anyone knows what's going on and who's who, it'd be Roberta. Or Bessie and Ada, once they get back."

"Oh, right. From Las Vegas." She moistened her lips. "So . . . are they big gamblers? Or do they just like the shows?"

Corinne opened the restroom door and threw Josy an amused glance as they walked back into the noisy dimness of the bar.

"I notice you're changing the subject. Listen, Chance is a good guy. He's going to track you down and ask you out again sooner rather than later, just so you know."

He'll be disappointed, Josy thought as they joined Roy and Roberta and several other people who had pulled up chairs around their table. She noted that Ty Barclay was nowhere to be seen and that his chair had been taken by the plaid-shirted man Roberta had danced with earlier. The next moment she spotted Ty striding out the double doors into the night.

Relief swept through her. She was glad he'd left. The less she had to do with anyone connected to the police, the better.

She sipped her wine, letting the others chatter around her. Corinne had a warm heart, Roberta was a stitch who seemed to flirt with any man within a half mile, and Roy was like a big, gregarious puppy dog, buying drinks and burgers and cheese fries for everyone at the table.

But she wondered what was going on with Reese and Jane and the studio. She wondered where Ricky was—if he was safe. And even, to her shame, where Doug was tonight.

Was he with his wife and his kids? Watching TV, reading a story out loud to his children, going out for ice cream? Or picking up another woman at a business party, telling her he was single, turning on the charm?

She set down her wineglass. It was still three-quarters full. But she suddenly needed to get away, get home.

She excused herself, said her good nights, and left the Tumbleweed. The air outside was cool, drenched with the scent of pine. And the hint of rain.

The moon was covered by murky clouds.

But she had enough light to see Ty Barclay sitting in a police cruiser no more than ten feet away. And to see that he was watching someone—two someones. Two men getting out of a black pickup. She saw his gaze trained on them as they ambled toward the Tumbleweed.

They glanced toward the cruiser once, but didn't slow their steps, just kept on walking, not even speaking to each other. As they passed her, she caught sight of their faces.

The taller of the two had the kind of tough, pock-marked face and hard, beady eyes usually found in B-movie bad guys. His nose looked like it had been broken more than once and his lips seemed stuck in a perpetual sneer. He looked to be in his midthirties. The second man, dressed in a black shirt and pants, cowboy boots, and a gray Stetson, had a square face, nondescript features, and a stocky build, with stringy hair that touched his collarbone. He looked to be a few years younger than his companion.

They both eyed her for a moment as they passed by, but neither spoke and then they disappeared inside the Tumbleweed.

As Josy entered her Blazer and slammed the door, Ty Barclay's cruiser suddenly roared to life and he took off, the car squealing out of the parking lot and onto the road with a blaring screech of tires.

At this rate he'll definitely beat me back to the Pine Hills, she thought, wondering vaguely why he'd been watching the two men. And why he'd taken off like that, like a bat out of hell. Not that it mattered. Nothing about Sheriff Ty Barclay mattered.

Making contact with Ricky did matter. And so did meeting Ada Scott. With any luck, she thought, driving home through the inky night, and doing her best to put Ty Barclay out of her mind, tomorrow she would do both.

Chapter 6

"LET HER GO, VERNON! OPEN THE DOOR!"

From inside the ranch house twenty miles from the nearest highway, Ty Barclay heard Sue Ann Watkins screaming. And he heard her husband bellowing, his voice a drunken roar.

"Go to hell, Sheriff!"

"Open the door, Vernon," Ty yelled back. "Now!"

There was the slamming thump of something hitting a wall, and Ty hoped to hell it wasn't Sue Ann. The siren of the state police cruiser shrieked down the highway in response to his call for backup, but Ty wasn't about to wait for them as he heard another high-pitched scream from Sue Ann.

He backed up a few feet, then placed a well-aimed kick that sent the door crashing in. He went in fast, his revolver trained and ready.

"Shoot me, go ahead, get it over with!" Vernon shouted, holding a kitchen chair frozen over his head, caught in the act of hurling it. He was a huge man, big as a linebacker, for all that he was past fifty. Ty's swift gaze took in Sue Ann cowering, white-faced and distraught, in the corner under the staircase, watching her husband through red-rimmed terrified eyes. But she didn't appear to be hurt, Ty noted as he centered all of his attention on the giant drunken rancher facing him.

"Put down the chair, Vernon. I'm not aiming to shoot anyone."

"I want you to put me out of my misery, damn it!" Vernon threw the chair against a wall and wheeled toward Ty, his face contorted with fury. His voice rose to an even more belligerent, thundering roar. "Shoot me, damn it, Barclay. I've lost everything anyway—damn rustlers. Even my wife, I know she's been sneaking around behind my back, I know it!"

"No, I never did!" Sue Ann shrieked. Her pretty, middle-aged face was wracked with grief and sobs shook her voice. Ty knew they'd been married for thirty years—he'd been invited last summer to their anniversary party.

"Vernon, you're drunk, you're crazy," Sue Ann cried. "Stop now before things get worse," she pleaded. "Sheriff, he just started throwing things, I've never seen him like this—"

"Freeze, Vernon. Don't move. No one wants to hurt you. We'll get this all straightened out—"

"The hell we will. I'm losing my ranch and my wife—you can't straighten that out, no one can!" Suddenly Vernon Watkins charged toward Ty like a maddened bull, howling with an anguished rage that shook the rafters of the house.

Ty waited until he was almost upon him before side-stepping deftly, and then, with a move as swift as lightning, he slammed the barrel of his gun down on the back of Vernon's neck and the man hit the floor like a sack of cement. Ten seconds later, it was all over.

Ty had him pinned and cuffed on the floor before

Vernon could even catch his breath, and then two state police officers burst into the room.

They pulled up short, staring at the huge rancher sobbing brokenly on the ground, at the woman weeping in the
corner, her hands covering her face.

"Everything's under control," Ty told a grim-faced
Hank Webber as the trooper came over and helped him
pull Vernon to his feet. Ty read him his rights, then
glanced over at Sue Ann.

"Take him outside and search him. I'll get her statement."

The troopers, Webber and Murdock, escorted the prisoner out of the house as Ty knelt beside the woman.

"You hurt, Sue Ann?"

"No . . . he never t-touched me, Sheriff." Her voice
quavered as Ty helped her up, steadying her as she swayed
a little.

"Vernon wouldn't ever hurt me. But he broke a bunch
of stuff . . . a bowl that was my mama's . . . and he busted
up some dishes and threw a lamp through the bedroom
window. He ripped out the phone cord." Her swollen eyes
were filled with tears, and she wiped at them with thin,
work-reddened hands.

"Sheriff, you know Vernon—you know he's not a bad
man, but things have been terrible lately. Those rustlers
have really hurt us. We've got a small spread here and
they've hit us hard."

"I know."

"We've been barely hanging on as it is . . . and we lost
more than a dozen cows last year. Now we've sent what's
left out to range again, and if the rustlers come back for
more before November . . ." She shook her head in anguish.

"Vernon's worried out of his mind. We just can't keep going much longer, not at this rate."

Ty's neck muscles tightened with frustration. The Watkins ranch wasn't the only one to be hard hit by the spate of rustling. With a single yearling cow being worth nearly a thousand dollars, losing a dozen such cows over a year to rustlers added up to a substantial loss, one that would hurt any rancher. But it especially hurt those with smaller spreads and tighter budgets. For people like Sue Ann and Vernon Watkins, a dozen rustled cows could mean the difference between making a profit and staying in business, or going under and losing everything—their home, cattle, and land.

"I know it's been tough," he told her grimly, knowing the words were woefully inadequate. Rustlers generally cost the state of Wyoming anywhere from six hundred thousand to eight hundred thousand dollars a year. But the human cost to the men and women ranchers who raised, branded, fed, shipped, and sold the cattle went beyond what any number could describe.

And last spring and summer, a particularly bad spurt of rustling had hit Thunder Creek. If small-scale ranchers like the Watkinses suffered the same kind of losses over the next few months, before the cattle were rounded up and brought in and counted again in the fall, a lot of them just wouldn't survive.

"We're working on it, believe me, Sue Ann. And Big John Templeton and Harlan Weeks have both volunteered their own planes and helicopters to fly over the back country on regular inspections. Deputy patrols are being stepped up too. I feel for you and Vernon, you know I do. But Vernon's not making things any better for himself here."

NIGHT THUNDER   83

He didn't add that money troubles were no excuse to go ballistic, terrorizing your own wife—but he thought it. When the call from Sue Ann had come through, she'd sounded scared out of her wits, and Vernon had grabbed the phone away from her before Ty could even tell her he was on his way.

"You're not going to arrest him, are you?" She was watching him anxiously.

"That depends. Do you want to press charges?"

"No. Course not. This wasn't like Vernon. He was upset, he was drinking . . . but he doesn't belong in jail."

"If that's how you feel, we'll take him over to the hospital for a psychological evaluation. And that'll give him a chance to sober up. It seems to me he'd benefit a lot more from some counseling right now than he would from staring at the walls of a jail cell. Let's see how it goes."

She nodded and wandered off in search of her purse, her steps slow and listless. She looked spent and all but broken, he thought, his eyes narrowing.

Not for the first time, Ty cursed the rustlers. State brand inspectors were a big part of stopping this particular crime, but they were spread thin and there was only so much they could do. With cattle left to graze for months within hundreds of thousands of acres of range, in canyons and sheltered valleys with nothing around for miles but sagebrush, grass, and scrub, it was relatively easy for thieves with a ramp and a rig to pick out a handful or a truckload at a time and simply drive the cattle off in the middle of the night. All they had to do was get them out of state, to Texas or Oklahoma, or one of the other states without brand inspections, and they could make themselves a tidy bundle of money.

And there weren't a whole lot of ways to stop it—especially if the rustlers stole unbranded cattle, or changed the brands, or took quarter horses instead, because those weren't branded at all.

While the enterprise was hugely profitable for the rustlers, it ran the gamut from pesky to devastating for the ranchers that were hit.

Ty hadn't been able to make much of an inroad against the spree—until lately. Some of the background checks he'd done recently on the license plate numbers of unknown vehicles that had been spotted in the back country had begun paying off.

Now he had himself a couple of suspects. But he wasn't ready to rope them in yet.

He'd begun putting some pieces together and he had a theory—one he needed to prove if he wanted to get rid of the rustlers at their source.

Ty suspected that this outfit was part of a large-scale ring operating in several states at once, not just a few locals rustling once in a while to pick up extra cash, like kids knocking off a liquor or appliance store. If his guess was right, this was a widespread, coordinated outfit, probably generating hundreds of thousands of dollars in the space of a year. After conferring with law enforcement and brand inspectors in Oregon, Colorado, and California, he was more convinced than ever that this was an organized crew of rustlers all working different areas, and all for the same employer.

And right now, Denny Owens and Fred Barnes, who'd both signed on last year as ranch hands at Ralph McIntyre's Double M ranch, were only two small pieces of the puzzle. But they could be his key to solving the bigger picture—and to nailing the big boss.

He'd already checked both of them out and what he'd found was fascinating. Both men had started work at the Double M within a week of each other. And they'd both done time.

Owens had been arrested two years ago for fighting and destruction of property in Montana, and Barnes had an assault record for beating up a woman in a bar.

On the surface, they looked to be small-time felons, but Ty had dug deeper—and hit pay dirt.

And he'd also hit upon a plan.

It was two hours later when he finally got back to the Pine Hills after seeing Vernon Watkins sedated for the night, getting a written statement from Sue Ann, conferring with the doctor at the hospital, and completing dozens of pages of paperwork.

He spotted Josy Warner's blue Blazer in the parking lot and found himself scanning the darkened building, wondering which unit on the second floor was hers.

Who cares, he told himself as he left the cool windswept night and went inside to the dusky hallway, lit only by a forty-watt bulb.

Yet for some reason, as he climbed the stairs he thought back to the dance he'd shared with her. It was odd that he remembered every detail about it—especially the way she'd felt in his arms. Soft, sexy, and cool as summer frost—except for the tension that had radiated from her. She was hiding something.

He hadn't been a cop all these years and not learned to trust his instincts. And his instincts told him that Josy Warner was not totally on the level. He wasn't sure what about her seemed off, but there was something.

He filed it away in the back of his mind. He wasn't about to start investigating her based on a gut feeling,

but . . . he sensed there was something there. Otherwise
he wouldn't be remembering so much about their dance
and their conversation . . . she wouldn't be on his mind.

And it wasn't because she was a slim, beautiful blonde,
or because he'd felt a flash of heat when he'd first drawn
her into his arms. It was because she had a secret, she was
afraid, or she was here on some agenda. That was the only
explanation.

He didn't think she was a criminal. Just a mystery.

So it wasn't as if it really mattered.

The rustlers picking on his town and who-knew-how-
many others did matter.

At least—until he caught them.

Chapter 7

THUNDER CREEK'S LIBRARY WAS A SMALL STONE building at the end of town, set in a small flower-bordered square with two hardwood benches, a drinking fountain, and a handsome six-foot-tall gleaming bronze statue of a wild mustang in flight.

Inside, the air-conditioning wasn't working but a wood ceiling fan kept the small lobby cool, and a spry woman of about fifty, wearing a pink blouse and a denim skirt, set aside a pile of papers, pushed her black-rimmed glasses higher on her nose, and called to Josy from behind the wooden checkout counter.

"Let me know if I can help you find anything. My name's Maggie Cartright. I'm the full-time librarian. We don't have too many customers this time of the morning, so don't be shy if you need something."

"As a matter of fact, I do need some help. I'd like to open a new e-mail account. Can I do that here?"

"Sure can, if you want to use one of those free servers like Yahoo or Hotmail. I'll show you what to do."

Maggie Cartright bustled around the counter, apparently deliriously happy to be of service to someone. "Course, I'll need to see some ID."

"Oh. No problem." Josy opened her purse, thankful she hadn't attempted to use another name while in Thunder Creek. She showed Maggie her driver's license and followed her to the single computer set up at a metal desk near the nonfiction bookshelves.

"It isn't hard, not a'tall. I took some computer classes at the university—they held a seminar for the librarians in five counties and we learned everything we need to know to operate these things. All you have to do is figure out a screen name and sit yourself down and . . ."

It was surprisingly easy. Only a few moments later, Maggie had retreated to her desk and Josy sat alone at the computer, staring at the screen, her fingers poised to type in her new screen name.

"Tootiebird." She typed it in with a small grimace. Ricky ought to instantly recognize that name. May Hammond had owned a parakeet named Tootiebird, a shrill, filthy little thing that had nipped at any finger that ventured inside her cage.

But when it came time to actually write the message she found herself hesitating, drawing a deep breath.

Middle name, Josy, Ricky had said. *You know the one. Middle name. Add my age.*

Oh, yes, she knew exactly what middle name Ricky meant. Karl Hammond's middle name had been Theobald—a fact that had inspired a great deal of derisive laughter among the foster kids in the Hammond house, perhaps in part because Karl himself was bald, or perhaps because Ricky led everyone in calling him Theobaldo behind his back. It had been the only defense she and Ricky and the other kids that had come and gone in the Hammond home had had against the man who'd thought noth-

ing of locking any of them in a closet if they didn't make
their beds neatly enough or if they spilled their milk on
the kitchen floor.

So . . . Theobald it must be. And Ricky, two years older
than she, was twenty-nine. She could only hope that
Ricky was continuing to use his Hotmail server—but with
a new account registered under Theobald29. But now that
she was ready, she hesitated, her fingers resting on the
keyboard as she inwardly debated how much to say.

She must be getting paranoid, because she was too
scared to say much that might get into the wrong hands.
The chances of anyone tracing one e-mail under a new account seemed slim, but she wasn't about to be too forth-
coming until she knew her post was going straight to
Ricky, no mistakes.

"Hope this gets to you," she typed. The silence of the
library was deep and complete, save for the whir of the
ceiling fan and the rustle of the librarian's paperwork at
the check-in counter.

And the tiny click of the keys beneath her fingers.

"I'm safe . . . I think. And I hope you are too. Write
back."

She hit *send* and watched her message disappear.

For a moment she just sat at the computer, resisting the
urge to write to Reese or Jane, to let them know she was
okay, to find out what was happening at the design studio.

It was frustrating to think that with a few keystrokes
and the *send* button she could be in touch with them, but
she dared not. For their sake as well as hers.

It was hard to believe she was in danger while she was
here in Thunder Creek. The town was peaceful, quiet, set
amid the lush, breathtaking openness of vast prairie,

flower-dotted foothills, and distant looming mountains. The people were friendly, the pace soothingly low key. She might as well be a million miles from New York, from the studio and the pressure-cooker of Francesca Dellagio Designs.

And from a dead body in Brooklyn.

Besides, no one there could possibly have followed her here.

So . . . she was safe. She must be safe, she told herself.

But she'd had a nightmare about Archie last night. Seen him again, the way he'd looked on that bloody floor, lying so still, his eyes closed. Closed forever.

When she'd jerked awake in the indigo darkness of her unfamiliar rented apartment, she'd been gasping for breath.

But now, as she emerged from the library into brilliant Wyoming sunshine and a sky bluer than an orchid, nightmares and danger and dead men seemed far away. It was daylight and the air was perfumed with the scent of pine and larkspur, wafting down on breezes fresh off the Laramie Mountains, and everywhere she looked was open land, endless and beautiful—full of nature's peace.

She backed the Blazer up, turned around, and headed toward Bessie's Diner.

As she drew nearer to town, though, it became more difficult to hang on to that precious sense of calm.

Knowing she might meet Ada Scott any moment set her heart tripping faster in her chest.

Ada was supposed to be back today, but that didn't mean she'd come right into work. Or that her flight hadn't been delayed. Or that she hadn't decided to stay in Las Vegas another few days.

She knew she was preparing herself for disappointment, bracing herself for it. But she was also trying to keep herself calm.

She was twenty-seven years old and she'd managed to live without a grandmother this long, she told herself. She might never even tell Ada Scott about their relationship at all. When the time came, she might not even choose to speak more than a casual hello to the woman. Still, as she parked the Blazer down the street and headed toward the diner, her stomach twitched—and it wasn't from hunger.

The diner was packed. Every booth taken. And three people were in front of her in line, all of them cowboys.

Then she saw Chance Roper, sitting in one of the front booths, only a few feet away, drinking coffee. Roberta was bopping from table to table. And . . .

Josy frowned as she caught sight of Ty Barclay at a table. There was a plate of eggs and sausage in front of him, but he was ignoring the food, engrossed in a conversation with Roy Hewett.

"Hey, Josy!" Chance grinned at her. "I hate to see a pretty lady waiting in line. Come have a seat."

The cowboys in front of her all turned and stared at her, grinning.

"Forget about him, ma'am, you can sit with us if you like," one offered, his brown eyes dancing.

"You don't want to sit with them. You don't even know them and believe me you don't want to," Chance shot back, laughing.

"And what makes you think she wants to know you?" a feisty female voice interjected.

Out of nowhere a small, gray-haired dynamo of a woman appeared at Chance's table, refilling his coffee cup with practiced ease and sweeping away his plate, fork, and knife.

"Hell, Bessie, why aren't you on my side? Aren't I your best customer?"

"One of my best," the woman acknowledged. Her eyes danced. "And certainly the biggest flirt. If you want to sit with him, go right ahead," she told Josy with a nod. "Course it's at your own risk. Otherwise, it'll be about ten more minutes until these tables clear and these cowboys get taken care of."

"I guess I can handle him all right. Especially if I get coffee right away." She sent Bessie a hopeful smile.

"Coming right up," Bessie promised, and bustled toward the kitchen as Josy scooted ahead of the line, slipping into a seat across from Chance who beamed with triumph, while the cowboys in line behind her playfully booed.

"I see you have a reputation in this town."

He held up both hands in a gesture of professed innocence. "Can I help it if women like me?"

"Help it? You gobble it up. You heard Bessie, you're the biggest flirt in town."

"I'll give up every single other woman if you'll have breakfast, lunch, and dinner with me today," he countered instantly.

Josy laughed. "Don't you have to work?"

"It's my day off. Once every two weeks I get a whole twenty-four hours to myself. Want to go hiking with me? Or for a drive? We could be in Casper in a couple of hours, take in a movie, and have a real nice dinner at the—"

He was interrupted by Bessie arriving with coffee. She handed Josy a menu before sweeping away again.

"Let's get through breakfast first," Josy suggested. "Any recommendations?"

"Yeah—everything. But the pancakes are about the best I've ever tasted."

"Pancakes," she murmured. She had a weakness for them, especially pecan pancakes. And there they were on the menu. "You've talked me into it."

Her gaze slid toward the cash register. A small-boned bird of a woman in her seventies was making change amd chatting with a middle-aged couple. She was no more than five feet tall, her face thin and soft-looking, beneath short tufts of white hair.

"Is that Ada Scott?" she asked Chance softly, without glancing away from the woman.

"Yep. She and Bessie just got back early today from Vegas. Ada won seventy-five dollars playing roulette. She's really tickled. Bessie's bummed because she lost thirty bucks at blackjack."

Roberta flew by the table, headed for the kitchen, a few men in cowboy hats moved toward the door, and Bessie brought a place setting and napkins. But Josy couldn't tear her gaze from the tiny, sweet-faced woman at the cash register.

She felt her throat tighten and reached for her coffee to wash down a rush of emotions unexpectedly making it difficult to swallow.

"Hey, are you all right? Why're you staring at Ada?"

She dragged her gaze back to Chance's face. "No reason. She . . . reminds me of someone. I'm sorry." Josy forced herself to focus on Chance and tried to smile.

But all she wanted to do was gaze at Ada Scott and try to imagine how and why she'd given her baby daughter away. She wanted to think about what would happen if she went over and spoke to the woman. But she couldn't think about any of that. Not now. Not yet.

She made small talk with Chance, batted away his compliments and lines, and in the end, turned down his invitation to spend the day with him. But when he invited her to go to a movie Saturday night in the nearby town of Winston Falls, she finally accepted. Why not? It was only one date, a movie date.

And she was pretty sure she'd made it clear that friendship was all she had in mind—and all she would allow.

He left the diner first, as she claimed she wanted another cup of coffee. Alone, she lingered over a fresh cup, casually studying Ada Scott at the cash register without being too obvious.

The crowd dwindled and soon only a few diners remained, among them Ty Barclay and Roy Hewett.

They were finishing up, though, Josy noted, watching as Ty moved to the cash register and spoke for several moments with Ada.

They seemed to be on familiar terms.

He left the diner with only the briefest nod to her, while Roy waved, came over, and made a point of telling her how glad he and Corinne were that she'd come to Corinne's farewell party.

Then she was virtually alone in the diner with Bessie, who had disappeared into the kitchen, Roberta, clearing empty tables, and Ada, counting money at the cash register.

Suddenly, Ada closed the drawer, locked it, and glanced her way. The next thing she knew the white-haired woman had picked up a coffeepot and was coming toward her.

"More coffee?"

Josy shook her head.

Ada was starting to move away before Josy found her voice.

"I hear you won some nice money at the roulette table," she blurted out, and Ada Scott paused and turned back to her with a surprised smile. "Who told you that?"

"Chance Roper. We had breakfast together."

"If that doesn't beat all." Ada returned to the table and cocked her head to one side.

"I'd think that man of all others would have more to talk to a pretty young thing like you about than my trip to Las Vegas," she mused.

"Oh, he only mentioned it because I . . . I thought you looked familiar."

"You don't say?" Ada peered at her with interest. Her brown eyes were faded, yet she managed to study Josy with a disconcerting keenness. "I can't say I recognize you."

"Have you . . . ever been to . . ." She was about to say "New York" but switched it at the last minute to "Chicago."

"Chicago? No, never." Ada shook her head as if the notion were absurd. "I've been to Cheyenne, to Casper, of course, to Las Vegas a dozen times . . . and lately to visit my grandson at the university in Laramie," she added, and Josy heard the note of fondness and pride in her voice. "Aside from that I've only been to . . ."

There was a momentary hesitation before she continued.

"I went to Denver once to visit a cousin," she said quietly. "Though that was a long time ago. But I haven't been too many other places. So I don't think we've met."

Suddenly she smiled. "I'd surely remember a young lady as pretty as you."

There was a crash in the kitchen just then and Ada

started. "Uh-oh. What in the world did Bessie drop now? I hope it wasn't the steak-and-potato casserole that's the dinner special for tonight."

She scurried toward the kitchen. Josy sat perfectly still, gazing with unseeing eyes at the empty coffee cup before her.

Shouldn't I feel something? she thought. *If this woman is my grandmother, shouldn't I feel something? Some pull, some connection? Shouldn't there have been some flash of something in her when we met, as well?*

Ada Scott seemed nice enough. A sweet, simple woman who'd traveled little from her own backyard, who worked among friends, who wore pink cotton pantsuits and sneakers. A woman who had treated her with the politeness you show strangers, and who had spoken of her grandson with obvious pride.

She's happy. She's at peace. She doesn't need or want a stranger in her life, Josy suddenly realized. *There's no need to go any further with this.*

Ignoring the icy disappointment pulsing through her, she slid out of the booth and asked Roberta for her bill.

"Coming right up, but I want to show you something." Roberta breezed toward the kitchen as Ada emerged. When Josy reached her at the cash register, Ada was shaking her head.

"Bessie dropped a pie. A strawberry-rhubarb pie. It's all over the floor. But will she let me help her clean it up?" Ada shook her head, her eyes sparkling. "The Templetons are all stubborn to a point, and she's one of them. Said she dropped it, she'll clean it, that's that." Ada chuckled. "I'm her best friend, have been for years, but do you think she'd let me help her? No, sirree."

Josy smiled. "You know her pretty well, don't you?"

"I surely do. You know how it is. You spend enough time with someone, they get to be like family. Me and Bessie, after all these years, we're like family."

"You mentioned your grandson." Josy didn't know why she was following up the conversation when she'd already decided to let it go. The words just seemed to stream from her mouth. "Do you have any other family besides him—and Bessie?"

"Well, all of the Templetons are like family to me. We go way back. Dorsey, Big John, and their daughter, Katy, of course. She's Katy Brent now. But I've been a widow for the past fifteen years, and my son died some eleven years ago, along with his wife."

Her eyes clouded. "There was a pileup on the highway during a snowstorm. Both my son and daughter-in-law were taken from me . . . and from Billy, my grandson. He was still a child then. I raised him after that, you know. He's all I have left. And he's a fine young man, if I do say so myself. He studies science at the university."

She shook her head. "Listen to me rattling on. You must have better things to do than stand around here—Roberta! Where's this young lady's bill?" she called toward the kitchen.

"Hold your horses. I've got it." But as Roberta came out and handed Josy her check, she also had a sheet of lined yellow paper in her hand. "Take a look at this, Josy."

It was the invitation list for Corinne's shower. Her name was there, at the very bottom of the list.

"Corinne wants you to come to the shower and so do I. So next time you come in here, I should have your invitation ready. But in the meantime, consider yourself invited."

Josy didn't know what to say. She'd only known Corinne and Roberta for a day—and a night—and they were including her, treating her as a friend, making her feel more than welcome in the town.

"This is so kind of you. I've heard of country hospitality, but you don't have to do this," she protested automatically, but Roberta folded her arms.

"No arguing, girl. My Luther used to say that arguing with me was a shameless waste of breath—and damned if he wasn't right. The shower is a week from Saturday, twelve o'clock. At Ada's place on Angel Road. You'll get to meet a bunch of ladies from the town, maybe you'll even get some decorating jobs out of it. I told Tammie Morgan yesterday that we had a decorator here from Chicago. She was curious as hell to meet you. Seems the Crystal Horseshoe wants to renovate a couple of their guest cabins—make 'em even ritzier."

She rolled her eyes. "She wants to talk to you. Bet she thinks you'll give her a deal—that decorator they got from Los Angeles cost them the sun and the moon."

Decorating jobs? Josy thought in dismay. *What have I gotten myself into?*

"Oh, my, Tammie Morgan." Ada snorted. She looked Josy straight in the eye. "Whatever you do, young lady, don't let that woman take advantage of you. She'll try to suck your brain and find some way to get you to work for her for free."

"Thanks for the warning. I won't let that happen." *Mostly because I know nothing about decorating dude ranch guest cabins,* Josy thought ruefully.

Her little deception was taking on a life of its own and she felt a twinge of guilt. At the same time, there was a small rush of warmth because Ada had warned her about Tammie Morgan. Even if it wasn't personal—Ada was just warning Corinne and Roberta's friend—it still made her smile at Ada with a surge of gratitude.

"Actually, I'm curious to meet her now." She laughed. "And I'd love to come to the shower. Thank you, Roberta, for including me."

"It's a good thing Corinne finally got me this list today or it would be too late to even have a shower," Roberta flung over her shoulder as she headed back to the kitchen.

Another customer had lined up behind Josy now, so she murmured a good-bye to Ada and left the diner.

But as she drove back to the apartment, she reflected that the shower would afford her a perfect opportunity to see Ada's home, to see if she recognized it as the same house she and her parents had driven to that long-ago day. Of course, Ada could have moved since then, but maybe she could find out about that too and casually ask where she'd lived before. It was an opportunity—an opportunity to learn more about her grandmother, to reconcile that memory of her parents and herself and the woman on that porch.

Even if she never told Ada a word about their relationship, even if they never had a real conversation alone together about anything except Thunder Creek chitchat, seeing her home and watching her interact with her friends and neighbors would provide a better sense of the woman to whom she was related by blood.

And that will be enough, she told herself.

But as she pulled up in front of her building she could still see Ada Scott's sweet, gently lined face in her mind. And she wasn't entirely certain she'd be able to leave

Thunder Creek without finding out one thing: why the plainspoken woman who worked the cash register at Bessie's Diner and had raised her grandson from the time he was a boy had made the decision more than fifty years ago to give away her newborn daughter.

Chapter 8

"ARE YOU TELLING ME THAT YOU HAVE NO IDEA where Ricky Sabatini is at this moment?"

Oliver Tate's voice was calm as he turned from the window where his children splashed three stories below in the shimmering free-form pool, and where his wife lounged on a pink chaise amid copper pots brimming with roses.

But for all the evenness of Tate's tone, Dolph Lindstron wasn't fooled. Not for a second.

Dolph was a big man—six foot six, 230 pounds of rock-solid muscle, and a brute strength forged in the slums of Copenhagen. But he wasn't stupid. Fear slithered through him like a snake when he saw the ice-chip green of his employer's eyes, the catlike way Oliver Tate pivoted from the window overlooking his estate.

For Oliver Tate, losing Ricky Sabatini was equivalent to a cardinal sin. And he was the sinner.

"No, Mr. Tate." Dolph stood at rigid attention. "Not yet, I don't. But I'll lock down Sabatini's whereabouts soon. And I *will* find him," he vowed, then tensed as he caught the flash of anger in Tate's icy eyes.

"And the woman—the woman with my property?" Tate asked silkily.

"Josephine Warner. We're still searching for her. She's nobody, not a professional, we should have her any day. And your property too, of course," Dolph added as his employer's eyebrows shot up, a sign he recognized. Tate was infuriated.

And Dolph knew it wasn't healthy to infuriate Oliver Tate.

"The Warner woman flew out of LaGuardia to Salt Lake City. She stayed two nights at the Best Western motel near the airport, paid cash for her room, made no phone calls. But the clerk remembered her—after I refreshed his memory, that is." Dolph smiled, his teeth gleaming whitely beneath his shaved head. But there was no responsive smile from Tate. Only two clipped words.

"Go on."

"She bought a blue '95 Blazer with Utah plates—paid cash again—and no one's seen her since. But we have people in Salt Lake City asking more questions, and I'm going back to interview the car salesman again personally—"

"I'm not interested in your tedious explanations, Dolph." The words flicked like a slow, slick whip. "I want results."

"Yes, Mr. Tate. Sure. I'll—"

The door to the office burst open suddenly and immediately Oliver Tate held up a hand for silence. Seven-year-old Eric Tate darted into the room in swimming trunks and sandals.

"Daddy, I swam. I swam across the pool. Stephanie can't swim, she'd drown if Mommy or Catrina didn't hold her up, but I can swim!" the boy announced, his hair still wet from the pool, though his feet were dry and clad in sandals, as required by Oliver Tate whenever anyone left the pool to enter the house.

"Good boy, Eric. You see? I told you swimming was easy." Oliver grinned down at the boy and tousled his damp hair. "You're strong, aren't you? A good, fast, strong swimmer."

"The strongest." Eric glanced over at Dolph, smiling. "One day I'll be as strong as Dolph," he boasted.

"Yes, you will. In the meantime, keep practicing your swimming so you'll be the best swimmer in the world. Or at the least in your high school when you're old enough to try out for the swim team. Daddy likes the best."

"Mommy is the best, right? The most beautiful?"

"Indeed she is. Out of all the women in the world."

"Stephanie isn't the best at anything."

"Not yet, she's only a baby. When she is older, she will be the best of daughters. Now see what I have for you."

Dolph kept silent as Oliver Tate reached into his desk drawer and pulled out a coin. He handed it to his son.

"Those who are best always get rewarded. This coin is worth a great deal of money, Eric. I want you to have it— put it away where no one will take it from you, and keep it. When you win your first swimming meet, I will give you a box of coins just like this one. All of them rare and valuable. But if you lose—I will come to you and take this coin away."

The smile faded from the boy's face. "You'll take it away?"

"Only if you lose. If you win . . . there will be more. Much more. And I know that you are strong enough to win."

Tate bent and kissed his son's cheek. "Go now. Put this in a safe place and then swim some more. Work at it. If you want to be the best, you must work very hard. Remember. Only the best is good enough."

The best, Dolph thought, and a tiny bead of sweat glistened on his shaved head. Oliver Tate was obsessed with the best. He insisted on it. Once upon a time, Dolph knew, his employer had been Olvan Tatrinsky, a starving kid from the slums of Helsinki, who lurked in alleys wearing rags and eating from garbage cans, until he started earning money by running errands for gangsters.

But as soon as he had enough money and the means to travel to America, Olvan left his native land, magically reappearing several years later as young, ambitious banking whiz Oliver Tate. His original backers were unknown, and probably dead, but now the boy who had lived in alleys infested with rats and garbage had far surpassed all those who had tutored him in the ways of crime.

Now his name, his fancy new name, was found in the registers of the best hotels, the business columns of the *Wall Street Journal,* and the invitation lists of all the best New York and London parties.

He was married to a former Miss World, had two perfect children—and the one that was imperfect, the brain-damaged eldest son who had been born first and in trauma after an automobile accident, had been shipped off to an institution, well cared for but ignored, as if he no longer existed.

And if Dolph didn't soon find what Ricky Sabatini had stolen from Tate, he knew he would no longer exist either.

Because Tate would decide he was no longer the best. There was always someone waiting to take his place, someone stronger, smarter, more ruthless and resourceful. Dolph had risen through the ranks in just such a way and he knew the drill.

Already, Hammer, who had gone trigger-happy with Archie Noon, and Lyle Samuels, the tech genius who had installed and been responsible for the Tate house's security system, had both been removed. Bloodily removed. Piece-by-piece removed.

Their bodies would never be found and no one would ever know. But Dolph knew—because he had disposed of them, exactly as Tate had ordered.

Hammer had screwed up. And Samuels's system had failed. His guards and dogs and alarms and buttons and lasers had failed.

And Mr. Tate loathed failure. Particularly when it hit home, and this particular failure had hit home in the most personal way for Oliver Tate.

Ricky Sabatini had stolen from him. Stolen something of immense value and beauty. Something Mr. Tate prided himself on possessing—especially since he himself had stolen it from an enemy.

And if Dolph didn't get it back, and soon . . .

He thought of what he had done to Hammer and Samuels. And knew that there were at least three men on his team who would be only too happy to do the same to him. And then to step into his shoes.

Men ready to prove that they were the best at whatever Oliver Tate asked of them.

Dolph waited until the boy ran from the room, the coin clenched tight in his hand, and then he spoke.

"I'm leaving in an hour for Salt Lake City to follow up on the Warner woman. I didn't want to tell you earlier in case it didn't pan out, but Len might have a lead on Sabatini and is checking it out. I'll know more from him by the end of the day."

"That's more like it." Tate nodded. "Keep me informed. I want him dead as much as I want what he stole from me."

"And the woman? If we find her and she doesn't have it after all?"

"Kill her regardless. It'll be a lesson to Sabatini and to anyone else who might try to go up against me. Don't come back here, Dolph, until she's dead."

Dolph nodded. He hoped he was the one to find the woman. It would prove his worth to Tate once and for all, and besides, he liked killing women. In addition to the stress, the pressure, and of course, the high pay and equally high stakes, this job had some special perks. Now and then he got paid to do what he liked best.

Standing before Oliver Tate, he struggled to keep from smiling. First he'd make her tell him everything she knew about Tate's little treasure and about Ricky Sabatini's whereabouts, likes and dislikes, friends, all the information they'd need to track him down—and then he'd kill her.

Slowly. Deliciously.

"Dolph, I'm tired of waiting. I want them both found and I want my property. You're to bring it back here personally. If you can't do it in a timely fashion, I'll have no choice but to turn the matter over to someone who can get the job done."

"That won't be necessary, Mr. Tate. I won't let you down."

Oliver Tate made no reply. He watched Dolph leave, thinking what a shame it would be to lose him—Dolph was quick and intelligent and ruthless, as well as being big as an ox.

But if he couldn't recover the prize, what good was he?

I can't afford inefficiency, Tate thought, turning back to the window. Far below he saw his wife applying sun-screen to Stephanie's back and legs. He liked watching them from above, surveying the kingdom he had created for them, for all three of them.

The sprawling Tudor house in Southhampton, the three acres of gardens, velvety cool and brilliant with flowers, the stables where only Thoroughbreds were allowed to dwell. Then there was the cabana and guesthouses, which were larger than the stinking ship he'd toiled on to earn his passage to America.

His children would never know what it was to be spat upon, beaten, dressed in rags. They would never know hunger or fear. They were born to lead, as he was leading, and they would lead from strength. Always from strength.

He'd teach them. Especially Eric. The boy would one day take his place and he must see what a leader needed to do to stay on top.

He must know. Just as Olvan Tatrinsky knew what he must do to those who had stolen from him.

The loss of one treasure was as bad as the loss of all. It could not be tolerated, and such an affront must be punished, rectified, and purged. The treasure was his, for as long as he chose to keep it. And someday when he decided it was time, when he had tired of looking at it, admiring it, anytime he chose, he would give it to Stephanie. She must have the best, only the best.

And no scum cop like Ricky Sabatini was going to cheat Oliver Tate and his family out of anything.

At least, not for long.

His secretary buzzed him from the reception area outside. The entire third floor of the house was set up as a home office with a reception area, conference room, and a private office suite. There was also a completely separate, private entrance for those admitted through the security gates with special passes.

"Yes, Linda."

Below he saw the housemaid setting up a tray on the patio beside the pool. No doubt crab salad and caviar and French bread and baby greens, as Renee preferred when dining alfresco. He expected there would be peach melbas for dessert. He was eager to go down and join them, to sit with Renee and hear her tell him about Eric's achievement.

But his secretary's words made him grimace, for he'd have to delay several moments before riding the elevator down to the pool.

"Wallace Becker is on line three."

"I'll take it."

NYPD precinct captain Wallace Becker spoke the moment he clicked onto the secure line. "We've got him—we've got Sabatini. My men are working him over as we speak. Any time now, he should be begging us to make a deal."

Chapter 9

ADA SCOTT WAS ENJOYING HERSELF IMMENSELY.
How she relished having all these laughing, chattering
women in her house—relished how pretty her parents'
oak dining table looked set with its lacy white cloth and
her Blue Willow dishes and the small cut-crystal bowl in
its center brimming with chrysanthemums.

The house smelled good too—thanks to Bessie's and
Katy's help with the cooking. They'd fixed chicken-and-
spinach quiche for lunch, along with a tossed salad of
baby greens, pecans, grapes, and mandarin oranges.
Roberta had insisted on baking her grandmother's cran-
berry muffins, and Ada had contributed dessert: her own
special pineapple upside-down cake, along with lemon
cookies and ice cream.

Sunlight beamed in through the ivory lace curtains and
seemed to crown her small cozy living room with a chest-
nut glow that made even the worn furnishings look almost
lustrous once more.

As much as she loved the peace and isolation of her
two-story frame house perched at the secluded end of
Angel Road, she often still missed the company of her

husband and her son when he was growing up—and of Billy and all his friends now that he was away at college.

She felt her throat closing suddenly and tears threatening. She blinked them back. *Silly, foolish, old woman.* There was nothing to cry over. She'd lived a good long life and there was still some more to go, if God was willing.

She had a good many friends, not to mention Bessie and the Templetons. And a job and a right smart grandson who was going to get a college diploma.

She had no right to cry at all.

Pouring icy lemonade from her mother's crystal pitcher into tall glasses, she glanced once more around the living room.

Corinne, bless her, seemed as happy as the meadowlark singing in the aspen outside the window. She'd waited a long time for Roy to get over Katy Templeton and get around to popping the question. She deserved to be happy.

"What do you guess she's thinking about right now?" Katy Brent murmured in her ear, so suddenly that Ada started and almost sloshed lemonade over the side of the glass.

"Who, honey? Corinne?"

"No . . . Josy. Over there by the window. Josy Warner. She looks almost hypnotized, doesn't she?"

Sure enough, the newcomer to town—who for some reason Corinne and Roberta seemed to have adopted—was admiring Ada's small array of old family photographs and knickknacks atop the small stone mantelpiece above the fireplace, studying each in abject fascination, as if it were a glittering gold bar dug out of earth and rock.

"Seems a bit odd, if you ask me." Ada shrugged. "Hard

to believe some fancy Chicago interior designer is going to want to copy how I display my little treasures."

"Why not? She could probably learn a thing or two from you. Your house is my favorite in this whole town—except for my own old home, and my cabin with Jackson and Mattie. I get the feeling Josy is . . ."

Her voice trailed off, and Ada glanced at her sharply. "She's what? Speak your mind, Katy."

"I was going to say she's . . . I don't know . . . lost. Or . . . looking for something."

"That one?" Ada adjusted the dessert plates so that they lined up evenly with the edge of the table. "She seems cool as a cucumber to me. Even if she is a fish out of water."

"You don't like her?" Katy stared at her in surprise.

"Now, I didn't say that. She's nice and quite pretty if you like that city-girl look. And I liked the way she stood up to Tammie when Tammie wanted her to take a look at those guest cabins and give her some ideas for redecorating. Said she charges one hundred dollars an hour for consultations and that included travel time and phone calls." Ada chuckled. "Did you see the look on Tammie's face? That did tickle me, I admit."

They both glanced over at Tammie Morgan, seated on Ada's faded chintz sofa between Ellen MacIntyre and Roberta. Tammie considered herself the epitome of Western chic and glamour and thought of herself and her husband, Wood, as the self-crowned royalty of Thunder Creek.

True, their ranch was one of the wealthiest in the county—even before they'd turned a ten-thousand-acre parcel into the Crystal Horseshoe Dude Ranch and now even more so—but Tammie tended to go overboard in the control freak and look-at-me-I'm-rich departments.

She'd hired a renowned celebrity chef, Elmo Panterri, to operate the Cowpoke Cafe, which had gone into direct competition with Bessie's Diner right after the dude ranch opened. Fortunately for Bessie, her customers had remained loyal, and Elmo had soon lost his taste for small-town living. He'd broken his contract within six months and some wannabe überchef had taken his place, but he hadn't lasted long either.

"I can't believe Tammie gave Corinne that tacky old weathered-barn-in-the-moonlight print that hangs in half the guest rooms in the dude ranch," Ada sniffed. "What in the world kind of a shower gift is that?"

"That's Tammie for you." Katy sighed. "But that crocheted tablecloth you gave her is lovely, Ada. She was thrilled when she saw it."

Ada nodded but she was barely listening, for she was distracted by the sight of Josy Warner reaching toward the small painted pitcher at the end of the mantel.

"Oh, no. Don't—" Ada began, but it was too late.

Josy was already lifting the pitcher by the handle, no doubt to take a closer look, but as she raised it off the mantel the china handle immediately broke off, separating from the rest of the delicate pitcher, which tumbled and crashed onto the polished wood floor.

Josy gasped and stared down at the cracked pieces of Ada Scott's beautiful little pitcher. The room full of chattering women had all turned to stare at her as the crash resounded through the living room and then a horrible silence filled the warm spring air.

"I'm sorry," she managed to choke out as Ada ap-

proached her and gazed sadly down at the pink and blue
and ivory shards.

"You had no way of knowing that the handle was broken." Ada knelt, gathering the jagged pieces. "It broke off
last week and I used a little Elmer's glue to keep it in place
until I could get something stronger to repair it. I
shouldn't have waited."

Josy stooped to help her pick up the shards, cursing
herself for having lifted the pitcher in the first place. "I
feel terrible about this. I'd like to replace it for you—"

"No need."

The words sounded curt. Angry. Josy's stomach
clenched.

Great way to ingratiate yourself with your grand-
mother, she thought miserably. *Break something she's*
probably cherished half her life.

Grabbing at pieces of china, she heard Bessie's and
Corinne's voices above her.

"It was an accident, that's all," Bessie stated.

"It's no one's fault," Corinne murmured.

Josy wanted to drop through the floor. "I'm so terribly
sorry," she said again.

For a moment it was hard to breathe. She was remembering the time in the Hammond foster home when she'd
dropped her milk glass on the floor after dinner. Not only
had the milk spilled all over, but the glass had splintered
into a hundred pieces.

May Hammond had screamed at her and then Karl had
stormed into the room, drawn from the television by his
wife's shrieks.

He'd grabbed her by the hair, nearly ripping her curls
from her head and dragged her downstairs into the damp,
dark basement crawling with ants and spiders.

"You'll stay downstairs until tomorrow morning when it's time to go to school. We don't want to see your stupid face for the rest of the night," he'd told her.

The basement had been terrifying—even with the single bare lightbulb over the sump pump turned on. It only served to show her the ants crawling across the cement floor, the cricket hiding in a dusty corner. There was no furniture down there, no place to sit except the steps or the floor—only boxes of old stuff and a broken grandfather clock.

But as soon as the Hammonds had gone to bed, Ricky had stolen down the stairs. He brought a chair for her, and a blanket. He stayed in the basement beside her the entire night, promising to kill any bugs that came close to crawling on her. He'd sprawled on the steps, dozing off now and then while she huddled on the chair, wrapped in the blanket.

In the morning he'd snuck back up before anyone saw him and returned the blanket and chair. Then, finally, after breakfast, she'd been sprung.

Karl Hammond had insisted she be sent off to school without breakfast, but as soon as she and Ricky were on their way, out of sight of the house, he gave her the Pop-Tart he'd stuck into his pocket instead of eating.

For a moment, kneeling beside Ada Scott in that charming house on Angel Road, gathering broken fragments of a once beautiful china pitcher, she felt just like that little girl who'd been banished to the basement, the little girl who'd so gratefully eaten a cold Pop-Tart on her way to school in the same clothes she'd worn the day before.

But she wasn't that little girl, not anymore. She'd come a long way from the Hammonds and from quietly taking whatever anyone dished out. And dropping the pitcher truly had been an accident, she reminded herself. She took a deep breath, set her shoulders, and gripped the shards carefully, consciously and deliberately pulling herself out of the past.

And at that moment, Ada Scott straightened, looked down into her face, and stretched out a cool, blue-veined hand.

"Come, child, I'll get my broom for the rest. There's no cause to look so mortified."

"Maybe not, but I wish I hadn't—"

"No, sirree, don't you think that way." Ada wagged a finger in her face. "People are important, not things. Didn't anyone ever teach you that?"

For a moment Josy was speechless. No, nobody ever had.

"Don't think you're getting off easy," Ada told her before she could reply. "You'll stay and help me clean up today after everyone's gone. Unless you have something more important to do," she added, but there was a gentle twinkle in her eyes.

"I can't think that you'd want me around all your pretty dishes and things after this," Josy said ruefully. "You're taking a pretty big risk, you know."

"Hmmm, is that so? Well, I'm a gambler—everyone knows that. Me and Bessie, we just love to beat the odds."

It was midafternoon before all the guests departed, and before Bessie and Roberta drove back to town to reopen Bessie's Diner, which had been closed from eight this morning until three in the afternoon in honor of the bridal shower.

Roy came by and had ice cream and coffee before helping Corinne load her gifts into his truck. Then Josy found herself alone with Ada as a few clouds drifted across the sky, momentarily obscuring the sun.

"Most of it's done," Ada pronounced crisply, surveying the aftermath of the party. "But if you'd shake that tablecloth out back and help dry some dishes, I'll be all set before my legs give out."

But she gave no sign that her legs were about to give out. Josy had never seen such energy in a woman—Ada swept the floor, cleaned the sink, plumped and tidied the cushions of her chintz sofa and the blue crocheted throw across the back of a mahogany rocking chair.

"Come over here and let me show you something," Ada said when Josy had carefully dried the last of the platters and serving bowls and set them on the small kitchen counter beside the dish drainer.

Ada led her into the living room and straight to the mantel. "That pitcher you broke belonged to my mother—this is her in this picture right here."

She pointed to a photograph in a square silver frame. The photo showed a woman and a man dressed in thirties-era clothing. Josy had examined the picture before and had guessed that it might be Ada's parents—and her own great-grandparents.

The woman was holding a toddler in her arms, and the toddler eyed the camera with what could only be called a wary expression.

"That's my mama, my daddy, and me. My brother was born about a year later. We weren't very well off back then, not many were—it was the Depression, you know. But we made it through. And once, just like you did today, I broke something—a little oval cut-glass jewel box that my father had given my mama on their second wedding anniversary. I sneaked into her room to play with it when

I was about five and I dropped it on the floor. She cried when she came in and saw what had happened, and I thought it was because her beautiful present was shattered all over the floor—but you know what?"

Still holding the frame in her hands, she looked intently at Josy. "She was crying because I'd tried to pick up the pieces and had cut my hand on the glass. My finger was bleeding."

Ada nodded, and Josy could see the memories floating across her gentle face. "Now, some mothers might have been furious, and mine had every right to be, but she was more upset that I had hurt myself, and she told me then— people are always more important than things. I've always remembered that."

Josy's throat ached. "That's a beautiful story. Your mother sounds like a very special woman."

"Oh, she was. She saw me through some tough times and she stood by me, which is more than some people do for their kin. I don't have patience with that kind. Now," she added, setting the picture frame carefully back on the mantel, "I saw you looking at all my little treasures up here earlier. Not that I mind, of course, but you seemed so caught up in them, I couldn't help but wonder why you were so interested."

"They're just so pretty," Josy said quickly. "And I wondered if any might be antiques."

"Well, they're old, let's put it that way." Ada chuckled. "Very few would be valuable to anyone but me. Everything here brings back memories for me."

"Did you grow up in Thunder Creek? In this house?"

"I've lived in Thunder Creek all my life, but my parents' house was north of town. My husband and I moved in here when we were married. I was twenty years old and

I fell in love with this spot of land the moment I laid eyes on it. Of course, this was a piece of Barclay land, so no wonder—they own some of the most beautiful land in the county. My husband and me were ever so grateful when they sold this little parcel to us."

"Barclay land?" Josy stared at her. "As in . . . Sheriff Barclay?"

"That's right."

"But . . . I thought he was from Philadelphia. Roy mentioned he was a homicide detective there."

"Yes, that's true, some of the present generation of Barclays live in Philadelphia now, but the land has been in their family for generations. They were ranching in Wyoming long before there were fences and automobiles and what passes these days for modern civilization. The Barclays go way back in these parts."

"I didn't know that," Josy murmured.

Ada nodded. "Roy is Ty's cousin, and he owns about five hundred acres, keeps it mostly for an investment, just like the Barclays do. But they've got over thirty thousand acres, and good water rights. They lease the water rights to local ranchers and someday maybe they'll sell off some more of the property, but they have a real fine family cabin up in the mountains and they still spend family vacations here—always have. I've known Ty and his brother and sister since they were knee high to a tadpole."

"You have my sympathies." The words somehow tumbled out without thought, and Josy could have bitten off her tongue as Ada's brown eyes fixed themselves intently on her face.

"What does that mean? Don't you like Ty?"

"I barely know him." She shrugged. "But he isn't exactly the friendliest person I've met in Thunder Creek."

She considered that a very tactful understatement, but Ada shook her head. "Ty Barclay's a good man." Her tone brooked no argument. "I grant he can be intimidating to some—especially those who don't know him, seeing as how he's so big, and looks like he could take a bear apart with his bare hands if he was riled—"

"I'm not afraid of him," Josy put in quickly.

"That's good." Ada smiled as she led the way across the living room and Josy realized they were now headed out toward the porch. "Seeing as he'll be here pretty soon unless I miss my guess."

Josy stopped short. "Ty Barclay is coming here? Why?"

"Did you see those horses in the paddock when you drove up today? The roan gelding and the buckskin colt?"

Josy nodded. She'd noticed the horses—gorgeous animals, chasing each other around the paddock facing Angel Road. She'd taken a good long look at the house at the end of the lane and was pretty sure it was the same house she'd gazed at all those years ago with her parents. Then she'd been distracted by the sight of those glossy, spirited horses frisking in the sunshine.

"I did notice them. They're beautiful." She hesitated only a moment. "I was hoping to have a chance to go over and take a closer look."

"That so?" Ada regarded her with interest. "Do you ride?"

"No. But I always wanted to."

It was true. Ever since she'd come to Thunder Creek with her parents that one time, and seen some children riding headlong across a meadow on the outskirts of town, she'd wondered what it would be like to race like that, fast as the wind, out in the open air with no one and nothing to hold her back.

Not that she'd ever had the chance.

"Those two horses belong to Ty," Ada continued, and pushed open the screen door, holding it for Josy. "He stables them here, rides them on the weekends, and in exchange pays me a little something and helps out with chores."

Her heart quickened. "So . . . he's coming here to ride? Today?"

"And to tend to the horses." Ada eased herself onto the porch swing and patted the weathered wood beside her, inviting Josy to have a seat. "During the week, or if he's too busy, young Tommy Hanson comes and takes care of them. But most every weekend Ty's around. Sometimes he rides up to the Barclay cabin and spends a night or two. Once a month or so I'll get him to stay and have Sunday supper with me. He likes to keep to himself these days, but he's always been good company—oh!" She broke off.

"Here he comes now—what did I tell you?" A satisfied smile wreathed her face, and Josy followed her gaze to where a black Crown Victoria police cruiser streaked toward them down Angel Road.

Ty Barclay braked sharply fifteen feet short of the porch steps and eased his long frame out of the car.

"Come on up here, Ty. I need a word with you," Ada called in the peremptory tone of an old woman, and Josy's stomach clenched. She glanced at her watch—she really did need to get going soon. Her dinner date with Chance was at seven o'clock and it was half past four already. She wanted to shower, and wash her hair . . .

But her mental list of chores flew right out of her mind as Ty Barclay strode up to the porch.

Damn, why did he have to be so supremely, irresistibly handsome? Especially today, in the late afternoon sunlight, he looked very much the rugged, modern cowboy in his jeans, black shirt, and cowboy boots, with the black Stetson sexily shading those brilliant blue eyes. Even his walk was sexy—long, easy strides, filled with confidence and a kind of edgy grace.

Too bad when it came to manners and charm, he was a big fat dud, she told herself. But her heart gave a strange lurch when those blue eyes locked on hers. His gaze was cool and decidedly brief. It immediately shifted to Ada and grew much warmer, she noticed with some irritation.

"What can I do for you, Ada?"

Addressing the older woman, he looked and sounded far more relaxed than Josy had ever seen him.

"I want you to tell me what's going to become of poor Vernon Watkins. But first, you've met Josy Warner?"

"Yeah." He gave Josy a curt nod. She returned it in kind. The air between them was frigid, but as Ada glanced sideways at the blonde woman on the swing beside her, and then over at Ty, she was sure she detected a sizzle beneath the frost.

"Don't tell me you haven't heard all about Vernon already." Ty took the porch steps two at a time and leaned his tall frame against the rail. "The whole town's talking about him."

"Well, of course they are. I heard it in Bessie's Diner all week and even at the shower today—both Roberta and Ellen MacIntyre brought him up. You heard about it too, didn't you, Josy?"

"I think so. Something about him going crazy and

tearing up his own house. 'Going postal' is the way Roberta put it."

Ada shook her head sorrowfully. "It's true, Vernon just up and went to pieces. It was a good thing Ty got there when he did. Now tell me"—she leaned forward, fixing her gaze on Ty—"was Sue Ann really all right? Vernon wasn't beating on her, was he?"

"He hadn't touched her by the time I got there, but she was plenty upset."

"That's what she told me. I stopped in to bring her some pie the other day and she just broke down, poor thing. She denied Vernon hurt her, said he just lost control and started smashing the furniture, all worried about the rustlers getting more of his cattle. But I wanted to make sure she wasn't covering up for him."

"No, she was fine, but scared out of her wits."

"And with good reason." Leaning her shoulders back in the swing, Ada looked weary for the first time all afternoon. "It's a damned shame, that's what it is. They were on the verge of bankruptcy a few years back," she explained to Josy. "And Vernon managed to get a loan from his son-in-law to keep going, but now . . ."

Her voice trailed off. "If those rustlers hit him again over the summer months, they're going to put the Circle Star Ranch under."

"Are you talking about cattle rustling—like in the movies?" Josy had heard some talk about rustlers here and there, but she'd been so caught up in her own problems she hadn't paid much attention. Cattle rustling was something that happened in old TV shows and movies, not in the twenty-first century.

"It's done with trucks and trailers now," Ty told her. She felt a twinge of alarm when her heart gave a little flutter as he looked at her, really looked at her, for the first time that afternoon.

He was too handsome in the hard gold sun. Too vividly, vibrantly male. She struggled to keep her attention on his words, not on the powerful line of his shoulders, the sharp planes of his face, or the low, pleasing timbre of his voice.

"But it still goes on," he continued, taking off his hat, turning it in his hands as he leaned against the railing. "Instead of stealing one or two cows or horses here and there, the rustlers load up a truckload of animals in the middle of nowhere and hightail it out of state."

"But where do they go?"

His gaze narrowed. "Someplace where they don't have brand inspectors and no one pays too much attention to the cows or quarter horses brought into the kill plants. Even with ranchers doing flyovers of the back acres when they can to check on their herds, most of the time no one's the wiser until the cattle have been rounded up and counted in the fall. By then it's too damn late."

Ada peered at him. "Have you gotten any leads?"

"One or two."

Shrewdly, she took a moment to study his face, reflecting on his coolly noncommital tone. "Ah, I bet you've got a suspect or two in mind," she said, delighted. "Not that you're going to tell *us.*"

A flash of amusement lit his eyes. "You got that right."

She gave a bark of laughter.

"Well." Ty tipped his hat to her, then set it back on his head. He turned those steady brilliant blue eyes on Josy. "I guess if you ladies have grilled me enough for one day, I'll just go saddle up."

Ada's phone rang from inside the house and she pushed herself out of the swing. "That could be Billy—he calls me every Saturday, you know. Ty, would you mind showing Josy the horses? She told me she'd love to see them up close."

Before either Ty or Josy could speak, she hurried into the house, letting the screen door slam behind her.

Not this again, Josy thought in dismay. *That's all I need—Ada channeling Roy Hewett.*

"Don't listen to her," she told Ty, a frozen smile on her face. "I'm not interested in seeing the horses."

"No surprise there."

She went still, then her gaze narrowed on him. "What the hell does that mean?"

He shrugged. "My guess is you've probably never ridden anything more feisty than a carousel horse in your life."

"So?"

"So you'd probably rather not risk your manicure hoisting your butt into a saddle." He looked her over lazily. That silky blue and white sundress that was wrapped around her body wasn't made for riding, but oh, man, it suited her. It was cool and shapely and enticing, just as she was. And equally out of place in the hard wilderness of hills and canyons on Blue Moon Mesa—which was where he was headed.

"You don't know what you're missing," he added, shoving away from the railing and sauntering down the steps. "But it's none of my business."

"You've got that right." She glared after him as he headed with that infuriatingly easy stride toward the stables. The nerve of him. She'd never in her life met a more irritating man.

"You think you have me all figured out, don't you?

Could you possibly stereotype me any more than you already have?" she called after him.

He turned back, his thumbs hooked in his pockets. "Hey, beats me. Could I?"

She shot off the swing, down the steps, and across the front yard, hauling up only a foot away from him. She notched her chin up, way up, so she could stare him in the eyes.

"For your information, I couldn't care less what you think about me."

"Same here. So what has you so upset?"

"I'm not upset. You just rub me the wrong way."

"Yeah. I have that effect on a lot of people."

"Well, golly gee, why am I not surprised?"

He gave her the ghost of a grin then and it nearly knocked the breath out of her lungs. His face changed subtly; it didn't soften exactly—that would be too much to ask—but it became . . . less hard. Less detached.

And if possible, even more handsome.

"You're not an easy person to get along with, you know that?" Ty said slowly. He resisted the urge to reach out and smooth a flyaway strand of silky blonde hair that had tumbled across her cheek. "Maybe you should consider lightening up a little."

"*Me?*" She gaped at him.

"Horseback riding is good for the soul. Especially around here." He spread his arm, encompassing the meadows and mountains looming behind Ada's house. "There's this one particular trail I know. You ride for a while along the banks of the creek, then veer across a gully, head up into the foothills. It's full of flowers, and the birds just sing all time and you can see for miles when you get to the top of Shadow Point. Then you head on to Blue Moon Mesa and that's where it really gets spectacular."

He pushed his hat back a little on his head and studied her with those keen eyes.

"Mellows me out every time. You ought to try it—I bet it beats meditation therapy and yoga and all that crap to hell."

"For your information I don't do yoga or meditation therapy," she snapped.

His eyes glinted in the sunlight. "Maybe you should."

Her mouth opened. And closed. She wanted to say something horrible to him, something every bit as rude as he had said to her, but she refused to lower herself to his level. While she struggled to come up with something mature yet stinging, he laughed.

"So are you game?"

"For what?" She eyed him with all the frozen dignity she could muster.

"For a little riding." He shifted closer to her, looming over her at the base of Ada's porch steps. She was astonished to see he was actually smiling at her.

"I promise not to let you fall off your horse. My two are pretty spunky—they'd probably be too much for you to handle, but Ada has an old mare—she's gentle as a lamb. You could probably manage her."

"Gee, thanks. I'm sure I could—if I wanted to."

Amusement flickered across his face. "Do you own any riding clothes?"

"I told you, I don't—"

"Jeans and a T-shirt should do it. Tell you what—I'll hang out here for a while. If you get back in the next hour, I'll take you up to Blue Moon Mesa."

"I can't." What was she saying? *I won't. I don't want to go riding with you,* is what she ought to have said.

Yet . . . did she? She pictured herself up on a horse, riding alongside Ty Barclay in the foothills. Then she pushed the image away.

"Why can't you?" he challenged, his eyes piercing into hers. "Too scared?"

"I happen to have a date."

A muscle tensed in his jaw. But his eyes were unreadable. For a moment she wondered if he was going to ask her who her date was with, but he remained silent.

He probably already knew she was going out with Chance. She'd gone to the movies with him last Saturday and tonight he was taking her to a real Western steak house in the nearby town of Winston Falls.

Corinne knew of their plans. Which meant Roy knew. Considering the size of Thunder Creek, there was every probability that Ty Barclay knew too.

"How about tomorrow? Say, twelve noon?"

She was flabbergasted. "Wh-why?" she sputtered. "Why on earth would you want me to go riding with you?"

She was frank, he'd give her that. She didn't beat around the bush, or play games. Ty felt a tug of admiration.

"Damned if I know. Let's just do it, not think about it."

Josy tried to form the word *no*. But she found herself nodding.

"Then let's meet right here. Noon tomorrow." He looked her over, his gaze roaming down her body.

"I don't suppose you own any shoes that aren't high heels?" he drawled.

Josy followed his gaze down to her stiletto-heeled

Manolo Blahniks. "In one minute I'm going to change my mind," she threatened.

A grin spread across his face. He didn't say a word, just grinned, then tipped his hat to her and strode away toward the stables.

She sank down on the porch swing, wondering what in the hell she was doing. There could be only one logical explanation for her agreeing to go riding with Ty Barclay.

She needed her head examined.

Chapter 10

LACING UP HER RUNNING SHOES, JOSY TRIED NOT to grimace. She was going to have an awful time today—she'd probably fall not only off her horse but off a cliff, despite whatever promises Ty Barclay had made to her, and she'd be lucky if she didn't break her neck.

Why on earth had she agreed to this?

Because Ty Barclay had the deepest, most intense blue eyes she'd ever seen? And the most intriguing, sexiest smile?

Two terrible reasons, she told herself.

She sighed and glanced out her balcony window overlooking the parking lot. It was a gorgeous day, of course. There were a few clouds over the mountains, but they looked far away and the sun was bright as a ball of melted butter.

Where was rain when you needed it?

Maybe if she got to Ada's late, Ty wouldn't bother waiting for her.

She pondered this option for a moment, then bolted to the full-length mirror on her bathroom door, took a quick glance at the image of herself in her jeans and a dark green T-shirt, her hair captured in a ponytail, and darted to the pantry. One glance inside, to the very back, just to assure herself that Ricky's package was still there, and she was out the door, a miniwallet hooked to her belt.

She felt very basic, very low-key, her only makeup a touch of lip gloss and a dab of mascara to darken her pale lashes. She wasn't trying to impress anybody, least of all Ty Barclay, but she was determined to show him she wasn't some frivolous Barbie doll, obsessed with soy lattes and nail polish and afraid to hoist her butt into a saddle, as he'd so inelegantly put it.

Besides, she asked herself as she hurried along the hallway, what else did she have to do? Her coffee table was littered with unworkable sketches. The change of scene had done zip so far to light a fire under her muse. And there'd been no word from Ricky—no response to her e-mail in all this time.

She was worried sick that she'd done something wrong in sending the e-mail and that she and Ricky would never connect. But even that was not as terrible a scenario as the other possibility that presented itself—that Ricky couldn't communicate with her. That he'd been caught by whoever was after him, and he was hurt—or dead.

That isn't what happened, she told herself as she ran down the stairs to the first-floor exit door. Ricky's on the move, and he simply hasn't had a chance to get back to you yet.

When she reached Angel Road she saw that Ty was already at the end of the driveway, leaning against his sheriff's cruiser. As she pulled up behind him, he glanced at his watch.

"Thinking about leaving without me?" Casually, she sauntered over and leaned a hip against the car.

"Didn't think you were coming."

She saw his gaze flick over her, from the ponytail down to the T-shirt, all the way down to her beat-up Pumas.

"You're missing something." He reached into his backseat and came up with a baseball cap, which he tossed at her.

"The sun'll fry you if you're out all afternoon without a hat. Wear this."

She grimaced, but pushed the Phillies cap on her head, grateful Francesca couldn't see her now. The very thought made her smile.

At that moment Ty Barclay happened to glance over at her. He wondered what had brought that cute little smile to her lips as he led the way to the corral.

Then told himself he didn't care.

He'd awakened this morning wondering why in hell he'd badgered her into going riding with him, then decided it had been a spur-of-the-moment mistake. But not such a costly one. He'd simply take her for a ride to Blue Moon Mesa, show her the view, then they'd ride back. He'd get her home by four and head over to Roy's to catch the Phillies game on ESPN. The afternoon would be over with before he knew it.

Yet he found himself glancing at her again as they walked toward the barn. She looked different today—younger, not nearly as coolly, distantly sophisticated. But she still looked good—and anything but ordinary. Even in jeans and a T-shirt and worn sneakers she was gorgeous as a model, and sexier than ever with that slight, catlike smile playing across her lips.

"You ought to try that more often," he commented. "Smiling, I mean."

"Look who's talking."

"In my line of work, there isn't much to smile about. Besides, why ruin my image?"

"Good point."

The tartness of her reply made him grin. He opened the barn door and held it wide for her. A soft whicker came from one of the stalls.

"You're sure you want to do this?" he asked as she stopped just inside. "I didn't mean to twist your arm the other day."

"You're going to feel real guilty if I fall off and break something, aren't you?"

"I told you. I won't let you fall off."

"Seems to me that's going to be between me and the horse."

He laughed, then studied her face, still looking amused. "Are you scared?"

"Not at all," she lied. Then as he held her gaze a moment, and those penetrating eyes pinned hers with a glance so acute it would have made Billy the Kid squirm, she sighed.

"All right, I'm scared. A little," she admitted. "But not enough to chicken out. Did Ada say it would be all right for me to ride her mare?"

"I didn't ask her. Actually, I thought I'd get you started on Moonbeam."

"Moonbeam?"

"My big roan you saw yesterday. I'll take the buckskin."

Panic skittered through her. "You said your horses weren't right for me, they'd be too much to handle."

"I was just trying to get a rise out of you when I told you about Ginger. That's Ada's mare," he added. "She's grown fat and lazy over the past few years and she's actually as slow as a turtle. I wouldn't put anyone over seven years old on her these days."

"But you said—"

"Look, you'll do fine with Moonbeam. He's well trained and if he likes you, he rides like a dream."

"If he likes me . . ." she muttered. "And how exactly am I going to get him to like me?"

"Sugar cubes. Moonbeam loves sugar cubes. I brought some along for you to feed him. Don't worry, you're going to be racing along the rim of Dead Man's Canyon in no time."

"Racing along the rim . . ." Josy glanced warily along the stalls, wondering if there was still a way out of this. "You're joking, aren't you?"

"Yeah." He grinned at her then, a slow, sexy, very male grin, and she wasn't sure if she wanted to punch him or kiss him.

"About the canyon," he added cheerfully.

Josy punched him in the arm as he laughed out loud. "You're a sadist, you know that?"

He chuckled. "Don't worry about a thing. We'll take it slow."

To her surprise, he turned out to be a surprisingly patient teacher. After several minutes of getting to know her mount inside the barn, with Ty demonstrating how to bribe him with sugar cubes, Josy stepped back and waited uneasily while Ty saddled both horses and led them out to the paddock.

She wished she could skip the lessons and get to the part where she flew across the meadow like the kids she'd seen on that long ago day, but she knew that like everything else in life, that sort of mastery only came in time.

Still, she started to relax as he showed her how to

mount on the horse's left, how to hold the reins, and explained how the stirrups worked.

When she was up in the saddle and he'd adjusted her stirrups, Ty led Moonbeam around in a circle to give her a chance to get used to the gait. After a while he mounted the buckskin, and they proceeded to walk both horses single file in another wide, sedate circle around the paddock.

"Just relax and get the feel of it," he told her, pulling up alongside. "Don't pull on the reins so hard, their mouths are sensitive. Here, hold them like this."

She tried to imitate the easy way he held the reins, the relaxed way he sat the buckskin, his feet resting easily in the stirrups. But she felt like she was about to topple off.

"You have a good sense of balance," he reassured her when she voiced this fear. "Are you an athlete?"

"Not really. Although I was on the track team in high school. And I took a few kickboxing classes last year. My friend Jane is a real pro at it and she convinced me to drop in a few times."

"By the time you go back home you might be able to add horseack riding to your jock résumé. But if that's going to happen, you'll have to graduate from a closed paddock to an open trail. So what do you say? Are you game?"

"Now? Already?" Panic rushed back and she nearly dropped the reins.

He studied her from beneath the brim of his black hat. "Unless you feel you can't handle it."

Josy took a deep breath. "Open the gate."

Her stomach was churning with equal parts excitement and apprehension when he unlatched the gate and led the way out of the paddock.

He was true to his word, though, Josy had to admit.

They took it slow. The horses remained at a walk as, side by side, they crossed the meadow behind Ada's house, heading toward the foothills north of Thunder Creek. Josy found her body adjusting to the horse's stride, and though she wasn't exactly relaxed, she was comfortable enough to glance around, appreciating the warm, sunlit air and the glorious open sweep of meadow.

"This must be boring for you," she said at last, aware that if Ty were riding alone, he certainly wouldn't be doing it at a walk.

She was surprised when he turned to look at her as he answered. "No. Not at all."

"Have you ever taught anyone else to ride?"

"Sure. My kid brother, Adam, and my sister, Faith. And Meg, my wife." He broke off suddenly, as if surprised that he'd even mentioned her name. His voice tightened.

"My . . . late wife," he amended tersely.

She almost heard the thunk as the wall around him shot up and locked into place.

Nice going, she mentally reproved herself. *Nothing like bringing up a sore subject.*

But now that she'd accidentally wandered into what must be forbidden territory, there was no point in pretending it hadn't happened. For years, Josy had tried to hide from everyone that she'd grown up in foster homes, until she'd forced herself to say it, over and over, to make it public, to accept it.

"When did you teach her? After you were married? Did you bring her here to Thunder Creek?"

For a moment she thought he wasn't going to answer her. There was a silence during which the wind raced through the tall grass and a hawk wheeled in the sky overhead.

"We did come here after we were married. Spent a week at my family's cabin—which happens to be on Blue Moon Mesa—but that's not when I taught her to ride. Meg and I knew each other from the time we were kids. She was friends with my sister. One year when we were teenagers she came up with our family for part of the summer—and that's when I taught her to ride."

"Faith already knew how by then?"

"Yeah. She learned when she was eight—we all learned young. Riding was a big part of the summers we spent here. I taught Adam first and then Faith. Since I was the oldest, when it came time for Faith to learn, it was left to me." He grimaced.

"You make it sound difficult. Was she afraid?"

"Faith?" He shook his head. "That brat's never been afraid of anything in her life. No, if it had been up to her, she'd have headed at a gallop for the mountains all by her-self the very first day. She begged me to put her on our dad's stallion, Fury. We had to keep watch at all hours so that she didn't saddle him up and sneak out for a ride when no one was paying attention. She finally did it when she was eleven, got herself thrown, and we had to search for her for five hours before we found her sitting with a sprained ankle halfway up Cougar Mountain."

He laughed, sounding so proud that Josy stared at him. "And is she still like that? Fearless? What does she do now?"

"She's a prosecutor. Goes after the bad guys. Nothing fazes Faith." He sounded pleased, and Josy had the impression that Faith Barclay was a woman to be reckoned with.

Just like her big brother.

"Was Meg fearless too?"

He shook his head. "Meg was adventurous and fun-loving, but she had a healthy respect for staying intact. She wasn't reckless like Faith—she thought things through. She paid attention. She wanted to learn the right way to ride, to handle a horse. Just like when she was in the police academy she wanted to learn the right way to shoot, to hit her mark every time, the way to talk down a suspect, to try to avoid violence if it was possible. She specialized in hostage negotiation," he added after a moment.

"It came in handy during domestic violence disputes. You know those guys who lose it and take their wives or kids hostage? Meg had a way of talking them down, a knack for getting through to them without anyone getting hurt."

"She was good with people," Josy murmured.

She saw the bleakness suddenly enter his eyes. "The best I ever saw. Everyone loved her." His tone had become curt.

But no one loved her as much as you did, Josy thought, a tinge of sadness pressing against her heart.

"Let's try a canter." He spoke abruptly, closing the subject. "Let Moonbeam follow Pepper's lead. Nudge his flanks lightly with your heels, but hold on tight with your knees. Easy does it."

The faster pace kept Josy busy balancing, but she tried not to bounce too much in the saddle and concentrated on not falling off. There was no more time to think about Ty Barclay or Meg or Faith, there was only the sensation of rolling movement, of air whipping past her, of the smooth flow of the horse's muscles beneath her.

After a while she felt like she was getting the hang of it, and though she wasn't quite flying, she was moving at a good clip, with only the flower-adorned foothills rising gradually before her, and seemingly endless meadowland surrounding her beneath the great aquamarine dome of the Wyoming sky.

Exhilaration surged through her. She was riding—riding across wide open spaces just as she'd always imagined all those years ago. Not galloping full speed, not bounding across the earth faster than the wind, but definitely riding.

A burst of sun ignited the larkspur and the tips of the leaves, and the scent of sage filled the air with a fresh fragrant aroma that made her feel intensely alive and almost connected to the very earth beneath her.

Ty slowed his mount to a walk and fell back so that they were riding side by side again.

"Had enough or do you want to go on?"

"To Blue Moon Mesa? Yes."

"It's at least another forty-minute climb," he warned. "The terrain's rougher. Think you can handle it?"

"No problem."

Was that a flash of approval she saw in his face?

"You really think I'm a wimp, don't you?" she asked.

His smile was slow and unexpected. "I'm not sure what I think," he replied, studying her face beneath the rim of the baseball cap. "I'll have to let you know later."

She smiled smugly. "You do that, cowboy."

Suddenly she urged Moonbeam forward, into a canter once again, surging past Ty Barclay and the buckskin. She heard his chuckle, and an answering laugh escaped from her own throat.

"Try to keep up," she called over her shoulder as she saw the start of a dirt trail winding upward toward the pines that rimmed the foothills.

Ty let her stay in the lead for a while, enjoying the view of her slender frame and rounded bottom ahead of him. She had good form for a beginner and she was a good sport too, he reflected.

And had a backside that was sexy as hell.

Not that any of that mattered. Inviting her to go riding had been a whim—a strange one at that—but he doubted they'd do it again. She might get ideas. Like they were going to start seeing each other or something and that wasn't about to happen.

Still, he might as well enjoy the day—she was good company and it was surprisingly easy to talk to her. She hadn't once started murmuring all kinds of platitudes about being sorry about Meg, questioning him about how long ago she'd died, telling him he'd get over it.

That was unusual. And refreshing.

For another few moments they rode in silence, until they neared the switchback that would take them to Shadow Point, and from there, to the trail that led to Blue Moon Mesa.

Ty spurred Pepper ahead and took the lead. "The path we want is this way—you can't see it outright unless you know it's there. Slow down here—the trail up to Shadow Point is going to be narrow."

They followed the switchback at a walk, and rode along an increasingly rocky trail, where buttercups and forget-me-nots dotted the sloping hillside.

"See that clearing up ahead?" Ty reined in Pepper and she drew up beside him, looking where he pointed to a wide ledge not far up the trail.

"That's Shadow Point. It's famous here as a makeout spot—has been for generations. Unfortunately, that's as far as we're going to get today. No way we can make it all the way to Blue Moon Mesa. Those clouds are moving in too fast."

He was right, she saw in surprise. She'd been so intent on the ride, she hadn't noticed that the sun was no longer beating hot on her shoulders, that the white puffy clouds had drifted away and been replaced by darker ones moving in from the west.

The air had changed too—it smelled of rain, and the breeze that whipped down from the hills felt cool against her bare arms. All of a sudden, it seemed, rain was moving in and moving in fast.

"Do you want to head back now or try to make it at least to Shadow Point?" he asked. "I can't promise you won't get wet."

"We've come all this way." Josy bit her lip, studying the clouds. "I like to finish what I start. And I'd like to see Shadow Point—even if we only stay for a few minutes."

"Okay then. Follow me. It's a little tricky just ahead—"

He broke off as Moonbeam suddenly reared up on his hind legs, snorting. At the same instant, Ty heard the deadly rattle from the side of the path.

It all happened in a flash. Josy shrieked, grabbing at the horse's neck to keep from falling off, but Ty was already seizing Moonbeam's reins, yanking the gelding down with a jolt, his muscles straining as the terrified horse tried to bolt forward.

"Whoa, boy. Whoa!" Ty's fist balled tight on the reins as Moonbeam danced sideways and tried to rear up again. Ty spotted the rattlesnake three feet away. Still holding the gelding under rigid control, he dropped his own reins, and in one swift movement reached back for his rifle, leaned over Moonbeam's neck, past Josy, and fired two shots.

He saw the shudder reverberate through Josy as the

gunshots boomed through the air, saw her close her eyes, wince, even as a few feet away, the rattlesnake collapsed into a lifeless heap.

Ty had his hands full for the next thirty seconds, keeping both horses under control with brute strength.

Finally, they quieted enough for him to spring down. He moved to Moonbeam's head, speaking softly. He had to concentrate exclusively on soothing the panicked animal until its quivering ceased, before he could finally turn his attention to the spooked woman still clinging to the horse's mane. She was white with shock, her green eyes wide and bright with fear.

"He's all right now. Let me help you down. It's okay, I've got you."

Shakily, she leaned toward him and felt herself being lifted gently to the ground. When her feet touched the earth, he didn't let her go. His arms stayed wrapped tightly around her, supporting her as he spoke to her in a quiet, matter-of-fact tone.

"The rattlesnake spooked him, that's all. Everything's all right now."

"One second he was f-fine, then . . . all of a sudden . . . he tried to throw me—"

"No, he wasn't trying to throw you. He just got scared and reacted. He forgot all about you," Ty said with a grim smile.

She was trembling, so he stroked a reassuring hand down her back. "It's all over now. You're fine. I told you I wouldn't let you fall—and I meant what I said."

She drew a deep breath, trying to slow her racing heart. It was true, he'd saved her from being thrown—or, possibly worse, from being trapped on a runaway horse bolting wildly up the trail. She'd have been lucky to hang on, much less able to bring him under control.

"Thank you," she gasped. "Now . . . can we . . . take a taxi home?"

He laughed. His arms were still wrapped around her and he was surprised when she suddenly leaned in against him and for a moment rested her head upon his shoulder.

They stood that way in silence for a moment, while a searing sensation rushed through him. Then she abruptly lifted her head, stiffened in his arms, and jerked back.

"Never mind. I . . . I'm sorry to be such a baby. I guess I am a wimp after all." She tried to smile. "I'm fine now. Really."

But she was gazing warily at the horses, and Ty knew exactly what was going through her head—she wasn't sure she could bring herself to get back up on Moonbeam again.

"You know what they say. When you fall off, you have to get right back in the saddle."

"Yeah? Who says?" She shook her head. "Whoever it was, he obviously never was thrown off a crazed horse and nearly eaten by a rattlesnake."

He laughed again. "You weren't thrown off either, and the rattlesnake wouldn't have eaten you."

"I'm not so sure."

Ty understood her distress. She was a raw beginner, and she was scared. But he knew one thing—if she didn't get back up on Moonbeam right now, she'd probably never ride again.

He took her hand in his, surprised by the iciness of her long, slender fingers. He folded his hand around hers. "If we don't get moving, we'll get soaked long before we get back to Ada's place. This looks like one of those fast-moving storms that comes when you least expect it, roars through, and then blows along on its merry way. And we're going to be smack in the middle of it. So we have to get the hell going. Shadow Point's going to have to wait for another day."

He was right. The clouds were getting darker by the moment and the sky was turning an ominous murky green. The sun had disappeared and the wind was turning colder every second they stood there.

She shivered in her T-shirt. "Okay."

Still, she hesitated, hugging her arms around herself and glancing uneasily at Moonbeam. The horse was quiet now, giving no sign of fear or nervousness. She wished she could say the same about herself.

"C'mon, you'll be fine. I promise," Ty said quietly.

She glanced at him. There was sympathy in his face, lending it a tenderness she'd never seen there before. As their eyes met, she felt an odd heat flare inside her and she drew in her breath.

Oh, boy. This fresh, sage-scented air was heady stuff. *That's all it is,* she told herself. *Too much space, too much nature, too much adventure for one afternoon.*

Too much man? a voice inside of her suggested. Josy tried to stifle the voice. "Well, if you promise, then what can I say? Let's do it."

She managed a smile, but it came out more as a grimace. Still, Ty Barclay smiled back as she started toward Moonbeam.

Right before she mounted, she glanced over her shoulder and saw the shot-up rattlesnake sprawled in the dirt. For one insane moment it brought back the hideous memory of Archie lying dead on the blood-soaked floor.

She closed her eyes, struggling to get a grip on herself.

"Not a pretty sight, I know, but he had it coming." Ty held her elbow to steady her as she prepared to swing a foot into the stirrup.

"I've seen worse." Josy braced herself, then swung up and over as Ty boosted her into the saddle. To her relief, Moonbeam stayed steady, merely lifting his head and snorting as Josy fitted both feet into the stirrups and settled herself.

"Good boy," she muttered in relief, and patted the gelding's neck before gathering up the reins.

Then Ty was mounted on Pepper, leading the way back down the trail the way they'd come. He kept the horses to a quick walk as they rode carefully to lower ground, working their way back toward the open, grassy land.

Big raindrops splattered down just as they reached the meadow.

"Don't gallop!" Josy called out worriedly, and he shot her an encouraging smile before urging Pepper into a trot.

By the time they reached Ada's house, the rain was hammering down like sleek silver nails and they were both soaked.

"Ada's not back yet, so you'd better head home to dry off," Ty told Josy over the rush of wind and rain as he helped her down outside the barn.

"What about you?" she called as he opened the barn door and led Moonbeam and Pepper inside.

"I've got to dry them off and rub them down and feed them before I leave. Don't worry, I'll be fine. But you'd better get out of those wet clothes."

Yet his eyes couldn't help lingering on her as she moved just within the barn door. Her jeans were molded tightly to the curves of her hips and to her small, rounded bottom. Just as her sodden T-shirt and bra were molded to her breasts.

He couldn't help it—he wanted to touch her.

Everywhere.

He wanted to lick the raindrops from that gorgeous, delicate face. To help her out of those wet clothes and into that sweet-smelling pile of hay in the corner.

Damn it, he was getting hard just looking at her.

He forced himself to look away and busied himself unsaddling the horses, but he sensed her still in the doorway, hesitating.

"I hate to just leave. . . . Do you . . . need some help?"

"From a tenderfoot?" He wouldn't let himself look at her again. Instead, he hoisted off Pepper's saddle. "Nope. Go home, Josy. Dry off."

It was the first time he'd called her by her name. For some stupid reason, her heart turned over in her chest.

"Thanks for the riding lesson. And for . . . everything."

"Maybe next time we'll make it to Shadow Point."

Next time? She opened her mouth, but it was hard to think what to say. Because all she could do right now was stare at him and try to get her feet to budge toward the barn door.

He was gorgeous. Waterlogged and gorgeous. His jeans were plastered to his body, what she could see of it. He held the saddle before him, covering one crucial part.

Not that she was interested, she told herself. But it was no use.

She couldn't drag her gaze from his shirt, which clung to his wide sculpted chest and to every bulging muscle on those powerful, corded arms.

Down, girl, she thought desperately, as a wave of hot yearning spiked through her.

"See ya," she finally managed to croak out, and then shivering, she darted out the door.

She didn't look back and didn't see him standing there, holding the saddle, watching her run away from him through the wind and rain.

He wasn't even aware of the smile on his face—at first. He caught it as the battered Blazer disappeared down Angel Road. Then the smile vanished.

Ty Barclay's mouth settled into a frown as he closed the barn door.

Chapter 11

"I BROUGHT A PEACE OFFERING."

Roy Hewett extended the six-pack of beer to his cousin with a grin. "And I could use one of these myself if you don't mind."

"Beware of family members bearing gifts," Ty growled, but he accepted the beer and stepped aside to let Roy enter his apartment.

He wasn't really angry anymore about Roy pushing him into dancing with Josy Warner, but he wasn't about to let his cousin off the hook too easily. It went against his general principle of keeping anyone from feeling like they had a right to mess in his life.

He'd come home from his rain-soaked ride with Josy about two hours ago. He'd showered, watched some TV, and had been just about to shove a frozen pizza in the microwave when Roy showed up. The rain had ended a short time ago and now, through the open doors leading to the balcony, the night glistened cool and still, filled with the scent of damp earth and sage. Somehow the fresh clean smell now made him think of her. Crazy.

"You want some pizza?" he asked as Roy dropped down into the easy chair and put his feet up on the coffee table.

"Naw, Corinne and I already ate. I just stopped by because she bawled me out again for what I pulled the other night at the Tumbleweed. She said I set up her new friend to get her feelings hurt. And that you had every right to be mad at me."

"Smart woman you're marrying. You ought to listen to her." Ty took the pizza from the freezer and tore off the cardboard packaging.

"Does that mean you're still pissed at me for throwing you together with Josy?"

"What do you think?"

"I think you need a kick in the ass to get your life jump-started again. And Adam and Faith both agree with me. So I did something about it, okay? Sue me."

"Just don't try it again or I might do something worse than sue you."

Roy grinned. He knew Ty was too basically good-natured to make good on his threats. Both Ty and Adam were tough as rawhide and there weren't too many men with any brains who'd go up against them, but Roy had once beaten Adam in a schoolyard fight in seventh grade, and he figured if he ever had to, he could at least survive a brawl with Ty. All the Barclay men could fight their way to hell and back and come out on top, but they also had famous soft spots for dogs, kids, and their own family.

"Fact is, you ought to have gotten down on both knees and thanked me," Roy retorted. "Josy Warner's a knockout. And she's only in town for a few weeks, according to Corinne, so it seemed perfect—no long-term commitment, no pressure. It's not like I wanted you to marry the woman."

"Stay the hell out of my life, Roy." Ty shoved the pizza

in the microwave and punched in buttons. "And you can tell Faith and Adam to do the same."

Roy helped himself to a beer and held his tongue until his big cousin had brought the heated pizza over to the coffee table, taken a bite of sausage and gooey cheese, and washed it down with a gulp of Budweiser.

"All right, you win. I won't pull anything like that again—at least for a while," Roy conceded. "So, come on, tell me. What did you think?"

"About what?"

"About Josy."

"I think you'd better drop the subject."

Roy gave up. Not only wasn't he going to get even a shred of information out of Ty, it also seemed obvious that the stunning new woman in town hadn't lit any fires under him. Damn.

"So what are you really doing here, Roy? And why did you say you could use a drink?"

"Oh, hell. It's all this wedding stuff. I'm sick of it. Invitations, writing wedding vows, picking out centerpieces. I can't wait till this thing's over. And I wanted to ask you something."

"Yeah?" Ty took another swig of his beer. "Shoot."

"How would you like to be my best man?"

Slowly, Ty grinned. A smile crinkled across Roy's face.

"I'd like it fine, so long as you don't try to set me up with any of the bridesmaids," Ty told him.

"Word of honor. But you'll need to rent a tux."

"Hey, anything for family."

Roy looked pleased. "Have you talked to your mom lately? Are she and your dad and the rest of the family coming in time for the prenuptial dinner?"

"I spoke to Faith yesterday. She said yep, they're all coming in early. And they're all eager to meet Corinne."

Roy nodded. "That's great. Speaking of which, now that I've arranged for my best man—item number five out of the fifty or so tasks she's assigned me for today—I promised to take her to the Tumbleweed tonight. I have to shove off. Want to join us? I promise not to torture you by introducing you to any more gorgeous blondes."

"Don't push your luck, Roy."

Roy laughed and stood up. At that moment, there was a knock at the door. Ty strode over and opened it.

"Hi." Josy stood in the hallway, smiling shyly. "I wanted to make sure you got home okay."

It sounded lame, even to her. She had to squelch the urge to run back to her own apartment as she gazed up at the tall man with the freshly washed hair slicked down over his brow, the clean black T-shirt and gray sweatpants, and the surprised expression on his face.

In truth she didn't know why she was here, but she'd been restless as a cat ever since she'd come home, soaked in a hot bubble bath, and eaten a handful of cheese and crackers. It was just about all she had left in her pantry—except for Ricky's stupid package.

"I got home fine." Ty was aware that Roy was less than ten feet away, listening to every word.

Now there would be hell to pay. The funny thing was, at the moment he didn't really give a damn. Josy Warner was drawing every ounce of his attention.

She looked as fresh and beautiful as a long-stemmed yellow rose. She was wearing white sweatpants and a pink tank top, and her pale hair was bound up in some kind of French twist arrangement that he found extremely sexy. It begged to be freed from the elasticized band that held it back from those exquisitely feminine features.

"And Moonbeam and Pepper?" she continued, still gazing at him with that slight hesitant smile on her face. "They're all right?"

"Good as new." Ty heard Roy walking up behind him. "You remember my cousin Roy?"

"Oh." A delicious blush rose in her cheeks. "Of course I do."

Roy Hewett was grinning from ear to ear—*looking exactly like the Cheshire cat in a cowboy hat,* she thought, shifting from one foot to the other as the heat in her cheeks told her she was blushing like a teenager.

"Nice to see you again, Josy." Roy's keen gaze shifted back and forth between her and Ty. "What's this I heard about horses?"

"We . . . went for a ride this afternoon—and got soaked." She suddenly remembered the baseball cap in her hand and thrust it at Ty.

"Here. I thought you might want this back. I didn't know you had company," she added quickly, starting to edge down the hall.

"Hold on." Ty's gaze held hers, then he glanced over his shoulder at Roy. "My cousin was just leaving."

"Yep, I sure was." Roy sauntered past him, out into the hall, his grin broader than ever. "I'm on my way to pick up Corinne," he told Josy. "We're headed over to the Tumbleweed. I'd ask you two to join us, but I expect you have better things to do."

From the twinkle in his eyes, Josy knew word would be racing like wildfire through the town in ten minutes flat that there was something going on between Josy Warner and Ty Barclay.

She suppressed a groan as Roy disappeared into the stairwell, and they heard the quick thump of his boots going down the steps.

Her gaze lifted to Ty's. "Oh, God. Sorry. Talk about bad timing." She shook her head with a wry grin. "Now he's going to think there's something going on between us. You know he will."

"Forget about Roy. He has the maturity of a second grader. Come on in."

She stepped inside, noting that his apartment looked just like hers. And it was almost as bereft of personal touches. There were no photographs, no art, except for the exact same moose and barn print, no flowers or candles or vases. Just a green sofa, two armchairs, a coffee table, and white walls.

"Nice place you've got here, Sheriff Barclay. It has about as much soul and character as mine. But I'm only here for a month—what's your excuse?"

"I'm not into interior decorating." He closed the door.

"Oh, right. I forgot. You're into . . . what was it? Guns, cuffs, Krispy Kremes." But she was smiling as she said it. "I think the only thing we have in common there is the doughnut thing."

"That'll work. I like to leave the guns and the cuffs at work anyway. How about a beer? Or do you only drink white wine?"

"More stereotypes, Sheriff?"

His eyes lit with amusement. "Don't be so suspicious. I happened to notice that's what you were drinking at the Tumbleweed that night. I'm a cop, remember? I notice things."

Another reason I have no business being here, Josy thought.

"A beer will be fine." She eyed the leftover pizza on the counter, wishing she knew just why she *was* here. "A slice of that pizza along with it would be heavenly," she murmured, trying not to sound too desperate.

His brows lifted. "All out of food?"

"Just about. I had cheese and crackers for breakfast and the last of it for dinner."

"I can do better than that."

He set the pizza on a black stoneware plate and zapped it, then brought the plate and a bottle of beer to the coffee table. He sipped his own beer, watching as she curled up on the sofa and devoured the food.

"I have another pizza in the freezer if you're still hungry."

"Give me a break. Do I look that starved?"

"Uh-huh. And my mother raised her kids to never let a guest go hungry. I'm just making sure."

She licked the last drop of tomato sauce from her fingers. "You're fond of her, aren't you?" she asked. "You're fond of all of them—your mother, your sister, and your brother. What about your father? You haven't said much about him."

"We get along." Ty's voice was calm, equable. "He's into business and politics a lot more than I ever will be. He'd have preferred it if I'd gone into either law or the FBI, instead of becoming a cop, but he let me make my own decision. Other than giving us unasked-for pieces of advice now and then, he's a fairly hands-off guy. Whatever makes my mother happy, makes him happy."

Despite his casual words, she saw the affection in his eyes as he spoke about his father and for a moment she wondered what it would have been like to grow up in that kind of big, active, happy family.

"What about you?" Ty asked. He sat down at the end of the green sofa and leaned his shoulders against the cushions, watching her. "Are you close with your family?"

"I think I would have been, but . . . I'm an only child and my parents died right before I turned twelve."

She waited for him to flinch, to offer some kind of awkward sympathy, but instead he just nodded and gazed at her, steadily, calmly.

"That must have been tough."

"Yes. They were in a car accident. It was . . . so sudden. One morning we all had breakfast together before I left for school, and the next morning . . . they were gone."

She picked up a napkin, twisted it in her fingers. "I couldn't even speak for a while after they died," she went on quietly. "For several months I was mute. The doctors said it was shock. It . . . it wore off eventually."

She swallowed, suddenly self-conscious. She'd told him far more than she'd told most people. Even Jane and Reese didn't know about her inability to speak.

"Were you taken in by relatives?"

She shook her head, shifting on the sofa, not willing to tell him more, about her life in foster care. *Don't turn this into a pity party,* she thought. Aloud, she spoke coolly. "Look, do we have to talk about this?"

"Not if you don't want to."

"I don't."

Ty nodded, came to his feet. "There's something I want to do."

He smiled as her head flew up and she regarded him with sudden wariness. For a coolly sophisticated, beautiful woman she had a way of turning skittish on a dime that intrigued him. And why not? A woman of contradictions . . . and secrets . . .

Pure magnetism for a cop.

He took a CD from a pile on the bookshelf and put it in his CD player.

Rod Stewart's jagged, raspy voice poured out. *If I listened long enough to you . . .*

"No Johnny Cash, Garth, or Dolly Parton?" she asked, surprised and a little nervous as he walked toward her and stopped beside the sofa. She had to crane her neck to look up at him, past that broad chest and those wide shoulders, past the five-o'clock shadow fringing his lean jaw.

"Country's fine, but I like to mix things up now and then. Ms. Warner, would you care to dance?"

Her laugh was soft, a little breathless. Ty felt his muscles tighten with a surge of one hundred proof lust.

"If you're sure nobody's forcing you into this."

"I'm sure." He took her hand and drew her up off the sofa. His gaze held hers as Rod Stewart's sensuous voice filled the room.

A whisper of heat shimmered through her as Ty drew her away from the coffee table, into the middle of the living room. When his arm slid around her waist and drew her close against him, Josy caught her breath.

Why in the world was her heart hammering like this? She'd danced with dozens of handsome men before—Doug Fifer had been plenty handsome—yet she'd never felt like she was going to have a heart attack when she danced with him, or any of them.

But none of them was like Ty Barclay, none of them had ever triggered an electric jolt to her heart when they touched her, or made her pulse race and burn, as if she were running naked beneath the sun on a golden July day.

They danced slowly, intimately, as Rod sang "Reason to Believe." Neither of them made any attempt to talk.

She could only wonder if he was as intensely aware as she was of the silence floating above the music, of the sweet languorous night, of the wind rustling in the darkness beyond the balcony doors.

The song ended too soon. Josy took a breath and searched for something clever and light to say, something that would help her recover from the heat flooding her body. But before she could say anything, Ty caught her face between his hands.

She stopped breathing, her gaze locked on his.

Five seconds passed. Ten.

His gaze searched hers. Then he swore under his breath, leaned down, and kissed her.

It was a deep, slow kiss. More gentle than she ever would expect from such a strong man. His mouth moved smoothly, deliberately, savoring hers. And she melted, melted into a puddle of sensations. All of them converged, flowed, swirled through her body at once.

Pleasure and need ached through her, even as a voice inside warned that this was crazy.

Crazy or not, she couldn't stop. She didn't want to. She lost herself in him, clinging to his mouth as he deepened the kisses, his hands roughly encircling her waist.

"Mmmm," she gasped at last, coming up for air. Dizzy and breathless, she stared into his eyes, reading the dark hunger in them. She dug her fingers into his shoulders, pulling him closer.

"Don't . . . stop," she whispered raggedly.

And then Ty's mouth was on hers again.

He was incredibly aroused. A part of him warned him to slow down, but he didn't. Couldn't. She tasted too sweet. She felt too good.

And she kissed him like a woman who knew what she wanted.

When he pressed his mouth to the pulse at her throat, her head fell back, and she moaned.

"Oh, baby," Ty muttered as his lips returned to her hot lush mouth, surprising her by sliding his tongue inside. Hers rose up eagerly to meet it.

Their kisses became hotter, faster, taking over what remained of reason.

This is insanity, Josy thought dimly, even as her tongue stroked against his, as her hands fisted in his hair. *Total insanity.*

And then she couldn't think of anything but him and *this* and she fought for breath against his wild, crushing mouth. Sensation built upon sensation and Josy gave herself up to them all.

Rod was singing "Downtown Train," but neither of them heard. Ty heard only her quick breathing and tiny mew of pleasure as he slipped a hand inside her pink tank top and bra, his fingers skimming over her nipple. He caressed her with soft, circular strokes, kissing her all the while. But when he started to lift the tank top over her head, she suddenly drew in a long, jagged breath and stopped his hands.

"Wait," she gasped. "No."

Ty's hands stilled. He let the tank go, a sense of loss enveloping him.

He fought for control of his body and emotions as she stepped back, straightening her bra, her tank top, taking deep breaths of air.

"You . . . pack quite a punch, Sheriff Barclay." She tried to sound flippant, but her voice was breathless. She couldn't let him see how shaken she was, how vulnerable she felt. Her knees were trembling, for heaven's sake, and her mouth felt bruised, tender, and scorched by his kisses.

"You pack a pretty big punch yourself, Ms. Warner." He reached a hand to her pale cloud of hair. A few strands of that French twisty thing had come loose and the soft tendrils framed her face. Gently, he brushed them from her eyes.

"I like you like this, Josy. Loose, relaxed, warm. Do you know you're sexy as hell?" He smiled, his body still tight with tension, still wanting her with a throbbing physical pain. She'd been letting her guard down, just as she had at the barn yesterday. It was making him crazy, for some reason he couldn't quite figure out.

"It must be the music," she murmured, trying to resurrect her defenses. "Rod Stewart's voice . . . just loosens me up."

"Rod's voice. Uh-huh. That's all it takes?"

She smiled at him, and his blood pounded. Her eyes were soft and dreamy as she reached up, tentatively touching his cheek.

"I should go," she whispered, not because she wanted to, but because she knew if she stayed five more minutes, if she let him kiss her again, she'd do something stupid.

When the day had started this morning she'd never dreamed she'd end up in Ty Barclay's apartment—dancing with him, kissing him. Never in a million years.

And all things considered it was a very bad idea.

"Sure you don't want to stay for one more dance?"

She shook her head, praying he couldn't see the truth in her eyes. A part of her wanted to stay there all night, in his arms.

But she couldn't afford to get lost in that hot blue gaze.

Or in that slow, sexy smile. She couldn't afford to end up in his bed.

"Let me walk you home then."

Her lips curved. "I think I can manage to get there without getting mugged."

"You never know." His hand smoothed her hair, slid down her cheek, resting there, very gently. "As a police officer, I'd advise you not to take those kinds of chances."

Oh, God, she was falling. For a cop. A sheriff. She couldn't do this to Ricky, to herself. It was too much of a risk, in so many ways. What was wrong with her?

She stepped back suddenly, too suddenly, and saw his brows shoot up.

"Okay, well . . . this was fun," she said lightly. "Thanks . . . for the pizza. And the beer." *And the kisses.*

"Not all that exciting for a first date," he said quietly. "I can do better. What about tomorrow night?"

"I can't."

A frown furrowed between his eyes. "Why not? Do you have another date?" *And is it with Chance Roper?* Ty wondered grimly.

There were a number of reasons why he disliked this idea. He didn't want to explore the most pressing one. "Break it," he suggested, his jaw clenched.

"I can't do that. It's Corinne. She asked me to meet her and give her some decorating tips. She wants to change around a few things in Roy's place to make it feel more like theirs, not his. She's cooking dinner for me and Roberta's coming too. We'll probably end up talking about wedding stuff."

"I can make you a much better offer." His thumb brushed her cheek again, then trailed down her throat, lingered at her collarbone. He felt the shiver go through her and his need for her heightened.

He had a wild fantasy of making love to her out on the balcony, then here on the sofa—and a third time in his bed, all night long . . . His chest was tight with the urge to pull her into his arms and undo that whole French twist thing so he could comb his hands through that gorgeous hair.

But his fantasy disintegrated when she shook her head again, offered him a forced smile, and edged back a step.

"Some other time." When she moved toward the door, he had no choice but to follow her.

But when he began to walk her down the hall, she pulled up short. "Don't be silly. I live thirty feet away. You don't have to do this."

He stopped, shoved his hands into his pockets. And nodded.

She was telling him to back off. Fine, he got the message. None of this was a good idea anyway. He wasn't even sure what he saw in her, other than that she was beautiful. And sexy. Then there was the fact that her mouth was incredibly lush and soft, like rose petals.

And she had guts.

Old-fashioned, saucy, ballsy guts. He enjoyed being with her, even when she was cold and snotty and feisty. But much more so when she was lounging in his apartment, eating his pizza and drinking his beer.

She's secretive, closed, and she's going back to Chicago in a few weeks. Forget it.

He waited while she pulled her key from the pocket of her sweatpants and turned it in the lock.

He heard her murmur good night and he grunted something in reply. It sounded like "See ya."

Ty dumped what was left of the pizza in the trash, opened another beer, then left it sitting on the counter as he paced back and forth, finally ending up on the balcony.

Cool air blew on his hot face and neck. *She isn't interested,* he told himself. *Or she's scared. Or she can't make up her mind.*

That's fine by me, he thought. *I don't have time for games or women who don't know what they want. I don't have the inclination to do that much thinking, or that much work.*

There were women in Thunder Creek who'd be easy on the eyes and a lot easier on the nerves. Women who wouldn't run hot and cold, women who weren't closed and secretive, who'd never been mute in their lives.

So why was he still thinking about Josy Warner?

Josy Warner was done. Toast.

"Over," he muttered aloud.

But something deep inside him knew that if he had to take a lie detector test right now, he'd sure as hell fail.

Chapter 12

SORRY THIS TOOK SO LONG, KIDDO, BUT I RAN INTO some trouble. Call me at this number as soon as you get this.

Josy stared at the computer screen, her stomach lurching. Finally—Ricky had written back. She was so excited she gasped aloud, then threw a quick, wary glance toward the checkout desk. Maggie Cartright was busy on the phone.

Quickly, she read the rest of the e-mail.

Be sure you're using a new cell phone, without an account, or any info that can be traced to you, like I told you. We'll set up a meet and I'll come pick up my stuff. Call now.

Tears pricked her eyes. Ricky was safe. He'd made it— and so had she. With any luck this whole nightmare would be over soon.

Please, she prayed. *Let it all be over soon.*

She scribbled the phone number on a scrap of paper and shoved it into her purse, then deleted the e-mail and signed off. She hurried from the library and got into her Blazer.

She didn't even want to delay calling Ricky until she

reached her apartment. Sitting in the parking lot, she locked all her doors, even though the area was deserted, and pulled the cell phone from her purse.

"Yeah." Ricky's voice gave nothing away. It sounded hard, cool. And slightly suspicious.

"It's me." She heard the quiver in her own voice and tried to steady it. "Ricky, I didn't know what happened to you. You didn't answer me for all this time—"

"Sorry about that, Jo-Jo. I ran into some trouble, but brother, was I glad to hear from you."

"Where are you?"

"You first, sweetheart. Talk fast, I never know when I'm going to have to run."

"They're still after you? Now?" Shock ran through her.

"Just tell me where you are, Josy."

"I'm in Thunder Creek."

"*Where?*"

"A little town in Wyoming. Thunder Creek."

"Man, when I said you should go far away, you took me seriously." She heard the chuckle of approval at the other end of the line. "Good going. Now I have to get to you."

"From where, Ricky? What's going on?"

"I'm in Boston, just blending in with the crowd. Looks like I'm headed west though. You still have that package, don't you?"

"Last time I looked, which was about an hour ago." She reminded herself that she wasn't a child anymore, dependent on big tough Ricky to get her through the hood and the Hammond house in one piece. "Look, Ricky, don't you think it's time to tell me what's inside it?"

"Better you don't know. Trust me. Now give me your number, in case I have to call you."

She did as he asked and waited while he repeated it back to her.

"You haven't had any trouble, have you, Jo-Jo?"

"You mean the kind of trouble Archie had?"

"Along those lines."

"No . . . or I probably wouldn't be talking to you right now," she said with more acid in her voice than she'd ever used with Ricky. She lowered her pitch, evened her tone. "I think I've covered my tracks pretty well. I haven't used any credit cards or my old phone. I haven't called anyone—even anyone from work."

"Good. And don't start now. Hopefully your luck will hold out until I get there. Once I take the package off your hands, they'll only be after me."

"Ricky, are you going to be able to get out of this mess? What's going to happen?"

"Don't know, babe, but I gotta go—"

"Wait—one more question."

"What?" She heard the sudden tension in his voice now, and sensed that he was walking fast, very fast. She could almost see him looking around and it dawned on her that he was probably about to run, to take off, probably down some alley or something. Maybe someone was closing in . . .

"Is Archie dead?" she nearly shouted, as his tension communicated itself to her. "Do you know?"

"Yeah, he's dead. And I will be too if I don't get moving. Stay safe, don't tell anyone else where you are, see you soon."

Josy drove to the store, stocked up on groceries, and went straight home. When she got there she drew the package out of the recesses of her kitchen cabinet, set it on the counter. Then she waited until all of her groceries were put away before she carried it into her bedroom and placed it on the bed.

Sunlight slanted into the room as she sank down on both knees on the bed, studying the parcel.

Ricky had told her not to open it—and she hadn't for the past two weeks. But she was neck-deep in this too, and much as she loved Ricky, she wasn't a kid who needed advice and guidance anymore.

She made her own decisions. And she'd decided while Ricky was talking to her that it was time to find out what had gotten Archie killed and set her and Ricky on the run.

She didn't feel the least bit guilty about defying Ricky as she lifted up the package and began tearing through the layers of brown wrapping paper.

Finally she reached a thin white cardboard box, which was sealed with tape. She used her apartment key to rip open the seal and carefully emptied out the contents— bubble wrap, tissue paper . . .

And inside four layers of the tissue paper . . .

She went very still.

It was a jewel.

Not just any jewel, Josy thought, her throat closing. It was a diamond. A glittering, dazzling, golden-yellow diamond—and it was big as an egg.

My God, where did Ricky get this?

It glittered brighter than the sun.

How many carats can it be? she wondered in awe, staring at it. *One hundred? Two hundred?*

Her hand shook as she reached for it, carefully picked it up. Her palm tingled. The jewel felt warm, vibrant against her skin. She'd never seen, much less touched, a jewel of this size, or this brilliance.

She knew it had to be real—and priceless. A man had already died for it. Another man had killed trying to get it back.

And she had it. Here, in her tiny rented apartment in the wilds of Wyoming. She had this . . . this amazing treasure that had brought Archie death.

She gulped, thinking of it stored all this time in her cabinet. With the Cheerios and cans of tuna and the jar of Jif peanut butter.

Where did it come from?

She didn't want to contemplate that; she only knew that if the men chasing Ricky didn't kill him first, she would do it herself when she finally met up with him.

It had to have been stolen. Had to be. But . . . whom had he stolen it from . . . and why?

She dropped the diamond into the box on her bed, sprang up, and began to pace around the room.

Ricky was in deep trouble, deeper than she'd even contemplated—and so was she. She'd expected the package to contain some kind of evidence, evidence that would exonerate him from the charges that had been made against him in New York. Evidence that would incriminate someone else.

But she'd never expected anything like this.

And now she was an accessory to whatever crime had put him in possession of the diamond.

Panic bubbled in her as she paced. *Okay, think. What can you do?*

She had to turn it over to the authorities. Immediately. As soon as she did, the danger would be over—for her, and probably for Ricky. Once word got out that the diamond had been recovered and was in police possession, surely whoever was chasing them would back off. Regroup.

She and Ricky could get out of this alive.

But . . . they'd both still face charges. Unless they could cut a deal. Maybe Ricky could explain, could get immunity. Maybe there were circumstances that had led him to this, circumstances that could be explained, justified.

There had to be—the Ricky she'd known all these years wasn't a thief. He must have had a good reason, she told herself, fighting back images of prison bars.

Josy went into the kitchen, poured herself a glass of water, drank one sip, and set the glass down. Her hands were still shaking. But she knew what she could do.

She could go to Ty Barclay. Turn the package over to him, let him contact the authorities in New York—and whatever else he needed to do. He would listen to her, she was pretty certain of that. Maybe he'd even help her, though she couldn't expect him to vouch for her. She'd lied about too many things already.

But she thought he would at least hear her out.

Only . . . Ricky had told her the cops couldn't get hold of the package. He'd insisted on it. And if she confided in Ty . . . they would.

She went back into the bedroom, threw herself down on the bed beside the box and the diamond, and covered her eyes with her hands.

Thinking back, she saw Ricky facing down the Callahan brothers for her. She saw Ricky sneaking into the Hammond basement, bringing her food, light, company.

She saw him teaching her how to kick a man in the balls to give herself time to get away if she was ever cornered, and insisting that she get familiar with the workings of a gun—even giving her one, already registered—as a welcome present when she'd moved into her first sixth-floor walk-up in the Village.

Of course she'd never used it. She'd given it to Jane, who'd been mugged one night at an ATM on her way home from work. Jane vowed she would use it if she had to—Josy had never wanted to even imagine having to use a gun. But she'd never told Ricky.

He'd only wanted her to be safe. Ever since she'd known him, he'd tried to keep her safe, tried to teach her how to get beyond being a mute victim of tragedy and of a system that was far larger and tougher than she was.

Ricky had been good to her. Was she really going to turn him in?

She knew the answer even as she peeled her hands away from her face. She gazed bleakly down at the diamond.

And suddenly she knew what she had to do.

Oliver Tate sipped a brandy as he strolled the length of his secret room. Hidden in the walls behind his wine cellar, this was his favorite room in the house, and the only room that even Renee was not permitted to visit without him.

It was thirty feet long and twenty feet wide, carpeted in black, with pearl-white walls. It was temperature-controlled, soundproofed, and lit by an extensive lighting system that dramatically spotlighted each of his many treasures from all over the world.

One of his greatest pleasures had always been to come here, anytime he chose, and survey everything he had acquired. He loved to touch them, all the beautiful pieces

worthy of a king. Even more, he loved remembering how
he'd acquired them and planning exactly where he would
place and display his next precious acquisition.

But tonight as he waited for Renee to finish dressing
for the AIDS charity concert at Lincoln Center, he was
disturbed, too disturbed to even remotely enjoy this room.

Nothing was right here, not now, not since the diamond
had been stolen. The Golden Eye had a reputation for being stolen that had been earned over centuries, and he
himself had stolen it from an enemy, a drug lord in
Malaysia. But it was not acceptable that the Golden Eye
be stolen from him.

He needed it back, not only because its place on the
black marble pedestal was empty now, but because it
would prove that no one could cross him and get away
with it.

Olvan Tatrinsky had learned long ago that strength, not
weakness, was the key to success. And that scum cop
Sabatini who'd wormed his way into his organization and
won Lyle Samuels's trust had made him look weak.

But not for long.

Dolph has had more than enough time, Tate thought
darkly, staring unseeingly at the luminous Rembrandt
framed in burnished gold upon the wall, near the
seventeenth-century Flemish tapesty that had once graced
the British Museum.

*If he can't handle this, it's time to find someone who
can.*

Tate paused to survey the soothingly quiet room, his
gaze restlessly skimming the paintings and statues and
objets d'art—from the glistening samurai sword dating
from the twelfth century to the antique pearl-handled Regency dueling pistols. He took in the exquisite Fabergé

eggs glittering on a gilt-edged Russian table, and the Renaissance pendant necklace said to have been worn at one time by the Empress Josephine.

But tonight he couldn't even be charmed by the array of golden, jewel-encrusted snuff boxes, or by his collections of Sevres vases or ancient Chinese jade.

No, tonight all he could do was curse the man who had pierced not only the secrecy of his organization—but also the privacy of his home.

Sabatini had somehow burrowed so deep undercover he'd been welcomed into the outer circle of Tate's organization. And that had enabled him to collect damning evidence linking Tate's business dealings to the very unsavory crime boss Julius Caventini.

And even Becker, Tate's own private cop-in-the-pocket, hadn't gotten wind of the undercover operation until it was too late. By the time Becker had a clue, Sabatini had already managed to turn over evidence that could send both Tate and Caventini to prison for the rest of their lives.

Tate scowled and polished off the last of his brandy.

He reminded himself that much of what needed to be done to rectify the situation had already taken place. With Becker's help, they'd managed to make the evidence Sabatini had collected simply disappear. And Sabatini had been cleverly discredited, making him look like nothing but a dirty cop on the take, trying to save his own filthy neck—a cop whose word wouldn't be worth a gram of crap.

But Tate hadn't anticipated that he'd strike back—and in the most in-your-face way imaginable: by stealing a diamond worth twenty million dollars from Tate's own private home.

Lyle Samuels, his so-called security expert, was to

blame for that. Before he'd died, Samuels had confessed that a week before Sabatini's cover was blown, he'd actually shown Sabatini the secret room, proudly displaying his security system's high-tech bells and whistles to someone he considered part of the team.

So now the Golden Eye was gone. One of the largest, most legendary diamonds in the world, snatched from the home of the man who had spent more than seven years trying to find it.

According to legend, the Golden Eye had originally been set in the eye of an idol. History had later tracked it—noting its possession by sheiks and sultans, pirates and kings. It had even made its way to the French court of Louis XV before it vanished in the bloodbath of the French Revolution.

But it belongs here, Tate thought, his green eyes narrowing to icy slits. *It was made to be mine.*

It's more than time to call in backup for Dolph, he decided as he left his treasure room and went to find Renee.

Armstrong would have his chance to get the job done.

He was tired of waiting, tired of excuses for Dolph not finding the girl. Let them both hunt her—and the diamond.

And may the best man win.

Chapter 13

THE BLAZER BUMPED AND ROLLED ALONG THE
rough gravel road as Josy drove slowly, making careful
notations on her sketch pad. She refused to let herself be
distracted by the stunning beauty of this rugged land, or
by the aquamarine radiance of the Wyoming sky. But she
did brake suddenly to stare when she saw a small herd of
pronghorn antelope on a ledge no more than a few hundred yards away.

Beautiful and proud, they stood perfectly still for a moment as if surveying their own private kingdom, then suddenly they turned as one and bounded away, disappearing
along the rocky bluff as if they'd been no more than a mi-
rage.

She glanced at her map again, took note of her surroundings, and jotted a brief description for herself, along
with a drawing.

Ledge at right . . . aspen tree . . . purple flowers beneath . . .

She'd been driving exactly sixteen minutes since she'd
left the highway, following the road into the foothills
about one mile south of Shadow Point and the trail she
and Ty had ridden the other day.

Not far enough yet, she decided, and drove on, climbing for another quarter of a mile. When she reached a side trail that wound around a gully, she turned onto it and proceeded slowly, watching for just the right spot.

Finally she stopped and got out, taking the package— rewrapped and retaped in its original brown paper—with her. She also pulled out the small shovel she'd bought at Merck's Hardware and her sketch pad and pencil, and set off toward a big rock nestled alongside a broken tree stump.

She knelt down in the grass a foot from the rock, dropped everything but the shovel in a little pile, and began to dig.

Turning down Angel Road an hour later, she wasn't surprised to see Corinne's car parked in front of Ada's house. She'd already stopped by Bessie's Diner, hoping to see Ada, and she'd heard all about the bad news.

"I'm jinxed, that's what it is," Corinne was saying in a low, desolate tone as Josy peered in through the screen door. They were sitting in Ada's living room, and Ada was pouring her a cup of tea.

"Maybe I'm not supposed to get married. Maybe I'm just not supposed to marry Roy. Maybe this is fate's way of telling me the wedding is a mistake—" Her voice cracked.

"Stop that now," Ada chided. Josy had never heard her speak so sternly. "You're talking nonsense." She caught sight of Josy on the porch and motioned her inside.

"Did you hear what happened?" Ada asked as Josy joined them.

"Yes, Roberta told me—the bridal shop went out of business. You don't have a gown."

"They just closed their doors. There was a message on their machine—all shipments have been suspended and they can't fill any orders dated after the first of last month. I'm so screwed," Corinne groaned, and tears shimmered in her eyes.

"Corinne, we'll figure something out," Josy soothed, sitting down beside her.

"That's exactly what I told her." Ada took a seat on the other side of Corinne. "There's that bridal shop in Casper. We'll go there and find you something pretty—"

"It's too late. There won't be time for fittings. I called and they're completely booked for the next three weeks. And their stock is low . . . I'm going to have to get married in my navy blue suit. It's short, it's too tight on me, and I'm going to look like a fat bluebird on my wedding day!"

Corinne gave a sobbing gasp as she struggled for self-control.

"Ada, you know about Roy's family," she said miserably as Josy stared at her, mystified. "They're related to the Barclays. And they're all rich. They own all that oil and natural gas, they have interests all over the world. I know Roy doesn't care about things like that—he loves me—but I don't want to humiliate him by walking down the aisle in a skimpy blue suit that hits above my knees . . . with a b-broken zipper—"

"You're hardly going to do that," Ada interrupted her. "We'll find you something in that bridal shop. And I'll do the fittings myself, if need be. I can still sew rings around just about anyone in this town, even if my eyes aren't what they once were. I'll get it done for you in time and you're going to look as pretty as any bride who ever walked down the aisle."

"I'll help," Josy said instantly. They both stared at her.

"I've been sewing for years," she said quickly. "I almost studied fashion design instead of interior design."

She squeezed Corinne's arm. "Between Ada and me, we're going to have you looking like you belong on the cover of *Bride* magazine."

A flicker of hope shone in Corinne's eyes. "Really? You think?"

"I *know*." Josy stood up, taking charge. "Let's go."

Two hours later they were plundering through the racks of Ceecee's Bridal Shop in Casper.

The selection was thin and the gowns picked over, because, as the salesgirl explained, it was between seasons. Most of the summer stock was gone, except for whatever gowns remained on the racks. The shipment of new fall styles wouldn't arrive until later in June.

Corinne's face had fallen when she'd seen the sparse selection but she turned toward the racks with something like desperation in the set of her mouth. Ada and Josy each picked a different rack and began eyeing the lineup of gowns.

There wasn't much there, Josy had to admit as she shuffled through padded hanger after padded hanger. Most of the leftovers looked like discouraged wallflowers. They were either too frumpy or too sexy, too plain or too glittery, or else too froufrou—nothing that would be right on Corinne. None of them caught her eye until . . .

"What about this?" she said suddenly, sweeping an ivory silk gown off the rack, carrying it over to Corinne. Ada scurried over, pursing her lips as she studied the gown.

"The fabric is beautiful," Corinne said slowly, "but the high neckline . . . I don't know. It looks so prim and old-fashioned. It isn't me."

"No, it isn't, but I'll fix it. We'll make it strapless, and I'll add seed pearls to the bodice and hem, jazz up the train . . ."

"You know how to do all that?" Ada asked incredulously, staring at her.

"Watch and see." Josy grinned. For the first time since she'd fled New York, she felt free. She felt like herself. She wasn't lying, evading, or pretending. And she could do something to really help Corinne, to help her have the wedding day she'd dreamed of.

"If you buy this dress, Corinne, I'll turn it into your dream dress. You're going to look like a movie star."

Corinne's eyes sparkled as she gazed from the dress to Josy.

"I'm buying it," she announced.

Ada shook her head. "I'll help with what I can, but what you're talking about is beyond me," she admitted.

"It would help a lot if you could sew in some of the seed pearls," Josy told her. "I'll make a pattern and show you where they go."

An hour later, after Corinne found simple white satin heels that she arranged to have dyed ivory, they headed over to a small restaurant called the Buffalo Grill for a celebratory dinner.

"You don't understand, Josy. I'm not usually neurotic. I'm a calm person." Corinne leaned back against the tan leather booth. "Aren't I, Ada?"

"Cool as a cucumber," Ada agreed. She cut her hamburger in half and reached for the catsup. "At least you were—until the day Roy proposed. Since then, you've been a basket case most of the time."

"It's partly because I thought Roy would never get over Katy Templeton, even after she married Jackson Brent. But he did . . . and then everything was wonderful because he truly wanted to marry me. But—" She broke off.

"It's okay, honey," Ada told her quietly as Corinne just frowned down at her plate. "I've been telling you, nothing like that is going to happen ever again."

Josy's brows shot up. "Nothing like what?"

"I was engaged once before," Corinne told her in a low tone. "Before I moved to Thunder Creek. He was a great guy and I was so madly in love I could hardly see straight—until he left me at the altar."

"What?" Josy gasped.

Ada jumped in quickly. "He didn't literally leave her at the altar. He called her the day before the wedding and told her he didn't want to get married. He'd met another girl three weeks earlier. He said he'd found himself attracted to her, and it made him realize he wasn't ready to get married."

"He called you the day before?" Josy repeated incredulously. "So tell me, how did you kill him? Slowly, I hope."

Corinne laughed shakily but there was still an echo of pain in her voice. "That was the last time I ever spoke to him."

"And now it's all behind her," Ada said. "But she's scared to death something's going to go wrong with Roy."

"Can you blame me? Look at all the trouble I've had with my wedding gown—maybe it's an omen. Maybe I'n not supposed to marry Roy either—or anyone—"

"Stop it," Josy ordered. "I've seen you and Roy together. If that isn't love in his eyes when he looks at you, I don't know what is. And you love him, Corinne. You guys are great together."

"I know. Roy is the best thing that ever happened to me."

"Then stop driving yourself crazy. And wait until you see the dress. I promise you—Roy's going to think he's died and gone to bridegroom heaven when he sees you."

Ada added something, but Josy didn't hear it. She was distracted by two men passing the window of the Buffalo Grill. They looked familiar . . . but for a moment she couldn't place them, then as one turned his head and glanced casually inside, it came to her with a jolt.

She *had* seen them before—the night she'd danced with Ty at the Tumbleweed. They were the two men in the parking lot, the ones Ty had been watching from his truck.

But even as the realization crossed her mind, another man joined them.

It was Chance Roper.

Chance said something and the one with the stringy hair shook his head. Chance was gazing through the window of the Buffalo Grill and Josy lifted her hand in greeting.

But he must not have seen her, for he didn't acknowledge her wave and in fact seemed to stare right through her before shifting his gaze back to his companions. He said something else, gestured, and then the second man nodded. Quickly, all three of them walked off down the street.

"Who'd you wave to just now?" Ada wanted to know.

"I thought I saw Chance, but maybe I was wrong," Josy murmured doubtfully.

"Chance is working today," Corinne said. "He's usually off work on Fridays. Come on, let's get the check and go home. I'm dying for you to draw me a sketch of how the dress will look—if you don't mind?"

"Mind? I can't wait to get it down on paper." Josy was surprised at how easily the image of the dress had come into her head. With a little cutting, shaping, and sewing, the result would be a sophisticated sexy confection that would perfectly suit Corinne. She suddenly couldn't wait to get started.

All during the ride home, ideas for other dresses began flitting through her mind. Ball gowns, opera gowns, cocktail dresses. The images flowed and she wished she had her sketch pad with her and could draw the ideas as fast as they were popping into her brain. She hadn't felt this way in months . . . maybe she was getting unblocked . . .

"So now you know my crazy history with men and marriage," Corinne was saying, stepping on the accelerator as they hit the highway and the prairie rolled past in a blur of spring wildflowers.

"You're not the only one who's been burned," Josy assured her. She thought of Doug, of his lies, his stories. He'd been clever and she'd been naive. Well, she'd never be quite that trusting again.

"No woman ever really knows what a man is thinking," she added darkly.

"Ain't that the truth." Ada, sitting beside Corinne in the passenger seat up front, gave a sniff. "Every woman past the age of fourteen probably has some story of a man doing them wrong."

"Even you, Ada?" Corinne looked over at the older woman as the sun filtered in through the windshield, edging lower in the rose and blue-tinged sky.

"Oh, honey, I've had my heartaches, if that's what you mean."

Josy went still. She studied Ada's profile from the back-seat, her attention suddenly centered on this woman who had given birth to her own mother.

"What happened?" she asked in a calm tone that betrayed none of the intense curiosity brimming in her.

"Oh, well, you know—what always happens. There was a young man."

She paused. Josy desperately wanted to press her, but decency kept her from asking for an explanation. She felt like she'd be prying—and under false pretenses. It felt wrong to pump Ada for information when she didn't even know that her granddaughter was sitting within three feet of her.

I should tell her the truth first . . . then ask her who my grandfather is . . . why she gave my mother away . . .

But not here, she decided. Not now.

Corinne, though, was oblivious and had no hesitation in urging Ada to talk. "Yes, there's always a young man," she agreed vehemently. "Usually a snake or a heel or one who's too stupid to know his own mind. So which was yours, Ada?"

There was silence for a moment. Then Ada spoke softly. "Mine," she said, "was a wild and handsome boy. He rode broncs in the rodeo, and he roped steers with the best of them, and he did a mean square dance. He also managed to hog-tie my heart."

Ada's tone was light, but beneath it, Josy detected the undercurrent of old pain.

"What was his name?" she asked.

"His name was Cody. Cody Ambrose Shaw." Her voice sounded odd. Tinged with sadness—and with pride. Though she seemed to be staring intently out at the sunset

sky, Josy had the impression she was really seeing something else. *Someone* else.

"Hey, girls, listen to us," Corinne broke in. "Talking
about dead love affairs and all the things that can go
wrong. Is this a sob fest or what?"

She grinned. Her mood had skyrocketed since they'd
found the dress, and she shot Josy a mischievous glance.
"Hmmm, I suppose you have a story or two yourself,
Josy."

"Nothing worth talking about." Josy winced at the
thought of admitting that she'd dated a married man.

"Then for Pete's sake," Ada said briskly, glancing at
Josy in the backseat. "Let's talk about happier things.
Like this wedding dress. How soon can you draw me a
pattern so I can get started? Far be it from me to hold up
the wedding because I haven't finished my part."

"Oh, Ada, you won't hold up the wedding," Corinne
assured her. "Now, my shoes—those are a different story.
If they don't get dyed and shipped to me in time, I'll have
to walk down the aisle barefoot."

"Or in sneakers," Josy suggested.

"Or in bedroom slippers," Ada put in. "We can always
get you a pair of fuzzy pink ones."

"Very funny." But Corinne was laughing and Josy saw
she was far more relaxed than she'd been on the drive to
Casper.

When she returned to the Pine Hills that night after
drawing a pattern for Ada and showing Corinne a sketch
of what the dress would look like when she was done with
it, Josy was tired, but she felt that things in her life were finally coming together. Her muse seemed to be returning,
she felt the old excitement about working on Corinne's
gown, and Ricky had gotten in touch with her at last.

Now all she needed was to try to avoid any further involvement with Ty Barclay. It could only lead to trouble. Big trouble.

Not only was he a lawman—not exactly an ideal lover for a woman who'd fled a murder scene and was hiding an undoubtedly stolen diamond—but he was also, in essence, still a *married* man.

Been there, done that, she thought grimly.

No matter how hungrily he'd kissed her the other night, or how good his touch had made her feel, it didn't mean a thing. Meg Barclay still owned his heart, as much as if she were still alive, and from what Josy had heard from Corinne, it sounded like she always would.

Don't be stupid, she told herself. *Getting any further involved with a man who hasn't gotten over the death of his wife would be pure masochism. The last thing you need is to fall in love with a man like that.*

Love?

Where had that word come from? she wondered, suddenly feeling cold with fear. *Sure, Ty Barclay saved you from falling off your horse, he set you on fire with his kisses, and he gave you pizza when you were hungry. But love?*

Get a grip, she told herself.

She needed to concentrate on what mattered. Like Ricky getting here soon and taking the damned diamond off her hands.

When that happened, her life would really get on the upswing.

She was putting the key in her lock when she heard footsteps pounding up the stairs. Ty Barclay burst through the stairwell door. He'd been running and he looked sweaty and hot and handsomer than any man had a right to in sweatpants and a black T-shirt plastered to his chest.

"I need to talk to you," he said in a curt tone.

"Well, good evening to you too."

He smiled but there was an edge of impatience in his eyes. "No time for the niceties right now." He came toward her and took the key from her hand, turned it in the lock, and pushed open the door. "Let's go inside."

Chapter 14

"WHAT IN THE WORLD IS WRONG?"

Even as Josy asked the question inside her apartment, a horrible thought chilled her blood—maybe he'd found out who she was, what she'd done, and all about Ricky and the diamond.

He was going to place her under arrest.

Cold fear grabbed her, but it turned to astonishment at his next words. "Listen to me, Josy. This is important. I want you to stay away from Chance Roper."

"*What?* Why?"

"I can't tell you that. Just do it, all right?"

Josy reached out and took her key back from him. "What's going on? What's wrong with my seeing Chance?"

His jaw clenched. "I don't want you to get hurt."

"Chance wouldn't hurt me. Why do you think he would?"

"How much do you know about him? Did he ever tell you his background? Why he's here . . . what he did before getting a job at the Crystal Horseshoe?"

"He's told me a little of it. He worked at a ranch in Tucson. He likes to move around, see different parts of the country. And he doesn't like to get tied down to one place. So what? What's it to you?"

"All I can tell you is that you don't know as much about him as you think. And what you do know . . . it's not all true."

She bit her lip, recalling her conversations with Chance—especially during their two casual, friends-only dates.

None of it had seemed off. None of it had seemed like lies or bullshit. She would have sensed that, wouldn't she?

Like I sensed it with Doug? Maybe she wasn't as good at reading people as she thought.

"He isn't married, is he?" she demanded suddenly.

"No. But you need to stay away from him, and that's all I'm going to say."

A ripple of anger ran through her. He had no right to push his way into her apartment just to warn her away from Chance, not without giving her a good reason. He had no right . . . and probably no basis for this stupid warning either. But then she remembered what had happened today in Casper.

Chance appearing outside the Buffalo Grill. And ignoring her.

So odd. He must have seen her wave to him, but he hadn't acknowledged it or come inside to say hello.

He'd stared right through her and then walked away with those two men. The same two men Ty had been watching the other night outside the Tumbleweed Bar and Grill.

A disturbing thought came to her. "He hasn't broken the law or anything? . . . " she began, then immediately bit her lip. "Oh, please don't tell me he's a suspect in the rustling investigation. *Is he?*"

"I didn't say that."

"But you're not denying it." Distressed, she stared at him, thinking of Chance's easygoing manner, his friendly flirtation with every woman under ninety. "He isn't a rustler. Or any kind of criminal." She shook her head. "He . . . can't be."

Ty was quickly reaching the conclusion that he'd only heightened her interest in Roper. He needed to distract her. For her own good, of course.

"You think I'm only trying to eliminate the competition?"

At her startled glance, a smile tugged at the corners of his mouth. "Now, *that* I see you can believe."

"Don't be ridiculous. Chance is just a friend. And you . . ."

"Yes?"

"I haven't quite figured out what you are," she told him tartly. As he continued to smile at her, she shot him a dark look.

"And I'm not sure I want to."

He laughed and reached out for her. His arms snaked around her waist and drew her close.

"I could help you out with that," he offered in a low drawl that sent shivers across her breasts.

Light flirtation, that's what this is, she told herself. *Calm down. You know how to do this.*

But did she want to? With the sheriff of Thunder Creek? A man she'd lied to again and again. A man she'd danced with and kissed—and with whom she'd nearly done a whole lot more.

A man who doesn't have a place for you in his heart, she reminded herself.

But . . . it didn't help that he was impossibly sexy,

especially with his hair mussed from his run. It didn't help that she was remembering the way it had felt to be held in his arms last night, or that right at this moment he was caressing her cheek very gently with his thumb.

Most of all, it didn't help that he was leaning down to kiss her again . . .

Today the kiss was hot, hard, and demanding. She kissed him back, unable to stop herself, and as she did a crazy picture popped into her head . . . an image of herself and Ty Barclay tussling naked on the floor . . .

That's not going to happen, she told herself, even as she abandoned herself to the heady power of his kisses.

He made a rough noise in his throat as her lips parted, welcoming him, and Josy felt everything slip away. All that remained was the heat of his mouth on hers, the musky scent of his skin. He was kissing her as if there were no one else in the world and nothing else that mattered. His hands sliding over her skin made every inch of her body come alive.

What had happened to getting a grip? She was lost in him, in his touch, in his heart beating against hers. She was half-crazed by those deep, devouring kisses until suddenly the phone rang.

It was in her purse and the sound was muffled, but she knew immediately what it was . . . and who it must be.

She jerked back from Ty. The color fled from her cheeks.

"Don't answer that," he said hoarsely, trying to pull her back, but she slipped from his grasp and seized her purse.

"I'll only be a minute," she told him breathlessly.

"Josy. Listen up."

It was Ricky. Her heart pounded as she flashed a shaky smile at Ty. *Oh God. Not now, Ricky. Not now.*

"Yes?" Even to herself her voice sounded high and tense, and it was no surprise that Ricky caught on.

"Is someone there with you?"

"Yes."

"Okay, stay cool, this will only take a second. I'm ditching this phone, getting a new one. I just wanted to tell you, I'll meet you three days from now, Thursday, in Medicine Bow National Forest. You've got a map?"

"Y-yes."

"Okay, 5 P.M. There's a rest stop a half mile north of the ranger's station on Laramie Peak. If I'm not there by five-thirty, get the hell out of there."

"Yes, but . . ."

"Bring the package, Josy. And be careful."

The line went dead. Just like the pleasure she'd been taking in Ty Barclay's kisses.

Ty was watching her, quietly, intently, as she set down the phone. She prayed he wouldn't ask her any questions.

But of course he did.

"Was that Chance?"

"No." The word hung in the air between them. Ty said nothing, just held her gaze with his own, waiting, and she could sense his curiosity—and his skepticism.

One thing was clear—he didn't look like he was in the mood to kiss her anymore.

Which is a good thing, she told herself. *For both of us.*

"Something has got you all shaken up."

"Maybe it's all that kissing we were doing." She tried a teasing tone, but he wasn't buying it.

"Obviously it's that phone call." He shoved a hand through his hair and took a step closer. For once his eyes didn't look shuttered and cool. They looked searching . . . concerned. He came to a halt right before her.

"Look, Josy, if something's wrong, you can tell me. I'd like to help. I've had this feeling all along that there's more to your visit to Thunder Creek than just a working vacation." He spoke quietly. "If you're in some kind of trouble, you can level with me."

"Don't be ridiculous. I'm not in trouble." She tried to laugh but the sound came out shrill and false, even to her own ears. Ricky's voice echoed through her head. *Bring the package. And be careful.*

It was almost over. She was so close. She'd get rid of the package and get some answers. But she couldn't afford to give Ty Barclay any—or to give in to the urge to sink into his arms and be held while she poured out all her guilt and doubt.

She couldn't do that to Ricky—not now. Not when it was almost over.

"I don't see why you'd think anything so silly." She shrugged. "Maybe your suspicious nature is getting the best of you."

"You think so? I happened to be in Bessie's Diner yesterday the same time as Maggie Cartright."

Josy froze. "So?" she asked, striving to sound unconcerned. But it was difficult to appear calm with Ty's razor-blue eyes fixed relentlessly upon her face.

"So she was talking to Katy Templeton, who had stopped in to see Bessie. Maggie asked her if she knew you. For some reason, she thought you and Katy might have known each other when Katy lived in New York."

"Katy . . . lived in New York? I didn't know that." She added quickly, "But I'm from Chicago. I told you that—"

"Yes, you told everyone that. And that's exactly what Katy said. But Maggie told her she must be mistaken. You see, Maggie had seen your driver's license and she distinctly recalled that it said you lived in New York."

Damn it. Couldn't a person get away with any stupid fib in a small town? And weren't there privacy laws involving librarians?

Not that she was in a position to file a lawsuit. But now Katy, Bessie, Roberta, *Ada*—everyone—would think she was a liar. Just as Ty Barclay did.

"She's mistaken." Desperately, she tried to brazen it out.

"Yeah? She seemed pretty sure. You know, Katy owned a restaurant in New York for a while, the Rattlesnake Cafe. Ring a bell?"

Josy's throat went dry. The Rattlesnake Cafe. She knew of it. She'd even dined there a number of times.

"Never heard of it," she said crisply. "Maggie Cartright must be mixed up. And why she was gossiping about me I have no idea . . ."

"She wasn't gossiping. She just seemed to think that maybe you and Katy had become friends, seeing as you had something in common. You'd both lived in New York and had successful careers there. But for your information, if you did live in Chicago, Josy, you'd know about the Rattlesnake Cafe too. That's where Katy opened her first restaurant, the original Rattlesnake Cafe. It put her on the map, led to her going national. You're sure you never heard of it—on Michigan Avenue?"

He's good, Josy realized. *Painfully good.* And she was still the most pathetic liar in the world.

"Is this an inquisition now? I don't know why you're giving me such a hard time and accusing me of . . . what? Lying? And something else? The next thing I know you'll have me arrested for being a rustler," she cried.

But Ty shook his head and took hold of her shoulders.

"I'm asking you to level with me, Josy. That's all. Because I know that's not the only lie you've told."

"What is that supposed to mean?"

"You said you're an interior designer. Corinne says you're decorating some penthouse for a big shot with a condo in the Loop. But these sketches aren't of sofas and end tables, are they?"

The blood rushed into her cheeks. She couldn't move for a minute, couldn't speak, but she knew without glancing down that her latest batch of lame sketches of women's cocktail suits and party frocks were spread across the wooden coffee table, right beneath Ty Barclay's nose. And he was too good a cop not to have noticed.

He sees everything, she realized, and that was a hell of a lot more than she wanted him to see.

"Do you want to level with me?" he asked quietly.

"What I want is for you to leave. *Now.*"

He stared at her. His face no longer reflected sympathy and concern. His eyes had narrowed and they looked flat. And hard.

The eyes of a professional cop.

Fear shot through her. Why had she let herself become involved with him in any way, shape, or form? He was dangerous to her and to Ricky. He could put them both in jail.

She tried to school her face, to keep the fear and the guilt from showing. She threw her shoulders back, stiffened her spine, and tightened her lips.

"I'd like you to leave right now," she repeated, when what she really wanted more than anything else was to throw herself into those strong, capable arms.

It was no longer possible to see the man who had

kissed her with such passion in the hard-eyed stranger who stood before her.

As she held her breath, afraid he'd actually tell her he wanted to take her down to the sheriff's department for questioning, he suddenly dropped his hands from her shoulders, turned away, and strode to the door.

"Whatever it is, I might be able to help—if you'd level with me. In the meantime, remember what I said about Chance."

Then the door slammed behind him and she was alone.

Chapter 15

"OH, MY LORD." TWO DAYS LATER, ADA STARED at the finished gown in wonder.

Corinne didn't say a word. She touched the satin fabric, brushed a finger along the seed pearls swirling across the strapless bodice, raised her gaze in mute awe to Josy's face.

"I can't believe it. This . . . is the same dress?"

"More or less." Josy smiled. The sun shone gloriously through the windows of Ada's house and set the ivory dress shimmering in a halo of pearlescent light. She was pleased with the results of her efforts, pleased with the sophisticated flair of the train, the glamorous strapless cut, and the rich sparkle of the seed pearls. She was even more pleased because in working on Corinne's gown, the lock inside her brain had somehow unlatched, and she'd almost magically envisioned and sketched four ball gowns and one knockout cocktail dress. All sexy and elegant and fresher than anything she'd seen on a runway in the past two years.

And they'd simply flowed onto the sketch pad, like wine pouring sweetly from an uncorked bottle.

"Don't you want to try it on?" she asked a still stunned Corinne.

"Do I ever," the woman breathed.

"Well, what are you waiting for?" Ada prodded. "Don't start crying now, because then I'll start too and I'm too old to cry."

Corinne turned to Josy, still holding the dress. She hugged her and whispered, "I can't thank you enough. You're like . . . my fairy godmother."

Josy laughed. "Try it on, Cinderella, and see how you like it before you thank me. Maybe you'll hate it."

But Corinne didn't hate it. She loved it, loved the way it fit her curves, hugged her breasts, the way it shimmered and moved with her when she walked or turned.

The gown needed only a final adjustment here and there. "I'll finish this up in two seconds tonight and bring it over to Roy's place for you tomorrow," Josy said.

She didn't mention that the next day she'd be disappearing from Thunder Creek, on her way to meeting Ricky. When that meeting was over, when the diamond was safely out of her hands, and Ricky told her it was safe to go home, she would be ready to leave Thunder Creek.

And a good thing too, she told herself. Her money was running low. She needed to get some sketches to Francesca.

And she had a life waiting for her in New York.

She glanced at Ada, her sweet lined face filled with pleasure as Corinne posed and twirled in the gown. Her heart ached suddenly. There was so much about Ada she still didn't know, had never had the chance to ask. And now she never would. She thought of Corinne's wedding, of missing it.

And then Ty Barclay's blue eyes and lean jaw swam into her mind.

She had so much unfinished business here.

But maybe it was best left unfinished. She sighed, not quite willing to explore why that idea made her unhappy.

"After tomorrow," she said as brightly as she could, "you're going to be good to go. Right down the aisle."

"Wait until Roy's family gets a load of this dress." Corinne struck a dramatic fashion pose. "Not that I need to impress them or anything," she added hurriedly, "but I sure won't feel like a freak who's getting married in a short, tight navy suit. I'll feel like a fricking princess!"

After Corinne changed out of the gown and left to meet with Roy and the minister, Ada poured two glasses of lemonade and handed one of them to Josy.

"You're a very talented young woman," she told her. "I can imagine what kind of marvels you do as a decorator. Hmmm, now. I wonder how you'd spruce up my old place if you put your mind to it?"

"This house?" Josy shook her head. She took a moment to answer, taking in all the little knicknacks on the coffee table, the rose-patterned rug, the fresh crisp white curtains. She glanced at the faded needlepoint cushions on the chairs, the stately oak grandfather clock near the staircase in the hall.

"I wouldn't change a thing." A lump rose in her throat. "I don't think I've ever seen a homier, cozier house in my life. It's perfect."

"Hah, you don't know about the leaky roof I just had fixed last year, or the threadbare carpet in the upstairs hall. There's always something to do in an old house." Ada set down her glass of lemonade on a lace coaster.

"What was your home like when you were growing up?" she asked.

"I don't remember much about my home with my parents before they died," Josy said slowly. She searched her memory, trying to see past the foggy brown veil of the past. "I remember my mother played the piano, and my father . . . he would sing. Off-key. It made her laugh. And I begged her to teach me how to play, and she did. When I was around six I learned 'Twinkle Twinkle Little Star' and 'Row Row Row Your Boat'—but then I lost interest. As children do," she added.

"So you had a piano," Ada prompted.

"Yes—and my bedroom had a cabbage rose comforter and matching curtains."

"Oh, that sounds nice. So cheerful and feminine."

A memory returned to Josy, one she hadn't thought about for years. "When I was about to turn twelve, though, I decided I wanted something more grown-up— fit for a teenager. I had my eye on a striped comforter and tons of throw pillows in red and black and purple . . ." She broke off. "But I never got it."

."Why was that?"

"My parents died in a car accident. And I . . ."

"You what, dear?" Ada was watching her, her eyes keen, despite their faded color.

"I . . ." Josy spoke slowly, her gaze still locked on Ada's face. "I was placed in foster care."

There was a silence. Ada nodded, her face oddly still and suddenly looking pale, but in her eyes Josy saw a sheen of sympathy.

"And was it . . . very bad?"

"I got through it."

"You certainly did, child. You're a beautiful, talented young woman. Even in the short time you've been here, folks in Thunder Creek have taken to you, some of us even feel like you've been here all your life. Which," she added softly, "you should have been."

"I . . . what?"

"You should have been here all your life." Ada's voice was low. "Since the time your parents died." She reached out a tiny, blue-veined hand toward Josy, then let it drop into her own lap with a grimace.

"You should have been living in this house with me. I am your grandmother, after all."

Ada's expression was calm as Josy's gaze flew to her face in shock.

Ada nodded. "Yes, child. I know." Her voice was quiet, almost matter-of-fact. "I've known since you first arrived. You're my granddaughter. Isn't that what you came to Thunder Creek to tell me?"

Chapter 16

CHANCE ROPER THREW SOME MORE WOOD ON the campfire and winked at the bright-eyed brunette in the tightest blue jeans he'd ever seen.

"If you think this is a pretty view, wait until the stars pop out in the sky," he told Shannon Monroe, the twenty-nine-year-old advertising executive who, along with two other young women from her San Francisco firm, was dude ranching it for the very first time.

"I can hardly wait." Shannon slanted him a smile as she added a few twigs to the fire. The three other Crystal Horseshoe hands escorting the party of twenty guests up Cougar Mountain were all busy setting up for the barbecue and seeing to the horses, while Cooky unloaded pots and skillets and equipment from the Crystal Horseshoe van, a literal kitchen on wheels.

"Save me a seat by the campfire, will you, darlin'?" Chance said softly, and her gorgeous brown eyes lit up.

"If you promise to roast me a marshmallow."

"Honey, I promise to do a whole lot more than that for you tonight." He winked at her, then laughed. "Be right back, ladies," he called more loudly to Marisa and Julie, Shannon's traveling companions, as he strode over to where the twelve-year-old Adams twins were scrambling up rocks, trying to get a closer look at some mule deer perched on a ledge high above the camp.

"Hold on, guys. Don't climb too high or we'll have to send out a rescue posse." At the sound of Chance's voice, Dale and Seth Adams both turned back, grinning.

"Are there mountain lions up here?"

"Might be."

"Is that why you've got a rifle in your pack?"

"Yep. You never know, we could meet up with a big cat, a grizzly, a snake, anything. Hey, your mom's waving at you. Better hustle over there and see what she wants."

As the twins ran off, Chance strode past the other families, couples, and the clusters of single women who were all busy enjoying the view and munching on the bags of trail mix that Slim was handing out. He passed the grazing horses and slipped down a path winding behind a boulder.

He walked about fifty feet down, out of sight and out of earshot, then punched buttons on his cell phone.

"Are we a go for tonight?" He spoke in a low tone, scanning the trail to make sure he hadn't been followed.

Denny Owens's voice rasped in his ear. "Damn straight. Midnight. You know the place."

"Have you thought about what I said? Asking for a bigger piece of the pie?"

"Me and Fred talked it over. But if we even mention something like that to the boss, he's likely going to shoot us right where we stand."

"Hey, we're the ones out here taking the risks," Chance argued. "He's cleaning up and we're doing all the work. Those quarter horses we're after tonight are some of the sweetest pieces of horseflesh I've even seen. They're worth ten grand easy. Now you tell me why we should even give him a cut—he's not out there with his butt on the line."

"Hold on."

Chance heard Denny repeating what he'd said to Fred Barnes. Then he came back on the line. "The boss is the one who owns the trucks and the horse trailers. He's got the buyers, the connections."

"That doesn't entitle him to a full fifty percent of our haul. Look, if you're afraid to deal with him, set up a meeting for me." Chance tightened his grip on the phone. "I'll talk to him. I'm telling you, we can do a hell of a lot better than this."

"Yeah, well, you don't know the boss. He's not the negotiating type."

"Introduce me. I am. I'll cut us a much sweeter deal," Chance assured him.

"Yeah? Well . . ." Denny sounded almost convinced. "We sure as hell are due for a raise. Listen, let us think about it some more and we'll talk strategy tonight when we meet up."

Denny disconnected. Chance clipped his phone back in his belt.

As he headed back up to the camp, where Sonny had begun to twang out a tune on his guitar, he smiled to himself. The way he figured it, he'd have plenty of time to rustle up some action with Shannon Monroe before he left to rustle Tammie and Wood Morgan's brand-new herd of quarter horses.

Shannon wasn't quite as gorgeous as Josy Warner, but hell, what could he do? Josy had spotted him in Casper with Denny and Fred. That had been a huge mistake, and in his line of work, mistakes could be dangerous.

He'd have to steer clear of Josy for a while—he didn't want her getting mixed up in this. It was true what they said—business and pleasure don't mix. And while Josy was definitely a pleasure, his rustling partners were strictly business.

Never the twain shall meet.

But they nearly had.

He'd have to be more careful. And cool it with Josy.

Besides, she'd told him she wanted to be just friends and so far, she'd stuck to it. Shannon Monroe sent out a whole different vibe.

Chance whistled as he tramped back up the path. Aside from that one near run-in with Josy in Casper, things had been going smooth as silk.

And soon he'd have the big boss right where he wanted him. The thought made him smile.

If there was one thing in life that Chance Roper loved, it was that moment of taking total control.

Chapter 17

"HOW COULD YOU KNOW?" JOSY'S CONFUSION showed on her face. "All this time—how could you possibly have known?"

Ada reached out and placed a small hand on Josy's arm. "The question is . . . were you going to tell me? Were you waiting for the right time? I'm sorry if I spoiled it."

"No, you didn't spoil anything. I didn't know how to tell you . . . or even if I would."

"I guessed as much." Ada sighed. Josy caught a flicker of pain in her eyes.

"I was afraid you'd decide not to say a word and you'd pick up and leave before I had a chance to say anything." Ada looked at her closely. "But you were probably waiting for the right moment."

"I guess I was. Perhaps I just didn't know how to say it." Josy shook her head, still stunned. "But you . . . how did you know? And . . . did you know from the beginning?"

"As soon as I heard your name. Josy Warner." Ada's hand fell away. She spoke quietly. "I'd done some research of my own starting about a year ago. I wanted to find my baby girl and see—oh, I don't know—see how her life turned out, if she was happy." She took a deep breath. "And I found out she was dead."

Josy said nothing. She watched Ada, watched her eyes cloud with sorrow, her hands tremble in her lap. Her own heart suddenly felt heavy as a stone.

"I also found out she left a child behind her. My grandchild. *You.*"

There was a silence. Josy couldn't speak for a moment. She was still digesting the shocking notion that all this time, Ada had known who she was.

"I suppose you have questions." Her grandmother— *her grandmother*—must have read her mind.

"Such as . . . why I gave my baby away. What would possess me to do something like that? A woman giving up her own child. Part of herself."

Ada sounded so heavy-hearted. Almost as if she were angry with herself. After all these years?

"I didn't want to. Lord knows, I wanted that baby . . . your mother, Josy. I wanted her with all my heart. But I knew from the start they would make me give her up. And that's what happened."

Ada's voice was so low Josy had to lean closer to hear her.

"They let me hold her . . . once. Just once. And then they took her away."

She blinked back the sheen of tears and faced Josy suddenly, her eyes filled with determination. "Let me tell you why it happened. And all about your grandfather. Your birth grandfather wasn't my husband, Guy Scott, bless his soul. You probably realized when I was talking in the truck who it was."

Josy moistened her lips. "Cody Shaw."

Ada nodded. "Cody Shaw," she repeated, as if saying

the name gave her a pleasure she wouldn't be denied. Her gaze fixed on Josy's face, studying it intently, her eyes almost hungry. "You have the look of him. I can't pin it down exactly—he was as male as a man could possibly be—and you are so feminine, but still . . . the graceful way you move, the way you hold your head, maybe the slant of your eyes . . . something about you speaks of Cody. Maybe that's why I took to you the moment I met you."

"You knew who I was even then?"

"I told you—yes. Billy helped me do the research on the Internet. He knows all about computers and search engines and such things, like all the young people do nowadays, and he found out all sorts of information. I found out that my baby was dead."

Ada's brown eyes filled with unshed tears. She blinked them back. "I was too late, you see. I'd waited all those years . . . never looked for her, never tried to find her . . . and when I did . . . it was too late. She was gone. She and her husband—"

Ada reached out again and this time closed her hand over Josy's, squeezing tight. "I'm sorry. So sorry you lost them, and that you had no one." Her voice quavered. "No one at all."

Josy swallowed. "I managed."

"Yes, I see that you did. I know that you did. I found out all about you too, with Billy's help. Not only did I learn that I had a granddaughter living in New York City, but that you were now a grown woman. That you worked at a fancy job. And not as an interior designer," she said drily. "You're the assistant to a famous fashion designer. Francesca somebody . . ." She wrinkled her brow.

"I've heard the name somewhere, maybe seen it in the

papers. But I didn't care about her. I wanted to know about you. Josy Warner. My Josy Warner."

Josy sat frozen, unable to speak, unable to move. All this time in Thunder Creek . . . Ada had known. She'd known about Josy even before Josy had begun to search for her.

"I admit to being a bit confused when you said you were an interior designer," Ada went on, her voice carefully neutral. "I guessed either my research was wrong, or you had a good reason for not saying what you really did for a living . . . or that you lived in New York and not Chicago. That puzzled me at first, let me tell you. But I've learned over the years that people usually have good reasons for what they do."

"You're right. I . . . I didn't want to lie, but I felt I had to. It's complicated."

"Most things are." Ada gave her a soft smile. "You don't owe me any explanations, honey. Lord knows, I owe them to you. I suppose you want to know why I did it. Why I gave your mother away."

"It sounds like you were in love with Cody Shaw. But . . . he . . . what? Broke your heart?"

"He did—but not like you might think. Not on purpose."

"But he wouldn't marry you. In those days, I'm sure single mothers weren't accepted as much as they are today."

"Oh, you can sure say that again." Bitterness glistened in Ada's eyes. "You're very right about that . . . but you're wrong about Cody not wanting to marry me. He might have, or might not—I always wondered—"

"He didn't know?" Josy stared at her. "You never told him you were pregnant with his child?"

"No. I never did. Let me tell you the reason though. You

need to understand your grandfather. You should know about him. I'm sure you've wondered."

"I have wondered. About both of you," Josy murmured.

Ada fell silent. Outside the window, a meadowlark sang its heart out, even as Josy realized that her grandmother was searching hers—and her memory.

"Cody Shaw," Ada said at last, a smile touching her faded eyes, "was the handsomest boy I ever did meet. And I met a lot of them. I wasn't always old and wrinkled and white-haired, you know. I was a pretty thing if I do say so myself and I loved to have fun. I liked to go to dances and rodeos and on picnics—and to meet my young man of the moment up at Shadow Point. That's where we always used to go to . . . what do young folks call it today? Make out?"

"Hook up," Josy corrected with a small smile.

"Oh, yes, hook up. I've heard Billy say that. Well, my generation probably invented hooking up at Shadow Point. And Cody and I, we did more than our share. It was the happiest time of my life—until, as you say, he broke my heart. You see, he didn't know I was in love with him . . . or that I was carrying his child."

She shook her head sadly. "He hadn't a clue that I was certain he'd want to marry me. He thought I was just having fun, like he was. All fun, that's what Cody was about. Fun, excitement, passion. He was passionate about life, about whatever he was doing at that moment. And about not getting tied down. Cody wanted to see the world. And I loved him so much, I didn't want to stand in his way."

"So you didn't tell him?"

"Not at first. I thought he'd come back and there'd be time."

"But he left you."

Ada's tone grew quieter. "He meant to come back. His home was in Thunder Creek and he thought he'd be returning once his tour was over. He rode on the rodeo circuit—and he died there too. In Butte, riding some wild bronc. He got thrown and broke his neck when he fell. His family brought him home and we all attended his funeral. Lots of girls were there. All of them weeping. Except me. I couldn't seem to cry. Maybe the tears were just stuck in my heart," Ada whispered, sounding as if she were speaking to herself.

She loved him more than she can even say, Josy realized. The glitter of tears in Ada's eyes brought a lump to her throat. She was young, pregnant . . . and the man she loved was dead.

"What did you do?" she asked gently.

"What could I do? I went to my mama and I told her the truth. She cried, but I didn't. I wanted Cody's baby. My folks, though," she went on with a grim set to her mouth, "they wouldn't hear of it. They loved me, true, and they didn't hold it against me, which was rare in those days. They stood by me, and when I started getting bigger with my child, big enough for folks to realize, they sent me away, supposedly to stay with cousins for a spell, but I was really at the Standish Home for Unwed Mothers in Denver . . ."

Ada looked out the window a moment, her gaze clouded, then turned back to Josy. "It was a decent enough place and they were kind to me there," she said with a shrug. "The only thing my parents insisted on—for my own good, they said—was that I give the baby up, give her away to a good home with two parents. They said I'd ruin my chances for a decent marriage if I didn't, that no respectable man would want an unmarried woman who was raising another man's baby. And in those days, in a small town like this, I guess maybe they were right. It didn't feel right to me, though. Never did."

Josy nodded, her throat dry.

"When I saw your mother—Cody Jean, that's what I named her in my head, you see—I wanted her more than anything I'd ever wanted in my life. I cried when they put her in my arms, and begged them to let me keep her, but my parents wouldn't give in. They kept insisting . . . and in the end I let her go."

"You signed the adoption papers?"

"Yes." The word held a well of sadness and regret. "Did she . . . have a good life with that family that took her? Was she happy?"

"Very happy." Josy nodded, recalling her mother's tales of Thanksgiving dinners and bedtime stories, how her father had taught her to play checkers and had never let her win, but when she did beat him on her own, he bought her a giant red lollipop.

"She fared better than you did, I'll wager," Ada said slowly. She seemed to shake off the old memories now and her gaze focused on Josy with heightened concern.

"After Cody Jean and your father died in that accident, you were sent to foster care. Foster care," she said again, the words seeming to roll in dismay on her tongue. "I've heard about those places. I can't picture you there."

She looked as if she didn't want to. Josy suddenly didn't want to tell her. "I managed," she said again.

Ada's expression sobered. "So you said. And so I see. But I want to know, Josy. It wasn't a picnic, was it?"

"No. Not much of one." She tried to shrug, but Ada wouldn't let her shrug off the pain.

"I want to hear about your life growing up," she said.

"Whenever you're ready to tell me. I don't need it sugar-coated. You're my blood, honey, and I'm yours. And if I had known what happened, if I had tried to find your mother sooner—I could have taken you in when you needed me, and you might have been spared a life with strangers."

She clutched Josy's hand. "I might have been a stranger to you at first too, but not for long. No, I don't think we would have been strangers for long. But those folks who took you in . . . did they treat you like their own . . . or like a stranger? I have to know."

Josy swallowed. "There was one home where the lady treated me like her own. Mrs. Palmer. But I was only there a few months, and then she took sick. Cancer. So I was moved. I went to two or three others, but the longest time I spent at any of them was at the Hammond house." Her mouth tightened. "I always felt like a stranger there."

"It was bad there, wasn't it?" Ada's eyes had grown rounder with a dawning horror. "Oh, you poor child . . ."

"No, no, it wasn't all bad. I had a friend. A . . . kind of brother—his name was Ricky. He looked after me. Even better, he taught me to look after myself. To stand up for myself."

"God bless him." Ada's hands were trembling now. "I wish I'd known. I wish I'd found you sooner, saved you from growing up with strangers. I wish . . ." She broke off, shook her head ruefully. "A lot of good wishing does at this point." Her mouth twisted, the age lines at the corners deepening. "I wouldn't blame you if you hated me."

"I could never do that."

Without thinking Josy reached out, clasped Ada's hand in her own. A rush of warmth surged through her. She didn't love this woman . . . not yet. She didn't even feel a true bond. But she felt something. Fondness? Sympathy? They'd both lived their lives apart and would always wonder what it would have been like to have spent them together, as grandmother and granddaughter in Thunder Creek.

A lump rose in her throat. "I have pictures in my apartment in New York. A photo album of my parents, including their wedding picture. Oh, and a small one in my wallet," she remembered suddenly.

Ada's eyes brightened. But they looked moist, Josy noticed as she dug in her purse for the wallet-sized laminated photo of her parents on their wedding day.

Ada studied it silently. Finally she spoke. "She was a beautiful woman. Like you."

"Like you." Josy smiled. "We came here once, years ago when I was very young."

"You . . . came here?"

"Yes, my mother and father and I. Somehow she must have learned about you and we all came to Thunder Creek. I believe we drove down Angel Road and saw you one afternoon on your porch. You were watering flower pots, as I recall. You looked up, saw us, and . . . and you set the watering can down."

"Oh, my Lord." Ada went pale. "Your mother . . . actually came here? Right down Angel Road?"

"Yes. I'm sure you don't remember—"

"I do." Ada gave a small moan, her hands pressed to her lips. "I do remember. I saw a strange car one day—it stopped, never came closer. That was odd; Angel Road is secluded, most people don't come down here unless they mean to. So it struck me when the car just stopped like that and didn't come any closer. I had a funny feeling," she whispered. "I didn't know why. But then the car just backed up and went away. I never thought about it any-more, not until just now. But for some reason, it stuck in my mind."

She drew in a deep, shuddery breath. "All those years ago . . . I never dreamed . . ."

"How could you?"

"Oh, my. Oh, Josy. If I'd known . . . don't you see, if your mother and I had reached out, found each other sooner . . . you might never have been sent off to live with strangers—" She broke off, choking on the words.

Josy put her arms around Ada, hugged her gently, as tears rolled down her grandmother's cheeks. "I know. I've thought the same thing so many times since I found out my mother was adopted. But . . . there's no point in won-dering about the ifs," she said quietly. "We can't change the past."

"True, but . . ." Ada closed her eyes with a great sigh.

Josy leaned back, a tightness in her own chest. She struggled to find the right words. "It seems to me that all we really have is *now*. Right now. You and I—we've found each other, haven't we?"

"That we have. What a wise young woman you are." Ada spoke approvingly as she wiped the final tears from her eyes.

"I've wondered so many times since I learned the truth—about you, and about my grandfather." Josy looked at her with hopeful eyes. "Do you still have any pictures of Cody Shaw?"

"Do I?" A slow, wide smile swept Ada's face. "I slept with his picture under my pillow every night while I was carrying Cody Jean—your mama. It was only when I knew I was marrying Guy that I finally boxed up all the pictures I had of Cody—pictures of him at rodeos, riding broncs, roping calves, lounging on my front porch. The box is in the attic, wrapped in pink ribbon inside an old chest." She pushed herself up off the sofa. "Would you like to see it?" Ada asked tremulously.

"Very much." Josy rose and followed her as the older woman led the way to the upper floor of the house on Angel Road.

Dolph was watching two hours later from the shelter of the trees as the blue Blazer rolled up Angel Road and out onto Lone Wolf Road. He melted back into the thickness of the trees until he reached his Explorer.

In less than a minute he had the Blazer in his sights. He kept a good distance behind it on the lonely road. No need to get too close and risk warning his quarry. He was pretty sure where she was headed. And he'd already scoped out her Pine Hills apartment.

The package wasn't there. He'd searched thoroughly, and in a way that left no trace to warn the woman he was tracking. But tonight, once Josy was back in that apartment, he'd have her cornered exactly where he wanted her.

Alone. In her bed. In the dark.

With no warning and no means of escape.

Dolph smiled, confident that in a short time he'd be able to report to Tate that his job was done. He wouldn't need to spend more than five minutes with Josy Warner in apartment 2D before she was begging him to let her tell him everything he wanted to know.

Chapter 18

JOSY PACED THE DARKENED LIVING ROOM OF HER apartment.

She was too restless, too wound up to sleep. She'd already made the final adjustments to Corinne's gown and had hung it carefully in the bedroom closet. But now her plan for meeting Ricky tomorrow filled her mind—along with the image of a twenty-year-old Cody Shaw, his dreamy good looks and cockiness captured forever in photographs.

All those photos Ada had shown her. They painted him clearly—a lean, tall, sinewy cowboy, all of twenty years old. Josy had marveled at how closely he resembled a ten-gallon-hat version of James Dean—except for his warm, dancing eyes. Even in the photographs they shone, not with sullen toughness, but with life, with humor, and with the passion Ada had described.

And they held kindness as well. Josy saw it and felt it as she stared at the young man leaning both arms against a rail fence, his cowboy hat perched on his head.

So now she knew who her grandfather was. And she had finally come clean with her grandmother—at least, about most things.

For someone who's terrible at lying, I've had to do an awful lot of it lately. But it's nearly over.

Tomorrow she'd dig up the package and take it to Ricky. Then . . . what?

There were answers she wanted from him. She needed to know what he planned to do with the diamond. And exactly what she'd been wading knee deep in. Maybe then she could finally leave it to him and climb out of the bog.

She couldn't even pin down yet exactly what she'd do next. Return to New York? Explain herself to the police? Or would Ricky have a way to keep her out of it?

No matter what, she realized as she paced, she had to go straight back. Jane and Reese must be worried sick about her, and Francesca needed the sketches and she needed them now.

Well, at least her muse had somehow danced back into her life and she was certain Francesca would flip over the ideas that had flowed onto her sketch pad after she'd redesigned Corinne's gown.

So, she'd go back. To work and to her ransacked apartment and her friends. She'd miss Corinne's wedding. That gave her a pang.

But I'll send a gift from Bloomingdale's, she told herself. *And maybe Ada will come to the city to visit sometime soon.*

For some reason, her heart sank in her chest. *It's only natural,* she reasoned, *to have conflicted feelings about leaving Ada when we've only just discovered each other, just when the fragile process of building a relationship has begun.*

Or maybe, she thought, pausing before the balcony doors, staring out into the night, *I'm not quite ready to leave Thunder Creek yet.*

That idea surprised her.

Josy lit a candle in the small glass votive holder she'd bought for the coffee table. She sank down on the sofa and pondered the flame. Its tiny brightness seemed to speak to her more powerfully than all the billboards and neon lights in Times Square.

But she wasn't sure what it was saying.

Actually, at this moment she wasn't sure about anything.

The balcony doors were open and she heard a sound from below. It sounded like the soft thud of a car door closing.

Instantly she thought of Ty.

It was late, after midnight, and she'd been aware all evening that his car wasn't parked in the lot. He could be anywhere, she knew—working late on police business, playing pool at the Tumbleweed, out on a date . . .

It doesn't matter to me, she told herself. She might never see him again . . . kiss him again . . . but it didn't matter. She didn't mean anything to him. That was especially true now that he knew how she'd lied to him, lied again and again.

Besides, she reflected, tensing her shoulders, facing the pain that squeezed around her heart, there was no chance of a future, any kind of future with Ty anyway. He'd never love her or any woman the way he'd loved Meg.

Haven't you had enough hand-me-downs? she thought angrily. *You don't want someone else's man—even if he wanted you. Which he doesn't.*

When she did fall in love—*if* she did fall in love— she'd always dreamed it would be everything. *Mean* everything. She wanted the kind of deep, giving love Ty had known with his wife. The kind Ada had felt for Cody Shaw.

She'd never have that with Ty Barclay. It was stupid to even think about it. About *him*.

Yet she moved to the balcony doors in the darkness and peered out to see if he was home.

The spot where he usually parked was empty. But there was another car, a dark SUV, parked across the lot, half hidden in the shadow of the flanking trees. And in the moonlight she made out the shadowy figure of a man moving swiftly toward the entrance of her building.

He paused and suddenly glanced up—straight at her balcony. She could feel him staring at her. In the darkness, she sensed surprise, but he kept moving, his head down now, his steps quicker.

She realized suddenly that with the candle burning behind her, he must have seen her—dimly, at best—just as she'd been able to see him.

A shiver ran through her, something deep and instinctive.

She was being silly. She was fully dressed, after all, in a white tank top and gray drawstring pants. Perfectly presentable. And yet . . .

She heard a footfall in the hall. He was on her floor.

Why? She'd never seen him before. He didn't live here, as far as she knew. And who would he be visiting after midnight . . .

She knew then. She didn't know how, perhaps some basic primeval instinct of self-preservation, but she knew as surely as if he'd hissed her name in the dark that he was coming for her.

The doorknob turned with a tiny click and she struggled to hold back the scream streaking through her throat.

Chapter 19

JOSY RAN TO THE SMALL ROUND DINING TABLE. Adrenaline flew through her as she shoved it over to the door, ramming it up against the doorknob even as the damned thing clicked again and she saw it turn. Her heart hammering, she spun around and glanced wildly about. She had to get out of here. And now there was only one way to do that.

She paused only long enough to blow out the candle, leaving darkness behind her, then she grabbed her purse from the sofa, slung it over her head and across her shoulder, and sprinted onto the balcony.

Her blood pounded in her ears as she climbed over the iron rail. She grabbed a toehold on the outside portion of the balcony, clutching the railing for dear life.

He was shoving against the door now—she heard a thump, and the creak of the table being shoved inward. No time to lose. Josy spared a swift glance downward—a row of shrubs was lined up almost directly below her but it was still a twenty-foot drop.

She twisted quickly around, took a deep breath, then let go of the railing and jumped.

Terror surged through her as she fell, then pain exploded as she hit the shrubbery and smashed through it.

But it cushioned her fall and after that first quick, brutal impact she rolled and tumbled free of the shrubs with only a grunt and a moan. She tried to stifle any noise, praying he'd search the apartment before he realized she'd jumped, hoping to buy as many extra seconds as she could before whoever was up there came out here to search for her.

She stumbled to her feet and dashed toward her car, digging in her purse for her key. But even as she found it and rammed it into the lock, she heard running footsteps behind her.

Terror filled her as she glanced up. He was plowing toward her like a linebacker. He was a huge man, with a shaved head, long legs, and a thick neck, and he wore all black . . .

Open the damned door!

She threw it wide, lunged inside the Blazer, and was trying to slam the door when he grabbed it, flung it back, and seized her with an iron grip. One hand clamped over her mouth, crushing her lips against her teeth as his other arm wound around her body, dragging her out of the Blazer.

"Nice try." A harsh voice cold as Alpine snow hissed into her ear. "But you're not playing in the kiddie leagues now."

Josy bit down hard on his fingers and tried to scream, but he refastened his grip after flinching no more than a millisecond—and this time the power of his grip across her mouth was even more agonizing. She thought every one of her facial bones was going to crack.

"I see you like to do things the hard way. Personally, I prefer to do them the easy way."

The next thing she knew, he slammed her head against the Blazer's door and pain roared through her.

Red stars danced in her eyes, agony sang in her skull, and then the world spun around. The pain and everything else instantly receded into deep liquid blackness that swallowed her up like the grasping waves of an endless midnight sea.

She awoke cold, wet, and shivering, greeted by a burst of white-hot pain. Dazed, Josy kept her eyes closed tight, clinging to the blackness, trying to slide back in. But the pain and the cold were insistent and she moaned, feeling sick and weak. Slowly, unwillingly, she opened her eyes.

Please let it be Ty, she thought. *He came home, saved me, he's reviving me . . .*

But it wasn't Ty who stood over her as she forced her eyes open. It was the huge ox of a man, with a satisfied smirk on his face, a man even more powerfully built than Ty Barclay. He held an empty plastic bottle of spring water in his fist as he towered over her.

"It's about time. I don't have all night. The sooner you give me what I want, the sooner you and I will conclude our business."

"I . . . don't know what you're talking about."

He threw the empty bottle of water down, narrowly missing her head. Before she could even gasp, he reached down and hauled her up by the neck. Pain swept over her in a great crashing wave and she felt as if her head were about to split open.

"You have something that belongs to my employer. He

wants it back." His breath smelled of mints and lemons all at once. Josy knew she'd never eat another Altoid again. His hands cut into her flesh, brutal as iron prongs.

"Tell me where it is and I'll let you go."

"I don't understand," she muttered through the pain splitting her skull. Dizzily she tried to glance sideways, to see where she was. It was pitch-dark, save for the frosted illumination of the moon, and all she could see was that they were in the middle of nowhere—she made out a hill, a weedy track where a dark SUV sat, a hulking shape in the shadows.

There were some shrubs around, looming trees, and the incessant song of crickets.

She could be ten miles outside of Thunder Creek—or a hundred.

How long had she been unconscious?

"Look, I don't know who you are, but—"

"Dolph," he said, showing his teeth in an eerie mirthless smile. "Call me Dolph. And you're Josephine Warner."

"You . . . you have the wrong person, Dolph. It's a mistake—I don't know what you're looking for, or—"

"I'm looking for the diamond. You know which one. The big fucking diamond. There's only one like it in the world. And if you don't tell me where it is by the time I count to ten, I'm going to have to take something that belongs to you."

In horror, she stared into his night-black eyes and saw the icy pleasure shining in their depths. An instant later she felt the knife pressed against her ear, its tip sharp and cold as he traced along the delicate shell.

"You won't look so pretty without this ear," he chuckled.

Josy's knees buckled, but he held her up, his smile widening.

"Talk, Josephine. *Now.*"

Ricky, I didn't sign on for this. How the hell did you get mixed up with someone like this—and whoever his damned employer is?

She had another vision of Archie, dead on the floor, the life bleeding out of him.

"Are you . . . the one who . . . killed Archie?" she heard herself ask in a voice that sounded raw and weak. He smirked at her.

"That was Hammer. He made a big mistake. He should have kept Archie alive, made him tell us everything we needed to know. This could all have been ended that night. But Hammer got stupid and screwed up." His voice rasped in the darkness.

"I don't screw up though, Josephine. I'm going to keep you alive and conscious and talking until you tell me exactly what you've done with that rock."

He pressed the blade harder against the lobe of her ear and she felt the prick of a cut. Warm blood trickled onto her bare arm. The man with the black eyes licked his lips.

"One," he said softly. "Two. Three . . ."

She was going to faint, which would be for the best. She didn't want to feel him cut her ear off . . . she needed to faint . . .

"Nine . . ." he was saying, and Josy still hadn't fainted.

"Okay," she gasped. "I'll take you to it. But get that damned knife away from me . . . now. Right now."

He laughed. She didn't like knives. None of them did. It made it all the more fun. He let her go for the time being, slid the knife into a sheath attached to his belt, under his light windbreaker. "Sure, blondie. You just take me to the diamond."

"I . . . need to know where we are. I hid it . . . in the foothills. I can't find my way there, unless I get my bearings."

"We're a mile west of your apartment. Six miles west of town. Nothing, nobody around but some hungry wild animals. And you and me."

Josy took a deep breath, trying to think past the pain in her head, past the fear and the shock of being at this man's mercy.

He kept watching her face, reading her. He wasn't stupid. Or gullible. This realization frightened her almost as much as the knife.

"It's after one in the morning. You're not going to find any help. So be smart and take me to the rock. It's the only way you're going to get out of this alive." His mouth stretched into a long, thin, creepy smile. "And in one piece."

Right—like you're going to let me go, she thought on a wave of desperation.

He wouldn't kill her until he had the diamond, so she could risk one more try . . .

But if it didn't work, it would cost her.

She swallowed.

"I buried it in a clearing . . . it's the other direction. Not far," she added quickly as his mouth drew back in a grimace of disbelief. "I'll show you."

"Oh, yes, you will. So quit talking about it and do it," he growled, and dragged her toward the car.

Her head was throbbing as he shoved her inside, but she tried desperately to think. If they passed another car, she could scream, open the door, jump out . . .

But they passed no one on the dark gravel road as he turned the car and headed east, one hand on the steering wheel, the other clamped around her arm. He was trying to keep her intimidated, she realized, and constantly aware of the fact that she was his prisoner, that she couldn't escape.

But she had to. And she would, Josy told herself, trying to ignore the bite of his fingers into her flesh, trying to form the sketchy outline of a plan.

"Where are we going?" he demanded as they passed within a few hundred yards of the darkened Pine Hills apartment building.

"Sh-shadow Point. It's very picturesque. You'll like it."

He looked like he was going to whip out the knife again, so she hurried on, "Take Old Wolf Road. It's coming up. I'll direct you as we go."

She prayed she could find Shadow Point in the dark— it was one mile south of where she'd really hidden the package. But she wouldn't take him *there*—not yet, not until she had no other choice.

There was a chance, a small chance, though, that someone might be at Shadow Point. It was a makeout spot, wasn't it? Thunder Creek's version of Lover's Lane? Maybe some couple would be there, or on the way back from there. If she could only come in contact with someone, she might be able to get some help or get away . . .

"Thought you were smart, hiding it, didn't you? If I'd found it in your apartment while you were gone, I might have just kept on going—taking it with me, of course. You made things worse for yourself. But your first mistake was getting mixed up with Sabatini."

"I can see that now."

"You know where he is?"

"No. I haven't heard a word from him since he left me holding the diamond. He only told me I'd better disappear—and not to go to the police." She stared straight ahead at the rough road the SUV was jolting over. "Believe me, I'd love to get my hands on him. I never bargained for this trouble."

"Don't worry. He won't be missing for long. The man I work for specializes in payback. We'll find Sabatini."

"Like you found me? How . . . how *did* you find me?"

He sneered at her. "How do you think? We traced your flight—once we knew you'd landed in Salt Lake City, it was all legwork. It took longer than it should have," he said darkly. "But it paid off, like it always does. One thing in our favor—men always notice a beautiful woman."

Her skin prickled as Dolph threw her a long look. His eyes gleamed in the lights from the dashboard and she turned away, shivering.

"You know that little flea-bitten motel you stayed at in Rock Springs?" He smiled in the darkness. "When you paid your bill, you set your map on the checkout counter. The big dumb clerk happened to look at it and noticed a red circle around Thunder Creek. I forked over a hundred-dollar bill and he told me everything I needed to know."

She closed her eyes. The clerk in Rock Springs. Why hadn't she kept the map in the car?

Because she'd brought it to her room, studied it before she went to sleep in that rock-hard double bed.

I wasn't cut out for cops and robbers, she thought bleakly. She opened her eyes, took a breath.

"Tell me about Ricky. What did he do to the man you work for—aside from stealing the diamond, that is?"

"That alone was quite enough." Dolph let go of her arm at last and held the steering wheel with both hands as the road grew more rocky and rough. She rubbed her raw skin, wincing.

"But before that he made a series of mistakes. He came to work for a business associate of my employer. And he got too close, too deep. He found out some things he shouldn't have. And then he turned out to be a cop."

He spat the last word out like it was filth. "Not very smart of Detective Sabatini. And he only made things worse when he stole the diamond. My employer takes that sort of thing very personally."

Why would Ricky have stolen the diamond? He was never a thief. Growing up, he bent the rules, but he didn't break them. He'd become a cop to do right—he wasn't on the take. Josy would bet her life on that.

Then she remembered she already had.

Her hands felt clammy. She was cold and sticky with fear. But she had to fight it, fight the fear as Ricky had taught her.

There had to be a way out.

It occurred to her she couldn't trust anything this man was saying . . . about Ricky, or anything else. But since she figured he was planning to kill her anyway, why would he lie?

Josy had no illusions about her captor. He was telling her too much, talking too freely. He didn't intend to let her live.

And she didn't intend to die. Her chest was so tight it hurt, along with her head, and the spot where he'd cut her ear. Blood still dripped, seeping onto the strap of her tank top.

If she didn't want to lose a lot more, she had to make her next move count.

"All right, where now? Don't fuck with me or you'll be sorry."

"It's up . . . that way to the right. There's a trail there . . . turn here," she instructed, her heart hammering as he followed her directions, steering the SUV onto the narrow winding track. She was pretty sure this would lead to Shadow Point—but she and Ty had only come so far, and they'd followed the trail, not the road. But the spot where she'd hidden the diamond wasn't more than a mile south of here, so it had to be right around here . . . a broad spot, overlooking the woods . . .

The night was lonelier than ever as they climbed the hilly road and it seemed the stars were brighter now, glowing like pearls in the sky. Josy prayed for the sight of other cars, but she couldn't see anything besides the looming trees, the desolate rocks, and brush.

Her heart sank. The hour was too late. If any couples had sought the romantic privacy of Shadow Point tonight, they must be gone by now. She cast frantically in her mind, and another plan of sorts came to her.

She pretty much knew her way from here, if she could only get away from him, make it down the trail to the meadow where she and Ty had ridden, and somehow get back to Angel Road.

She didn't want to bring this man anywhere near Ada's house. But if she lost him . . . or hurt him . . .

Fear jarred her senses alert as they crested the hill and pulled onto the clearing. No one was here. Shadow Point was deserted.

Her pulse racing, she scanned the thick darkness, looking for embers from a leftover campfire, sticks, branches, or rocks she might be able to use against him.

"Here?" He braked and stared at her through the nearly opaque darkness. Those black eyes slid over her almost as sharply as the blade of the knife had flicked across her ear.

"Yes. Here . . . over there." She pointed past a lone aspen.

He opened the car door.

"All right, blondie. Showtime."

Chapter 20

TY CROUCHED IN THE DARKNESS BEHIND A clump of brush. With his gun drawn, he listened to Chance Roper, Denny Owens, and Fred Barnes arguing less than twenty feet away from his hiding place.

"I'm telling you, Barclay's not stupid, whatever you think," Chance was saying. "He's got deputies and ranchers like Big John Templeton and Wood Morgan and the like patrolling their back country—and one of these times they're going to see something and then bam, you're dead."

He pointed a finger at Fred as if it were a gun, but Barnes's tough, pockmarked face looked merely contemptuous as he shrugged.

"Maybe you're the one who'll be dead," he suggested.

Denny, his voice as calm and nondescript as his square, even features, spoke in a steady tone. "That's why we moved on to the smaller guys, Roper. We'll hit them for a while before switching back to any of the big shots. They can't afford to keep up those copter patrols for long."

"Yeah, well, I still think it's time to move on," Chance growled. "I get nervous hitting the same area too long."

"Yeah, well, tell that to the boss," Barnes sneered.

"Damn straight I will. Soon as I meet him." Impatience crept into Chance's voice. "I thought it was going to be tonight."

"You thought wrong." Barnes's lip curled. "BJ don't want to meet you—not yet."

"Why not? I got ideas—ways we could make this whole operation better for everyone."

"Actually, Roper, BJ's kinda pissed at you." Denny yanked a Camel from his shirt pocket and lit up. "You've been pushing too hard. Making waves."

Barnes's tone was a low growl. "And BJ doesn't take kindly to anyone thinking he's smarter than the boss."

"To hell with you. What'd you tell him?" Chance's voice had sharpened.

Behind the bushes, Ty strained to see the three men, willing his eyes to pierce the darkness. This smelled wrong. Something was going down. His muscles bunched and tensed in the darkness, his finger curling around the trigger of his gun.

"Told him everything." Fred Barnes was jeering now. "He was mostly interested in how you want to quit and go into competition if he doesn't meet your terms."

"You asshole." Anger had crept into Chance's voice. "I thought you agreed with me that we weren't getting a big enough cut."

"Yeah, that's what you thought all right."

The tip of Denny's cigarette glowed orange in the night. "But BJ thought you were starting to sound like a troublemaker. We got no room for troublemakers in this outfit. Things have been going along just fine. You're hired help, Roper, like us, no more, no less. Guess you kinda forgot that."

"BJ's taking advantage of both of you, big-time,"

Chance shot back. "He's playing you for suckers. And here I thought you were smart, I thought you'd want to look after yourselves."

Crouching in the dark, Ty had to hand it to him. Chance sounded pretty damned cool for a man who'd just been betrayed by two of his partners. Instead of turning on their boss, Owens and Barnes had ratted Chance out. But he was still plugging away.

Chance Roper was no lightweight. He knew what he wanted, and he didn't sweat easy.

Ty ignored his cramped muscles, focused on the three men beyond the bushes, and waited.

Things were about to get interesting.

Goose bumps prickled along Josy's arms as Dolph tugged her out of the car and toward the tree.

It was much colder up here, closer to the mountains, and the wind bit right through her drawstring pants and tank top. Her teeth were chattering as she stumbled along with Dolph over the rough earth.

"Where'd you bury it?" he demanded, giving her arm a shake, and Josy met his gaze squarely.

"By that big rock. Beside the tree stump." She yanked her arm free, and pointed. "There."

He shoved her toward the rock, then pulled a narrow-beam flashlight from his windbreaker pocket, pointing it at the dirt.

"Start digging."

"You're not going to help me?"

"You buried it, you find it. And I'll take it."

Josy squatted on the ground beside the rock. She

glanced quickly out over the valley below. Darkness, silence.

Except . . .

She thought she heard something. Voices. But they were faint, so faint she could almost be imagining them. They seemed to be coming from someplace below in the wooded valley—but she couldn't tell from where, and the wind kept snatching them away. There were no lights. Just the tops of the trees, the flanks of the hillside, the incessant song of the crickets . . .

And every so often, the low, indistinct sound of voices. Men's voices.

Dolph heard them too. "What the hell?" he muttered, spinning toward the valley. "Who the hell is down there?"

The warning glance he flicked her way chilled her blood.

"Don't get any ideas. I can cut out your tongue quicker than you can scream," he warned, and on the words, the knife flashed out again. He made a slicing motion in the air with the swiftness of someone comfortable wielding all manner of deadly things.

"Don't try anything stupid," he said in a low tone. "Whoever it is must be a good quarter mile away. Much too far away to help you. So *dig*."

Josy picked up a short stick lying on the ground near the rock and began gouging out the dirt, even though she knew her lie was about to come back and bite her.

The diamond wasn't buried here. She'd hoped there might be someone here at Shadow Point to help her, and she'd gambled that Dolph wouldn't kill her—even now— not until he had his prize.

But as soon as she was forced to admit her lie, there

would be a reckoning. Fear nearly paralyzed her fingers as she clutched the stick. A dreadful reckoning.

Unless . . .

The voices from below had stopped. Now there was silence, but for the crickets and the low moan of the night wind.

But someone had been there—she and Dolph had both heard them.

"How the hell deep did you put it?" She heard the impatience and suspicion edging his voice and tried not to think about the knife.

"Pretty deep. I didn't want anyone stumbling over it accidentally. Or an animal digging it up and—*here*!"

He reacted instinctively, just as she'd hoped. He leaned over her, shining the flashlight, peering down into the hole.

It was now or never and he'd just given her the opening she needed. As he bent forward she scooped up a handful of dirt and flung it in his eyes, then sprang up and stabbed the stick straight into his face with all of her strength.

He fell back with a groan, blinded momentarily by the dirt and the sudden unexpected pain in the center of his forehead.

That moment was all she needed. She dashed past him in a blur, hurtling down the track toward the valley.

"Help!" she screamed into the blackness, praying there was still someone out there to hear. "Help me—someone!"

"You made a big mistake, Roper," Denny said slowly. There was a hint of regret in his tone.

"Meaning?" Chance demanded.

Barnes spat a wad of tobacco through the air. It landed on Chance's boot. "It's this way, Roper. The fact is, the boss doesn't want to meet you, or negotiate with you—and he sure as hell doesn't want to have to worry about you."

"He just wants us to take care of you—before you become a problem." Denny threw down his cigarette, ground out the butt with his heel. "You see, when the boss has a problem, we take it sort of personal."

I'll say, Ty thought, clicking off the safety on his gun. *They're going to waste him.*

He surged up and leveled the gun. But before he could order them to freeze, a woman's scream tore down the hill.

"Help! Help me—someone!"

What the hell? Josy? Adrenaline rushed through Ty's body as the three men in the clearing all swung toward the sound.

"Police! Freeze!" he shouted, through sheer will focusing all his attention on the rustlers, his adrenaline pumping.

Shots exploded, and Chance hit the ground. Ty saw Denny and Fred bolting toward their horse trailer twenty yards back.

"Freeze!" Ty yelled again, but they kept running and he fired in the darkness. There was a yell and a thud as Denny Owens went down.

Chance had his gun out and was trying to stand. Then all hell broke loose as a spotlight blasted from the trees and three sheriff's deputies closed in on Fred Barnes from the other direction.

"Police! Don't move! You're under arrest!"

It's about damn time, Ty thought, but he was no longer paying attention to the takedown—he was sprinting toward the track that led up to Shadow Point, where he could hear the sound of someone crashing down the trail.

"Help!" That frantic scream pierced the air again, more ragged and desperate than before. *It can't be Josy,* Ty thought, but it sure as hell sounded like her. Suddenly her voice cut off in midshriek and fear knifed through him.

He charged up the track at a dead run, his feet slipping on loose stones, his muscles bunched with tension as he listened for more sounds.

At first he heard nothing but the commotion from below and his own hard breathing in the darkness, then the sounds of a scuffle reached him from the trail above.

"Josy!" Ty yelled. "Where are you?"

No answer, but at that moment he rounded a turn and saw them.

A man with a gleaming shaved head was dragging Josy toward the underbrush, his hand clamped across her mouth as she struggled to break free.

Ty dove at him and he went down, Josy falling with them in the tumble. Somehow Ty managed to shift his weight so that neither he nor the stranger fell on her. An instant later, she was scrambling desperately aside as Ty smashed a fist against the thug's head, slamming it against the ground.

But suddenly the man elbowed him in the jaw, then with an adroitness born of brute strength and experience, he twisted more neatly than anyone his size had a right to, and threw Ty off.

He rolled to his feet—Ty grabbed for his ankles and missed. The bald-headed man plunged back up the track like a fleeting nightmare, melting into the darkness before Ty's eyes.

Ty bolted after him, but twenty yards up, the trail

branched off in two different directions, and the man had vanished down one of them.

Ty stared through the darkness in both directions, but didn't see anyone, didn't hear anything.

He paused, panting, all of his senses on edge. Josy was still down there—alone. What if the bastard doubled back?

Wheeling, he ran back down the trail, skidding down rocks and past brush. He found her exactly where he'd left her—alone, sprawled on the ground, gasping for air.

She looked like hell and she was shaking. There was blood on her ear, on her shirt and arm, and she looked to be freezing. Cursing, Ty stripped off his jacket and slid it around her as he knelt down on the grass and took her in his arms.

"You're okay. You're safe now," he said, his own breath coming fast. He resisted the urge to hurl questions at her, though God knew he had a million of them. But not yet. She looked to be in shock. Fear shone from her eyes.

She threw her arms around him and clung to his neck.

"He—He . . . he broke . . . in . . . my apartment . . . I tried . . . to run . . ."

"It's okay, Josy. You did good. You escaped . . . and you found me. By some miracle," he added, stroking her hair as her entire body trembled against his. "He hurt you. Damn it, you're bleeding. We need to get you to a hospital."

"*No* . . . no hospital. Just hold me, another minute. One more minute."

"I'm not going anywhere. I've got you, Josy."

He couldn't believe how calm he sounded as he held her close and moonlight spilled down on the jagged trail.

He was trained to be calm, to react professionally to violent situations, but this all felt different. Gut-wrenchingly, staggeringly different.

The sight of Josy shivering and frightened and bleeding swamped him with emotions he hadn't felt in . . . a long time.

Since he'd shown up at the precinct that day . . . since he'd seen Meg one final time after that lunatic got through spraying bullets into her . . .

He fought to keep his feelings under control. "Tell me what happened," he said quietly, though all hell was breaking loose inside him. How the hell had Josy ended up battered and bleeding on Shadow Point? What garbage was she mixed up in?

What happend? Ty, don't ask me that. Please don't ask me that, Josy thought, feeling tears sliding down her cheeks. She didn't answer him, merely nestled closer, clinging to his warmth and solid strength. *I need one more moment,* she told herself, wishing she didn't have to let him go at all.

Her head was still throbbing and she ached all over. She heard men's voices down below in the valley, and she didn't understand why those men were here, or why Ty was here. She only knew that by some miracle, she'd escaped that monster Dolph and his damned knife.

And he hadn't found the diamond.

She drew a breath and looked at the sky. It would be dawn soon. She had to get the diamond, get it to Ricky . . . today.

She needed to pull herself together.

"Josy?" Ty shifted her away from him, holding both her arms carefully as if she were a rag doll who would flop over if he didn't keep her up. Which, at the moment, she might very well do, she reflected weakly.

"I need you to tell me what happened," he said more firmly. "I can't help you if I don't know—"

"Sheriff," a curt voice suddenly interrupted and Josy tensed as a uniformed deputy appeared around the curve in the trail. "There's something you need to see down here. Owens has a leg wound and needs to get to a hospital. And Roper's hurt pretty bad. Ambulances are on the way."

"Roper?" Josy stared at the deputy. "Chance Roper?"

"Yes, ma'am." Deputy Frank Tanner nodded politely, but his attention swiftly returned to Ty.

"There's some evidence in their vehicle you might want to take a look at."

"Right. Coming. Stay with Ms. Warner, Frank."

"Sure thing."

Ty looked back at her. "This won't take long. I'll be right back—"

"What's going on, Ty? And what happened to Chance?"

"We busted the rustlers tonight. A couple of them, anyway. With any luck, it will lead us to the rest."

"So . . . it's true," she breathed, dismay rushing through her. "Chance is one of them?"

"No." His gaze was cool and grim now as he studied her distressed face. "Chance is a cop. He was working undercover. This is going to have to wait, Josy; I have to get down there."

"I'm going with you," she said quickly. "I want to see Chance."

His mouth tightened. "Suit yourself. But don't touch anything."

He escorted her down the trail in silence, steadying her

when her foot slipped on a loose stone. She blinked at the scene before her, the spotlight bathing the area in eerie brightness, the police cruisers with their blinking red lights, the men swarming about a man on the ground with a blanket across his shoulders—and Chance, wrapped in a bloodied blanket ten feet away, his eyes closed.

As Ty moved off toward a horse trailer nearby, she rushed toward Chance, her heart thudding. Memories of finding Archie surged through her. *But this isn't the same,* she thought. *Chance isn't going to die.*

But he looked bad.

"You're going to be fine, Chance." She leaned down, whispering in his ear. "Hold on and you'll see. You're going to be just fine."

For once in his life, Chance Roper had no quick and easy comeback, no charming compliment flowing from his lips. His eyes remained closed.

She heard the blare of an ambulance siren and felt a dazed sense of unreality. A moment later Ty returned and took her arm. He steered her away from Chance as the EMTs rushed to get him onto a gurney.

"We need to talk, Josy. Now. I want to put an APB out on that guy who hurt you, so you need to tell me—"

"I can't." She broke free of him and stared miserably into his eyes.

"Can't what? Describe him? Then tell me how he got to you, where this started, what he wanted. What he *did* to you." He gripped her arm, his tone laced with impatience. "Don't you want him caught?"

"Yes. No. I mean . . . not yet. Ty, I can't tell you. Please, no APB, no questions. Just . . . let me go home."

"What's this all about, Josy? You've been hiding something from day one. You're mixed up in something, aren't you? And it's nothing good."

She didn't answer, just gazed back at him, agony in her eyes.

Ty's gut clenched. He'd known all along that some things didn't add up with her, that there was some mystery about her, but he hadn't expected it to be anything serious—and he sure as hell hadn't thought it would be criminal. But a man had hurt her tonight and probably had intended worse. Who the hell was after her?

Frustration ripped through him and he didn't know what he wanted more—to get his hands on the man who had attacked her, or to stroke her face, her hair, and erase the pain from her soul.

"Whatever it is, I'll help you," he said in a taut tone. "If I can. I can't do anything, though, if you don't level with me."

"You can't help me, Ty. I mean it. This is something I have to do myself." She shook her head. "Trust me, you don't want to be involved in this."

"I am involved." He grabbed her arm as she started to back away from him.

He saw her wince, and glanced down, seeing the bruise already forming on her pale skin. Not from his touch— from that animal who'd been trying to drag her into the brush.

He dropped his hand, controlling the rage that leapt through him. "I want to get this guy, Josy. I want to help you. I'm asking you to trust me."

She wanted to. She *did* trust him—with her own life.

But not with Ricky's. Ricky would go to jail. She couldn't tell Ty about what he'd done, or about the diamond.

"It's not that I don't trust you." She swallowed. "But there's someone else involved. I made a promise—"

"Damn it, Josy!" He seized her hand this time and pulled her toward his cruiser. She didn't have the strength or the will to resist. She felt safe just being with him, and she needed to feel safe for a little longer. She wouldn't tell him about Ricky, but she'd let him take her home. Then she could clean up, get to her car—and dig up the diamond before first light.

"Are you taking me home?" she asked wearily as he helped her into the passenger seat.

"No." Ty slammed the door and came around as she stared at him in surprise.

"That's the first place he'll come looking for you again. I'm operating on the assumption that you and that thug had unfinished business. Am I right?"

She nodded wordlessly.

"I'm taking you somewhere you can get some sleep. Somewhere he won't find you."

"Where?" she whispered as he started the engine. She'd never seen his face quite this set, his jaw thrust out so aggressively.

"Blue Moon Mesa—my family's place. The Barclay cabin."

Chapter 21

THE ENTICING AROMA OF FRESH COFFEE GREETED her as she stepped out of Ty's bedroom wrapped in his thick black terry-cloth robe. It was three sizes too big for her and reached nearly to her ankles, but it was cozy and warm and clean, and smelled like Ty—that sage and Dial-soap smell that she associated with him, a scent that pleased her somehow more than Doug's designer cologne ever had.

"I hope you don't mind," she said quietly, when she padded barefoot into the kitchen. "It was hanging on a hook in the bathroom, and I didn't want to climb right back into my dirty clothes."

"Mind?" Ty, who was pouring beaten eggs into a sizzling fry pan on the stove, shook his head. His gaze skimmed over her appreciatively. "It looks a helluva lot better on you than it ever looked on me," he grinned.

Josy shook her head in rebuttal. She felt like a mess, inside and out, but at least she was a clean mess. It had felt heavenly to take a shower, to rinse away the dirt and blood of this night, to soap her hair and scrub the soil from beneath her fingernails. She'd found her comb at the bottom of her purse and pulled it through her towel-dried hair. It was still damp, but would have to dry naturally since she hadn't seen a hair dryer.

She didn't care, though—all she cared about now was the fragrant, steaming coffee Ty had poured into two blue mugs set on the kitchen table, and the scrambled eggs he was scooping in equal measure onto two matching plates.

"Headache better?" he asked as she slipped into a chair and picked up a fork.

"Much. Thank God for Advil. There's only a slight throb now. I can't believe I'm hungry, but this looks delicious."

"I'm always famished after the adrenaline stops." Ty took a seat across from her at the table, and took a gulp of coffee.

"Is that what it is? I feel like I'm running on empty— totally drained—so it must be. I suppose the coffee will take care of that."

"No—it's decaf. We're better off without the caffeine at this point—both of us ought to try to get a few hours' sleep before the sun comes up. Something tells me it's going to be a long day."

Josy didn't say anything. But she knew he was right. It would be a long day. A god-awful day. A day she might not live through—and that Ricky might not live through either.

A spurt of fear closed her throat and she nearly choked on a forkful of eggs.

Ty regarded her with concern while she gulped some coffee and managed to swallow.

"I'm fine," she gasped. "Don't . . . worry."

He set his fork down, frowning.

Don't worry, huh? Just because I found you out in the foothills in the middle of the night, being dragged into the underbrush by some shaven-headed thug? Just because you're nobody to me, some woman who could disappear tomorrow, as if you'd never popped into my life, and I'd never think twice about you again?

Yeah, right. Sorry, babe, it's not like that between you and me.

That fact shocked him, but it was true. When had things changed, when had this curvy delicate blonde with her green cat eyes and careful smile become someone he cared about, thought about all the time? When had she become a woman he was desperate to keep safe?

"I made some calls." He poured her more coffee. "Chance is in surgery—the bullet lodged in his rib cage and he has a collapsed lung, but they think he'll make it just fine."

"Thank God. When I saw him lying there, I thought he was dead. Or on his way." She bit her lip and looked Ty in the eyes. "You said that Chance is a cop? You've known that all along?"

"We've been working together on the rustling investigation. He's actually a sheriff's deputy in Oregon who had only recently transferred there from Denver. We started out comparing notes on the rustling situation in Oregon and here in Wyoming, via e-mail and phone. Then I started putting two and two together. I ran some stuff on the computer and found there was a distinctive pattern to the thefts that have occurred over the past year and a half. Enough of a pattern to make me think this could be the same outfit operating in multiple states. Not a small-scale operation like most spates of rustling, but a big one, well organized, well planned—and well coordinated."

Ty took a sip of coffee. "Wyoming, Oregon, and Montana have all been hard hit over this eighteen-month period of time—and it could be the rustlers are rotating from one area to the next. When things get too hot, they move out for a while and hit another section or another state—confounding and harassing overworked brand inspectors as they go."

"Do you have any idea who's behind it?"

"That's the million-dollar question. And that's why Deputy Roper volunteered to go undercover. He managed to get himself hooked up with two of the rustlers, but so far he hadn't gotten them to give much away about the big boss. All we know are his initials—BJ—if those are even the initials of his real name."

"But now at least you know who some of the rustlers are," she pointed out.

"We'd suspected for a while that Denny Owens and Fred Barnes were involved, but it wasn't until Chance got them to trust him that we had proof. We also have reason to believe that Owens and Barnes are aliases—their identification checks out on the surface, but not everything adds up. Now that they're in custody we can check their prints and fill in some of the blanks."

Josy nodded. "So that's why you were watching them from your car that night—the night we met—because you suspected them."

"It wasn't the night we met." Ty set down his mug, and looked straight at her, his gaze holding hers. "It was the night we danced. We met the night before that, on the stairway at the Pine Hills."

Josy was caught off guard by the intensity of his gaze. She couldn't look away . . . not that she wanted to.

"Yes. You're right. I . . . didn't think you remembered."

"I remember all right. You looked like an exhausted fawn who'd been swimming upstream and was finally nearing the bank . . . ready to climb out. You could barely get your suitcase up the stairs. So I gave you a hand." He drew a breath. "I had a feeling right then that you were running away from something. Hiding from something. But I didn't know it was something dangerous."

Josy fell silent. She simply stared at him, thinking how wonderfully handsome he was and how warmly he was looking at her—and wondering how he would look at her when he found out, very soon, no doubt, about the full extent of her lies.

What would Ty Barclay, hero lawman, sheriff of Thunder Creek, think of her when he heard that she was involved in a diamond theft and protecting the thief?

If indeed Ricky *was* a thief, she told herself. She only had Dolph's word on that. He could have been lying.

But his story made sense, and she had an awful suspicion it was the truth.

Ty would probably have to arrest her if he knew the facts. He'd force her to turn the diamond over to him. And that would get Ricky in even deeper trouble.

Her fingers clenched around her fork. She'd been hoping to keep Ty on the subject of the rustlers for as long as possible, but he'd already shifted it to her. She searched her mind for some way to deflect his focus.

"Tell me something—why did those men shoot Chance?" she asked, biting her lip.

His brows lifted. He knew what she was doing. But for the moment at least, he seemed to be humoring her. "He was pressing them too hard, trying to find out who their boss was," Ty explained in an even tone. "I guess they caught on—or didn't like how he talked about their boss. They're apparently loyal and interested in protecting him for some reason. That's significant in itself."

Ty pushed back his chair, stood up, and carried his plate to the sink. "And now," he said matter-of-factly, "don't you think it's time you told me what you're mixed up in?"

Her heart skipped a beat. "Trust me. It's better if you don't know."

"I disagree."

He strode back to the table but didn't sit down. He regarded her unwaveringly and she could feel the heightened tension radiating through the cabin.

"Let's have it, Josy." Though his tone was quiet, it held an edge of unmistakable determination. "What are you hiding from?"

Slowly, she lifted her gaze to his. It was obvious that she couldn't put him off any longer. And suddenly, for some reason, she didn't really want to.

"It's not what I'm hiding from," she murmured. Her heart turned over at the way he was studying her. Not like a cop, a policeman, but like a man trying to read into the heart and mind of a woman.

"It's *who*," she said softly. "And I don't even know who he is."

"Even now? When he's shown up—tracked you down?"

She nodded. "Even now. You see, he—that man back there, Dolph—works for someone. I don't know who . . . or how many more might be out there—but they're not going to stop until they get what they want. And I can't give it to them, Ty. I won't!"

She pushed back her chair and paced away from the table, into the big open living room of the cabin. It was a soothing place, and in other circumstances it would have felt sublimely homey and comfortable with its tan and beige upholstered sofa and ottoman, the rust-colored curtains at the wide window, the assortment of authentic Western saddles hung upon the wall.

Ty had a fire roaring in the stone fireplace and the blaze sent out reassuring ribbons of warmth, but she couldn't get warm—suddenly she felt cold, cold and frightened. Even here, even with Ty. For all she knew, a gang of armed men who all worked for Dolph's employer could have followed them to this cabin, they could storm in any moment now—

"Ty, I shouldn't be here. You're in danger while you're with me. I have to leave. Please, take me back to the Pine Hills so I can get my car and . . . and do what I have to do. You don't need to be involved in this, and believe me, you don't want to be."

"You're wrong about that, Josy."

Ty closed the distance between them. His hands gently gripped her shoulders. "I am involved. And I want to be right where I am. With you."

She stared at him. "But . . . why?"

His arms swept around her waist. He pulled her close to him, touching her damp hair with his fingertips, gazing down into those anxious green eyes.

"Don't you know why? Hell, Josy," he smiled, "I'm starting to wonder if you're really as smart as I think you are."

"I guess I'm not. You're going to have to spell it out for me," she managed to say despite the huge lump in her throat. He was looking at her with bemusement . . . and with tenderness. Such tenderness. It made her ache in a place deep inside.

No one had ever looked at her that way. Not Doug, not Ricky, not her high school boyfriends. No one.

Ty spoke softly. "Because I care about you." A muscle clenched in his jaw. "And because I'm not about to let some goon—or a whole herd of goons—hurt you. And because I'm a cop—and cops are curious. We find something that doesn't make sense, something we don't understand, and we have to figure it out. I've been trying to figure you out since day one."

She froze. "So . . . it's the mystery that intrigues you. Not me. Just the question marks—"

"No. Hell, no." Ty couldn't believe that such a beautiful, smart woman could be so insecure. "It's not just this, or just that. Life should only be so simple. It's everything, Josy." He hauled her up against him and his voice was rough with emotion.

"Everything about *you*. Yeah, it might have started with the mystery, but pretty quickly it became a lot more." He smoothed a tousled curl back from her brow. "Like the way your head tilts to the side when you smile, and the way your hair smells like wildflowers. Then there's the way your jeans hug your body. When I saw you walking toward me that day we went riding—" His eyes glinted dark as cobalt, haunted by desire.

"Even the way you spoke to the horses, the way you bite your lip when you're concentrating hard. And then there's this . . ."

"This?" she asked, her heart beginning to thud as he traced the outline of her lips with his finger.

"Yeah. *This*." His head dipped lower and his mouth slanted against hers. It was a long kiss, and a searing one. After that first startling impact, it was tender. Bone-meltingly tender.

The heat of it jolted through her. Josy lost herself in the

texture of his mouth on hers, in the hardness of his chest as she pressed against him.

She felt a wave of indefinable loss when he slowly pulled back. "I thought you'd have figured it out before now," Ty said.

He pressed another kiss against the fragile white skin of her throat and felt her shiver.

"I'm not going to let anyone hurt you. But I can't protect you if you don't tell me what this is all about. Trust me, Josy, just trust me."

"I do." She reached up, touched his face, stroked a finger over the sexy dark stubble on his jaw. A tremble went through her. Being this close to him made it hard to think straight. It made her want to tell him everything, to lean on him, and to finally share this burden that she'd been carrying alone these past weeks.

But that was impossible.

"It's not just about me, Ty. There's someone else involved. Someone I owe big-time. And I can't betray him . . . even to you."

Her words stirred something dark and fierce inside him. Jealousy. Who was this jerk she was so loyal to? A lover, a husband? A ball of barbed wire tightened in his chest. Somehow he managed to keep his expression neutral. It cost him, though.

"I said I'd try to help. If he's important to you, I'll do my best to protect him too. But you have to look out for yourself."

"You don't understand." She pushed away from him and stalked to the window, her stomach churning. Then she spun around to face him.

"This man has played a big part in my life. If not for

him, I don't even think I'd have much of a life. I'd have fallen apart a long time ago."

"Are you in love with him?" He forced the words out. They seemed to cut his tongue.

She looked at him like he was crazy, then threw back her head and laughed. "No. Oh, no. Ricky is like . . . a brother to me, a best friend. A guardian angel," she added with a strangled laugh.

"He's been there for me since my parents died, since I was placed in my third foster home. But I could never be *in love* with him."

The relief Ty felt was like a full-grown grizzly leaping off his chest. He walked over to Josy, took her hand in his, and led her to the sofa. Sitting down beside her, he began to very gently rub his thumb across her long, slender fingers.

"Okay, then. Tell me about him."

She hesitated a moment, then nodded. Ty wasn't going to let up until she told him. And part of her knew that with Dolph on her trail, she needed all the assistance she could get.

But she had to make him see why Ricky deserved his help too. Why she couldn't do anything that would hurt Ricky in any way.

And as she talked, and told him about how Ricky had been the one person to help her overcome her muteness when no one else could, even the therapists hired by the state, how Ricky had made her laugh, and looked out for her, how he'd kept her company in the Hammonds' basement the night Karl had banished her to the darkness, she saw the expression on his face tighten, and a flash of understanding in his eyes. He held her hand all through her story, and his fingers closed around hers as she told him about the Callahan brothers.

"They were the neighborhood bullies. Dean was the oldest, he thought he was really hot stuff. James was a year younger and he was the meanest of the three. He . . ." She swallowed hard. "He killed a stray cat one day when he was bored. Set it on fire."

Ty said nothing, just held her hand more tightly, and she was very grateful he was there with her, not interrupting, but letting her explain about Ricky at her own pace.

"The youngest brother was Frank. Little Frankie. He was the runt of the litter and laughed like a hyena at everything his brothers did and said. Frankie would have gone along with murder if Dean or James suggested it."

She closed her eyes a moment, seeing their faces again, reluctantly reliving that hot summer day.

"They used to ride by the Hammond house on their bicycles and stick their tongues out at me when I was in the front yard. I tried to stay out of their way, but one day I was walking home from a friend's house—her parents had invited me over for dinner and Mrs. Hammond had allowed me to go—when I saw them playing catch in the street. It was early September, still warm, but starting to get dark earlier. I didn't want to walk past them, so I ducked down another street, to try to circle around."

She grimaced. "That was my first mistake. Dean saw me cutting through that street, and he knew I was avoiding them, that I was scared." She paused a moment and took a deep breath.

"The next thing I knew they had headed me off one street over. I was trapped—I couldn't go forward, and when I tried to run away, back the way I'd come, they ran after me. Frankie was whooping, like it was a big game and they were winning, but James told him to shut up. That's when I really started getting scared."

She glanced at Ty. His mouth was grim. His eyes burned with anger, but she knew it wasn't directed at her. He let go of her hand and his arm slid around her.

"What happened?"

"They grabbed me. Dean held his hand over my mouth. I could hardly breathe, much less scream. They dragged me to the garbage dump. It was four blocks over and there was this rusted fence, this horrible smell. They shoved me inside, dragged me far away from the street so no one could see. It was getting dark. I was terrified. Then they told me to take off my panties," she said, her voice so low Ty had to strain to hear her.

"I refused, and I . . . I tried to scream, but we were too far away for anyone to hear." Her voice wavered ever so slightly, but she quickly brought it under control. "Dean and James picked me up and threw me into a Dumpster. It stank and there was this garbage all over, up to my hips. Every time I tried to climb out, they pushed me back in."

She looked up at him, her eyes stark with memory. Ty's gut churned. He had the insane wish to be able to go back in time, to step in and spare her from an ordeal no one should ever have to suffer.

But now, all he could do was listen, and try to bear the pain he saw in her eyes, heard in her voice.

"They told me if I took off all my clothes, they'd let me out. I was screaming, but there was no one to hear. Or so I thought."

She shifted her shoulders. "Ricky had seen them dragging me into the dump. He was several blocks away, but he saw what was happening and he came charging in there like . . . like a one-man SWAT team," she finished on a shaky laugh. "He tore into Dean, and hit him so hard he broke his nose. Before James and Frankie could go after him, he grabbed up a tire iron and told them to scram before he beat their brains in. Ricky was a year older than Dean, but he wasn't nearly as big. He was thin and wiry, but he could fight. He . . . he had this way about him . . . this confidence . . ."

She stopped suddenly, casting another quick glance at him. Ty had that same kind of almost arrogant physical confidence too.

It must be a cop thing, she decided.

"He faced down James and Frankie. Dean was bleeding and crying on the ground. When he ordered them to take Dean and get out of there, and never go near me again, they did it. They all ran off and Ricky pulled me out."

Ty nodded. But before he could say anything, Josy hurried on, eager to bolster her case. "After that, Ricky told me that he was going to teach me some things I needed to know. Like how in every situation there's a time to run and a time to fight. He said he'd teach me the difference—and what to do when I had to fight. 'Use what you can,' he always told me. 'Look around, see what's there. Use what you can.' "

Her eyes shone in the firelight as she rested her shoulders back against the sofa. "After that night, the Callahan boys stayed away from me. They never even spoke to me again—or stuck out their tongues. But if it hadn't been for Ricky . . ."

Her voice trailed off.

"Yeah. I get it," Ty said. "Good thing he was there. Those punks deserved even worse." At the contained fury in his tone, Josy inched closer to him and rested her head on his shoulder.

He frowned and held her, trying to rein in his surge of protectiveness. "Okay, I understand. You're loyal to Ricky. Now what's his connection to the guy who came after you last night? What's this really about?"

Lifting her head from his shoulder, she took a long breath. Then she told him.

She told him all about Ricky's suspension from the police force, about the internal investigation, the rumors and accusations—and about his phone call telling her he'd left a package with her doorman. She recounted everything that had followed, including how she'd found Archie dying on the floor in his own blood—and how the man with the dark blond hair had entered the house in Brooklyn, carrying a gun.

And she told him how her apartment had been ransacked and how Ricky, in that last urgent call, had ordered her to run.

Ty's expression had grown steadily grimmer.

"I wanted to stay and call the police—God knows, I wanted to try to help them find whoever had killed Archie," she said in an agonized tone. "But Ricky told me I couldn't trust the police. And I was afraid that if I turned the package over to them and told them everything, it would be even worse for him. I just couldn't do that to him. He needed me, so . . . I had to help him."

"That bastard." Anger tautened Ty's face.

"No, Ty, don't say that. Don't you see—"

"I see that he involved you in one hell of a dangerous situation. He put you in danger, Josy. I don't care what he did for you before, you're a civilian and his friend. He never should have let you get mixed up in whatever mess he made for himself."

"You're wrong. Ricky's being framed, I know it. And he needed my help—I'd do it all again," she exclaimed, pulling back from him.

Ty launched himself off the sofa. He paced around the cozy firelit room, his boots thumping on the hardwood floor. "What was in the package?" he demanded, suddenly wheeling back to face her.

"What will you do if I tell you?"

"Damn it, Josy, this isn't a game." He raked a hand through his hair. "Your old friend Ricky is mixed up in some very dirty business. Now, I don't know if he's clean or dirty himself and right now I don't care. But if I'm going to keep you safe, I need to know who—and what—I'm up against."

"I won't tell you about the package—not until you promise me something."

His eyes narrowed. Josy threw back her shoulders in the too-big black robe and met his gaze squarely. If she didn't know that Ty Barclay was on her side, she would have been very frightened indeed. But she happened to know that beneath that tough, uncompromising, intimidating cop exterior, Ty Barclay had a heart and a soul. And a tender side few would ever guess.

He would listen to her. She just had to make her case.

"What kind of promise?" he bit out.

"Promise that you'll let me deliver the package to Ricky. You won't try to stop me."

For a moment he looked like he was going to explode. "No."

"Then take me home. I have . . . things to do."

She stood up from the sofa, but he reached her in a quick stride and seized her shoulders.

"This isn't kid stuff anymore, Josy. It's bad news. You're smart enough to know that. I'll try to help Ricky through this if I can—I'll even help him cut a deal, though I'd like to kick his ass from here to Tennessee. But I need to know what I'm dealing with."

"What we're dealing with," she corrected him.

His breath hissed out in exasperation. "Tell me about the package. When and where are you giving it to him?"

"First promise me you'll let me deliver it."

Standoff. Ty took her measure, fighting for patience even though he was worried as hell about what she'd gotten into—what her dear old friend Ricky had *gotten* her into. She was as frustrating and stubborn as any woman he'd ever met and that included Meg, and even his sister. Faith would like Josy Warner, no doubt about it.

From the upward tilt of her chin, and the determined glint in her eyes, he knew this was one round he was going to lose.

"All right. I won't stop you from delivering it." Even as he said the words, he knew he was going to regret them.

She smiled at him. This slender blonde who'd been ambushed by a pro, threatened and cut with a knife, and then dragged around Shadow Point half the night was beaming at him with the sweetest expression of triumph and relief he'd ever seen.

I've got it bad, he thought, his stomach roiling. How had this happened? How had he gone from being mildly interested in the new woman in town to *this*? It was unbelievable and pathetic . . . and damned crazy. He wanted to kiss her suddenly, but he knew he couldn't. He had to interrogate her first.

"Okay, I promised, so let's have it," he said with a scowl. "What's in the package?"

She sank down on the sofa again and he joined her there, waiting as she looked up into his eyes.

"A diamond," she said. "The biggest diamond you ever saw."

"How big?"

She curled her fingers and thumb into a big C. "This big. It's a major *rock*."

Shit. Ty kept his tone level. "And you put it where?"

"In the ground. Once I saw what it was, and realized it had to be real or why would everyone want it so badly, I decided burying it was the safest thing to do in case anyone came looking for it. Don't worry, as I drove out into the wild I made exact notations where I hid it."

"And where did you put these notations?"

"I memorized them after I got home and tore them up into itty-bitty pieces and flushed them down the toilet." She slanted a glance up at him. "How'm I doing so far, copper?"

"You're scoring an A in Criminal Theft 101. Any idea where this diamond came from?"

"Dolph said it belonged to his boss. He accused Ricky of stealing it. Which—if that's true, I know Ricky must have had a good reason," she added quickly. "Obviously Dolph's boss is a criminal himself. He probably stole it to begin with so—"

"Hold it. I want you to start from the beginning. I want you to tell me everything about Dolph, everything you remember about the way he looked, the car he drove, what he said."

So she spent the next half hour reliving the events of the evening, searching her memory for descriptions and details and telling Ty everything she could recall. When he finally nodded, ending the questioning, she sank back exhausted on the sofa.

Ty placed his hand over hers. "You did good, Josy. One more thing. Was that Ricky who called you the other night when I was in your apartment? Was that him setting up the meet?"

She nodded.

"So when is it?"

"Tomorrow. I mean, today. Five o'clock."

"Where?"

"The rest stop one-half mile north of the ranger's station on Laramie Peak. In the Medicine Bow National Forest. I suppose you're going to insist on coming with me." She hated the hopefulness in her own voice, but she couldn't hide it. She didn't want to be dealing with this alone anymore.

"Oh, I'm going with you all right. Count on that."

"Actually, I am." She smiled wanly. "After tonight, I'm glad to have some reinforcements. I don't know who else might be out there looking for the diamond."

"I have a proposition for you. Why don't you let me drop you off at the courthouse and put you in protective custody? Just for the day. Then I'll meet Ricky on Laramie Peak and—"

"No!" She bolted upright, her eyes wide with alarm. "Ty, you promised." Her voice rose. "You can't tell anyone about this. And you have to let me deliver it! I thought I could trust you—I haven't trusted anything a man said since . . . since . . . well, for a long time now, but I trusted *you*. Don't you dare go back on your word!"

"Take it easy. It was just a suggestion." He eased her back down on the sofa and took a seat beside her. "I'll keep my word, even though it's against my better judgment."

As her heartbeat slowed and the panic died down, Josy felt the tension slide from her body. She suddenly felt too weary for words.

"Okay, so now what?" she mumbled.

"Now we get some sleep. In the morning, I'm going to make a few phone calls. Maybe I can find out some background on what we're dealing with."

"But you can't tell anyone about Ricky or the diamond."

"I'll just ask some questions. I have a friend from Philly who transferred to the NYPD a few years back when he married a girl from Staten Island. I'll talk to him, but I won't give anything away."

"Okay." She sighed, and offered him a tentative smile. "I trust you. I really do. It's just—"

All at once her gaze clouded. "Is this going to cause trouble for you? You're a cop—you're helping me. And I'm involved in something that's probably a felony—"

"*Probably* a felony?"

"Oh God. This could ruin your career, couldn't it?"

"Let me worry about my career."

"The last thing I'd want is for you to get fired or—my God, arrested—for helping me—"

"Hey, did anyone ever tell you that you think too much?"

"All the time." She answered his smile with a rueful grin. "Don't change the subject, Ty. I couldn't bear it if after everything you've done—"

"I haven't done anything yet."

"Yes, you have. You rescued me from that . . . that

monstrosity up on Shadow Point. And you brought me
here."

She glanced around. "This is a wonderful cabin. I actually feel safe here," she added, surprised.

"You are safe here. This place is pretty well tucked
away and I made sure we weren't followed. For tonight,
you can sleep without any worries. I promise."

"Thank you." She leaned over impulsively and kissed
his cheek. Ty felt her warm breath on his face and a surge
of desire ran through him, like an electrical volt charging
all his batteries at once. She smelled like flowers and
woman and shampoo, and she looked sexy as hell in his
robe. And more beautiful than he'd ever seen her with her
damp golden hair tumbling around her face and her eyes
soft in the candlelight.

Her gaze was locked on his. He wanted her with a fe-
rocity that burned through his blood.

Something had changed between them.

She wasn't holding back anymore, she wasn't even trying to be aloof, to keep him at arm's length and hide her
secrets. The woman with him in the cabin now, looking at
him with those beautiful searching eyes, was real and vulnerable and more desirable than any woman had a right
to be.

"It's almost three-thirty in the morning," he heard himself saying in a hoarse tone. After what she'd been through
tonight, it wouldn't exactly be fair to push anything more
on her. She'd want to sleep, he was sure of it, not to get involved in . . . whatever.

This isn't the time, his conscience told him, even
though his body ached to touch hers.

"Tomorrow's going to be a long day."

"I know." Josy nodded, yet her gaze still held his. "We should . . . go to bed."

"We should."

She knew she ought to look away right now, while she still could. But she had no desire to look away from him. Quite the contrary.

She had opened up her whole life to him tonight and he hadn't judged her. He was going to help her. Emotions and sensations charged through her. Slowly, her hand crept up, touched his face.

Her heart was trembling and she couldn't think of anything right now except how much she wanted him. Needed him.

Just for tonight.

"Take me to bed, Ty," she whispered, and abandoned all caution as she kissed him softly on the mouth.

Chapter 22

THE CABIN ON BLUE MOON MESA WAS DARK BUT for the flickering flames of the fire and the single lamp on the table. There was no sound but the crackling of the logs and the small moans and greedy sighs of the two people locked in each other's arms.

Josy was almost unaware of her surroundings. They simply didn't matter. Ty did. *This* did. This warmth and pleasure that shivered through her as Ty took the kiss deeper, and wrapped her in his arms.

She clung to him, tasting him, breathing him in. She welcomed the smoothness of his tongue, the feel of his hands skimming over her body.

She clung to him as his hand slipped inside her robe, cupped her breast. Her nipple tightened into a taut peak at the teasing strokes of his thumb. He did this until her head fell back and a moan escaped her throat. Then they were caught up in more long, dark, swirling kisses, and Ty parted the robe, sliding it off her bare shoulders with ease.

It fell in a heap to the floor and she stood naked before him, all smooth pale curves, golden curls, and big green eyes glimmering in the firelight.

"My God, Josy, you're beautiful." He caught her to him and his hands roamed her body, igniting wildfires everywhere he touched. Need ached through her and she tore at the buttons of his shirt, yanking the ends of it from his trousers.

"You are, cowboy," she whispered against his lips. All the while her hands worked frantically, dragging the shirt down the slope of those broad, powerful shoulders and tossing it aside.

Then her hands explored that broad bare chest that was lightly matted with dark hair, and all the while he was kissing her mouth, her jaw, her throat—hot, hungry kisses—and then his mouth trailed down to her breasts.

Slowly, his tongue circled a nipple. Half crazed, Josy groaned with pleasure and grabbed onto his arms, hanging on for dear life as delicious sensations swept over her and she felt herself going under.

"Ty," she breathed in a hoarse, desperate voice totally unlike her own, and heard him chuckle thickly.

Then his mouth closed over her nipple and she gasped. She plunged her hands through his hair and held on tight as he nipped and licked and suckled her.

A fire built inside her as he moved to her other breast. More, more, more . . .

She gave herself up to the storm of pleasure and when he scooped her into his arms and carried her naked into his bedroom as if she weighed no more than a wisp of silk, she was as flushed and hot as a peach split open on a grill.

He kissed her lips as he lowered her onto the bed with its black and green comforter. Very gently he set her down and leaned over her, gazing into her brilliant eyes.

"You all right, Josy?" He kissed the bruises Dolph had put on her arms. "I'd never want to hurt you."

"You didn't. You won't." She drew him down to her, her fingers gripping his belt buckle.

"Just don't stop now, whatever you do," she breathed as she loosened the belt.

His stomach was so lean, so hard. All of him was hard. He took off his boots, and together they got rid of his pants, then she pulled him down on her, her soft mouth locking on his. A few hours ago she'd thought she was going to die. Now she had never felt more alive.

"Make love to me, Ty," she whispered as he nibbled at her shoulder. "Don't stop here or I'll never forgive you."

"Does it look like I'm stopping?" Grinning, he returned his attention to her swollen mouth and kissed her more deeply than she'd ever been kissed. He knew exactly how to drive her crazy and when his big hands finished tormenting her breasts some more and slid down her thighs, she quivered all over.

His smile was deep and hungry, dark with the longing for her.

"We don't have to rush this, Josy. We have all night," he said. His fingers stroked the soft curls between her legs, enjoying her quick intake of breath.

But the words cost him. So did the waiting. He wanted her so badly it hurt. His muscles were clenched, his heart pounding, and he felt like a fever was rushing through his blood. She was exquisite and the touch of her fingers on his flesh burned his skin and made him taut with need. But he went slowly, deliberately, taking raw male pleasure in the touch and scent of her, in the arousal that glazed her eyes.

"I don't think . . . I can wait all night," she gasped, as her fingertips rubbed his nipples, her body starting to arch against him.

"Damn, I can't either." He grinned and gently chewed the corner of her mouth, then dropped his head once more to her throat.

By the time he'd stroked a finger inside her and found her slick and ready, their bodies were both gleaming with sweat and Ty's muscles were almost painful with built-up tension.

Josy was utterly beautiful and deliciously sexy and it was all he could do to enter her slowly, to force himself to hold on awhile longer. He filled her slowly, watching her eyes turn a dark wild green, listening to her rushed breathing.

He moved gently inside her, and made love to her slowly, until her back arched and her legs wrapped around him and her entire body strained against him. Then his thrusts intensified and a raging savage pleasure tore at him as they rocked together, panting and needy, their bodies joined in sweat and fire. Time spun away as they bucked and danced and galloped together, becoming one—one heart, one soul, one body, fused in a shattering, pounding heat.

They climaxed togther in an explosion of senses almost beyond what they could bear.

As the storm crashed and broke and ebbed, he rolled off her and pulled her into his arms. Closing his eyes, he took deep breaths, his heart still thundering.

She was exquisite, both elegant and wild, turning him on in a way he'd almost forgotten. Making love to Josy had completed him in a way none of his casual emotion-free flings with women, or occasional nights with hookers, ever had.

He'd almost forgotten how it felt to hold a woman he cared about, to watch her eyes as she came while he was inside her.

He stroked Josy's hair, pushed himself up, and leaned over to kiss her. Her face was flushed, glowing, but she looked exhausted. And yet, she was smiling up at him, more beautiful than ever.

"If you keep looking at me like that, we're never going to get any sleep," he chuckled, and gently kissed the tip of her nose.

"Promise?" She wound her arms behind his head and pulled him down to her.

"Whoa, baby, careful what you wish for," he chuckled, his hands stroking her beautiful breasts.

"Forget it. I'm tired of being careful," Josy whispered back. "I'm going to wish for the moon and the stars."

"Might as well add the sun while you're at it. It's going to be morning soon."

"Bring it on." She buried her lips in his neck as he snuggled down beside her. She felt wonderful and dreamy, almost drunk. She knew she should stop talking, but she couldn't help it.

A combination of sated satisfaction, pent-up tension, and exhaustion from the entire night seemed to loosen her tongue.

"Give me ten minutes and I'll be good to go again," she murmured, vaguely aware that he laughed as if from a great distance, and that he was lightly fingering her hair, gently rubbing her shoulder . . .

She dropped like a rock into sleep.

Ty studied her face in repose. That fine-boned, elegant

face, the long lashes sweeping against her skin. Silken hair spread on the pillow.

His chest tightened. Josy Warner was in a lot of trouble. Someone was trying to kill her. She'd aided and abetted a fugitive.

And what they'd done tonight might make things tougher than ever for her. At the very least, more complicated.

His mouth twisted into a frown. Reality slammed him in the stomach.

He should have kept his distance. He shouldn't have given in to the chemistry between them. He cared about her, but something told him she cared more. More than he could give.

Josy was a loving, giving woman, loyal to a fault, with a heart as big as the whole state of Wyoming. And for all her sophistication, she'd want more than just fantastic sex. A lot more.

She'd want a relationship. A home, the kind she'd missed out on growing up. Children. The whole nine yards.

Pain wrenched at him. He'd tried that once. If it had been going to work, it would've worked with Meg. He didn't think he could risk it again, loving someone that much, wanting their child that much, losing everything . . .

That part of him had died with Meg. Maybe he should have explained that to Josy before they'd slept together. But she was a big girl. He hadn't made her any promies or declarations. He hadn't once mentioned the *L* word.

He just hoped she didn't expect love.

He could only love Meg. He hoped like hell she realized that. Maybe he ought to have spelled it out . . .

He fell back on the pillow and forced himself to get

some sleep while he could. Tomorrow he'd have to try to keep Josy alive—both of them alive. And then he'd have to deal with the rest. He'd back off subtly. Let her down as gently as he could.

And hope to hell she saw it the same way he did.

Chapter 23

"YOU FOUND HER—AND YOU LET HER GET away?"

The controlled fury in Oliver Tate's voice was not lost on Dolph. He swore silently, clenching the cell phone tight against his ear.

"She won't get far, Mr. Tate. I've called in reinforcements—Len, Morley, and Armstrong will be here in an hour." He didn't want to get into exactly what had gone wrong last night. Mr. Tate loathed explanations every bit as much as he loathed mistakes. Tate wouldn't be happy to know he'd stumbled into a bust while he was chasing the girl, and that some goddamned hick cop had nearly caught him.

That guy who'd hit him had known what he was doing. Dolph had seen stars and his face still hurt. He'd barely had the wits to get away, but had known that in his dazed state, it wouldn't be smart to stick around.

Much better to attack in his own time, in his own way.

That's what he'd do today.

"The four of us will fan out to find the girl. We'll have her and the diamond by noon."

"You sound quite confident."

"I am." Dolph was sweating, though, as he sat inside his car on a steep, lonely road in the foothills. Tate didn't give second chances too often. One slip-up and you were through.

Like Hammer. Like Lyle Samuels.

He held his breath, waiting for the verdict. "I'm going in fully loaded this time, Mr. Tate. I'll be on a plane home tonight with your property."

"See that you are, Dolph. See that you are."

The phone clicked in his ear. Dead air. A reprieve.

Dolph took a deep breath, opened the glove compartment. He grabbed a PowerBar from inside and a bottle of water from underneath his seat and made short work of both, tossing the wrapper and the bottle out the window when he was done.

It was 7 A.M. In another hour he'd have Len, Morley, and Armstrong combing the town, foothills, and valley by helicopter, motorcycle, and automobile.

They'd find the girl. They had to.

If she wasn't dead by tonight and the diamond wasn't on its way back to Tate, he'd be the one buried.

Tate might occasionally give one of his employees a second chance, but he'd never been known to grant a third.

When I catch the bitch, she's going to pay big-time for all the trouble she's caused. I'll make sure she dies little tiny bits at a time. Lots of pain, even more blood. That babe's going to fade away like paint drying. She's going down real slow.

Chapter 24

"ARE YOU SURE THIS IS THE SPOT?"

Ty dropped down on one knee beside the tree stump and glanced up at Josy in the milky-gray morning light. "Right here?"

"I'm positive." She handed him a stick. "It's down at least a foot."

As he started to dig, Josy hugged her arms around herself in the chilly morning air. The day had dawned cool and cloudy. There'd been a misty rain earlier. Now it was dry, but the air smelled of earth and damp grass and more rain on the way. She shivered in her tank top. But not only from the chill in the air.

She was exhausted from the harrowing events of the previous night, and in the clear light of day, her fear was returning. She was afraid not only for herself, but for Ty and for Ricky. And there was a definite tension—an awkwardness—between her and Ty that had communicated itself to her the moment she woke up.

He was already showered and dressed, and in the kitchen making a pot of coffee when she opened her eyes.

She woke up alone in the big carved-oak bed.

And he'd been in such a hurry to get started that they

hadn't even talked much. He'd kissed her once, a quick peck, after she'd made the bed and hung his robe back in the bathroom.

But his mind had been elsewhere.

On the diamond. On Ricky. Not on *us,* she'd realized as she'd gulped the coffee, grabbed her purse, and followed him out to his car.

"Ah. Got it."

She stared in silence as he tugged the brown-wrapped package from the dirt hole. Those strong fingers swiftly unwrapped the layers of paper, and then he was holding the diamond in the palm of his hand.

"Talk about a hot potato."

The diamond glinted with cool crystal fire even in the pallid daylight. "Whoa, baby." Ty shook his head. "I can't even begin to guess what this is worth."

He got to his feet, still studying the diamond. "But I'd bet my pension it's a bundle. Something this size? It has to be a famous rock."

"Do you mean . . . like the Hope diamond?"

"Exactly. When your pal Ricky turned thief he didn't exactly do it in a small-time way, did he?"

"I'm sure he has a good explanation." She bit her lip. "Maybe it's evidence or something."

He slanted her a skeptical glance. "Yeah. Maybe."

Ty stuffed the diamond back into the wrapping and dropped it into his jacket pocket. "Let's get the hell out of here. Dolph's bound to be searching for you all through this area. We'll be safer once we get into Albany County."

There was silence between them for nearly the entire first hour of the drive. Josy tried to concentrate on the scenery, the low hills that grew gradually steeper, the greasewood brush, the sky billowing with charcoal clouds.

Ty had switched on the radio, perhaps, she thought, to fore-stall any conversation, and Willie Nelson was singing "Al-ways on My Mind."

She refused to let herself dwell on what had happened between them last night. Today it seemed like a dream, a sensuous, wildly erotic dream, nothing at all like the cool, casual reality of them driving toward Laramie Peak, silent as strangers.

Better to think about today—about handing over the diamond to Ricky, finishing this horrible business at last. There was one aspect of it that she hadn't considered be-fore, but as the silence dragged on and she cast a quick glance over at Ty, she realized she'd better deal with it now. She didn't want any unpleasant surprises later.

"I'm going to ask you to make me another promise." Her voice sounded loud after such a long silence. She took a breath as Ty switched off the radio, his eyes still on the road.

"Why do I think I'm not going to like this?"

"You can't arrest Ricky. Or hold him in any way. I'll give him the diamond, and then we leave and he—"

"Gets away with it? We hand him stolen merchandise and let him run? I don't think so."

Josy heard the grimness in his tone and her stomach roiled. "You promised me you'd let me deliver it."

"And I will. But I never said I'd let him just walk away scot-free."

"So this is a trap?" Dismay swept through her. "You're setting him up, aren't you? You called your friend on the NYPD this morning and arranged for the police to be there—"

"You ought to be a writer, Josy. You have a vivid imag-ination." He shot her a tight smile. "Relax. It's only going to be you and me. I'm not planning to arrest him—I just want to persuade him to do the right thing. He needs to turn himself in and let me help him get this straightened out. According to my friend in New York, your old pal Ricky's in shit up to his shirtsleeves. It'll go a lot better for him if he faces it and quits running."

"Ricky doesn't run from things," she protested sharply. "Not unless there's no other way. We don't know the whole story, and when we do, you'll see that he's been framed, just as he said."

"Maybe he was." Ty switched on the windshield wipers as a slow rain began to drip from the sky. The day had grown increasingly gray, the air whistling past the windows was thick with dust and grit.

She turned in her seat and stared at him. "You believe he was framed too? Tell me," she said quickly. "What did you find out?"

"I spoke with Tommy Berger while you were still asleep. Ricky's a wanted man in New York, all right. Big-time. The national media hasn't picked up on the story yet—but the suits in the city want him back. Do you know why he was being investigated?"

"I know what the newspapers said about him. They said he was working undercover on a case involving some crime boss."

"Not just some crime boss. Julius Caventini."

"Yes—Caventini." She nodded. "But the police accused him of going over to Caventini's side. They said there was evidence he'd done a hit for Caventini and taken money for it. And that he'd accepted a payoff for tipping Caventini off to the investigation and helping him conceal evidence."

"Right. Actually it was a precinct captain, a twenty-five-

year veteran named Wallace Becker, who made the accusations and had Ricky arrested. According to Tommy, Ricky
claimed to have evidence implicating not only Caventini
but Becker and some cops in two other precincts, and—get
this—he also pointed the finger at a big-shot businessman
for being part of the organization. The businessman, Oliver
Tate, has a squeaky-clean rep. He gives to all the right char-
ities, is active in New York social circles, and is rumored to
be on a short list of potential candidates for governor down
the road."

"Oliver Tate? That part wasn't in the papers," she said,
feeling slightly dazed. "I know who he is. I've never met
him," she added, "but his wife attended some of
Francesca's runway shows. She always has a front-row
seat. She was a former Miss World and is absolutely stunning. And I saw them once at a party one of Reese's ex-
husbands threw at the Rainbow Room. They're one of the
city's power couples."

"Well, according to Tommy's sources, your pal Ricky
thinks Tate is in bed with Caventini and Becker. So to
speak. Married to the mob."

"I wonder which one of them hired Dolph to find me."

"Could be any of the three. And you were probably
right when you said there might be others coming after
you too. If Ricky's telling the truth, all three of these men
have a lot to lose. They're playing for very high stakes,
Josy."

"But Ricky had evidence, right? It wasn't only his
word against Tate and Becker—"

"A funny thing happened on the way to internal investigations," Ty said drily. "The evidence he turned over
somehow disappeared."

Josy's mouth dropped. "What do you mean, disappeared?"

"There was a theft from the evidence room."

"How convenient." Anger darkened her eyes. "Don't tell me that didn't send up a red flag for the guys doing the internal investigation," she exclaimed.

"Tommy didn't have any scuttlebutt on that end of it. Though I'd think it would—if internal affairs is paying attention. But Josy"—he paused, choosing his words with care—"that still doesn't explain why Ricky had this rock. Or where he got it—and how."

"There has to be a good reason," she insisted. "We'll get all those answers today."

"Yeah, if we make it that far." Ty slowed for a sharp curve in the road. "Have you noticed that chopper?"

She hadn't. But now that he mentioned it, she became aware of the steady whirring hum of a helicopter in the distance. Glancing through the windshield she saw a helicopter flying low in the sky ahead, coming right toward the car. As it glided overhead it changed direction, circling away to the east.

"What about it?" she asked, a sick feeling in the pit of her stomach.

"I noticed it earlier. It appeared to be following us briefly—then disappeared. Now it's back. Could be Dolph or one of his friends."

"Do you really think so?" Her breath caught in her throat. Now she'd put Ty in danger. And if they were being followed, they were leading Ricky's enemies straight to him.

"Can you lose it?"

"We're about to find out."

Ty twisted the wheel and the car veered off the main

road onto a gravel path. The cruiser jolted over the rough road, flanked on either side by stands of lodgepole pines.

"We've got time to kill, so let's take the back roads for a while. This will take us to Bitter Gulch—we can get lunch there and switch cars."

"How are you going to manage that?"

He pulled out his cell phone and shot her a grim smile. "Watch and learn."

An hour later the car bumped onto a narrow paved road. Soon she saw a weatherbeaten wooden sign that read *Welcome to Bitter Gulch*.

"Talk about off the beaten path," she murmured. "This town looks smaller than Thunder Creek."

"It is, by about a hundred people. They've got a nice little diner here, though. Not as good as Bessie's place, but we can get a decent burger."

A burger sounded wonderful. Josy had barely even sipped her coffee this morning. Her appetite was coming back, especially since they hadn't seen or heard the helicopter again since they'd turned off the highway.

"I'm so hungry I just might eat two burgers," she muttered.

"Nothing like a woman with a healthy appetite."

She spoke lightly. "Ah, so that's what you like in a woman."

Without turning her head, she could sense his glance shifting to her. "Among other things."

"Such as?"

"Oh, soft blonde hair." He shot her a smile, and her stupid heart fluttered like a butterfly on speed. "Beautiful green eyes. And, oh yeah, the softest lips in the West."

She smiled back, some of the tension ebbing from her. "Oh, really," she drawled.

"Yep. And don't forget a talent for getting mixed up in more trouble than she can handle."

"Some of us are just born lucky." Deliberately, she kept her tone light and flip. "There's one more thing I think you neglected to mention. Knowing how to keep things uncomplicated."

"That helps." There was a short silence and then he added, "Uncomplicated works for me."

Sure it does. Heaven forbid anyone should actually fall in love with you, or take those heart-wrenching kisses seriously.

"Me too. My last relationship was a mess. I learned my lesson."

"Are we talking about the cop who was your ex-boyfriend?"

Ty was surprised by the stab of jealousy he felt at the mental image of Josy with another man. He didn't like the picture it made in his head. Not one bit.

"He wasn't a cop. I just told you that to cover up how alarmed I was when I found out *you* were a cop," she explained.

Ty didn't say anything. He didn't have to. She knew what he was thinking.

So many lies.

How had she ever—even for a moment—thought anything beyond the most casual of affairs would be possible with a man she had lied to about almost every aspect of her life?

"He's an investment banker," she hurried on. "A *married* investment banker." She turned her head away from him, staring out the passenger window. "I had no idea. When we met he told me he was single."

Okay, the jealousy was gone. Now he just felt angry. "It must have been rough on you when you found out."

"I was in shock." She didn't know why she was opening up to him. Or why he would believe a word she said after all the lies. But somehow the words began pouring out. "I never would have guessed he was such a lying bastard. He said he traveled for his job and worked a lot of nights and weekends, schmoozing clients and CEOs. At least that's what I thought. He managed to squeeze me in a few times a week. We had a lot of nice romantic dinners, and rented movies at my place. Once we even went away to Puerto Rico for a weekend. I found out later that he'd told his wife he was at an investment symposium in Miami."

She sounded bitter. Ty could hear the brittleness in her voice, even though she struggled to keep her tone even. He parked on a small side street alongside the Country Goose Diner. "You must have gone through hell when you learned the truth."

"I did. I hated the idea that he was hurting his wife and his children. The worst part was that he'd tricked me into hurting them too. I felt like . . . like a total sleazebag."

"That's crazy," Ty said sharply. "He's the sleazebag, Josy, not you." He shut off the engine and turned toward her.

"You're anything but that. And you deserved a hell of a lot better than what that asshole did to you."

For some absurd reason, tears threatened. She blinked them back. "I grew up with secondhand clothes, secondhand schoolbooks," she said quietly. "I've always hated anything secondhand. But that's how Doug made me feel once I learned the truth. I didn't come first with him—and

neither did his wife. He came first. His own selfish, imma-
ture whims."

She met Ty's gaze squarely, speaking past the lump in
her throat. "I won't ever be someone's secondhand
woman. Second choice, second best. I won't do that to
myself—not for any man."

Her eyes sought his, and they were filled with regret—
and determination. "I thought Doug loved me, that we
were building something solid and good together, but it
was all a lie. And I swore after I found out that I'd never let
anyone use me again. I won't be a substitute wife or girlfriend. It's first choice, or bust. I owe myself that, Ty."

Her words hit him like a barrage of rocks. He stared at
her, his gaze narrowed. "You think that's what I did last
night? That I used you . . . as a substitute for my wife?"

"No, that's not what I'm saying." She shook her head
as pain squeezed her heart. She couldn't let him see how
stupid she'd been. He hadn't used her—what had happened between them had been real and powerful. But not
powerful enough. He didn't love her. He still loved Meg.
He'd always love Meg. And she'd known that all along.

"I think you enjoyed last night every bit as much as I
did." She forced herself to speak lightly. To smile. "It was
wonderful. But we both knew going in that there couldn't
ever be anything more. I've known from the beginning
that you've never gotten over your wife's death. Corinne
told me that the first night at the Tumbleweed. So last
night—well, don't worry about it." She shrugged. "No
complications. No strings. End of story."

Even as she said the words, she wished to heaven they
were true. Yes, she'd known the situation going in—but
she'd forgotten it every time Ty Barclay touched her,
kissed her. She'd forgotten as soon as his hands stroked

her skin, as soon as his lips took her to that hot, delicious place where common sense floated away. Somehow during these past few weeks in Thunder Creek, her heart had started responding to Ty Barclay as much as her body had. She'd opened herself up to feeling much more for him than mere attraction.

She'd been idiotic enough to fall in love with him.

"Once this business is cleared up, assuming we get out of it alive, I'm going back to Manhattan." She spoke matter-of-factly, praying he hadn't detected the slight tremble in her voice. "And you're staying in Thunder Creek. But I'll never have any regrets about last night."

"That's damned comforting," he growled. His eyes had turned a dark, dangerous blue.

"What's wrong with you? I thought you'd be relieved."

"I am. Can't you tell? Let's get some lunch."

"Don't tell me you're angry."

"Why should I be? But let me get this straight, you're saying essentially that last night meant nothing to you. Have I got that right?"

"Last night was unforgettable," she said simply. So unforgettable that her chest was tight and she was afraid any moment that she'd start to cry. She touched his hand, lightly, then pulled back.

"And I'll always be glad for it, even when I'm back in Manhattan charging through the rat race and you're here catching the bad guys. But I knew it was only one night. And so did you."

He stared at her, scowling. "Yeah. I knew you'd be going back—as soon as this deal is over." He was reminding himself, he realized, more than her. He knew he should be relieved, but instead, he felt irritated as hell.

"Assuming you don't end up in Sing Sing." He opened

the car door abruptly. "Let's eat, we don't have all day. I want to be ready to roll as soon as Roy gets here."

They didn't talk much over lunch. Ty's mood had done a 180. She wasn't sure exactly why. They lingered in silence over their coffee, killing time until they could switch cars. Josy kept glancing at her watch. Not long now and she'd be meeting Ricky. If, she told herself, nothing—and no one—got in the way.

It was another half hour before Roy arrived. He sauntered into the Country Goose Diner carrying a duffel bag.

"Here you go. Got some bottles of spring water in there, and a few beers, like you asked. And some ammo and grub. What's this all about? Who's following you in a copter?" he asked as he dropped into a seat next to Josy and directed his question to Ty.

Ty gave him no details. But he warned Roy to keep to the back roads on his way home to Thunder Creek and not to tell anyone what was going on.

"No problem, but are you two okay?" Roy turned to Josy, studying her in concern. "What in hell has my cousin got you involved in?"

"It's what I've got him involved in." Josy managed a wan smile. "Ty's taking good care of me."

"He'd better. Corinne wants the two of you at the wedding—and I don't want anything upsetting my bride." Despite his casual tone, there was a worried frown between Roy's brows. "Hey, cuz, want me to hang around, come with you . . . wherever you're going? I'm not a cop, but I watch them on TV. I know how to do backup."

"No, thanks, Roy. Not necessary." Ty hoped to hell he was right. He drew out his wallet to pay the lunch check. "Letting me use your car is a big help. Keeping your mouth shut about this is even bigger."

"I hear you. Lips are sealed."

"Thanks. All right, I need to make a pit stop," Ty said, after paying the waitress for their lunch. "Roy, wait here with Josy, will you?"

"No need," Josy said, realizing that a restroom visit was probably a good idea. She slipped out of her seat and headed toward the ladies' room. There she took deep breaths, suddenly feeling that the hamburger she'd devoured was corroding her stomach. She needed to splash some water on her face, put on lipstick, calm herself down. This day was only in the early stages—she still had a long way to go.

By the time she came out, Ty and Roy were already waiting outside. Roy handed Ty the keys to his white Ford Ranger and then gave her a hug before heading to Ty's car.

"Whatever's going on, you two stay safe."

He shot Ty a speaking glance and walked away.

The moment he left them, Ty took the brown-wrapped package from his jacket pocket and transferred it into the duffel bag, which he stuffed on the floor near Josy's feet.

Time for the last leg of the journey.

A light rain began to fall as they swung back onto the main highway and headed toward the huge area of protected land known as Medicine Bow National Forest. They saw a helicopter in the distance, but it never turned their way, instead disappearing to the south.

No one appeared to be following them, though a motorcycle did pass them once, the burly young driver glancing over momentarily before he roared on ahead.

Ty's mouth thinned into a hard line, but he said nothing, and Josy tried to relax back in her seat.

But that proved more impossible as each mile flashed by. She didn't know what the next few hours would bring, and after last night, she knew that Dolph was capable of anything. Anything at all.

"That's Laramie Peak up ahead. We can only take the car so far—up to a point near the campgrounds. Then we'll have to hike it."

"Well, so will anyone else trying to get their hands on the diamond—and on Ricky," she said. She was staring at the sloping, pine-covered mountains, silhouetted against the murky sky. On a clear day, the view would have been breathtaking. Even today, with the sky wet and gray and a heaviness hanging in the pine-scented air, Laramie Peak was magnificent.

But she forgot all about the view and everything else when her cell phone rang. Josy jumped, then grabbed it from her handbag.

"It's me," Ricky said curtly. "Change of plans."

"But we're almost—"

"*We?*"

"I'm bringing a friend with me. Someone I trust."

"Goddammit, Josy—"

"Last night I was attacked, Ricky," she interrupted him. "And now they're after me—"

"Shit! Sorry, Josy. Did they hurt you? You all right?"

"Yes, thanks to my friend—"

"Listen, this is all the more reason to switch our plan around. Forget Laramie Peak. Right now, head to Wheatland. There's a bar a quarter mile outside of town. Slattery's Saloon. I'll come to you."

He hung up without waiting for her reply. Feeling chilled, Josy looked at Ty. "Change of plans."

"I expected as much," Ty said drily. "That happens a lot when guys are on the run, afraid for their lives. A moving target, constantly changing direction, going serpentine, is harder to hit. Where to?"

She told him, and he grimaced, then did a U-turn toward the interstate.

"Slattery's Saloon, huh? That place is a big-time hangout for drug dealers and degenerates. Nice friends you've got, Miz Warner."

Josy clenched her hands together. She was getting a very bad feeling about this. Ricky had been sounding less and less like himself each time she'd spoken to him.

So much had happened in the past day. Suddenly she thought of Chance. He was in the hospital, recovering from a gunshot wound. And at least one of the rustlers was doing the same. And Ty could have been back in town, in the thick of the investigation, questioning his suspects, examining evidence. Instead he was here with her.

Risking his life.

She spoke suddenly. "Whatever happens today, I want you to know—" she began, but he interrupted her with a reckless grin.

"Save it for my eulogy if I don't make it out of Slattery's Saloon alive."

Ty floored the car as they zoomed onto the interstate. As if to mock his words, the sun broke through the clouds with a burst of golden promise.

Chapter 25

SLATTERY'S SALOON WAS A LONG, LOW, RAM-shackle building that squatted at the edge of a weed-choked dirt field on the outskirts of Wheatland.

There were only two cars parked outside, neither of which was a black Explorer like the one Dolph had been driving. *So far, so good,* Josy thought, as she got out of the pickup and watched Ty seize the duffel from the floor.

They started toward the saloon in silence. The air was eerily quiet and heady with the scent of sage. The silence was broken only intermittently by the cry of hawks wheeling through the sky. But inside her head was a rush of sound—the roaring of her own blood in her ears. Now she was finally going to get some answers—and rid herself of the damned diamond.

She only prayed she'd be able to persuade Ricky to let Ty help him, to turn himself in and work once again with the police.

The saloon was dimly lit and there were only two other patrons. A husky kid of about eighteen chewing tobacco and playing pool, and a paunchy, sour-eyed cowboy in a plaid shirt and jeans straddling a stool at the bar. Ty led the way to a round table near the dartboard. It was a few feet from the restrooms and the rear exit, and as Josy slipped into a chair, he took a seat facing the entrance, turning it slightly so he could also see the exit door.

He set the duffel down beside him as a tough-looking waitress with spiky red-streaked hair strode over to the table.

"Two Buds," he said curtly, keeping an eye on the door.

The waitress loped off.

"Nervous?" Ty asked. But Josy never had a chance to answer him, because at that moment the door opened. She saw Ty's gaze swivel to the entrance and turned her head in time to see Ricky slouch through the door.

He spotted them immediately and moved toward their table. As he drew closer she felt a ping of shock. Ricky's lean, sharp face was bruised—he had a black eye, and a nasty cut across his chin. He also walked with a limp, as if he'd been kicked in the kneecap.

"Oh, God," she murmured as he ambled up to her.

"Hey, kiddo." He managed a tired smile as he reached her and Josy launched herself out of her seat and threw her arms around his neck.

"Are you okay?" she whispered.

"You're asking me that? Me?" A dry laugh. "I'm asking you. Are you okay?"

"I'm fine—thanks to Ty. Ricky, what the hell is this all about?"

"It's about some nasty guys who tried to screw me. And I tried to screw them right back." He answered in a low tone, speaking directly to her, ignoring the dark, strapping man sitting two feet away, watching him with cop's eyes.

"I never meant this to involve you. Things got royally screwed up, Josy, I swear. I'll explain it all, but not now.

Not *here*. I've gotta get outta here and so do you. Where's the package?"

"Not so fast, buddy." Ty spoke up softly, but his voice was as cold and hard as a slab of granite.

Ricky's smile faded. He drew back from Josy and glared at the other man.

"Who's this guy, Jo-Jo?"

"The name's Ty Barclay." Ty didn't extend his hand. "Sheriff Barclay," he added, watching the other man's face.

"You brought a cop?" Anger whistled through Ricky's low, strained voice.

"He's a friend first, and a cop second," she said quickly, praying like hell it was true. "Come on, Ricky, sit down. We have to talk."

"Are you crazy?"

"He's not going to arrest you," she said, slipping into her own seat as Ricky sank down, scowling, on a chair. "He and I have a deal. He's trying to protect me and to help you. Ricky, I need you to tell me, where did you get that diamond?"

"Shit, Josy. Keep your voice down. So you unwrapped it, huh? And then you told him about it?" He glowered at her, and Ty leaned forward, a hard light entering his eyes.

"She told me enough to know you're in way too deep to keep running."

"I can run as long as I need to, Sheriff." Ricky's tone was as hostile as Ty's.

"Maybe. But you'd damn well better give Josy an explanation for why the hell you involved her in something like this."

"You think I wanted to involve her?" Ricky snapped. "It was supposed to go down a completely different way."

"And Archie wasn't supposed to die, either, was he?" Ty said.

Ricky's skin turned a little grayer. "What'd you do, blab the whole thing to him? Jesus, I thought I could trust you."

He shook his head at her and Josy felt herself flushing. But for the first time, anger burst through her.

"Ricky, some goon nearly killed me last night. I've been involved in a murder—I watched a man die while I was standing right next to him—" Her voice broke, but she recovered it after a moment and continued more strongly. "I've had to hide out for my life, leave my job, my friends—"

"Well, you made some new ones, didn't you?"

She stared at him. "What's happened to you? You're different."

His laugh was so jaded, so full of cynicism, it made her shiver. "Life happened to me, Jo-Jo. I did my job and I tried to get the bad guys, and look what happened. They set me up. And you know why they were able to get away with it? Because another cop—a precinct captain, some asshole named Becker—was in the back pocket of the man calling the shots."

"All the more reason you need to go back. Ty and I will help you. There has to be some evidence to—"

"Not anymore—Becker got rid of it first thing."

"If you're telling the truth, there's other ways of verifying it. Running away isn't the answer."

"Yeah? I didn't think so either, until I realized that these guys are a lot bigger than little old me. And they have a lot of money to throw around, a lot of people working for them. Sometimes you gotta fight, kid, and sometimes you gotta run."

"And the diamond?" Josy asked quietly. "What was that for? To help you run?"

"Yeah. Insurance. If I couldn't prove my case and I was going down, I needed enough money to get out of the country and live wherever the hell I wanted—so long as it was someplace with no extradition." He shot Ty an ice-cold frown. "I've got a buyer lined up, ready to pay me a fortune once I deliver the diamond. Good thing, too, because my case is a lost cause. I don't know how many people Tate and Becker paid off, but the evidence I had is long gone, and now it's my word against theirs. You tell me, who's a judge going to believe?"

"Internal investigations is checking it out," Josy protested. "Shouldn't you wait and give them a chance to—"

"Josy, I wanted to wait. I wasn't planning to run at first, but then . . . oh, hell. I can't explain it all now. Just give me the diamond and this will all be over."

"It's not that easy." Ty's gaze bored into Ricky. His voice was pure flint. "Your pals found Josy. She's in danger until you turn yourself in, until they know for certain they can't get the diamond back."

"Once I'm gone—with the diamond—they'll leave her alone," Ricky snapped.

"Who'd you steal it from? Caventini? Or Tate?" Ty prodded.

Ricky studied the other man a moment, as if evaluating his determination, then apparently realized he wasn't about to be put off. He shrugged.

"From Tate. He's the one pulling the strings. He's as bad as Caventini, maybe worse. And Becker is zipped up tight in Tate's thousand-dollar Gucci pocket. Tate's a fanatic collector—he's got a treasure room in that Southampton mansion of his that you wouldn't believe. It's got a secret door, security cameras, the works. There's art in there, jewelry, antique weapons, you name it. All of it is rare and some of it's priceless. And most of it's stolen."

"Including this diamond?" Josy whispered.

Ricky nodded. "He stole it from a Peruvian drug dealer who made a fortune and hired someone else to steal it from a legitimate private collector. For some of these guys, the millions, the houses, the cars aren't enough—they want more possessions, they want what no one else in the world has, things that no one else can ever touch or even see. Tate is like that. I stumbled onto him during my investigation into Caventini and started connecting some dots. But as soon as his name turned up in one of my reports to my contact—bingo. Everything went haywire."

Ricky shifted restlessly in his chair, like a man unaccustomed to staying in one spot too long. He glanced over his shoulder at the doorway before continuing. "Caventini tried to have me killed, and I knew the gig was up, but when I turned over my evidence and wanted protection, Becker suddenly claimed I'd gone over to the other side. They framed me but good, Josy."

Hunching over the table, Ricky spoke even faster. "I needed a backup plan in case I couldn't prove my innocence. And that included the means to get out of the country, somewhere none of them could find me. To make that happen, I needed the diamond."

"Not to mention that stealing the rock was going to be a poke in the eye to Tate," Ty remarked. "Am I right?"

"Damn straight." Ricky smacked his fist softly on the table, revealing bruised knuckles. "And I had it planned perfectly. I had no problem bypassing their security system all to hell, but there was one little hitch. Tate and his wife and kids were supposed to be in their villa in Cancún for a whole month when I took the diamond. I figured by the time he came back and found out it was missing, I'd either have hit on a way to prove I'd been set up, or I'd be long gone." His eyes shone dark as a wolf's in the dim light of the saloon.

"But the bastard came back early—one of his kids got sick and they wanted him checked out in the States. He found out only five days after I took it that the diamond was gone and it didn't take him longer than a New York minute to figure out who was responsible."

"So this guy who's after Josy works for Tate?"

"Describe him to me." Ricky turned to Josy.

"He's huge—six foot two or three, shaved head, sharp features, eyes like an arctic lake. He likes knives—"

"Dolph," Ricky interrupted her. "He's Tate's number one guy. Shit, did he hurt you?" He peered at her intently all of a sudden, and for a moment, Josy saw the old Ricky there—the Ricky who had looked out for her all those years ago.

"Not too badly," she mumbled, aware that her hair hid the scratch Dolph had put on her ear.

"But he'd have done a lot worse if not for Ty." Her hands were clenched, her nails digging into her palms. "I haven't been able to stop thinking about Archie."

"Yeah. Archie." Ricky rubbed his neck. "Don't you think I feel bad too?"

"How was he involved in all this?" Ty asked, his gaze still trained on the other man's beat-up face.

"He used to be an informant of mine." Ricky's lips twisted. "He was this decent kid who'd been hanging with creeps. Hanging on the sidelines kind of stuff. After he started snitching for me, I tried steering him in another di-

rection. He got a job at a community center, then decided
to take some paramedic classes—you know the drill. The
kid was actually turning his life around. When I found out
Tate had come back early and knew the diamond was
gone, I knew I needed to get it out of your hands fast,
Josy. I was too far away to get it myself, but I set up the
meet with Archie at his uncle's place so you'd at least be
out of it. I never dreamed they'd be on to you so soon.
These guys . . ."

He shook his head. "They've got too much to lose—
they don't fool around."

"Then it's time you stopped doing just that," Ty said
curtly.

"You mean turn myself in? I'd be dead in forty-eight
hours. Becker's men caught up to me once—after Josy
ran. How do you think I got these bruises? They wanted
Josy—and the diamond. After they worked me over for a
while I gave them a false lead, and while they were checking it out, I managed to get away. Next time, Barclay, I
won't be that lucky. So next time . . . it ain't gonna happen. I'm outta here."

Ricky eyed the duffel bag. "Is it in there, or is that a de-
coy?"

"It's there," Josy replied, but as he reached for the bag,
she touched his arm. "Ricky, you said before there's a
time to fight and a time to run. So think about this again—
it really is your time to fight. You have me on your side—
and Ty."

"Josy, come on. A hick sheriff from Nowhere Creek?"

She glared at him, but Ty looked unperturbed.

"He happens to be a former Philadelphia police detective—who's been decorated—and he has friends at the
NYPD. If you go back with me—with *us*—if you let us

call in the authorities, we'll make sure you get a fair hearing. If all three of us go in together and tell everything we
know, surely someone will listen. Every officer in internal
affairs can't be under Becker's thumb—"

"Maybe you're willing to take that chance but I'm
not!"

Suddenly, even as he spoke the words, Ricky made a
grab for the duffel, but Ty moved faster, jerking it out of
his reach. In that instant, the doors to the saloon burst
open and a dark-complexioned man with long wiry black
hair and a face like a ferret crashed inside, a second man
with crew-cut red hair close behind him. Both carried
guns, and the moment they spotted Josy, Ty, and Ricky
across the room, they started shooting.

Ty was already dragging Josy down below the table before Ricky yelled, "Get down!"

Shots exploded through the saloon. Ty knocked the
table onto its side and ducked down behind it along with
Josy, drawing his revolver and returning fire. Ricky was
shooting too, as the other men dove for the floor and
rolled, while the waitress, the kid at the pool table, and the
paunchy cowboy all scrambled behind the bar.

Josy's heart was in her throat as she squatted on the
floor with Ty, the duffel bag in front of her. The two men
had taken cover behind a bigger, rectangular table that
they'd shoved onto its side, and somehow Ricky had
edged into the alcove that led to the exit door. There was
now a cautious lull in the shooting as everyone held his
position and looked for an opening.

"Give us the diamond, Sabatini, and we'll let you go,"
the ferret-faced man shouted.

"Like hell you will," Ricky yelled back.

Ty wondered how many of Tate's men were closing in

on Wheatland this very minute, headed to this very bar. He had to get Josy out of here and as far away from the saloon as he could.

"I'll draw their fire," he instructed softly, his tone so low only Josy and Ricky could hear. "When I do, Josy, I want you to get back there with Ricky and get the hell out of here. Sabatini, what are you driving?"

"A red Jeep."

"If I'm not out there in one minute, take Josy and head back to Thunder Creek. I'll call ahead and have the state troopers meet you on the interstate. Ready?"

"No, you can't do this, Ty, it's too dangerous." Her face was whiter than chalk. "I won't go without you. I'll stay here and we'll call the troopers—"

"I'll be right behind you, baby," he said swiftly. "Soon as I nail these guys. Now *go*."

He leaped from behind the table and sprinted, dropped, and rolled in a blur as rapid-fire shots rang out.

Josy dodged back into the alcove with Ricky, her blood pounding in her ears. But instead of dodging outside in those precious seconds Ty had bought them, Ricky unexpectedly lunged back toward the table and scooped the duffel bag from the floor, then he shoved Josy out the exit door into the cloudy afternoon light.

She glanced back at the last instant and had a final glimpse of Ty, sprinting behind the jukebox, drawing more fire.

"Run!" Ricky ordered, seizing her arm as he sprinted toward the car, dragging her with him. But they never made it that far. As they raced toward the parking lot at the front of the saloon, they both froze.

A helicopter was zooming toward the field, and a deafening clamor enveloped them. The copter was landing,

Josy realized in shock, but as she and Ricky spun toward his Jeep, they were confronted by a motorcycle roaring up the road toward them.

Ricky fired at the driver as the din from the helicopter blasted across the field. But his shot missed and the driver braked behind the Jeep. He jumped off the bike, taking cover, a Luger materializing in his hand.

"Drop your weapon, Sabatini," he yelled above the din. "Or I'll shoot the woman."

Behind them the helicopter had set down on the field, and as the motor shut off and the noise died away, she heard another voice, rusty as old nails.

"You heard him. Put your weapon down *now*."

The pilot of the helicopter, a stocky blond man with sideburns, ran out at a crouch from beneath the spinning blades, an automatic rifle slung across his shoulder.

And suddenly in the complete and utter silence that filled the parking lot, Josy spotted the other car—the car that hadn't been there before, the big black Explorer that would always be in her nightmares.

It was parked right outside the doors of the saloon and she realized in horror that the men shooting at Ty inside had come here with Dolph. Dolph had waited in the parking lot, in case they ran, hoping they'd run . . .

Her knees wobbled as he slid out of his car and smiled at her.

"So," he said in a pleasant tone that sent needles of terror ripping down her spine. "Josephine Warner, we meet again."

Chapter 26

"YOU DIDN'T THINK I'D FORGET YOU QUITE SO easily, did you?"

Dolph's smile deepened as he saw the terror flash through Josy's eyes. Realizing this, she fought back the fear. She forced herself to ignore her racing heart and the tightness in her chest, and spoke in a voice that sounded every bit as even as his.

"If you touch me again, I'll make you sorry."

The motorcycle guy laughed and came out from behind the Jeep, his gun still aimed and ready. "Oooh, Dolph, you scared yet?"

"Shaking in my boots." Dolph's eyes were still riveted on her face. They held a gleam that made her stomach turn over.

The stocky blond man near the helicopter had started walking forward with slow, easy strides, the automatic rifle trained on Josy.

"She doesn't have anything to do with this anymore," Ricky said roughly. "Now it's between you three and me."

"Think so? Why don't you hand over the merchandise you stole," the stocky man suggested. "And then we'll see."

Instead Ricky swerved, pointing his gun at Dolph. Josy didn't know how his arm could be so steady.

"It's not going to work that way, Len," Ricky said. "First you let her go. She drives away in my car—I stay and turn over the diamond."

"What's to stop me from shooting you right now and taking the diamond—and her?" The stocky guy—Len—demanded. The smug smile on his face reminded Josy of a college fraternity jock playing a prank, except that there was something chilling and off in his searing blue eyes.

"This baby right here." Ricky kept his gun trained on Dolph. The motorcycle guy was edging closer. "Hold it right there, Armstrong, or I shoot him," Ricky barked.

Armstrong paused.

"Dolph's top dog here. If you shoot me, he'll die too," Ricky promised. "I'll take him out before I fall."

"Yeah? And what's to stop me from shooting the bitch?" Len demanded, keeping the gun level with her chest.

"Same thing. I take out your leader. Tate wouldn't like that. Dolph's his number one guy." Ricky hadn't taken his eyes off the big man with the shaved head. "Isn't that right, Dolph? Or are you ready to die?"

"Give me the diamond and the girl, and you can go," Dolph said softly.

"Not going to happen." Ricky stared him down.

Her stomach clenching, Josy flicked a glance at the saloon. What was going on in there? She hadn't heard gunfire in the last minute or two. She prayed that Ty hadn't been shot. But he hadn't come out—and neither had the other men . . .

"Seems like we're at an impasse," Len said. "Except . . . we're really not. Armstrong?"

"Yeah?" The motorcycle guy brought the Luger up a few inches, smiling.

"Kill him," Len ordered. "Now."

Armstrong aimed the gun—at Dolph—and as Josy watched in shock he pulled the trigger.

Chapter 27

"STAY DOWN!" TY YELLED TO THE PEOPLE crouched with the bartender behind the bar. The bullet in his arm burned like hellfire, but he ignored it, just as he ignored the blood soaking his shirtsleeve, dripping onto the floor.

"I just called 911," the waitress shouted back. "You bastards are all fried."

Tate's hit men answered by pumping more shots toward the jukebox. "Come on out," the ferret-faced man called. "Or we'll kill all those nice folks behind the bar."

"Try it. You'll be dead if you so much as stick your nose in the air," Ty said coolly.

But he felt anything but cool. Josy was out there with Ricky and who knew what the hell they were going to find outside. These two shooters might not have come alone. And he sure as hell didn't trust Ricky Sabatini—not when the stakes were this high. And not when Ricky found out—

The roaring whir of a helicopter interrupted his thoughts. Ty swore under his breath. It sounded like the damned copter was landing right on the roof. He had to finish this and get out there to Josy.

"Hear that?" one of the shooters yelled above the whirring din. "We've got company. More of us any minute now—coming through that door. You can't watch your back and us at the same time!"

"Those are cops, you idiot," Ty shouted back. "My backup. You're surrounded."

Maybe they'd believe him. One instant, one opening, that's all he needed.

"You're screwed," he called out, his tone deliberately arrogant. "They're coming in those doors and the back exit, and you're sandwiched in between. And meanwhile, Sabatini's gotten away with the diamond. All you've got here is me. I'm nothing to Tate."

There was silence from outside then—the helicopter must have landed, Ty thought tersely—and the men waiting to pump him with bullets had fallen silent as well.

"If I were you two dumbasses, I'd cut my losses and try my luck on the road while you still can," Ty followed up roughly.

He listened, bracing his reflexes to react if Tate's men came storming through the exit behind him. But no one came through . . . not the main double doors or the exit.

Not yet.

What the hell was going on outside?

Sweat dripped down his neck. In his mind he saw Josy, frightened, hurt . . .

Fear for her cut through him like a dagger.

He had to get out of here.

Then they blinked. The two shooters apparently realized they were wasting their time here with him instead of following the diamond—or maybe they bought his story of the cops getting ready to storm the saloon. For whatever reason, they made a run for it, spraying bullets behind them as they sprinted for the double doors.

It was the opening he'd been waiting for. Using his good arm, Ty fired five shots in rapid succssion. He saw the red-haired man spiral down, screaming, and ferret-face convulsed as a bullet plunged into his shoulder. The impact stunned him into hesitating for a split second, poised just feet from the doors.

Ty fired again. This time the bullet ripped through his back. Ferret-face thumped to the ground with a crash like a tree cut down at its base.

"Everyone stay down behind the bar!" Ty shouted. He raced toward the fallen men. Crew cut looked critical. He'd been hit in the chest; he was moaning, his eyes glazed. He wasn't going anywhere, but Ty scooped up his gun just the same.

The other guy was gone—a mass of bone, blood, and flesh. Dead as a doorknob.

Ty leapt past both bodies, his attention centered on what he'd find when he opened those doors.

Dolph's huge, muscular frame lay twisted and still in the gritty dirt. Josy swayed in shock, unable to look away.

They'd shot him—just like that. And he was on *their* side.

Her stunned brain tried to make sense of what had happened.

Ricky figured it out first. He now had his revolver trained directly on Len. "Tate's orders, right? Because he let Josy get away."

The blond man's lip curled. "Mr. Tate doesn't like mistakes. Or cops who cause trouble. Okay, Armstrong," he

said, flicking a glance at his partner, who looked as unperturbed after shooting Dolph as if he'd merely kicked a
rock out of his path.

"Now the girl. Count of ten. Unless Sabatini drops his
gun."

Armstrong aimed at Josy, his expression so coldly non-
chalant her heart nearly stopped.

"Len, if she dies, you do too." Ricky's voice was a
harsh rasp. "Are you ready to go to hell right this minute?
If not, let her go."

Len shrugged. "Okay, Sabatini. She can go—after she
brings me the diamond. Is it in that bag? *Is it?*" he demanded of Josy.

"Yes." Her tongue trembled over the word and she saw
him smile. Bastard.

"Good. Bring it to me. Then I'll let you go."

"No deal," Ricky snapped. "Josy, don't move."

She knew why he didn't want her moving toward Len.
It was a ploy, a trap. If she got too close to either Len or
Armstrong, they'd grab her, use her as a shield, and force
Ricky to drop his gun.

But she had to do something to tilt the odds in their favor. And she was desperate with worry about Ty. Somehow she had to give Ricky the upper hand.

"It's okay, Ricky," she said quietly. "I'll do it."

"No."

"I've been wanting to get rid of this diamond all along.
I don't want it one more second." She let her voice go
shrill, emotional. It wasn't difficult, considering she felt
as if she were going to collapse at any moment. "Besides,
he said he'd let me go. Please, it's my only chance."

She hoped that would tip Ricky off. At least he didn't

protest again. As she walked quickly toward Len she prayed Ricky was ready for what was coming next.

"Use what you have," he'd always told her.

Well, she had this duffel.

She held her body rigid as she moved toward Len. But suddenly another barrage of gunshots thundered from inside the saloon, and she stopped breathing, her heart freezing in her chest.

Please God, let Ty be all right, she prayed. Then she quickened her pace and reached Len, but as he stretched out a hand for the duffel she suddenly shoved it with all of her might into his stomach, knocking him off balance.

As he staggered back, two paces away from her, enough to give Ricky a clear shot, she heard it. Thunder, once, twice—and blood sprayed from Len's chest. She felt warm droplets on her neck and shoulders, splattering across her tank top as the blond man crumpled into a heap on the weedy earth. Bile rose in her throat and her knees sagged as she half-turned and saw Ricky firing again, this time at Armstong. But Armstrong was shooting back, and as she watched, Ricky sagged to the ground, blood spurting from his thigh.

"No!" she screamed. But Ricky's shot had gone true— Armstrong was hit, hit worse than Ricky. He twisted with a groan and fell facedown.

He didn't move. Oh, God, was he dead?

Confusion, fear, and desperation clawed at her—then she spotted the rifle in the weeds near Len's body.

She sprang forward, grabbed it up, casting a panicked glance at Len's unmoving form, then at Armstrong's, before staggering toward Ricky. A hawk screeched overhead and she heard sobs—then realized that they were coming from her own throat.

"How bad are you hurt?" she cried, kneeling beside Ricky.

"Only . . . a scratch." But his breath was rasping in his chest and pain laced his voice.

"Help me up. Get . . . the duffel, Josy. Let's get . . . outta here."

"But Ty—"

"You heard him, he said . . . not to wait. Get the duffel."

She didn't want to leave, not without Ty. She glanced uncertainly toward the saloon again, then jumped when Ricky's fingers closed hard around her arm. Startled, the rifle tumbled from her grasp.

"Get the goddamn duffel, Josy. *Now*."

"Fine, you can have the duffel, but I'm not going with you."

Clamping her lips together, she averted her eyes from the scattered bodies and ran back toward the crimson space where Len's blood soaked the dirt.

She needed Ricky to leave her with the rifle, or one of the guns. For when Ty came out—in case he needed help . . .

Seizing the duffel she dashed back to Ricky, casting an uneasy glance at Armstrong. He hadn't moved . . . he was still facedown. He must be dead . . . or unconscious.

Where was Ty?

Ricky was starting to limp toward the car. Blood drenched his pants leg, his shoes, puddled in the dirt as it flowed from his wound.

"We should wrap that, stop the bleeding—"

"Later." He kept on walking, his stride uneven. When they reached the car, he put the rifle on the floor and holstered his gun. "Give me . . . the duffel."

"Here." She thrust it at him, not caring about anything,

certainly not that stupid diamond, not when Ty was still in the saloon and she had no way of helping him—

Suddenly, more gunshots boomed from the saloon, a burst of them, and cold fear surged through her.

"No," she breathed, "please, no." A tremor rocked her body, but suddenly, beside her, Ricky let loose a stream of oaths.

"What the hell! Where's the damned diamond?" he yelled.

He was squeezing the brown wrapping paper in his fist and staring furiously into the duffel. "There's nothing but a few bottles of water and beer and ammo and junk in here! And this goddamned brown paper. What did you do with it?"

"It was in there." In shock, she stared into the duffel. "I saw Ty put it in there myself . . . oh, God."

Ty. She had seen him put the wrapping paper in the duffel bag—but he must have already taken the diamond out, she realized dazedly. *He must have done it when I was in the restroom.*

And then it hit her. Why hadn't she thought of this earlier? He had given the diamond to Roy.

When she'd come outside, the two of them were already standing by the car. It wasn't until Roy drove off that he'd removed the wrapping paper from his pocket and stuffed it into the duffel. But by then, the diamond was no longer wrapped inside . . .

"It doesn't matter, Ricky," she said hurriedly. "You don't need the diamond anymore—you have to turn yourself in. After all that's happened, they'll believe you—"

"Damn it, Josy, I trusted you. You betrayed me too!"

"No! I didn't. I didn't know—"

"I can't go back," he snarled at her, his face twisting

with fury. "I know too much. They'll find a way to kill me, I have to get out of the country. The diamond was my one hope—you just signed my death warrant—"

Suddenly, there was a rush of sound behind them and Josy turned in time to see Dolph springing at her.

She tried to leap out of his reach, but he moved faster, grabbed her with arms like iron bands. One arm snaked around her throat and held her tight, nearly cutting off all her air. She gasped, struggled in vain, and then felt the butt of a gun against her temple.

"Hold still, Josephine, or I'll give you something to squirm about."

Ricky was staring at Dolph in shock. His bruised face had gone gray as dust.

"Kevlar," he said dazedly. "You're wearing . . . a Kevlar vest. I should have known."

Dolph's black eyes glinted. "I know how Tate operates. He doesn't give many second chances. Do you think I'd get within one hundred yards of his men after everything that's happened and *not* wear a bulletproof vest? Len's been drooling to take me down—and to take my place."

He tightened his grip on her throat even more and Josy's vision turned black. She struggled uselessly, slammed her foot against his instep, tried to elbow him, but nothing seemed to touch him. Red spots danced. She heard his laughter as if from a great distance.

"You're killing her—let her go!" Ricky yelled.

"Drop your gun, Sabatini. Kick it over here. Now, or I'll snap her neck."

Ricky set his gun down and kicked it. It skidded through the dirt, landing inches from Dolph's feet. "Now let her go, damn you!"

Dolph laughed. He loosened his grip suddenly and

threw Josy to the ground. She fell heavily, a rock scoring her cheek as she hit the hard-packed dirt.

"Now I'm going to shoot her—and you get to watch. Then it's your turn, Sabatini."

Josy lay stunned, trying to catch her breath. She smelled the dirt, saw an ant crawling over her finger. Her throat felt as if it had been pulverized. She couldn't move. And couldn't speak.

"The diamond is what you're after, Dolph." Ricky was talking fast. "Forget her, it's that bastard sheriff holed up inside the saloon you want. He snatched the diamond from under her nose—and mine. If you want it, you'll—"

"I want her dead more. And you too. I'll get the diamond, don't you worry. But it's for me now—Tate will never see it again."

He pointed the gun at Josy and she felt a faintness wash over her. She tried to brace herself, wondering if she could roll aside at the last moment, somehow avoid the inevitable. But how would she know when to move? Dear God, how?

"Don't!" Ricky cried hoarsely.

"You're next." Dolph smiled. He held the gun and watched Josy's terrified eyes for a moment longer, savoring the moment. The bitch had cost him his job, but he would take her life. He only wished he had time to do it slowly. A bullet at a time . . . a finger, limb, organ at a time.

But Sabatini was right. He still had to get the diamond . . .

A muscle twitched in his jaw. Ricky saw it and sprang forward a fraction of a second before the huge man pulled the trigger.

For one agonized instant he stood between Josy and the

killer. Face-to-face with Dolph. Then the shot roared and his eyes rolled back and death exploded through him.

Josy screamed as Ricky crumpled backward to land a foot from her. Horror surged through her—he was still alive, his eyes glazed, blood pooling at his mouth.

"Nobody ever taught him to take his turn," Dolph murmured.

Josy rolled to her knees, touched Ricky's brow.

"Ricky, no! No, no, no," she screamed.

"No need to miss him. You're joining him. Now." Dolph smiled at her.

A shot rang out. Dazed, Josy closed her eyes. She flinched. Gasped. But she hadn't been hit. Dolph had.

The bullet from Ty's gun shattered Dolph's kneecap and the big man went down screaming. He collapsed in the dirt, blood streaming down his leg, but there was more fury than pain in his face.

Ty stood ten feet away, his gun leveled, and cool murder in his eyes.

"Police. Throw down your weapon. And put your hands above your head."

"Go to hell," Dolph muttered thickly. "You won't kill me. You need me. I'm the only one left . . . to testify against Tate. Or this bitch will go to prison." He laughed, an ugly sound.

"Want to bet?" Ty shot the gun out of his hand. He sprinted toward Dolph, scooped up the weapon. But Dolph wasn't done yet.

He lunged forward with what appeared to be superhuman effort and sliced at Ty with the knife that had suddenly materialized in his hand. The blade narrowly missed Ty's throat.

Ty slugged him, one punch, then another, the blows

echoing sickeningly in the silence outside the saloon, and Dolph went down.

And stayed down.

Ty took the knife, threw it a dozen yards away, and knelt beside Josy.

He was no longer aware of the fire burning through his arm, or of the weakness overtaking him as his blood spilled out. All he knew was that Josy had a cut on her face, bruises on her throat, and her eyes were dazed with horror and grief.

"Ricky," she whispered to him. "We need to help . . . Ricky."

Ty's glance flitted over Ricky Sabatini. The only one who could help Sabatini now was the undertaker.

"Come on, Josy, let me help you up. I have to call—"

He broke off. Sirens pierced the afternoon air. Finally. What the hell had taken them so long?

The kid who'd been playing pool and the bartender came out warily and surveyed the scene. The waitress and the older cowboy edged out behind them. The wail of the sirens came closer.

Ty licked his dry lips and looked down at Josy again. She stared at him with raw grief and a pain that rent his heart. She looked like a pale, broken doll, crouched among the weeds, anguish glistening in her eyes.

"Help Ricky," she whispered again.

Ty smoothed the hair back from her brow. His voice was thick. "Ricky's dead, sweetheart. I'm sorry. The police and the ambulance are coming. You don't have to get up if you don't want to. Everything's going to be all right."

Tears streamed down her face. Ty took her in his arms. He held her close against him, stroking her back and her pale hair that felt gritty with dirt and dust. He listened to her sobs and her pain ached through his chest.

She didn't speak to him, not one word. The only thing she said, over and over, was the name of a dead man.

Ricky.

Chapter 28

SPECIAL AGENT THOMAS BEAUMONT TOSSED
the bulging file folder onto Ty's desk, his piercing gaze
filled with skepticism.

"All I can say is that it's a lucky thing for the Warner
woman that Dolph Lundgren lived," he snorted. "And that
he's agreed to testify against his former boss. Otherwise,
she'd be looking at a prison term right now. Accessory after the fact, aiding and abetting . . ."

"Neither one applies," Ty responded, his voice hard.
"And you know it. Josy Warner didn't even have a clue
what was in the package Sabatini left with her doorman
until a scant few days ago. Then she turned it in—to me.
That hardly makes her an accessory to the theft."

"She was planning to give it back to Sabatini in that bar
in Wheatland," Beaumont pointed out. He looked like a
taller, fair-haired Tom Cruise. But something about the
way he held his shoulders and the curl of his lips oozed an
off-putting, hard-nosed arrogance. "That sounds like aiding and abetting to me."

"Give it up, Beaumont. She turned the diamond over to
me. I turned it over to my cousin with orders to hand it
over to the Feds. What more could you ask? Josy Warner

even accompanied me after that, to assist in locating and questioning Sabatini. She nearly lost her life by cooperating with my investigation and because of her, you now have a chance at taking down Caventini and Tate for good. Plus, the Golden Eye gets returned to its rightful owner in Zurich."

"She kept it hidden for weeks," observed John Snow, the other FBI agent who'd been working on the case since the melee at Slattery's Saloon. "Even after Sabatini skipped bail and disappeared. She also fled a murder scene. Sorry, but that doesn't look to me like she's some hapless innocent—"

"We've been over this before. She trusted Sabatini. That's what it comes down to." Ty locked gazes with the low-key Snow. After spending the past seventy-two hours going over every detail with these two, as well as with the pair of detectives from the NYPD who had arrived in Thunder Creek yesterday to question Dolph in his hospital room, he had succeeded in taking their measure. Beaumont was ambitious, stiff-necked, and by-the-book. Snow was more laid-back, on the surface at least, but his receding hairline, comfortable paunch, and mild brown eyes belied a razor-sharp mind.

"Look, Snow, you need her cooperation. She's nothing but an innocent bystander who got dragged into the muck. If you really want to go after a woman who has absolutely no connection to organized crime or corruption in the NYPD, that's your choice—but it looks to me like a losing proposition. You've got big fish on the hook—if you're smart you'll go ahead and fry them and throw the minnows back."

"We don't need a two-bit sheriff telling us what to do," Beaumont snapped.

Ty ignored him. "Seems to me the taxpayers would be better served by your putting away a supposedly respectable business tycoon who not only commissioned an international diamond theft but is in bed with New York City's top crime boss—rather than persecuting a woman who got dragged into something that had nothing to do with her."

"You make it sound easy." Snow sighed. "It won't be." But deep down he knew Barclay was right about pursuing the woman. Beaumont was just being his usual asshole, pit-bull self.

Snow had already concluded that pressing charges against the Warner woman wasn't going to accomplish much. She'd been loyal to Sabatini, and he'd gotten some bad breaks and made some bad decisions. But the big prize here was Caventini—and Tate. If they could make the charges stick against those two . . .

If.

"No one's ever been able to get a conviction against Caventini before," Beamont pointed out caustically. He ignored Snow as the older man took a turn around the sheriff's office.

Beyond the window the golden Wyoming day contrasted with the ugliness that Snow and Beaumont dealt with on a daily basis. But unlike Snow, Beaumont wasn't interested in the view. He was only interested in nailing as many suspects as possible, and getting the maximum amount of credit for it.

"Tate's connection is going to be even tougher to prove. You can bet your ass he'll have a dream team of high-profile superlawyers defending him—and they'll sue our asses when it's all over if we don't make the charges stick."

"Then make them stick. You've got Dolph's testimony."

"A hit man? You really think he's going to be believable in front of a jury?" Beaumont scoffed.

"Miss Warner's testimony will help," Snow pointed out thoughtfully.

Ty nodded. "If you don't mess up her reputation by filing charges against her."

Beaumont and Snow exchanged glances. *Match point,* Ty thought with grim triumph.

He tried not to think about how Josy was barely speaking to him. Or about how pale and drawn she'd looked when he sat in on her interviews with the FBI and the NYPD detectives who'd flown in to question her. They hadn't had a chance for a private conversation since their lunch in Bitter Gulch at the Country Goose Diner.

Between all hell breaking loose after the Wheatland shoot-out, and keeping up to speed with fast-breaking events in the rustling case, Ty had barely slept. And Josy had been tied up full time with investigators from one official branch or another.

He doubted if she'd want to talk to him anyway. He'd tricked her about bringing the diamond to Sabatini—and he hadn't even had a chance to explain that he'd given it to Roy for her own good, to minimize her risk of felony charges. From the moment he'd first heard about this entire mess Sabatini had dragged her into, Ty's priority had been to keep Josy safe, and to keep her the hell out of jail.

He'd gone out on a limb to try to help her find Sabatini and save his life too—but that hadn't turned out very well.

And now she wouldn't forgive him for that. He'd realized it as soon as he saw her face when Sabatini lay dead beside her.

Too much history there, too many recriminations now.

It didn't really matter, he tried to tell himself. She'd be going back to New York Monday after the wedding was over anyway. That's what Roy had heard frm Corinne. She already had a plane ticket booked.

Ty's chest felt heavy, like there was nothing but dead weight inside as he sat with the two FBI agents.

It's just the letdown after a big bust, he tried to tell himself. There'd been nonstop repercussions after the shoot-out at Slattery's Saloon. In New York, Caventini and Tate had both been arrested. Dolph was in custody and ready to spill his guts. And although he hadn't been formally charged yet, the cops in NYPD's Internal Affairs Division were looking very seriously at the allegations against Captain Wallace Becker.

Ty's role in the case was almost over—until and if they needed him to testify at trial.

After the wedding, he'd probably never see Josy Warner again.

Which is good, he thought, as Snow's cell phone rang and Beaumont left the room in search of coffee. There was no future for the two of them. Especially not after what had happened to her hero, Sabatini. Ty's stomach twisted.

No future, he repeated to himself, as if somehow repeating it would ease the sense of loss he felt.

He'd never even thought about a future with Josy before, never even been able to imagine what that would look like. Especially since they lived in two very different worlds and . . . hell, she'd made it clear from the way she practically looked through him ever since the shoot-out, that whatever brief glimmer of connection might have existed between them was over and out.

Done.

Which was just as well.

Who am I trying to kid?

"Yeah, I got it," Snow was saying rapidly into his cell. "Right away. Keep me posted."

He snapped the phone shut and wheeled toward Ty. "You're not going to believe this. TB!" he shouted, and Beaumont rushed back into the room.

"Wallace Becker committed suicide an hour ago at his home in Staten Island, New York," Snow announced. "A suicide note has been found. We don't know the full contents yet, but preliminary investigations have revealed a link to activities that have a bearing on the present case."

"Hot damn." Beaumont whistled. "Talk about manna from heaven."

"NYPD Internal Affairs has already dispatched an investigator, due here late this afternoon to question the Warner woman," Snow said.

"It looks more and more like Sabatini was telling the truth. I don't think you need to worry too much about your Ms. Warner at this point," Snow said to Ty. "I suspect that with the evidence Becker will have left behind, she's pretty much home free."

"She's not *my* Ms. Warner. My interest in her isn't personal," Ty said sharply.

"Yeah?" Beaumont's lip curled.

Snow grinned outright. He had seen Thunder Creek's sheriff cast more than one glance at Josy Warner during the interview process and those glances had held more than professional curiosity. A great deal more.

"If you say so," he told Ty Barclay with a shrug. "But . . ." A sly glint shone in those keen brown eyes. "I have to tell you, Sheriff, you sure as hell could have fooled me."

Chapter 29

JOSY PARKED HER BLAZER DOWN THE STREET from the sheriff's department building and sat behind the wheel for a moment, bracing herself for what she had to do next. Not only for the meeting with an internal affairs official from the NYPD who had flown out to interview her, but for yet another encounter with Ty.

She didn't want to see him anymore. She just wanted Corinne and Roy's wedding to be over. She wanted to leave Thunder Creek, go back to New York, and try to tear Ty Barclay out of her heart through distance, work, and time.

And she'd do it too. Even if it killed her.

But first she had to get through more police interviews today—and the wedding tomorrow.

The past few days had served up another kind of ordeal. Every night when she tried to sleep, nightmares woke her. She kept seeing Ricky jumping in front of her, taking the bullet meant for her, saving her life.

And falling dead before her eyes.

She kept hearing the thunder of that shot that had left him lying flat in the dirt, gone forever from the world—and from her.

She'd wake up chilled and crying. And filled with grief as deep and jagged as the steepest Wyoming canyon.

Finally this morning she'd managed to sleep until ten, and then get to the hospital to visit Chance. She'd stopped at Bessie's Diner on the way, bringing him a bag of warm sweet rolls and one of Bessie's blueberry pies, and it had cheered her when she walked into his room to see him sitting up in bed, relentlessly zapping through all the channels of the television suspended from the ceiling.

"How come none of my nurses are as gorgeous as you?" he complained as she came over to the bed and leaned down to kiss his cheek.

"Oh, puh-leeze. Don't you ever stop?" she'd chided him. "I look like hell and you know it." But as she'd begun setting out the pie and the sweet rolls on a foam plate on his bedside table, he'd told her he'd never seen a more beautiful woman and that if he wasn't under doctor's orders he'd be down on the floor, on one knee, ready to propose.

"Propose what?" she'd shot back, but she was laughing when she said it, the first genuine laugh Josy had managed in days. "Never mind," she'd told him, handing him the plate with both a sweet roll and a generous slice of pie. "I don't want to know."

Somehow or other, in the course of an hour-long visit she'd actually been able to engage him in a semi-serious conversation. She'd soon realized that beneath his buoyant charm and jokes he was frustrated more than he would ever willingly reveal. It rankled him no end that he'd failed to learn the identity of the brains behind the rustling operation. Even knowing that he'd helped identify and capture two of the major players didn't satisfy him. And no matter how she tried to praise him or buck him up, she still detected the gloom of defeat in those normally good-natured eyes.

"I thought I was so close," he grumbled, raking a hand through his hair. "But they weren't really ready to throw in with me, or to turn on their boss. They were this close to killing me. If I hadn't had Ty backing me up you'd be crying over my grave right now."

She shuddered. "So you didn't find out who the big boss was. You still captured two of the gang. And maybe some more evidence will be found that will point at whoever is in charge."

"Well, it hasn't yet—not from what I hear. And so far, Owens and Barnes aren't talking. If they'd start squawking, they might even be able to cop a plea, but they haven't opened their damn mouths."

"Sounds like they're either very afraid of someone . . . or very loyal to that person," Josy remarked. She thought of all she'd done and risked out of loyalty to Ricky. And of what he'd ultimately sacrificed out of loyalty to her.

She probably knew better than most how powerful an influence loyalty could be. And just how dangerous.

Loyalty to Ricky had led her to where she was today— now—outside of the sheriff's office in Thunder Creek, trying to find the strength to go inside.

Just get it over with, she told herself, and opened the door of the Blazer.

"I'm back." She walked through the paneled lobby of the one-story brick building and offered a wan smile to Ty's efficient, birdlike secretary, who looked up from her desk, peering at Josy through oval, pink-rimmed glasses.

"So I see." The woman returned her smile, clucking her tongue sympathetically. "I'm sure you must be pretty darned sick of this place, aren't you? Wait just a moment, he's expecting you—"

The door to Ty's office opened then and the two FBI agents, Snow and Beaumont, strode out. They'd questioned her for four hours yesterday, and two the day before. Ty walked out right behind them.

For a moment when he first saw her, she thought she glimpsed something in his eyes, something human and warm and possibly even concerned, but that absurd impression quickly vanished, leaving her certain she must have imagined it.

Especially when he nodded at her in a businesslike way that cut her to the quick.

"Good, you're right on time. Detective Rossman is waiting inside."

She nodded, schooling her face to match his impersonal expression. But as she edged past him into the office, which she had come to know all too well in the past few days, she suddenly stopped dead, shock sweeping through her.

"It's him." She clutched Ty's arm, her fingers digging into his flesh. "That's the man I told you about!"

"What man?" He moved closer to her instinctively.

The detective had risen to his feet. He was tall and leanly built with dark blond hair and he wore a conservative dark suit. She had seen him once before. It seemed like months ago, but it had only been weeks.

"You're the man in Archie's house—the one with the gun!"

"And you're the one who got away." Bemused hazel eyes swept over her, and the man stretched out his hand.

"Detective Ron Rossman, NYPD Internal Affairs."

Ty steered Josy to one of the chairs facing his desk. He

closed the office door. "This is the man you saw in the house in Brooklyn? The one you ran away from?"

"Yes. I thought . . . I thought he was one of the bad guys."

"Why weren't you in uniform?" Ty asked Rossman.

Rossman sat down in the chair next to Ty's desk, addressing his answer to Ty. "I was officially off-duty. There was already an ongoing internal affairs investigation into the charges made by Ricky Sabatini, but I wasn't assigned to the case. Still, I had my own suspicions that if Captain Becker *was* involved in corruption, his influence could have possibly extended even into internal affairs. I met with my boss, who shared my concerns, and he put me on special assignment."

"So you were following me? Or . . . who? Ricky? Archie?" Josy asked, a hint of skepticism in her tone.

"I don't blame you for being suspicious, Ms. Warner. In fact, I respect it. But let me assure you, I did not have you under surveillance at that time. The night Archie McDonald was killed, we had a tip that something big was going down. Oliver Tate had returned early from Cancún to find that the Golden Eye diamond he'd stolen from yet another criminal was missing. Apparently it didn't take him long to deduce that Ricky Sabatini had taken it—and he gave orders for his men to find Sabatini and the diamond ASAP."

Rossman picked up a pencil from Ty's desk and tapped it absently against the palm of his hand. "Ricky was nowhere to be found," he continued, "but as we learned later, Tate's thugs paid visits to nearly everyone Ricky'd had semifrequent contact with over the past six months—and that included, among others, Rafe Terrell, his retired ex-partner; a woman he'd dated for several months; his snitch, Archie—and you. Your apartment was ransacked that night not because they knew the diamond had been hidden there—only because they guessed someone close to Ricky was either hiding him or the diamond or both—and they were covering all their bases at once. Unfortunately, the tip we got was limited—it hinted that something related to Tate and Sabatini was going down in Brooklyn. So we tracked down Archie, but we got there too late. Hammer had already killed Archie. And you had been there and gone, taking the diamond with you."

"When I saw you in that house that night, with a gun, I just assumed you were after the diamond too—" She broke off, shaking her head.

If she hadn't run away, if she'd stayed and Detective Rossman had taken the diamond from her right then, maybe Ricky would still be alive, she thought, clenching her hands in her lap.

Or . . . maybe not . . .

"We've been able to piece together a lot of evidence backing up the version of events Ricky told us during our initial questioning. We still have a lot more to do, especially now in light of what's happened with Captain Becker . . . but I think it's safe to say Ricky's name will be cleared. At least in regard to everything besides his theft of the diamond."

Rossman glanced at Ty, standing with his arms folded across his chest, listening grim-mouthed to the explanations.

"The good news is," Rossman told him, "we now have evidence to prove that Becker did have an accomplice in internal affairs—he's the guy who removed Sabatini's evidence from the evidence room. And he is being questioned even as we speak."

"So why do you need to see Ms. Warner today?" Ty asked. "She's already told me and the FBI her story a dozen times. And she's returning to New York in a matter of days—or so I've been informed." There was an edge to his tone.

Josy stared at him. He sounded bitter. Or angry. Why in the world should he be either one of those things? Because she was leaving? And she hadn't told him directly?

He was the one who'd made it clear he wanted as little to do with her as possible following the terrible events at Slattery's Saloon. Aside from being present at all of her interviews with the FBI and police officials, he had virtually ignored her, and hadn't given any sign of wanting to exchange more than polite formalities with her.

And even before then, she reminded herself, Ty was the one who'd been all business the morning after they made love at the Barclay cabin. Obviously, he had realized he was getting in too deep—or that she was—and he'd backed off.

That hadn't changed, not as far as she could see. It hadn't changed even when they'd both almost died out in that field of dirt and weeds.

So why should it matter to him now that she was leaving Thunder Creek?

"You know how these things work, Sheriff Barclay." Rossman shrugged his shoulders. "The sooner the witness is interviewed, the better. Details tend to fade with time. And I need to turn in a preliminary report by Monday. Ms. Warner's statement will be of value to me in writing that report. And since someone apparently pulled some strings allowing her to remain in Wyoming for several days before returning to New York for further questioning," he paused briefly and shot a meaningful glance at Ty, whose face remained as dark and impenetrable as rock, "the powers that be shipped me out here to jump-start the process."

"They wanted me in New York sooner? How... who... I wasn't told," Josy said, surprised.

"We'll talk about it later," Ty told her tersely.

"I didn't think we had anything further to talk about—now or later," she replied, her tone as brusque as his.

For a moment those cobalt eyes pierced hers and she saw once more the flicker of something beneath, some emotion she couldn't quite read.

"Neither did I," he returned abruptly. He broke the glance and turned swiftly to Rossman. "Let's get this over with then, detective. I still have a rustling investigation demanding my attention and suspects being bound over today for trial."

Yes, Josy thought bleakly as the questioning began anew, *the rustling investigation. Back to business as usual for Sheriff Barclay.*

An hour and a half later Rossman finally thanked her for her cooperation, gave her his card, and instructed her to call his office for a follow-up interview after she returned to New York. She left the office quickly and was surprised when Ty excused himself and walked her out to her car.

They paused at the Blazer in silence. Neither had said a word since they'd left the building. Above, the sky was as beautiful and clear as it had been the day she first arrived in Thunder Creek. When Ada Scott had still been merely a name on a sheet of paper, when she had never set eyes on the sheriff of Thunder Creek.

"What was that Rossman said about someone pulling strings to keep me from having to return to New York?"

she asked, breaking the uncomfortable silence that loomed like an invisible wall between them.

"I made a few calls." Ty shoved his hands into his pockets. "Basically I vouched for you to the authorities in New York. It was just a matter of persuading them that another few days wouldn't hurt, and that you'd contact them as soon as you returned from Thunder Creek."

Josy thought she knew exactly why he'd gone to the trouble. "The wedding," she said quietly. "You knew it would upset Corinne—and therefore Roy—if I couldn't be there. And you're right, it would have. Corinne already thinks the wedding is cursed." She mustered a polite smile. "I'm sure you wanted them to get off to as smooth a start as possible."

"There was that," he began. The tension in his tone made her lift her gaze to his face.

"Was there another reason?"

"Yeah." He was studying her, his expression unreadable. "I wasn't ready to—"

"Ty!"

A short, wiry deputy popped out of the building behind them. "The DA needs a meeting pronto. Judge Mason wants to see all the parties in chambers prior to the hearing. We gotta hustle to the courthouse."

Ty's jaw clenched. "Sorry. Can we finish this later?"

"If you'd like." She wasn't sure she saw the point. Every time they spoke like this—uneasy, careful, and strained with each other—a little part of her died inside.

To think that they'd made love with so much passion and joy, that they'd held each other all through the night and through the dawn—and now . . .

Now they were like strangers. Ty was striding back to his office and she was sliding into the driver's seat of the

Blazer, watching him walk away from her. She couldn't remember the last time she'd felt so empty. Or so alone.

There were so many things she wanted to say to him and couldn't. And there were a thousand things she needed to do before Corinne's wedding and before she returned to New York.

But right now all she wanted to do was cry.

A strange feeling came over Josy as she turned onto Angel Road and eased the Blazer toward Ada's house at no more than twenty miles per hour.

This might be the last time she came down this road for a while. Ada had invited her to visit over Christmas and she'd accepted. But right now, Christmas seemed a long time away.

And she was startled by the ache already gnawing inside of her because after the wedding tomorrow she wouldn't see her newly discovered grandmother again until snowflakes tumbled from the sky and Rockefeller Center was brimming with ice skaters.

Odd how she had become attached so quickly. To Ada, to this small, cozy house on Angel Road, to Corinne and Roberta and Bessie . . . to Thunder Creek.

Not to mention Thunder Creek's sheriff. But thinking about leaving him hurt worse than all the rest.

Don't think about him. Don't even try to guess what he was about to say before. Think about going back to New York, to your own apartment, trashed as it might be—to work, Francesca . . .

But the only bearable aspect of work was the thought of seeing Jane and Reese again. Even though the fall sketches were nearly completed, and she ought to be able to finish them in the next twenty-four hours, she couldn't drum up any enthusiasm for turning them over to Francesca. What was wrong with her?

As she expected, Roberta's Jeep was parked at the end of the lane. In Bessie's Diner that morning, Roberta had told her that she and Ada were leaving work early to assemble favors for the wedding dinner—small pieces of candy wrapped in lacy bags and tied with lavender ribbon. She'd invited Josy to stop by and lend a hand.

Josy only hoped the task would take her mind off the desolation filling up all the spaces in her heart.

She tapped on the screen door but didn't hear any voices and there was no sign of Ada or Roberta in the living room.

"Anybody home?" she called out, trying to sound cheerful, but the dead silence inside immediately struck her as odd. "Ada? Roberta?"

Maybe they're working out back in the garden, she thought, but even as she turned to go around to the back of the house, Roberta called out cheerily, "Come on in, Josy. We're in the kitchen."

She pushed open the door and hurried across the living room. "Do you still need help with the favors—"

She faltered at the kitchen doorway, her mouth frozen in astonishment.

Ada was seated in one of the kitchen chairs, her hands strapped to the arms of the chair with gray duct tape, and another strip of duct tape covered her mouth.

Roberta stood beside her chair. She held a rifle and it was pointed at Josy's heart.

"Took you long enough to get here. Come on in and sit down. I have a phone call to make."

Chapter 30

"SHERIFF, SORRY TO INTERRUPT YOU, BUT Roberta Hawkins is on the phone—she says it's vital that she speak to you right now."

Standing inside the air-conditioned courthouse with his cell phone to his ear, and several deputies and the assistant district attorney gathered in a knot around him, Ty frowned.

"Helen, this isn't a good time. I'm waiting for the DA to come out of the judge's chambers. Take a message and tell her that whatever it is, I'll get back to her."

"Sheriff, you don't understand." The birdlike secretary's normally composed voice sounded high-pitched, almost breathless. "She says it's urgent. She says she needs to talk to you right away or . . . somebody will *die*."

What the hell? Baffled and annoyed—and suddenly, as a dark premonition spiked through him, filled with foreboding—Ty spoke in a clipped tone. "Put her through."

Roberta's voice on the line sounded upbeat and breezy. "Sheriff, it's me. Roberta. Glad you took my call. It means your little girlfriend might just live."

"What the hell are you talking about, Roberta? Where are you?"

"I'm at Ada's house, of course. I know how fond you are of Ada. And guess who's here? Josy Wosy pudding pie."

He heard her laugh suddenly, a harsh, nervous laugh that sounded very different from the good-natured waitress at Bessie's Diner.

"I have a rifle pointed right at her sweet little heart. And I'm going to pull the trigger too. Unless you get your butt over here, Sheriff."

"What's this all about, Roberta?" He managed to ask the question in an even tone, despite the fact that every muscle in his body was coiled with tension. Cold fear had replaced his initial shock. He'd have thought this was some kind of sick joke, except that Roberta didn't sound like she was joking. She sounded odd—almost as if she were high. There was a note of desperation beneath the bravado in her voice that chilled him to his core.

"It's about getting what I want. And what I want is my boys set free. You're not locking them up like their daddy. Not unless you want me to blow your little girlfriend's head off. And Ada's too."

"Take it easy, Roberta. I think you need to explain this to me some." The DA walked out just then and Ty snapped his fingers over his head to get the man's attention. The DA quickened his steps and approached, watching him in tense silence.

The chilling expression in Ty's eyes and his carefully calm tone speaking into the phone had already alerted the deputies that something was wrong. Everyone fell silent, watching him with grave expectation.

"Bullshit, Sheriff." Roberta's voice rose. "You know all you need to know. Just get my boys—you know 'em as Denny and Fred—out of the lockup and bring 'em over to

Ada's place. You let us all get in my Jeep and head out of town, with no one following us, and I promise you, I'll let Josy and Ada go just as soon as I feel safe. You've got twenty minutes."

The phone went dead.

Ty was already shouting orders as he sprinted to his car.

"Let me take the tape off her mouth," Josy said quietly, as Roberta dragged a kitchen chair toward the window, where she could sit in the corner and see the road. "You don't need to keep her gagged anymore."

"True enough." Roberta shrugged. "Go ahead. Just don't try anything. I've been shootin' tin cans, foxes, and rabbits since I was eleven and I never miss."

Josy knelt down beside Ada and as gently as possible peeled the gray tape from her lips. "It's going to be all right," she said softly, her eyes locking with her grandmother's. To her surprise Ada didn't look nearly as pale or frightened as she would have expected—instead, she was flushed. Anger steamed from her faded brown eyes.

"Roberta, you are fired," she snapped the moment the duct tape was gone.

"Fired?" The woman shot her a thin smile. "Well, I don't know what you and Bessie and ole Katy will do without me. I'm the best damned waitress who ever worked at Bessie's place—everyone knows it. But I'm never waitressing again. Me and my boys—we're going to live in style."

"Denny Owens and Fred Barnes are your sons? Why didn't you ever tell anyone?" Josy asked, straightening up. She was wondering frantically how she could get that rifle away from Roberta. The woman was bigger than she was, and no fool.

But it had to be done.

"It served my purposes for no one to know, that's why. Things worked out much better with no apparent connection between us. No one—including our dear sheriff and that low-down sneaky cop, Chance—even knew our real names. That way no one could catch on by finding out the boys had a record."

Roberta shook her head and her dangling turquoise earrings clinked around her face. "I didn't count on Chance being a cop, not at all. He made a pretty good rustler—he almost had us fooled—until he kept pushing the boys to tell him the name of their boss. I figured at first he was trying to horn in on our operation—and to turn the boys against me, but then . . ."

Her eyes grew crafty. "I started wondering if he was a cop. He just wouldn't give up, you know. Either way, we decided he had to be dealt with." She stared ruefully at Josy. "Too bad that you and Ty Barclay got in the way that night. If my boys were still free, you and Ada wouldn't be in this pickle."

Ada sent the other woman a scornful glance. "Rustlers are scum of the earth. You needn't look so proud."

"I am proud." Roberta stuck out her chin defiantly. "I'm as proud of me and my boys as you are of that smarty-pants grandson of yours at the university. Let me tell you something—we took over the family business when my husband couldn't run it anymore, and we grew it even bigger than it ever was. Thanks to me, I guess. When Luther was in charge, we were small potatoes. I found ways to outsmart or outbribe the brand inspectors Luther never dreamed of. And I made a lot more money rustling cows and horses than I'd make in a hundred years waiting tables at Bessie's."

"Where is Luther now?" Josy asked, stepping casually around Ada's chair, trying to position herself in front of it.

But Roberta jerked the rifle toward her. "Hold on, pumpkin. Back up. We don't want you getting too close now, do we? I need you—to get my boys back."

"Where's Luther?" Ada spoke up, her voice frostier than Josy had ever heard it. "He walked out on you, didn't he?"

"Like hell he did." Roberta flushed. Anger and resentment blazed in her eyes. "He got arrested over in Oregon two years ago. He's in prison for rustling, that's where he is. And I miss that man more'n you'll ever know. But he'll get out in another couple of years and when he does, we'll have a cool little fortune ready for his new start—for our new start too. We'll just go underground until then, and come up somewhere else with brand-new names and IDs and presto, get on with livin' the good life."

"So all this time, you've been the one behind the rustling operation. You're BJ, the big boss," Josy said.

"Bobbi June, that's me. Don't look so surprised." Roberta glanced quickly at the road, then back to her two hostages, her grip steady on the rifle. "My Luther taught me everything he knew, and I figured out even more on my own. I'm a real independent twenty-first-century woman," she added, her lips twisting. "Of course it helped dating some of Thunder Creek's most eligible ranchers."

She spoke quickly, her gaze flitting back and forth between the road and her hostages. "It wasn't at all hard finding out what those nice older gentlemen were up to— where they wintered their cattle, when they were setting out patrols. And they knew all about their neighbors' stock too. Once a man's been divorced or widowered, he enjoys a woman's company and the chance to tell her all about how smart he is and what a good businessman and every little problem he encounters. Luther never had the inside scoop I did, and he didn't think as big as I do, but he still did pretty well. Until he got caught."

"Your sons got caught too," Josy pointed out. "Do you see a pattern here?"

Roberta's gaze sharpened and her lips stretched into a thin, hard line. "You'd best watch what you say, Miss New York City," she snapped.

"If I were you, I'd want to cut my losses and take off," Josy went on doggedly.

Roberta shook her head. She looked grim, tense, and somehow older, the deep lines around her eyes and mouth standing out in bright relief in the sunshine that streamed through the kitchen window.

"Not without my boys," she stated flatly. "Once Sheriff Barclay trades 'em for the two of you, we'll be out of here quicker than ice cream off a spoon."

"You're going to miss Corinne's wedding," Josy said in a low tone, all the while listening for the sound of sirens. She thought she heard them, far in the distance, a muted jangle.

"Can't be helped. Poor Corinne's going to be real shook up. But my boys come first. Now, let's go into the living room, ladies. We got company comin' any minute now."

She ordered Josy to cut the duct tape that bound Ada's wrists. "There's a vegetable knife in that drawer—take it out, nice and slow. Just cut the tape and then set the knife down in the sink. No quick moves. Nobody has to get hurt here—not if I get what I want."

Josy followed her instructions exactly, then helped Ada to stand up. She was shaky on her feet, no doubt sore from the bonds and the lack of blood circulation in her wrists, but her chin was high and there was a blaze of anger in her eyes.

"It's going to be okay," Josy said under her breath as she slipped an arm around her grandmother's shoulders. "Ty will be here soon."

"Quit whispering!" Roberta barked. There was a wild wariness in her eyes. "You're not allowed to talk to each other. Now get in the living room—quick. Don't go forgetting that I'm right behind you and my finger's on the trigger."

As they crossed the braided rug, the sound of sirens wailing down Angel Road filled the house and Josy glanced back to see the color draining from Roberta's cheeks.

"Okay, now. You'd better pray he brought my boys. Go stand in front of the window, both of you. I want them to see that I can pick you off anytime I choose."

Chapter 31

TY RACED THROUGH THE TREES WITH SINGLE-minded purpose, not even glancing back as he out-distanced the deputy trying to keep up with him by a good ten yards. His strides were long and powerful, his eyes fixed on his destination. He'd left his car on the main road when everyone else had turned down Angel Road, and had veered off at a dead run, sprinting across the ridge like a man possessed, then circling a quarter mile through the brush and around to the line of trees that backed Ada's house. He ran as he'd never run before, his feet thundering furiously across the damp grassy earth.

This—*now*—was his only hope, his only chance to get into the house without being spotted.

Only a short while ago he'd thought he'd have time to talk to Josy, to tell her how he felt, to see if they could ever bridge the chasm that had sprung up between them with the death of Ricky Sabatini.

But now they might not have any time at all.

He sucked in air and ran faster.

Every second was going to count . . .

• • •

"Move it, faster!" Roberta snapped as the stream of police vehicles and two ambulances roared down Angel Road. Ada moved slowly, stiffly, toward the windows, her spine rigid. Josy lagged behind, taking one step, two . . .

"Lord," Roberta muttered nervously behind her. "Did he bring my boys or just every damn cop in the state of Wyoming? He'd better have them out there or he's going to need both of those ambulances," she blustered.

The first few vehicles turned sharply right and screeched to a halt in the drive, positioned sideways as a barrier. Officers spilled out, crouching behind the cars, drawing guns.

A voice called out through a bullhorn. "Roberta. This is Deputy Frank Tanner. You served me bacon and eggs yesterday at Bessie's. You know me—I gave you a big tip. And you know I don't want you or anyone else to get hurt."

"To hell with you, Tanner, where the hell is Barclay?" Roberta shouted.

"He can't hear you." Josy twisted her head slightly so she could look at Roberta. "Maybe we should go outside."

"Shut up! Get up there by the window!"

"Roberta, I'm going to call you on Ada's phone now. Pick it up so we can talk. No one needs to get hurt."

"The hell they don't. I want to see my boys!" Roberta yelled again just as the phone rang. "You get it, bring it to me!" she ordered Josy.

Josy went to the cordless phone on the side table near the sofa and lifted it from its cradle. It had already rung four times.

"Don't answer it, bring it to me!" Roberta commanded. Sweat glistened on her face. "Ada, don't turn around. Stay right where you are."

Josy moved back over the braided rug, toward Roberta,

but suddenly her hands fumbled and the phone fell to the floor.

"Sorry," she muttered, kneeling quickly. But instead of picking up the phone, she grabbed the edge of the rug and yanked it toward her with all her might.

Roberta's feet flew out from under her. She went down, the rifle tilting sideways, but she squeezed the trigger as she fell.

"Run, Ada!" Josy screamed and dove toward Roberta.

She threw herself on the woman just as she landed on the floor. As adrenaline pounded through her, she wrenched the rifle away and threw it as far as she could across the room. There was no time to hesitate—she slammed her fist into Roberta's jaw at the exact moment that Ty bolted in from the kitchen, his Glock in hand.

But there was no need for his gun. The impact of the punch had sent pain throbbing through Josy's arm, but it had also sent Roberta's head snapping back.

She lay on the floor, unmoving. Unconscious.

Josy rolled off her, her breath coming in ragged gasps. She stared up at Ty. She was trembling all over, but the expression of relief and joy on his face made her heart go still.

"Thank God." His voice was hoarse. "Are you hurt?" He knelt beside her, raised her to her feet. And folded her into his arms.

"I'm fine . . . but Roberta . . ."

"She's breathing, you didn't kill her, but you decked her good, didn't you?" His hands were threading through her hair, sifting through the soft strands, while a raspy laugh came from his throat.

"I almost forgot how tough you are—you didn't even

need me, did you?" he whispered, and his hands suddenly cradled her face, his eyes so tender she couldn't breathe.

Suddenly everything else fell away. Everything else ceased to exist. She spoke without thinking, without holding back. Straight from the heart.

"How can you say that? I'll always need you." Sudden hot tears brimmed from her eyes and then she was crushed against his chest.

"Oh, my God. You don't know how much I wanted to hear you say that." Ty kissed her mouth, gently, hungrily, and with a need that made her body melt. "Because I need you too. These last few days have been hell, Josy. But now you're back in my arms." He stroked her head, resting against his chest. His voice shook. "And it feels too right for me to ever let you go."

They were interrupted by voices from the door and people rushing into the house.

"Um, Ty? Ada Scott is safe outside with Kevin. Hate to interrupt but . . . this *is* a crime scene," Deputy Tanner said drily.

He was grinning, and all the officers behind him were grinning. Deputy Ed Carter, who'd burst through the kitchen door a good thirty seconds after Ty, was grinning too.

"Roberta's out cold," Ty responded, looking at Tanner, though he hadn't released Josy or even loosened his hold on her.

"Cuff her first and then let the paramedics get a look at her. Carter, you take Ada's statement. Tell her that Josy's okay. I'm going to . . . question Ms. Warner personally."

Josy heard guffaws and chuckles as Ty draped an arm around her waist and led her out of the house.

They stood in back, near the barn, and held each other.

"We need to get a few things straight," Ty said, his lips brushing against the top of her head.

At the down-to-business tone of his voice her heart splintered. For a moment she'd thought everything was all right, after all, between them, but now she knew. Things weren't all right.

They couldn't be. Perhaps in the moment they'd both gotten carried away, but . . .

She dropped her arms from his neck, lifted her chin. "I know. I know exactly what you're going to say." She forced a pallid facsimile of a smile. "This is never going to work out."

She tried to sound matter-of-fact and mature. *Pretend you're Reese,* she told herself dully. Reese, to whom short-term, doomed relationships were as common as cabs in Times Square.

"I know you don't love me and that I could never replace Meg in your life. You don't have to spell it out," she said quickly, not giving him a chance to interrupt. "And I know that I'm going back to New York and you're staying here in Thunder Creek and I've already told you I wouldn't be happy anyway, being second best, second pick. I need more than that, I *want* more than that. So as much as I love—I mean, care for you," she amended quickly, "it won't work. For so many reasons—"

"Like hell it won't."

"What?" She stared at him blankly.

"Were you about to say you love me?"

Her chin shot up a notch higher. "I'd like to know what that has to do with anything."

"Give me a break." He studied her beautiful face, uplifted to his, all the while stroking her cheek with his thumb. "I thought this was going to be about Ricky."

She could only stare at him, speechless. How could it be about Ricky? Suddenly, understanding struck and she felt her heart sink into the pit of her stomach. "You mean, things can't work out because I tried to help him. You can't get past that, can you?"

"No, sweetheart. It's not that." His somber eyes glinted into hers even as his big hand cradled her nape.

"I thought you were the one who couldn't get past what I did. I was too late, I let Ricky get killed. I know how much he meant to you and I let you down—"

"Ty, no!" She shook her head. "It wasn't your fault. You risked everything to try to help me save Ricky. I'll never forget that." She drew in a breath. "He died protecting me from Dolph. And for that, and so many other things, I'll always be grateful. You can't imagine how much I'm going to miss him. It's going to take time . . ."

Her voice cracked and she struggled for control. "I wish *I* could have been the one to save him. I wish that with all my heart. But I don't blame you. You have to believe me."

Ty studied her face, and slowly nodded. He wished there was a way he could soften the grief tearing through her. But he knew something about grief—and he knew everyone had to cope with it in their own way, their own time.

"So," he said evenly, "if you don't hold Ricky's death against me, what's the problem?"

"You have to ask?" She laughed shakily. "There's too many to count." Her eyes darkened. "Starting with all the lies I told you."

"I don't remember you lying to me about anything that really mattered." He pulled her closer, his arms winding around her waist. "Like what happens when we do this."

He bent down and kissed her. The kiss made her dizzy and hot and hungry for more, a lifetime more, but she felt the prick of tears in her eyes again and pushed him away.

"There's still Meg. There will always be Meg. And I told you—"

"You don't want to be second pick. Second best. Bull-shit."

"What did you say?"

"You heard me. Bullshit. Do you love me or not?"

What was wrong with him? Didn't he understand any-thing? "What difference does that make?"

"Meg is dead." He said the words quietly, so matter-of-factly that Josy could only gaze at him in surprise. "She and I had something special and wonderful and now . . . it's gone. She's gone."

His eyes glinted at her, warm, direct, full of dazzling blue light. "But you know what I realized? I'm still alive, Josy. You made me realize that. You made me want to be alive again. No one else has ever been able to do that— only you. You remember when I was pinned down, shoot-ing it out with Tate's men in Slattery's Saloon? It struck me for the first time then, that I actually cared if I lived through it. And I did . . . because of you."

His voice thickened. "I love you, Josy. I think I've loved you since the day we went riding. Since the moment you let me hoist you up on Moonbeam, even though you were scared to death. You gave me my life back, and . . . my heart." He shook his head. "I'm only sorry it took me so long to realize it. But I do now." He searched her eyes.

"So will you please tell me, did you or did you not start to say that you loved me?"

"Actually, I did." Her hands crept up around his neck. She felt dazed by everything he'd said, but not so dazed that she didn't feel a bounce of joy jumpstarting her heart. "I *do*."

"Remember those words. We're going to be saying them again very soon."

Everything was happening too quickly. And not quickly enough. "Take it easy, there's still *issues*. We have jobs in different cities—"

"I'll transfer to the NYPD. We can come back to Thunder Creek whenever we want, stay in the cabin. See how Corinne and Roy are getting along, if they're as happy as we're going to be—"

"Ty, no, I don't want you to have to quit your job. You love it here. Your horses . . . the cabin . . . I could move to Thunder Creek. I can design clothes anywhere. And I'm sick of working for Francesca, I think she's the one jamming my creativity. I want to design ball gowns and wedding gowns and tea gowns and I can sketch and sew anywhere. Maybe I can start my own company . . . it would be small, of course, at first, but Reese might back me. I'd have to go to New York periodically of course, but . . ."

She paused as Ada's voice broke into the relative quiet near the barn. "Oh, dear Lord, thank God you're all right!"

Ty stepped back as Ada threw her arms around Josy. "Honey, that was quick thinking with that old rug. How'd you get to be so brave? And smart. You take after your grandfather, you know. He was quick as a wink, had reflexes like no one else I ever saw."

She kissed Josy's cheek, and hugged her, and Josy kissed hers in return. "I almost fainted when I saw you strapped to that chair. Did she hurt you?"

"Only my pride, honey. I'm embarrassed that I never

caught on to Roberta in all this time she worked at the diner. Imagine, our own Roberta was queen of the rustlers. Wait until Bessie hears about this."

"What was that you said, Ada—about Josy taking after her grandfather?" Ty looked puzzled.

Josy laughed, color popping into her cheeks. She and Ada exchanged glances.

"It's very simple actually. There's just one more thing you don't know about me, Ty. The real reason why, when I ran, I ran straight to Thunder Creek."

Josy slipped an arm around Ada's shoulders and leaned her cheek against the other woman's.

"I came to find Ada. You see, she's my grandmother."

Chapter 32

"HERE, SHE WANTS TO TALK TO YOU." TY HANDED Josy his cell phone as she lay cuddled against him in the bed. Her hair was draped like gold lace across the pillow, and her face was flushed petal pink in the moonlight that streamed in the window. Their lovemaking brought out the glow in her eyes, he concluded with satisfaction.

He'd never seen anyone look so beautiful.

Far below the bustle and roar of the New York City evening blared through the streets, but here in Josy's soon-to-be ex-apartment, a feminine haven from the rough world if ever he'd seen one, there had been only the sounds of unfettered pleasure and joy and intense physical exertion until a short while ago when they'd both collapsed into exhausted sleep.

Then the phone rang. His mother. Josy had become her new best friend.

"And as soon as you decide if you want to get married in New York or Thunder Creek—or here in Philadelphia, whichever you prefer—we'll all get together and draw up the plans. I know you—and Ada, of course—will have plenty of ideas, but if there's anything I can do to help, anything at all—"

Ty, who could hear his mother's excited voice, rolled his eyes, grinning, but Josy was listening with avid pleasure.

"I appreciate that so much, Mrs. Barclay. I'd—"

"Anne, please."

"Anne. I'd love to have your help. I'm going back to Thunder Creek just as soon as I pack up my stuff here and arrange to sublet the apartment. Yes, it's true, my friend Reese is looking for a loft in Soho we can use as a factory and showroom, and Jane—by the way, I really want you to meet her—is going to be in charge of the New York office and she's also one of my bridesmaids. No, I haven't asked Corinne yet. I'd like to ask her in person when we get back there. That's right, it will be Faith and Corinne and Jane and Reese standing up for me."

Ty reached for the bottle of champagne on the bedside table and topped off each of their glasses.

"Oh, my studio? Ty has a million ideas for that," Josy was saying with delight. "Your son could have been an architect—he's drawn up some incredible plans. I'm going to have a mountain view. Yes, to the west, so I can watch the sunset while I'm drawing. We'll stop in Philadelphia before going to Thunder Creek so we can show you the plans. No, no, I wouldn't dream of moving into the cabin—it belongs to all the Barclays. I know how much you all love going there and—"

Ty tossed back his champagne and felt peace enveloping him as he listened to Josy. He loved how animated and happy she sounded, and how delectable she looked in the moonlight—especially since she was lying naked beside him, the sheet draped temptingly just across her breasts.

Every once in a while he tugged it away, and managed a few quick sweeps of his tongue over those luscious red peaks, before she laughed and gasped and pushed his head away, trying to keep the breathlessness from her voice as she answered his mother's questions on the phone.

His family had taken to Josy quicker than a finger snap.

His father pronounced her "every bit as classy as your mother and equally smart."

Adam had punched him in the arm and said Josy was too good for him, and he'd better realize how lucky he was.

Faith had threatened to tell her all the family stories over Thanksgiving when there would be enough time to explain to his future bride exactly what she was getting herself into.

And though Josy had seemed a bit shy at first, sooner than he'd thought likely, she'd started feeling at home with them.

If he'd didn't know better, listening to her chat with his mother about the wedding right now, he'd almost think she'd been raised in a big, noisy, and very nosy family herself.

It seemed she was going to like being part of the Barclay clan.

Finally, it seemed his mother was winding down. Josy handed the phone back to him.

"Good talking to you, Mom," Ty said lazily, "but now we've got some betrothal business of our own to attend to, if you know what I mean. What? Yes, absolutely. Before the night is over."

Josy watched the muscles ripple across his back as he reached to set the phone down on the nightstand.

"What's going to happen before the night is over?"

"I'll give you three guesses." He handed her champagne glass back to her and watched her take a sip of it, all the while her eyes were studying him thoughtfully.

"We're going to make love again?"

"That goes without saying."

"We're going to start packing up the apartment?"

The mock dismay in her eyes made him laugh.

"Not on your life. Tomorrow's soon enough for that. We're not doing anything tonight that requires more exertion than getting ice cream from the fridge. Except . . . you know."

Oh, yes, she knew. Laughing, she reached for him, pulled him down to her, and kissed him with deep happiness.

"Then, what is it? I give up." She slid her hands down his chest, her fingers exploring.

"Okay, you get one hint. What goes with champagne?"

"Roses. You already brought me some."

He had. An exquisite bouquet of American Beauty roses graced her dresser.

"Try again. You'd never make detective, not if you're this slow on the uptake."

She nipped his shoulder, and then chewed her bottom lip. "We've got moonlight already, so it can't be that. Let's see. Chocolates? Champagne and chocolates."

A wide smile crossed his face. "Good enough. Hold on."

He slid from the bed, all six foot two of sinewy, muscled male, and strode naked to the corner of the room where he'd dropped his briefcase.

Her gaze ran over his splendid body as he unclasped the case and withdrew a signature gold Godiva box. Pure lust jolted through her. Ty was not only far and away the sexiest man she'd ever seen, he was also the most tender lover.

And he was hers. Ty loved her, and he'd proved that over and over during the past eight days.

Throughout all the interviews and questions, both in Thunder Creek and back in New York, when she'd faced another trio of detectives from internal affairs, he'd stood by her, backed her, supported her.

And so had everyone in Thunder Creek, once the truth had come out about Ricky, the diamond, Roberta, all of it. Roy and Corinne, Katy and Jackson Brent, Bessie Templeton, and everyone else had rallied around her once the whole story had raced like wildfire through the town.

Corinne had freaked out at first that Roberta, her matron of honor, was really Bobbi June Byrd, the brains behind the rustling ring—and that she was going to jail for at least the next ten years. But Corinne had managed to calm down in time for the wedding, and in the end nothing else disastrous had happened except that Tammie Morgan had fallen down the steps of the church and broken her ankle and Corinne's father's flight from Texas had been delayed due to storms and he'd only reached the church Sunday morning an hour before the ceremony was to start.

Aside from that, all had gone smoothly and Corinne and Roy had looked ecstatically happy as they spoke their vows, cut the cake, and shared their first dance before a crowd of family and friends.

Corinne had even managed to see to it that Josy caught the bouquet.

Now as Ty tossed the box of Godivas on the bed and sat down beside her, she felt a surge of wonder at how much her life had changed since she'd arrived alone and weary that first night in Thunder Creek.

She'd survived danger and near-death—and she'd knocked a rustler out cold. She'd found her grandmother—and she'd lost Ricky. She'd finished her sketches and turned them over to Francesca for the last time. And she'd turned a whole new corner in both her life and her career.

Last and best, she'd met the man she'd love with all her heart for the rest of her life.

There was something else that had happened, something more subtle and unexpected—perhaps the strangest thing of all. She'd found an entire town that somehow had come to feel like home, a place where her heart felt at peace. A place where the pace suited her more than she'd ever thought possible, and where her creativity had been reborn.

It was Ty's home, and soon it would be hers.

And one day, it would be the place they raised their children.

Thunder Creek.

Josy opened the gold Godiva box, intending to seductively feed him the first chocolate as a prelude to another round of hot and luxurious sex. But her attention was caught by a breathtaking glitter in the center of the box.

Surrounded by tiny exquisite chocolates, nestled in its own fragile veil of paper, just as if it were a chocolate-covered cherry or a caramel cream, rested a diamond ring.

It was a brilliant pear-shaped diamond within a shimmering platinum setting. It winked like a star in the moonlight, a star Ty lifted and slipped gently onto her finger.

"What's moonlight, champagne, chocolate, and roses

without an engagement ring?" His smile was at once tender and mischievous.

She stared at him and at the diamond, a surge of emotion leaving her speechless.

"Will you marry me, Josy Warner?"

She flung herself against him, her hands twining behind his neck. "You know I will. I told you that day after Corinne and Roy's wedding, when we rode out to the cabin."

She pulled his head down to her and kissed him lingeringly. Heat circled through her as the kiss turned deeper, and his hands caressed her breasts.

"I didn't need a ring to know that you love me," Josy whispered, trembling as his hands slid lower down her body, and as she felt his hard shaft pressed against her.

"Well, I happened to think it would look pretty good on your finger. Unless you want me to take it back?"

"Just try it, cowboy." Then she moaned, as his hand dipped lower, awakening a cascade of delicious sensations deep in her core. "You'd have a better chance of fishing on the moon than getting this ring off my finger," she added breathlessly.

Ty's eyes had darkened to a fierce lusty blue. He traced his tongue around the soft curve of her lips. "I've no desire to fish on the moon. Or to ever take that ring off your finger. There's only one thing I do desire right now—and you don't need three guesses to figure out what that is."

"No," she agreed, her laugh ragged, as she felt rational thought and control slipping away. "I definitely know that answer."

She pulled him down and climbed atop him and their bodies clung and rocked. They touched each other everywhere, kissed and held each other until there was no way to tell where she left off and he began. Hungrily, deliciously, they made love by New York City moonlight and later, much later, they lay entwined in bed and whispered of their future—of the life, the family, the love that awaited them—in the place called Thunder Creek.

About the Author

JILL GREGORY is the *New York Times* bestselling author of more than twenty-five novels. Her novels have been translated and published in Japan, Russia, France, Norway, Taiwan, Sweden, and Italy. Jill grew up in Chicago and received her bachelor of arts degree in English from the University of Illinois. She currently resides in Michigan with her husband.

Jill invites her readers to visit her website at www.jill-gregory.net.

TOLEDO PUBLIC LIBRARY

0 4444 0059867 8

7/04

"SPECTACULAR WRITING.

	DATE DUE	
JUL 2 2 2004	AUG 0 1 2013	
AUG 1 0 2004	APR 1 3 2014	
AUG 3 0 2004	APR 2 0 2015	
SEP 1 4 2004		
SEP 3 0 2004		
OCT 0 5 2004		
DEC 1 4 2004		
FEB 0 7 2005		
MAY 5 05		
JUL 2 1 2005		
OCT 2 5 2005		
MAR 4 2006		
AUG 0 7 2006		
DEC 1 2		
MAR 2 2007		
MAY 2 0 2009		
11/6/09		
JAN 1 2010		
SEP 1 9 2010		
OCT 5 2010		
NOV 1 5 2012		
JAN 2 9 2013		

DISCARDED

THE LIBRARY STORE   #47-0120

Plea........ costs:
$5.5........ ble
sale........ .... object to
allow........
chan........

Bar........
Att........
400........
We........

Nar........

Add........

City........

Daytime Phone (_____)

ROM 8 7/0.